AUTUMN JONES LAKE

*A steamy standalone romance featuring a swoon-worthy single dad and the
one woman he absolutely shouldn't fall in love with.*

ABOUT WARNINGS & WILDFIRES

By Autumn Jones Lake

Sullivan

It's a hot summer morning and I'm already running late.

I'm no one's white knight, but when I see a damsel in distress, I have to rescue her.

I didn't know it would be Aubrey Dorado, the girl I swore was off-limits.

Now she's under my skin and I can't get her off my mind.

So, I did the worst thing possible and hired her to work in my gym.

Lusting after my new employee breaks my number one rule.

But each day she tempts me with her sweet personality and clever mind.

I've been burned by love before.

Romance is a risk I can't afford.

But how much longer can I resist the attraction simmering between us?

Aubrey

I don't walk my neighbor's dog often, but when I do, of course, he knocks me off my feet.

Even better? The one to come to my rescue has to be my swoon-worthy self-defense teacher, Sullivan "Sully" Wallace.

I'm so broke that when he offers me a job, I jump at it.

Now I'm spending way too much time with my untouchable crush.

Worse, he makes it clear he has no romantic interest in me.

And just when I think he's changed his mind, the biggest mistake of my life returns to ruin everything.

ACKNOWLEDGMENTS

It's been…a year so far. I'd be lost without the continued support and encouragement from certain people.

First, thank you to my readers. Your love of my characters, continued support, and eagerness for each new book continues to amaze, humble, and inspire me.

Iza, thank you for your continuing friendship. I'm so happy we finally met this year!

Andrea, thank you for reading this early on and encouraging me to continue.

Liz, thank you for the final seal of approval.

Daniele, thank you for those last final catches!

Thank you to my crit partners for the valuable insight.

Thank you, Ellie for a smooth editing process.

My Lost Kings MC Ladies Facebook group, thank you so much for spending time in my world. Your questions and theories fuel me and your demand for the next book keeps me motivated. I'm so grateful that you're willing to embrace a non-Lost Kings MC book. Thank you.

Mr. Lake—thank you for everything always.

DEDICATION

If you're still punishing yourself for past mistakes, forgive yourself.
Let those mistakes guide you, not define you.

CHAPTER ONE
SULLY

CRAPPY COFFEE BEATS no coffee every morning.

If I don't stop at the post office, I can still make it to the gym on time. It would be nice if I could count on my younger brother, Jake, to open Strike Back on Monday mornings, but let's be honest, he's most likely running later than I am.

I push open the coffee shop door into the thick August humidity. It's not even nine a.m. and the freshly-paved village road in front of me is already shimmering with heat.

A yellow and black butterfly flutters in front of my face for a second before flying away. A brief reminder of why I'm rushing to work. Of what's most important to me in this world.

I'm half-way to the curb where my Jeep's parked when a tiny figure catches my eye.

A hooded sweatshirt covers her face, but something familiar about her body keeps my attention riveted on the woman jogging toward me. Tight leggings, curvy legs, wide hips, small stature.

You don't have time for this. Stop being a creeper.

Even though I consider myself a dog person, the big white pit bull jogging at her side makes me think twice about approaching the woman. I open my door and set my coffee in the console cup holder. Before climbing in, I take one last glance at the jogger.

Several things happen at once. A squirrel darts into the road. The pit bull's ears perk up and he lunges after the confused critter, yanking the jogger off the sidewalk. She trips and slams into the pavement, her palms striking asphalt with a hard *slap*. The dog continues charging after the

1

squirrel, leash trailing behind him.

"Gambler, no!" the woman shouts, her voice choked with pain. She seems unaware of the sports car barreling toward her at exceeding-the-speed-limit miles an hour.

At the last minute the car jerks to the right, zipping by, missing her by inches.

A startled scream tears out of her throat. My gaze darts between the galloping dog and the girl in the road.

Help the girl or grab the dog?

"Please! Get him!" she shouts.

I'm already moving toward her, but I stop and force out a loud, piercing whistle. The dog stops and cocks his head. I repeat the whistle and he breaks into a run, stopping in front of me. His whip-like tail sweeps over the pavement in a quick, eager rhythm.

"Hey, boy. Are you friendly?" Casually, I lean over, pick up his leash, give it a gentle tug, and hurry over to help his owner.

"Are you okay?" I call out.

She tips her head up and the hood slides back, revealing her face.

Her beautiful face flushed from exercise or embarrassment. Big brown doll eyes, and pink, pouting lips.

Aubrey.

I knew I recognized those sexy legs.

Shy, but sweet, Aubrey comes into my gym once a week for the low-cost self-defense class I teach. Cuter than hell, she's too young for me, not that it matters.

My life consists of a number of rules. At the top of my list: don't date clients. Don't date at all, if I'm being honest.

"Sullivan?" Her cheeks turn even redder.

I offer my hand to help her up and she winces.

Dropping my gaze, I understand why. The fall ripped a huge hole in her tight, black leggings at the left knee. Blood and dirt ooze from multiple scrapes and the skin is already turning shades of red and purple.

She hisses in a pained breath and her eyes water.

"It's okay, Aubrey." I wrap an arm around her waist and encourage her to lean on me. "I've got you."

"Ooo…it stings so bad."

"Do you want me to take you to the emergency room?"

"No." She glances down at the wriggling mass of muscles and fur. "Thank you for catching him. I'm dog-walking and apparently I'm not cut out for it."

There's a note of shame in her tone I don't like. "He's a strong boy. He'd be a handful for anyone," I say, tugging the leash.

"No kidding." Her lips twist in a pained imitation of a smile.

"Come on, my Jeep's right over there. I'll give you two a ride home."

"Thanks."

I wrap the leash up in my free hand and keep my arm around her waist. She limps the whole way and aware of how inappropriate it would be, I have to fight the urge to pick her up and carry her.

Gambler happily jumps in the back. I hold the passenger side door open for Aubrey and she hesitates. Her eyes shine. Her cheeks turn even redder.

"What's wrong?"

She drops her head, staring at the sidewalk.

Finally, it occurs to me, she's not sure how to climb into my lifted Jeep with her torn-up knee. "I'm too short," she whispers.

Short my ass. She's perfect.

"Here." I show her the oh-shit bar in the right corner. Before thinking it through, I fit my hands around her waist and boost her up.

A squeal erupts out of her. "You can't!"

"Can't what?"

"Lift me."

"I just did." I settle my hand on her leg to stop her from turning in the seat. "Wait."

Her big, brown, questioning eyes meet mine.

"Your knee." I reach past her and snag a bottle of water out of the middle console. "We need to clean it up."

"I'll be fine," she protests.

"You went down pretty hard. I don't want it to get infected." I brush

3

her hand aside and survey the damage. Blood and dirt trail down her leg, seeping into the ragged material of her ruined pants. "This is bad," I mutter, squirting water over the non-shredded parts of her leg first.

I grab a wad of clean napkins out of the glove compartment and dab at a few spots. Once I wash some of the blood away, I note the bits of gravel and dirt embedded in her flesh. Her injury is more than I can treat on the side of the road with a bottle of water and some cheap, paper napkins.

"How far is your place?" I ask, meeting her watery eyes.

She points down the road. "Not far."

"Buckle up." I nudge her into the seat and pull the seatbelt around her. She shakes her head, but buckles in while I close the door.

When I climb in on the other side, a warm wet tongue lashes the side of my face. I reach back and pat Gambler's head. "Thanks for the tongue-bath, fella."

"He seems to like you. You must remind him of Tyler."

Who the hell is Tyler?

Yeah, here I am with my rigid rule about not dating clients, poor girl's bleeding and in pain, and *I'm* itching with jealousy the second another man's name comes out of her sinful mouth.

Good job, jerk.

"Is that your boyfriend?" I ask striving for a neutral tone.

Her soft laughter reassures me before she even says a word. "No. He's my neighbor. He needed a dog-sitter, and I needed the money."

"Where's your house?"

She points up ahead. "Third right."

I recognize the area. Cheap apartments contained in three square brick buildings three stories each. I follow the road around to the parking lot located in the back.

"The last one," she directs.

I pull into a spot in front of her building and open my door.

"Oh, you don't have to—"

"What floor do you live on?" There's no chance in hell I'm letting her limp her way inside all by herself. I'm still not convinced she doesn't

4

need to go to the hospital.

"The second."

"How are you planning to get the two of you upstairs?"

I don't wait for an answer. Jogging around the Jeep, I open her door and help her out. "It's getting hot," she mutters, slipping off her sweatshirt and tying it around her waist.

Fuck me.

Hot's an understatement. The long, loose T-shirt she's wearing has no business being that sexy. The round neckline hints at a tight-fitting sports bra underneath and shows off a lot of flushed skin covered in a fine sheen of sweat, nudging the dirtier part of my mind into wondering if that's what she'd look like after sex.

"Sully? The dog?" Her soft voice draws me away from my filthy fantasies.

"Sure. Yeah."

I open the back and Gambler falls into my arms, body wiggling, tail wagging, tongue licking. "You're just one big ball of energy aren't ya, boy?" I set him down and rub his head.

Aubrey moves to take the leash and I stop her. "I've got him. Go ahead."

She doesn't protest, and I stop to dig out a first aid kit before catching up with her.

Every step makes her flinch and the urge to scoop her up comes raging back.

"Here." She holds her hand out for the leash at the top of the stairs. "I need to let him into Ty's place."

How close is she with this guy? Why does she have his apartment key?

Not your concern, jackass.

I wait outside while she takes care of the dog. When she backs out of the apartment and sees me, her eyes widen.

"What are you still doing here?"

"Waiting for you."

A brief smile flickers over her face. "You don't have to do that."

As if I'd leave her alone limping and bleeding. We stand there staring at each other for a few seconds.

"Well." She points to the door in front of us. "That's me."

Aubrey

ATTRACTION IS A funny thing.

I've been attracted to Sully from the moment we first met. He's never looked at me with anything other than professional interest. Even though our mutual friends Bree and Liam have hinted several times that we'd make a cute couple.

Fate has a terrible sense of humor.

Here, I'm trying to do a nice thing and walk my neighbor's dog so I can earn extra money.

Instead, I end up falling, barely miss getting run over by some asshole, scraping most of the skin off my knee, and looking like a fool in front of my crush.

Now, he wants to come into my apartment too? Can my morning take more of a sucky wrong turn?

"Uh, sure."

Deep breath. In. Out. Everything's okay.

My cheeks heat up as he follows me inside. The apartment is tragically tiny. Worse, I share it with my sister, because even if I wanted to, I couldn't afford it on my own. All of those embarrassments are muffled by the screaming inferno now known as my left leg.

"Where's the bathroom?" he asks.

I point down the hallway. The only direction it could be. Each step burns and I'm mortified Sully not only witnessed my clumsiness, but now he's in my home.

It's a tight fit in the bathroom, but he doesn't seem to mind.

"Sit down," he says, nodding at the closed toilet seat.

Realizing protests will get me nowhere with him, I perch on the seat.

"Scissors?" he asks.

"Cabinet." I point, you know in case he can't tell the big square box in front of his face is what I'm referring to. I'm not sure my hair-stylist sister will appreciate me using her fancy scissors, but they're the only pair I can think of at the moment.

Methodically, he lays out each item he plans to use on the counter and my stomach flutters. "I think I'm going to be sick," I whisper.

He runs his hand over my head, pulling me closer, so my cheek rests against his leg. "Deep breath, Aubrey. You're okay."

It's corny, but all my fears settle down with his touch. He's a solid guy. Muscular and strong. Not too tall. I'm five-foot-three on a good day. He easily has nine or ten inches on me. Enough to be comforting, but not overwhelming.

He crouches down in front of me and I have a chance to study his eyes. Bottomless and rich, like my favorite Spanish roast coffee. Sympathetic and warm.

His strong, steady hands wrap around my calf, gently lifting my foot. I hiss at the pain racing over my skin.

"May I?" he asks, tapping my sneaker.

"My feet probably stink." Nervous laughter follows my idiotic words.

He shakes his head and eases my sneaker and sock off, setting them on the floor. "Hmm, nothing looks broken or swollen, so that's good. Do you have an ice pack in your freezer?"

"That's probably all we have in the freezer."

He raises an eyebrow. "We? Do you live with your parents?"

"No, my sister." The one who took me in after my parents tossed me out.

My gaze drops to my shredded leggings. "My sister's going to kill me," I mutter. Realizing he has no idea what I'm talking about, I add, "The pants. I borrowed them from her."

One corner of his mouth lifts. "Little thief, huh?" he teases. "Jake's always pilfering my stuff too."

The teasing works and pulls a chuckle out of me.

He returns to studying my injury, while I contemplate running my fingers through his dark brown hair. Not to be creepy or anything, just to verify if it's as silky as it appears.

"I hate to say it, but I either need to cut off the fabric around the wound or..."

Sully's too much of a gentleman to suggest what's extremely obvious. It would be easier if I strip down. "I can take them off," I offer.

My T-shirt's long enough to cover me and with his help, I stand. Pretending his face isn't up close and personal with my lady bits is rough. My hands shake as I hook my fingers into the waistband and slowly roll the stretchy fabric over my hips. A grunt of pain pops out of me when I try to bend my leg and Sully helps by dragging the pants down my legs, carefully pulling the material away from my cuts.

For a moment neither of us speak.

His warm breath skates over my bare skin, easing my pain.

I glance down and find his gaze riveted to my lower body.

"Sully?" I whisper.

As if in a trance, he slowly drags his gaze up to meet my eyes. "Do you have a bucket? I need to clean the wound and don't want to get water all over your floor."

Bucket. First aid. Of course. Sully is all single-minded focus and none of that attention is on me as anything other than an injury to be treated.

"Under the sink, there's a foot bath. Will that work?"

"Yup." He curls his hands around my thighs, his fingers dangerously close to my butt and nudges me back to the toilet. Heat sears every inch of my skin where we're touching. He seems to feel it too and jerks away. "Sorry."

Oh my God. Light tingles race over my skin. A shivery sensation that tightens my nipples.

From having his hands on my *legs* for five whole seconds.

If that's how my body responds to a such a simple touch, what would—

"Aubrey?" Sully's voice interrupts my speculation. "Are you ready?"

I'd like to say I don't cry or act like a baby while he treats my cuts and scrapes, but I don't believe in lying. It hurts like a bitch. Especially when he deftly uses a pair of long, skinny tweezers to pluck out the more stubborn bits of gravel embedded in my flesh.

Tears silently roll down my cheeks and I swipe them away before Sully sees.

"Almost done," he murmurs.

I exhale a long slow breath as he smooths ointment over the whole area. Finally, he tapes a piece of gauze into place and declares me finished.

"Thank you so much. I don't think I would've been able to do that myself."

"No problem." He finally meets my eyes and there must be a stray tear or two, because he uses his thumb to whisk it away. "I'm sorry. I tried to be gentle."

"Digging gravel out of flesh is going to hurt, no matter what," I say with a wry twist of my mouth, trying to make a joke to cover my embarrassment at being caught crying like a baby.

He holds out his hand and helps me up. "Let's put that ice pack on your knee to keep the swelling down."

"I-uh, I'm going to put some pants on."

"Need help?"

I wish. "No, I've got it."

I limp my way into my bedroom, closing the door behind me. Is this really happening? Sully's in my apartment?

Because he feels sorry for you, klutz.

Shaking my head, I push away from the door and grab the first pair of shorts I see. My T-shirt is longer than the shorts, so I trade it for a tank top, then slip my feet into my favorite fluffy slippers.

Sully's in the living room holding a small blue ice pack in one hand and a kitchen towel in the other. "You weren't kidding about the empty freezer. Not even a pint of Ben and Jerry's?" he teases.

I almost say "It's not that time of the month yet." But thank God, my brain to mouth function kicks in. Instead, I shrug. "I'm more of a Stewart's Chocolate Chip Cookie Dough ice cream girl."

"Upstate New York girl through and through. I'm partial to the Crumbs Along the Mohawk myself."

"Adventurous," I tease, drawing a smile from him. Maybe this is my chance to slip in a casual not-a-date invitation. "Maybe we can stop by there after class next Sunday?" I force a light chuckle to cover my nerves. "I at least owe you some ice cream for taking care of me today."

His smile fades. "You don't owe me anything, Aubrey."

Right. He's not interested. Not even in a thank-you-for-rescuing-me ice cream cone.

He motions for me to take a seat on the couch and crouches down in front of me, gently pressing the towel-covered ice pack to the red lumpy area on the side of my knee. "Twenty minutes on twenty minutes off," he says in a low voice.

Is he planning to stay here the whole time?

Do I want him to?

I've been dying to be alone with Sully for weeks now. But not like this.

"So it's just you and your sister?" he asks. "Are your parents nearby?"

I clench my teeth. "How old do you think I am?"

The question seems to startle him. He sits back and allows his gaze to sweep over my body. "Eighteen? Nineteen?"

I lift my chin, as if that will make me appear older. "I'm twenty-two."

A glimmer of something—interest?—passes over his face. "Sorry. You—"

"Yeah, I'm short." I try to laugh it off, but it sounds forced. "I get it all the time."

The smoldering look in his eyes must have been a hallucination. Pity is the only thing shining there now as he attempts to explain himself. "Aubrey, I didn't mean—"

Being bitchy isn't the way I pictured this chance alone with him, so I fake a casual smile. "I guess you don't read those forms you make all your clients fill out."

He ducks his head. "Guilty. If we did more one-on-one training or you used the weights or something, I would've looked at it closer."

One-on-one. Good Lord, is that an option?

Or was that a hint that my big butt could stand to do a little more cardio?

The door opens, putting an end to our awkward conversation. My sister, Celia, slips into the living room unaware of us at first. She's so engrossed in reading the mail in her hands, she jumps when she notices Sully. Her wary gaze slides between the two of us finally landing on me. "Hey, Aubrey. Everything okay?"

"This is Sully—"

"Oh, the self-defense guy." The tension drains from her face and she takes a step closer, holding out her free hand. Sully stands and greets her. Inwardly, I groan. Celia's beautiful. Taller, skinnier, prettier. Introducing her to a guy I'm interested in never ends well for me.

After they say hello, Celia's gaze settles on the ice pack covering half my leg. "What happened?"

"I was jogging with Gambler and fell."

"Shoot, Aubrey. I told you to wait until I got back. Are you okay?"

"Sully fixed me up. I'll survive, but your new leggings didn't. Sorry. I'll replace them."

Celia shakes her head, chestnut-brown curls bouncing everywhere. "Don't be silly." She rushes over and scoops me up in a hug. "I'm just glad you're okay."

"He's a strong dog," Sully says.

"Gambler?" Celia chuckles. "Yeah, his owner, Ty, is a big brute himself. He can handle him. My little sister can't."

I roll my eyes and barely restrain myself from sticking my tongue out at her.

Sully takes a step back. "I should get going." He nods at my sister, but his gaze doesn't linger, igniting a spark of hope inside me. "Nice to meet you, Celia."

"Thank you for taking care of me," I say.

"Anytime." He reaches over and squeezes my shoulder. "I hope you're able to come to class Sunday."

Our eyes meet and all I'm able to do is stammer out a, "Me too."

After he leaves, I slump back against the couch.

"Wow, you weren't kidding." Celia's hushed tone and bright eyes suggest she's interested in an afternoon of girl talk.

"Well, if he wasn't interested before, he's definitely not interested now. He not only witnessed my epic slam into the pavement but had to listen to my sniveling while he picked gravel out of my skin."

Her gaze drops to the bandage covering my knee. "Ouch. He must like you a little or he wouldn't have helped you out."

"Doubt it. He's just a nice guy. I'm sure he felt obligated."

"The world needs more nice guys. All the guys I know would've whipped out their cell phone to take a video instead of helping out a girl."

"You know a lot of assholes."

She smirks and throws herself into the easy chair on my left. "True story."

I groan, remembering I never offered Sully anything and Celia raises an eyebrow. "I didn't even offer him a soda. I'm such a jerk."

"I'm sure he understood." She raises an eyebrow. "So you like him? I can see why."

Uncomfortable with the question and my feelings, I glance away. "I'm not the best judge of character."

"Aubrey," she sighs.

"Anything good?" I ask, gesturing at the mail in her hands.

She flips through the stack. Her eyes narrow and she shakes her head. Disappointment clouds her eyes when she hands over one long white envelope in particular. "Please tell me you didn't contact him, Aubrey," she says in her best big-sister-disapproves tone.

Embarrassed, I snap the letter out of her hand. I don't have to read the return address to know who it's from, but I still glance at it quickly before tucking the letter under my thigh.

Ice swirls in my chest, making it hard to breathe.

A single tear runs down my cheek and I swipe it away before Celia sees. She's spent enough time worrying. And I have a much bigger problem.

Somehow he found me.

CHAPTER TWO

SULLY

DID I PRACTICALLY have my face shoved in Aubrey's crotch this morning and not do a damn thing about it?

The brief moment has been replaying on a loop in my head all day. *So close.* When she rolled her leggings off, I was treated to a quick glimpse of pink cotton panties. The primal urge to rip them off and bury my tongue in her almost overwhelmed me. I managed to keep myself in check and tend to her instead of mauling her. Barely.

"Earth to Sully." Jake snaps his fingers in front of my face and I bat his hand away. "What's got you so twisted?" he asks.

About five feet three inches of plush curves I want to explore.

"Nothing." No, I didn't share my morning with my brother. He's prone to saying something obnoxious about Aubrey that will make me want to punch him.

I hook my arm around his neck, drawing him closer.

"Hey, why you trying to choke me?"

"Smile." I hold out my phone to snap a selfie.

Knowing who the photo's for, he pulls a total goof-face.

"Maddy's the only person I'd take a selfie for in the middle of our favorite bar. Makes us look like douche-wads," he mutters as I send the picture.

"Hey, hero," someone says behind me.

"Officer Hollister!" Jake shouts. "Join us."

"What are you talking about?" I ask as soon as he sits across from me.

His mouth tips into a grin. "Heard all about your heroics. Rescuing a dog *and* a girl in one morning."

"What girl?" Jake asks.

"Never mind."

"At least that explains you being off the grid this morning," Jake says. He elbows Liam in the side. "He was late to open the gym. Had a line of pissed-off gym rats waitin' outside when I showed up."

"Maybe if you *ever* showed up on time, it wouldn't have been an issue," I grumble.

Ignoring me, Jake focuses his eager-puppy face on Liam. "Explain."

Liam signals our waitress and orders a beer before answering my brother. "Bree was on the phone with Aubrey for close to an hour hearing all about how you rescued her and played doctor."

I groan and sit back. Liam's fiancée, Bree, hasn't been subtle about trying to set Aubrey and me up. "She was hurt. What was I supposed to do, leave her bleeding in the street?"

My brother's watching me with an amused expression that I kind of want to wipe off his face. With my fist.

"Aubrey's the cute, tiny one, right?" he asks, holding his hand up about an inch above the table. "With the fantastic ass?" he adds, complete with an obscene grabby-hand gesture.

"Shut up."

"Did you get any?" Jake insists.

Liam groans and shakes his head.

"She's a client," I say through clenched teeth. "I don't date clients."

"Who said anything about dating?"

Liam throws a narrow-eyed glare at my idiot brother. "She's Bree's friend. Knock it off."

"Hey, I'm single. Doesn't Bree have any hot friends she can—"

"No," Liam answers before my brother even finishes the question.

Bored with us, Jake motions for Liam to move so he can prowl around the bar seeking out a bedmate for the night.

"Sorry," I say when Liam returns to his spot.

He shrugs. "He grows on you after a while. Like fungus."

I laugh at the stupid joke and Liam grins.

"Thanks."

"All kidding aside, Bree wanted me to say 'thank you' for being so nice to Aubrey."

"They're pretty tight now, huh?"

"They talk a lot," Liam says.

"Bree doing okay after everything that went down?"

He shrugs. "I don't know if you ever get over something like that."

Isn't that the truth.

"But," he continues. "Classes started and she's throwing herself into that and adjusting to the new house."

"How's your new job?"

Another shrug. "Starting back at the bottom kinda sucks, but it won't be forever."

Liam gave up his relatively quiet deputy sheriff gig to join the much livelier Empire City Police Department. All so Bree could remain close to her grad school.

"You're a hero. She's lucky to have you."

He snorts. "She's her own hero."

I pick at the label on the bottle in front of me. "Yeah, I guess she is." I grin at him. "What's she keeping you around for anyway?"

"Hell if I know." He laughs but then turns serious. "I should thank *you*. Your class probably helped save her life."

"That and your shotgun lessons."

He groans and looks away. "Yeah."

After a few minutes of silence, he sits forward. "Don't take this the wrong way."

"Nothing good ever comes after those words."

He ignores me and continues. "Don't give Aubrey mixed signals if you're really not interested. She's a nice girl and she's been a good friend to Bree. Don't make me kick your ass."

Offended that he thinks I'm such an asshole, I open my mouth to tell him to fuck off.

"Don't tell me to fuck off, either. I'm serious," he adds.

I groan and shake my head. "No signals, officer. Promise. She's been

15

taking classes at my place for a while. I'm serious about not dating clients."

"Uh-huh," he grunts in that disbelieving tone that sets me on edge.

Keegan's big voice booms over the bar noise, rescuing me from this stupid conversation. "Figured you guys would be here." He stops and slaps a hand on each of our shoulders.

Liam shrugs him off and tips his head back. "Where you been?"

"Working. It's like every fucking idiot in Empire decides to set their backyard on fire this time of year. 'Don't burn shit outside when there's a drought.' Why is that so hard to comprehend?" He shoves into the booth next to Liam and nods at me. "I'm glad you're here. I'm supposed to ask if you want to teach *How to subdue a suspect with minimal force* to some new recruits? It actually pays, unlike all your damsel-in-distress classes."

"Sure." I can always use the money and the networking opportunity.

"Bro," Jake says, walking up and slapping my shoulder. "Amy's looking for you."

I groan at the same time my dick perks up. Amy is *not* a client of mine. She's never even set foot inside my gym. Hell, she might not even know I own a gym. We have an occasional good time together, then go our satisfied, separate ways.

Across from me, Liam shakes his head but doesn't bother to comment as I slide out of the booth. Keegan isn't so polite.

"Slave to the pussy much?" he says with a wide grin.

"Fuck off."

I tell myself I'm only heading to the bathroom to splash some water on my face and figure out what the hell I'm doing tonight, but I know better.

Amy doesn't disappoint. She pops out of the ladies' room as I enter the hallway. "Sully! Jake said you were here."

"How've you been?"

She moves in closer, slinging her arms around my neck. "Missing you."

The corner of my mouth tips up and I brace one hand against the wall. "Yeah?"

She nods and pulls me down close enough to smell the beer on her breath. "We're always *so* good together." She reaches up and whispers in my ear, "Remember the time we snuck in the closet and you made me put my hands against the wall while you took me from behind? That was *so* hot."

Yes, it was. And I can picture it perfectly. What a helpful memory. Exactly what I need to erase the image of Aubrey's perfectly thick little thighs out of my head. All day long, I've been fantasizing about what would've happened if I'd peeled her panties off along with her leggings.

I squeeze my eyes shut to banish Aubrey from my brain. Thinking of fucking one woman while I'm planning to fuck a different one is a dick move.

She slides her hand between us, cupping my package. "Mmm…feels like we might not make it to the closet." Her hand slides into mine and she tugs me down the hallway. "Do you have a condom?"

"Wait, Aubrey," I say, stopping dead.

Her eyes widen. "What did you call me?"

Shit! Why did I say that?

If *thinking* about another woman when you're about to fuck one woman is a dick move, actually calling the girl you're about to fuck by another girl's name makes me dickhead of the century.

I blink, taking in Amy's long, lean frame. The sky-high, red heels will put her at just the right height…

But I can't shake the image of Aubrey's sweet, trusting face as I tended to her injury this morning.

I should've checked on her after I closed the gym. What if she needs something? She can't make it up and down those stairs with her bum knee. Does she even own a car?

Fuck. I drag my hands through my hair, so frustrated I'm close to yanking it out.

"Sully?" Amy's bright red cheeks highlight that I'm not only being a rude asshole, but I've also embarrassed her.

"I'm sorry, Au…Amy." Goddammit, what is wrong with me? "It's not you—"

"Clearly." Her pinched expression, crossed arms, and tapping foot suggest she's moving from embarrassed to seriously pissed.

"I'm sorry. I have to go."

Like the dick I am tonight, I hurry away from her and back to my friends.

"Where's Amy?" Jake asks when I stop at our table.

"I don't know," I mumble, whipping out my wallet and throwing some bills on the table. "I'm heading out."

"Seriously?" Jake bitches. He jabs his fist into my bicep. "Don't forget Wrath's dropping off that equipment for us later in the week."

"Aren't you going to be there?"

"I'll try, but I got a lot going on."

A lot going on probably means borderline criminal activity I'd rather not know about.

"We'll talk later." Now that the idea's in my head, I'm way too eager to leave to sit around talking about work.

Liam tips his head up and lays his cop stare on me. "But Keegan just got here," he says. The unspoken, *Are you really leaving us here with your asshole brother?* sort of hangs between us.

"Sorry, bro." I seem to be apologizing to everyone tonight.

Keegan shakes his head. "I can't believe I drove all the way over here for this."

Amy takes that exact moment to walk by and hiss "asshole" at me loud enough for the whole table to hear.

And promptly mock me for.

"Whoa!" Jake howls with laughter. He tips his head with fake-serious concern. "Quickdraw tonight? Don't worry, it happens to the best of us. Well, not me, but—"

"Shut up."

Shaking his head, Liam slides out of the booth. "I want to get home before Bree anyway. I'll walk out with you."

"Fuck you both," Jake says, flipping us off. He throws his arm around Keegan's shoulders, making Keegan send a wrinkled-brow-side-eye Jake's way. "Keegan's got my back."

I return the gesture before following Liam out the door. On the sidewalk, he turns and gives me a more serious appraisal. "Sure you're all right?"

"Just something I need to take care of."

"Something or *someone*?"

"Don't worry about it."

He pins me with the hard cop stare again. "Don't forget what I said."

Ignoring the reminder, I hustle over to my Jeep and get the hell out of there.

I should bring her something, right? What's even available at this hour?

Shit, what if she's asleep? I don't have her number. I hesitate behind the wheel. I could go back to the gym and look it up, but that'll take too long.

I need to see her. *Now.*

Aubrey

POPCORN, CHECK.

Movie, check.

Sad girl all alone tonight, double-check.

I'm about to hit *play* when someone knocks on my door.

I duck down on the couch as if whoever's on the other side of the door has X-ray vision.

"Aubrey?"

Am I hallucinating or is that Sully's voice?

"Just a minute!" I shout, jumping off the couch. A slap of pain vibrates down my leg. "Ow!"

"Are you okay?" Sully asks through the door.

I limp my way over and open the door. Sure enough, he's standing in front of me.

"Sully, hi. What are you doing here?"

He holds up a brown paper bag. "I couldn't stop thinking about your empty freezer."

I blink a few times. "You brought me ice cream?"

"Well, I wanted to check on you." He cranes his neck, trying to see inside the apartment and I feel like an idiot for not inviting him in already. "Is that okay? I would've called, but I don't have your number."

"Come in. Thank you. That's so nice."

"Is your sister here?"

"Nope. She's working."

He sets the bag on the counter and pulls out three pints from Stewart's. "Cookie dough, right?" he asks, handing me a pint.

"Wow, uh, yeah. Thanks."

"I didn't know what your sister might like, so I went with plain ol' chocolate," he says, opening the freezer and sticking one of the pints inside.

He brought ice cream for my sister too? Just in case? I'm in danger of melting into a puddle of goo.

"Spoons?" he asks.

Still too surprised by the sweet gesture, I point to the drawer in front of me. Instead of you know, opening it myself.

He slides it open, brushing his hand against my hip in the process and I back away.

"Sorry," I mutter.

I take the spoon he offers and hobble back to the couch. He follows and stares at the popcorn on my coffee table for a second.

"I didn't mean to interrupt—"

"Trust me," I say, holding up the container. "This is *way* better than popcorn. I've been dying for ice cream since we talked about it this morning."

"Looks like I made the right choice."

He swivels his head between the chair and the couch. My stomach flips as he takes the space next to me on the couch, his warm, muscled thigh lightly pressing against mine.

"What are you watching?" he asks.

"I was about to watch Atomic Blonde."

"Really?"

I lift my shoulders. "I still haven't seen it."

"Neither have I."

I raise an eyebrow. "Really? Hot chick in an action movie? Figured a big, buff guy like you would be all over that."

If I'm not mistaken, he almost seems embarrassed. This man has a thousand reasons to be cocky or arrogant...yet, he isn't.

"No special girl you wanted to take to the movies?"

He snorts and stabs his spoon into his just-barely softened ice cream. "I don't have a ton of free time."

"Oh."

We settle into the movie and half-way through, no matter how hard I fight it, I end up falling asleep.

I'm not sure how much later I wake up against Sully's arm to the sound of someone knocking on my door. He glances down with a soft smile. "Hey, sleepyhead. You expecting anyone?"

Embarrassed, I sit up and wipe the drool off my chin. "No."

I move and he places his hand on my leg. "Stay there. I'll get the door."

At some point, he must have pulled a blanket over me and I tuck my feet up under it as I turn my head to watch him.

SULLY

IT'S NONE OF my business, but it bugs me that Aubrey's alone in the apartment so late at night. Or would be if I hadn't decided to stick around.

That's why I answer the door. If anyone thinks she's easy prey, they're in for a shock.

It's a good thing I answer too. With his hood pulled up, I can barely make out the guy's face. He's got a few inches on me, but I'm already calculating which spots I'll strike if he makes a move toward Aubrey.

"Hey." He scowls at me, attempting to step forward. "Is Aubrey home?"

I block him from stepping across the threshold. "Who are you?"

"Who are *you*?" he asks, placing his hands on his hips. "Where's Aubrey?"

"Tyler!" Aubrey calls, struggling to get up off the couch.

"Are you okay, honey?" he asks.

Honey?

Obviously she knows the guy. My urge to tell him to get lost and slam the door in his face almost wins, but I step aside and let him enter.

It occurs to me I've never asked if she has a boyfriend. He's too old for her, but no one's asked my opinion.

"Sully," Aubrey says. "This is my neighbor. Gambler's his dog."

"You might want to invest in some obedience classes for him," I say instead of hello. My mama raised me with better manners than that, but as far as I'm concerned, this guy's responsible for Aubrey getting hurt so I'm not feeling very polite.

"I know," he says, shaking his head. "Celia called to bitch me out. I wanted to make sure you're okay. I'm so sorry, hon."

Maybe he's not a total douche. Maybe he's *Celia's* boyfriend.

"It's not your fault," Aubrey says. "I'll be okay." She throws the blanket back and Tyler's eyes widen.

"Shit, Aubrey. Your leg's a mess."

"I'm fine," she insists. "Sully fixed me up."

Tyler finally glances at me and with his hood now down I recognize him. "You're Keegan's buddy? The dog rescuer?"

"That's me." He holds out his hand and I shake it. "Sullivan Wallace, right? You own Strike Back?"

"Yeah."

Now that we've established we have a friend in common, Ty's posture relaxes. Mine doesn't. The mild urge to punch him still lingers.

"I've only had Gambler for about a week. He's friendly as hell but strong. I should've worked with him more before having Aubrey handle him on her own. I was in a tough spot though."

"It's fine, Ty. Really," Aubrey insists. "I'm just lucky Sully was there to catch him, so he didn't get hit by a car."

"Thanks, man," Ty says. He turns back to Aubrey. "You need me to get anything for you?"

"No. I'm fine."

He shakes his head and pulls his wallet out of his pocket, flipping it open and grabbing a wad of bills that he hands to Aubrey.

"Ty. That's way more than we agreed on."

"I didn't know you were gonna get hurt," he says, refusing to take any of the money she pushes at him. Aubrey finally gives up and stuffs it in her back pocket.

"Thanks."

"If you need anything, let me know. Okay?"

"I will."

Ty's gaze slides between Aubrey and me. "You sure everything's okay?" The, *Do you need me to get rid of this jerk* expression on his face isn't lost on me.

Now I really want to tell him to back off, but at the same time, I'm glad Aubrey has someone looking out for her.

Aubrey ducks her head. "I'm fine. Thanks, Ty."

He gives us one last inspection before saying good night.

I'm burning to ask about their relationship, but don't know how to phrase the question without giving Aubrey the wrong impression.

Keep telling yourself you're not interested in her.

She lets out a big yawn and stretches, showing off all the curves I want to memorize with my tongue. "Sorry I fell asleep on you," she says in a husky voice.

"Glad you were comfortable enough to fall asleep." I glance at the clock. "I should go. Will your sister be home soon?"

She stands and hobbles over to me. "She probably went out after work. I'll be okay."

I'm not sure what possesses me, but I reach out and tuck a piece of hair behind her ear. She ducks her head. "I'm probably a mess."

"Messy looks good on you." Makes me think what it would be like to wake up next to her in the morning. All her long, silky, coconut-scented hair spilling over my pillows.

It's official. I've reached the knows-what-her-hair-smells-like level of creepiness.

She tilts her head back.

Her full, cherry-red lips part. So close. So kissable.

My pulse quickens.

She closes her eyes.

Waiting for the kiss this moment demands.

Instead, I squeeze her hand, let myself out, and pretend I don't notice the disappointment clouding her eyes.

CHAPTER THREE

Aubrey

Dearest Aubrey,

Remember the beautiful conversations we used to have? No one knew you better than me. No one knew me better than you. I miss those days and dream of you often.

You've made so many changes in your life. Moving in with your sister. Drifting aimlessly from one menial job to another. You once had so many higher aspirations. What happened?

Is it because I'm not there to guide and support you? For that, I'm so sorry, sweetheart.

I don't blame you anymore. I need you to know that.

You & me for infinity, Aubrey.

Soon we'll be together, and I'll make up for all the time we've lost.

All my love,

D.

I saved the letter. It's been sitting on my desk for three days. Taunting me.

Now I wish I'd thrown it away the second my sister handed it to me.

My hands shake as I fold the letter back into its envelope and tuck it away in my desk drawer.

A trickle of fear runs down my spine. I should've kept better tabs on him.

Instead of pretending I could start over fresh.

Celia's already left for the day. Once again I'm alone and it's starting to weigh on me.

There's a thump in the hallway outside the apartment and I practically jump out of my skin. It's not an unusual noise. Things bump and bang all hours of the day and night here.

But it's enough to snap me out of my fog.

I need to get out of here.

A safe place, preferably with lots of people sounds perfect.

Sully's studio. Not because of him. Well, because of him, yes. It's more than that, though. Taking his self-defense classes has given me back some of my confidence. I'm not stupid enough to think a few afternoons learning to punch, kick, and evade a would-be attacker make me invincible. But at least he's given me a fighting chance against a harsh world.

Strike Back is dead quiet when I open the front door an hour later.

Sully's behind the front counter talking with a terrifyingly large blond man in heavy black boots, jeans, a T-shirt that shows off thoroughly inked and muscled arms, and a leather vest covered in various patches. The man exudes strength and power, similar to Sully, but darker, almost menacing. He shifts and I glimpse the grinning skull wearing a crown covering the back of his black leather vest.

No 'almost' about it. Definite menacing vibes surround this guy.

Did I walk in on something sinister? Is Sully in deep with the local mob? Is he about to have his knee-caps broken? Does that actually happen in real life?

Perhaps I should skip the true crime documentaries next time I'm laid up.

Neither of them notices me right away. They're speaking in low tones, but I catch the name *Jake* more than once.

Uncomfortable going unnoticed and eavesdropping for so long, I finally clear my throat.

"Oh, hello there." The blond giant smiles down at me, suddenly not looking so terrifying. "Am I in your way?" he asks, stepping back.

He's so polite, and doesn't so much as drop his gaze below my face, that a guilty flush spreads over my skin for assuming he's a criminal.

"Hey, Aubrey, what's up?" Sully asks, throwing a scowl at his friend. "This is Wrath, Jake's business partner."

Wrath lifts his chin but doesn't offer to shake my hand which is fine. His hand would swallow mine up anyway.

"Uh," I stammer like an idiot, my gaze darting between them and finally landing on Sully. "I wanted to talk to you for a minute. But you're busy, I can wait."

"No. No. Customers first," Wrath insists, holding up his hands. There's a devilish smile playing over his lips, but I get the feeling he's mocking Sully, not me. With a more serious expression, he jerks his thumb over his shoulder. "I'll be out back. Come find me when you're finished."

SULLY

As usual, I'm lost in Aubrey's big brown doll eyes and only mumble to Wrath that I'll be out in a minute.

Shake it off.

I'd have to be completely dense to not know Aubrey's interested in me. And I can't say the attraction isn't mutual.

I don't date clients. Quickest way to get a sleazy reputation in this business. I've sunk every last penny I have into my studio and need it to succeed. The last thing I need is to be fodder for the gossips in this town. Too many people depend on me to let myself get caught up on one girl. No matter how much she intrigues me.

Too bad I have to remind myself of all those reasons every time I see her. Too bad I've been thinking of her non-stop since Monday night.

"How's your leg?" I ask.

"Better. I mean, it's bothering me now. After the walk but—"

"You walked all the way down here from your place?"

"It's not that far."

Hell, it's probably less than a mile and it's a relatively safe area. It still bugs me.

"So, the reason I wanted to talk to you is that, while I love the classes, I'd like to take something more intensive. Or maybe one-on-one lessons?"

When I don't answer right away, she fidgets. "Never mind." She hesitates. "It doesn't have to be you if you don't have time. If you know of someone else. Or maybe Jake?"

Hell fucking no.

If anyone's touching Aubrey, it's me.

Teaching. If anyone's *teaching* Aubrey, it's me.

No way am I allowing my brother to touch her. Nor am I sending her off to let some other guy put their hands on her curvy little hips or wrap their arms around her.

Shit, I'm getting hard just thinking about it.

So inappropriate. This girl will have me breaking my rules in no time.

Which is exactly why I need to turn her down.

In a way that won't leave her seeking out someone else.

Wallace, you've officially reached a new low.

"Jake's more of a personal trainer. You don't want him bulking you up." My smooth-guy tone even makes me want to roll my eyes.

She screws her face into the cutest mask of confusion.

"I have a waitlist for private lessons. I'll put your name on it."

"Oh. I guess that would be okay."

A noise from the back door catches my attention. "Excuse me, Aubrey. I need to help Wrath carry some equipment inside. If I don't get out there, he'll do it by himself."

She chuckles. "I'm not surprised since he's so big."

So she noticed my friend, huh. Not sure I care for that. I can't help it. I reach out and squeeze her arm. "Stay here. I'll be back in a few minutes."

I was right. Wrath already has two of the benches unloaded from his truck.

"I said I was coming."

"I'm fine," he says, waving me off. Except he's here doing me a favor so I should do my share of the heavy-lifting.

"Who's the little pixie?"

"What?"

He jerks his head toward the gym. "Amber?"

Everything in me tightens up. "Aubrey."

He nods as if I answered some secret question for him. "She your girl?"

"Don't worry about her," I snap. "She's not your business."

Wrath's the enforcer for the Lost Kings MC, the motorcycle club that runs this part of upstate New York. Someone you do *not* want to piss off if you want to continue breathing. I've known him a long time and he's my brother's business partner. I'm not a coward, but I'm usually not stupid either.

Lucky for me, he's more amused by my outburst than angry. "First, you *know* my girl. Why you riskin' me beating your ass?"

Right. Lethal biker or not, I don't think I've seen him even notice another woman since he and Trinity got together.

"Second, is she even legal?"

"She's twenty-two."

"Fuck, I feel old." He shakes his head. "She's obviously into you."

"Nah, she just wants to take some extra self-defense classes."

"Sure," he says, drawing the word out to mock me. "What's your problem?"

"I don't date my clients."

He rolls his eyes toward the sky. "Are you sure you're related to Jake?"

I snort but don't answer the question, since he's not expecting one anyway. "I don't need the reputation your gym has."

"Fuck you." His entire expression darkens into a menacing scowl. "Whisper and Jake fuck around with clients. Not me."

Yeah, that was a dick thing to say. He runs a pretty well-known afterschool program for at-risk kids out of his gym and has been after me to set one up here. Except, I haven't had the time or resources to work it out.

"Sorry."

Wrath doesn't hold grudges. He'll either punch you in the face or let it go. Today he's in a forgiving mood and my face remains unblemished. "Come on. I need to get back to Furious," he says placing his hands on either side of the bench. "Which way you wanna go?"

"I'm fine." I walk it in backward with him steering and we get it set up in the empty space I'm setting up for weightlifting.

"You need some money now?" I ask when we're finished.

"Nah," he waves it off. "We'll work out a payment plan. I'm not worried about it."

I'll admit I'm eager to return to Aubrey and not too subtle about it. My gaze scans the room, seeking her out.

Wrath smirks and shakes his head.

Aubrey

SULLY SAID TO stay, but I feel pretty useless standing around doing nothing.

The phone behind the counter rings. And rings.

I crane my neck, but can't see Sully anywhere.

When the ringing starts up again, I pick the phone up.

"Strike Back Studio, how can I help you?"

All the caller needs is a time for the evening classes. I have to search for a calendar with current schedules, but finally give them the information and hang up.

Wrath and Sully are walking toward me when I pick up my head. Sully with a furrowed brow and Wrath with a wry twist to his lips.

"Who was that?" Sully asks.

"Uh, someone who plans to attend your Mixed Martial Arts class tonight. She needed a time." I scurry out from behind the desk. "I hope that's okay. It wouldn't stop ringing."

"Yeah. Thanks for doing that."

"You really should hire someone," Wrath says to Sully.

"Thanks, I'll take it under advisement." Sully not-at-all-subtly glances at the door. "Don't you have somewhere to be?"

Amused, at what I'm not sure, Wrath widens his stance and crosses his arms over his massive chest. "Nah. I can hang with you kids for a bit."

"Asshole," Sully mutters under his breath, making Wrath laugh.

The three of us stand there awkwardly looking at each other. Well, awkward for me. Wrath seems to be enjoying Sully's irritation.

"What do you do, Aubrey?" Wrath asks.

"Uh...I." The intensity of his stare, while he waits for me to answer, makes me stutter. "I work at the coffee shop down the street and go to school part-time."

He smacks Sully's shoulder with the back of his hand. "You can come up with some flexible hours for her."

"I'm really not looking," I protest. It's a lie. I can definitely use the money, but standing here watching Sully try to come up with excuses not to hire me isn't exactly a confidence booster.

"Well," Wrath finally says, turning to Sully. "I gotta go."

"About time," Sully mutters.

Wrath grins even wider. "Let me know if you want to take over that class while Murphy's on the road."

"Will do."

They engage in some elaborate man-shake that ends with Wrath thumping Sully on the back a few times.

"Nice to meet you, Aubrey," he calls out on his way to the door.

Sully's still shaking his head when he turns to face me. His neutral expression makes it hard to tell if he's happy I'm still here or he'd rather I get lost.

"Waitlist," he says, stepping behind the counter and pulling out a notebook.

"You know, I was thinking, I'd really rather start as soon as possible. So if you have someone else you recommend, maybe that's better?"

He cocks his head and his gaze roams over me long enough that I question whether or not I measure up.

"What's your rush?" The corner of his mouth twitches. "Gang initiation coming up?"

"What? No." He's teasing, so I feel silly. "Nothing like that."

He still seems hesitant and it occurs to me that the class I take with him has a sliding fee. For private lessons, he probably charges a lot more.

"I uh, can pay you." Actually, I'm not sure that's true since whatever money I make at the coffee shop and doing odd jobs—like walking dogs who can drag me down the street—goes to helping my sister with expenses and the two classes a semester I take at the local community college.

"It's not that." He reaches up and rubs the back of his neck and I have the insane urge to massage it for him. Mercifully, I keep my hands fisted at my sides.

The phone rings again and I reach over to grab it without thinking. "Strike Back, how can I help you?"

Sully keeps his gaze locked on me while one of his clients explains she thinks she left a valuable watch behind this morning. "Mrs. Pine wants to know if anyone turned in a watch," I explain.

He nods to the desk. "There's a lost and found box under there."

I pull out the box and dig through, finding a tiny old-fashioned wind-up watch with a stretchy metal band. I hold it up and Sully shrugs.

"Ma'am, we have a few watches. Can you describe yours to me?"

She describes it right down to the date "1942" engraved inside. "Yup. We have it."

I slip the watch under the counter, so it's safe until she arrives. "She's on her way to pick it up."

Sully doesn't say anything. Instead, he watches me with that unreadable expression that both heats my skin and makes my stomach flutter.

"Uh, I'm sorry. I didn't mean to overstep."

"Stop apologizing, Aubrey," he says softly. He motions for me to come out from behind the desk.

"Wrath was trying to bust my balls, but he's right. I need someone to manage the phones. It's not busy now, but in the afternoon, things can get hectic. I don't know what your schedule—"

"I can do it." I practically jump at the chance. Not only to spend more time around Sully but because I need the money. "I'm at Busy Beans a couple mornings a week or whenever they call me in. I'm in class on Monday afternoons and Wednesday evenings. Otherwise, I'm available." God, I sound pathetic. Too eager.

"That'll work. Jake comes and goes between here and Furious Fitness down in Empire."

So desperate to say yes, I didn't think of what the job would actually entail. Good God, what if he expects me to prance around in some gym version of a Hooters waitress uniform? "What exactly do you need me to do?"

"Answer the phones. Some light cleaning. Post some ads. Little stuff I don't always have time for."

"Oh, I can do that."

"I know you can," he says in a more serious tone.

"In our downtime, I can give you some of those lessons."

Shoot, here I thought he planned to pay me in actual money.

"Here," he says, reaching under the counter and flicking a piece of paper on the top. "Fill that out so I can get you set up with payroll."

Oh thank God.

By the time I'm finished filling out the forms, I'm feeling pretty good about my new job.

I try to ignore the fluttering in my belly and warmth over my skin whenever I think of all the time we'll be spending together.

CHAPTER FOUR

SULLY

I'VE LOST MY damn mind.

It's official.

I'm already attracted to Aubrey. If dating clients is a no-go for me, dating an employee of mine is an absolute no-fucking-way. A line I'd never cross.

But damn, she's a natural. The job's not rocket science, but the reason why the position's been empty for so long is the last few people I hired were either too lazy to do any useful work or too stupid to figure out basic things. Like answering a ringing phone.

Aubrey's the perfect mix of initiative and smarts.

She officially starts working for me on Tuesday.

I already spend way too much time thinking about her. She's supposed to be off-limits and now I'll have to resist temptation on a regular basis.

No girl's ever had me so twisted up.

A towel whaps me in the face, pulling me away from my thoughts of Aubrey.

"What the fuck, bro? Pay attention," Jake snaps.

"Motherfucker," I growl, jerking the towel out of my brother's hands. "Do that again and I'm gonna kick your ass."

He laughs at the threat. Probably because he's heard it at least twice a day for the last twenty years or so. Love my brother, but damn he's a pain in my ass some days.

Like now.

"What's got you so messed up?" he asks.

"Nothing."

"Does it have anything to do with the new employee you hired without consulting me?"

He picks up the new hire form Aubrey filled out the other day and waves it in my face. "I'm assuming this *Aubrey Dorado* is the same one you're so spun up about." He taps his finger against his bottom lip. "Hmm…Dorado, doesn't that mean golden? Weird, she's not a blonde."

"You're an idiot. Give me that." I snap the paper out of his hand and chuck it in a drawer. "We needed the help. I don't have to consult you on personnel issues."

"You gonna fuck her?"

"No, you dick. I don't hire people to harass them."

"I didn't say take her into your office and whip out your dick like a creep."

The bell over the front door rings, interrupting us and probably saving Jake's life.

Aubrey.

Hasn't even started the job yet and she's the first one here for class.

At least she's with Bree, giving me a buffer.

"Morning, ladies," Jake calls out. He winks at Bree, risking a beating from Liam later. "Ready to get sweaty?"

"Hell, yeah," Bree shouts, pumping her fist in the air.

"That's the spirit," Jake says, circling the girls. "Morning, Aubrey. I hear my brother made you part of the Strike Back team."

Red creeps up her neck to her cheeks. "Uh, just a few days a week." Her gaze darts to me. "Sully said you needed the help."

"We do. From the schedule he's been diligently drafting, looks like he plans to keep you all to himself."

"Don't you have somewhere to be, jackass?" I wedge myself between him and Aubrey bumping him out of the way.

He laughs and heads to the front of the room.

"I'm going to have to come visit more often," Bree says. She throws one arm around each of us and squeezes. "This is great."

More people join the class and I step away from the girls. Without having to ask, Aubrey brings me the few things I need for the class and lays them out.

"Thanks, Aubrey."

She nods and rejoins the group.

It's an easy class. I've taught it hundreds of times. I use Bree to help me demonstrate some of the moves because I can't trust my hands if I put them on Aubrey right now. She's too damn cute in her red and black fitted top and black leggings with big red roses that end below her knee, covering most of the bandage she's still wearing.

Nah, cute doesn't cut it with Aubrey.

After class, Jake renews his quest for an ass-kicking by asking Aubrey to stick around so he can "show her a few things."

Her wary gaze darts between Jake and me. "Bree drove me here."

"I can take you home later," Jake offers.

Bree gives him a cool look. "You really need her to work today?"

"Actually," I interrupt. "We can work on some of those private lessons if you want and I'll give you a ride home later."

A hesitant smile tugs at the corners of Aubrey's mouth. "You're sure you don't mind?"

"Not at all. Jake's closing tonight."

"Wait a minute—" Jake says.

"Go collect the towels, bro." I cut him off, slapping my own towel against his chest.

Jake chuckles and snatches the towel out of my hands. "I can give you lessons too, Aubrey."

"Sully already promised." Aubrey's a sweet woman who clearly doesn't want to hurt Jake's feelings. What she doesn't realize, is Jake doesn't *have* any feelings that go beyond one night.

I really like hearing my name from her lips. Maybe too much.

Bree pulls Aubrey aside and they talk for a few minutes before Bree waves and takes off. Jake huffs and disappears into the locker room.

"Do you need anything from class clarified?" I ask when Aubrey returns.

"Well." She flicks her gaze over my shoulder and shifts from foot to foot. "We spent a lot of time on how to get out of a wrist grab."

I cross my arms over my chest and nod. "It's a common technique."

She bites her lower lip and almost seems embarrassed to ask the question. "What if someone tackles me from behind?"

Jesus Christ, *I'd* like to tackle her from behind.

Rein it in, cowboy.

When I actually think about her question, combined with her eagerness to start these lessons, it bothers me. "Aubrey, be straight with me. Is someone hassling you?"

"What? No," she answers too quickly for my comfort.

"Aubrey." I level a more serious stare at her. "You seemed to be in a hurry for the private lessons. And you've got real specific scenarios in mind. What's wrong?"

She hesitates and her cheeks turn even redder. "Look at me, I'm short. People think I'm an easy target. Too small to defend myself."

"You look fine to me."

Unprofessional much? "Sorry, what I meant was, I understand."

"How could you understand?" Her gaze roams over me, taking in my arms, and chest, then dropping to my legs. "You're a big, strong man."

I'm not the kind of guy to waste a second puffing up my chest at the observation. "I mean, that's why many women take self-defense classes."

Her pillowy lips push into a pout and it takes a lot of strength to hold back and not kiss her. "I want to be able to make someone regret messing with me." There's a touch more conviction in her tone.

Something's still not right about her motivation and it occurs to me that I may know her favorite flavor of ice cream and have her employee application practically memorized, but in reality, I know squat about Aubrey and her past.

It makes me want to protect her. I'm usually all about teaching women to protect *themselves* and not depend on someone else to keep them safe.

But Aubrey?

I want to wrap her up in my arms and murder anyone who looks at her sideways.

Aubrey

SULLY DOESN'T HOLD back and I appreciate that. He doesn't *hurt* me, but he doesn't go easy because I'm so much smaller than him either.

I do my best to ignore the way his muscles effortlessly bulge with every move. Not even his easy manner hides the raw strength he holds. More than once my eyes linger where they shouldn't.

I'm flushed and sweaty when a buzzer goes off near the front counter.

"What's that mean?" I pant out the words.

He still has his arms around me. His eyes search mine, but neither of us speaks for a second. "Private lesson's up," he says without pulling away.

"Oh."

This heavy, heady moment hangs between us. Lips almost touching. Sharing a breath. Our eyes meet. Impulse takes over and I reach up on my tiptoes, pressing my lips to his.

His posture stiffens. *Not* returning the kiss. Not even moving. His hands drop to his sides, away from my body.

Oh, shit.

What am I doing?

I stumble backward breaking our one-sided kiss. "I'm so sorry." My voice rises in pitch. "I don't know why I did that."

"Aubrey," he says, reaching for me.

No. I can't take his kindness. Not after doing something so foolish.

"Give me a minute and I'll drive you home," he says, slowly backing away.

"Th-that's okay. I can walk."

"Aubrey." He reaches to grab my arm, but I skirt by him, jerking my bag off the floor and running for the exit.

"Aubrey, wait," he pleads.

"I'll see you Tuesday," I mumble on my way out. He doesn't follow.

On the sidewalk, I sling my backpack over my shoulders and break into a run.

I can *not* believe I kissed him!

And worse, he recoiled as if a spider had crawled up his leg.

Okay, maybe not that bad.

But he definitely wasn't happy to find himself in a lip lock with me.

CHAPTER FIVE

SULLY

A LL MORNING LONG, I watch the door, waiting for Aubrey.

I spent yesterday punishing my body in the weight room. Trying to work off the need to see her.

A hundred times I thought about swinging by her apartment. Just to talk.

Or to kiss her for real.

Yeah, that sweet, awkward kiss she planted on my lips after our private lesson?

Can't get it out of my head.

My dick's gotten way too well-acquainted with my hand since that kiss.

She took me by surprise and I handled it so badly I'm afraid she won't show up for her first shift.

Jake wisely decided to spend his afternoon somewhere else.

To my relief, Aubrey arrives on time. Nervous and awkward at first. Pretending it didn't happen. But I recognize embarrassment when I see it. She tries to hide it by asking me generic questions about the job. The pink blush staining her cheeks says more than the words coming out of her mouth.

"Come on, let me give you a full tour."

"Is this okay?" she asks, pointing to her outfit.

Because I'm a jerk, I've kind of been avoiding looking directly at Aubrey. Once I do I won't be able to drag my gaze away from her.

Her request forces me to take her in. All of her. The tight black leggings with blue and green stripes running down the sides. They happen to match the colors of my sign out front. So does the snug blue polo shirt she picked out.

"It's perfect. If I ever design a uniform for the place, that would be it."

A relieved smile spreads across her face. "Good."

She has her long, dark hair pulled into an elaborate braid but a few pieces have sprung loose and before I realize what I'm doing, I brush them off her cheek.

"I wanted my hair out of the way," she says, tucking the strands behind her ear.

"You look pretty...I mean, professional. Thank you for taking the job seriously."

"Of course I take it seriously."

"Well, you'd be surprised."

"You've just hired the wrong people."

"Can't argue with that."

There's a lull in the studio around one o'clock, so that's usually when I eat lunch. I toss a menu on the desk and ask her to pick what she wants.

"It's okay. I brought something."

"Save it. I want to buy you lunch on your first day."

She's tense as she scribbles down her order and hands the menu back to me.

It's not until we're sitting behind the desk together about to dig into our sandwiches that she breaks.

"I'm sorry about the other day, Sully," she blurts out.

I sigh and sit back, dropping my sub on the wrapper and wiping my hands off before answering. "I'm not. It was sweet. You just took me by surprise."

"I don't go around kissing everyone I interact with. I want you to know that."

"So, I'm special?" I tease.

She doesn't even crack a smile. "Yes. I like...I like you a lot. And I haven't liked anyone in a long time."

Jesus, she's killing me here. "I like you too, Aubrey."

"I feel a 'but' coming on."

"But, you work for me. I don't want to complicate things." Could I be a bigger asshole?

The disappointment in her eyes intensifies my guilt, but Aubrey's brave. She flashes a quick smile. "Well, I guess that's that. I'll follow the rules and keep my lips to myself from now on."

I only have one response in mind. Thankfully, I don't say it.

Rules are meant to be broken.

Aubrey

I SURVIVED LUNCH with Sully. I didn't choke on my sandwich or embarrass myself in any other way.

Most importantly, I didn't kiss him again.

The job isn't bad. He wasn't kidding about things picking up in the afternoon. I'm busy greeting customers, answering the phone, and signing people up for classes.

I expected to feel a little self-conscious among all these fitness-focused people, but the only ones who pay any attention to me are the guys who show up in the afternoon.

Sadly the only person who interests me is Sully.

He pretty much defines drop-dead sexy. I'm not the only one who notices either. His sinful mouth, ripped body, and dark, brooding eyes have every woman who takes a class with him stumbling over their sneakers.

"You're doing great, Aubrey," Sully assures me after closing.

"Thanks." I drop into the chair behind the front desk. "I'm exhausted, even though I don't feel like I did very much."

"You did plenty." He glances at the front door before turning back to me.

Lost in the intensity of his penetrating gaze, I don't stand a chance.

"Everything okay?" he asks, his warm voice full of sincerity. Even if he's aware of the effect he has on women, he never seems to exploit it.

"I'm fine."

"Do you need a ride?"

"My sister's supposed to pick me up on her way home."

He glances at the front door again.

"I can wait outside," I say, grabbing my stuff from under the counter.

"No," he says quickly. He motions for me to follow him. "Let's set you up with your own locker."

I follow him into the locker room and he throws his arms wide, turning in a half-circle. "Your pick." He hands me a lock and a card with the combination.

"Thanks. Now I feel official."

He reaches out and squeezes my shoulder. "You're very official."

The second he touches me, my body trembles. Maybe he notices, I'm not sure, but he hurries out of the locker room.

Rattled, I stumble to the first locker in front of me and slip the lock in place. I practice opening it a few times to make sure the combination works, then head outside.

My sister's near the entrance talking to Sully and smiles as soon as she sees me.

"Why didn't you call?" I ask, hurrying over.

"I finished early." She glances at Sully. "I wanted to say hello to your new boss and make sure he's taking good care of you."

Even though Celia's teasing isn't meant to hurt, it makes me feel about five years old.

"I'm fine," I mumble.

"She's terrific," Sully says, giving my shoulder a squeeze. "I'm lucky she had time in her schedule."

Celia beams and my anxiety spikes. I hold up my bag. "I'm ready to go."

"Bro, what are you still doing here?" Jake calls out from the back entrance. "Oh, hey, Aubrey." His gaze shoots to Celia and lingers. "And hello to you too."

He slows down and adopts his usual cocky swagger, and I groan. While I find Jake charming in a harmless-flirty way, my sister has no patience for overconfident player types.

Jake's danger radar must be defective because he circles my sister like a shark until Sully gives him a not-so-subtle shove. "You'll have to excuse my brother, Celia. I dropped him on his head a lot when he was little." He wraps an arm around Jake's neck, dragging him closer in what looks like a brotherly embrace until you notice Jake's eyes bugging out from lack of oxygen. "This is Aubrey's sister, Celia." He gives him one final warning squeeze before releasing Jake.

Jake coughs but shakes off the choke-hug quickly. "Now that your sister works here, you'll have to stop by for some classes."

"Do you teach any?" she asks.

He hands her his schedule and she folds it up without reading it, stuffing it in her back pocket.

"Maybe I'll try your Sunday class, Sully. Aubrey says she gets a lot out of it."

"Any time," Sully says.

"I don't teach that one," Jake says.

"I know," Celia answers without looking at him.

Sully ducks his head and cough-laughs.

"Good to see you again, Sully," Celia says, grabbing my arm and tugging me toward the door. "But my feet are killing me."

"Night, girls," Sully calls out. "Thanks, Aubrey."

"Nice meeting you, Celia," Jake says.

"Did you have to be so rude to my boss's brother?" I ask once we're outside.

She rolls her eyes at me. "I'm sure his ego survived. Besides, Sully seems to know what his brother's about." She gives me a more serious look. "Be careful around him."

"Jake?" I open my car door and slide in, waiting for her to get in her side. "He's harmless."

"He's got smooth-guy written all over him. I deal with jackasses like that all day long at the salon." She shimmies her shoulders. "Ones who 'accidentally' shove their face between your boobs when you're cutting their hair."

Now she's being ridiculous. "You don't even know him."

"Neither do you," she points out.

"I love you, but the over-protective big sister thing is super annoying."

She rests her hand on my leg. "I don't think I'll ever outgrow it, so just deal."

SULLY

"I THINK I'M in love," Jake mutters.

"Shocking," I grumble, locking up the front door and flipping off the lights.

"She's a taller, older version of Aubrey. And that a—"

"Don't," I warn, cutting him off before he starts singing the praises of Celia's ass.

"She picking Aubrey up every night?"

"I don't know." I cock my head and study him for a second. "Stay away from her."

"Why?"

"Seriously? Her sister works here now. I don't need you charming her into bed, then never calling her again."

"I gotta be honest, bro—"

I hold up a hand, cutting him off. "Stay. Away."

"All right, all right." He throws his hands up in surrender. "But if she moves on me, I'm not turning her down."

"I won't hold my breath."

Jake's not insulted. He never is.

"You coming over for dinner?" I ask.

"Is Mom cooking?"

"Yes," I answer in my *don't-be-a-moron* tone.

He ends up following me home, parking in my driveway and walking over to our mother's house with me.

I'm sure Mom had dinner hours ago, but she's used to us coming and going at all hours.

"Give me a few minutes," she says after greeting us at the door. "I had to run to Stewart's for more milk."

"Why didn't you tell me?" I ask, following her into the kitchen. "I would've stopped at the store for you."

She clucks her tongue. "I'm not an invalid, Sully."

"Never said you were."

She waves me away. "Go sit at the table."

"Sully's got a girlfriend," Jake announces.

I shoot a glare at his end of the table, but he ignores it.

"Oops, I mean, he hired a girl to work at Strike Back," Jake amends.

Mom raises her eyebrows. "What's her name?"

"Aubrey," I answer before Jake starts up again. "It's only a few hours a week."

"That's good. You work too much." It's a common complaint of my mother's even though she knows if I don't keep myself busy, I'll go nuts.

My mother turns to Jake. "What about you? Keeping out of trouble?"

"I haven't knocked up anyone if that's what you're asking," he mumbles, shoveling a fork full of mashed potatoes into his mouth.

My mother leans over and whaps him with a dishtowel. "That's not funny."

We talk about other stuff throughout dinner and my mother yawns as we're clearing off the table.

"Sorry it's so late."

"It's fine, Sullivan. I have to be up early tomorrow, so I might head to bed in a few minutes."

"Sure. I'll clean up." I take her arm, stopping her. "Doctor?"

She blows out a frustrated breath. "Yes."

"One of us should go with you."

"It's just a regular exam," she says, tapping her cheek right below her good eye. "Same thing I do every month."

I let out my own sigh. Years of guilt, I suppose. "I still feel better if you don't go alone."

"I'll go," Jake says, joining the conversation. "Where am I going?"

"Dr. Kersaw's."

Jake's never seemed to remember the incident that left our mom blind in one eye, so I doubt the same wildfire of anger, fear, and guilt blaze through him every time Mom has to go for her check-ups.

"Same time as usual?" Jake asks.

Mom confirms the time and gives both of us a quick kiss on the cheek before heading to bed.

Jake stretches and twists. "I'm gonna crash at your place since I'll just be back early in the morning."

"Yeah, no problem. That's why you have a room, jackass."

"Sullivan!" my mother shouts from the other room.

Jake sticks out his tongue and points at me like a deranged five-year-old and I roll my eyes.

Some things don't change all that much.

CHAPTER SIX
Aubrey

IN GENERAL, I enjoy people-watching, so I expected to be entertained working at Sully's place.

And it's definitely been entertaining. I mean, *wow*. Strike Back is a magnet for hot guys.

Unfortunately, some have more muscles than manners.

Sully's quick to rectify that situation each time it comes up.

Other than chasing off guys who stop to give me inappropriate uniform tips, Sully's a man of few words. Which has been weird, because I'm used to him barking out instructions during class. But when he's not teaching, he doesn't say much beyond "Yes," "No," and "Thanks" in response to my questions. He might be short on words but he's polite.

The men I know from my job at the coffee shop love to talk about themselves, so I find Sully's silence both relaxing and intriguing.

His brother, Jake, is the exact opposite. Always talking. Always flirting.

Always determined to annoy his big brother.

While Jake's fun to be around, he's also exhausting and I'm relieved that most afternoons he leaves to work at the gym he owns with Wrath and one other guy.

Jake's been gone for a few hours and I'm about to take my break when the front door chimes. I glance up, smile in place, ready to help whoever it is.

Apparently, today is leave Aubrey tongue-tied day. Two muscular guys around my age saunter inside. My gaze slides over the one on the left, who's busy scanning the room. He has close-cropped red hair and the faintest hint of auburn scruff covering his chin. His friend has dark, curly hair and determination brewing in his brown eyes. Unlike the majority of the clients, they have a presence that commands attention. No goofing around from these two. They're both serious and focused.

Focused on *me*.

The dark-haired one strides up to the counter and lays his hands on the glass. "New girl," he says, staring down at me.

"Well, aren't you observant?" I smile sweetly and grab a bottle of Windex, aiming the spray to the left of where his sweaty palms are marking up my glass.

Rude? Probably, but I have the feeling if I don't assert myself with these two, they'll steamroll right over me.

"Now I understand Jake's rambling," dark-hair says, sweeping his gaze over me.

His red-headed friend comes up next to him and slaps his shoulder. "Back off," he says in a voice almost too low for me to make out the words.

Dark-hair flashes a grin that I'm sure drops lots of panties for him, but he reminds me too much of the jocks I went to high school with to be impressed. "Aubrey, right?"

He knows my name?

Should I be worried or flattered that Jake's been talking about me to his friends?

"Jake's not here, but I can go grab Sully for you," I say, stepping out from behind the counter.

He stops me by throwing his hand out, grazing my arm. "No hurry, darlin'." He flashes another grin. "We came to meet *you*."

"Me? Why?"

"You're Sully's girl, right?"

I wish. "Hardly. I work for him."

"Remy!" Sully calls out, striding over. "What do you need?"

Sully's presence fills the space behind me and I almost jump out of my skin when he wraps an arm around my waist, settling his hand on my hip.

There's no battle for dominance between the guys. Dark-hair smirks and raises his hands in surrender.

"Remy, Griff, what do you need?" Sully asks again.

"Sullivan," Remy says in the same serious tone. "Looking for Jake."

"He'll be back later."

"And I'm looking for a new ring girl," Remy says, his gaze landing on me again.

Before I even have a chance to ask what the hell a ring girl is, Sully answers for me, "No."

Remy shakes his head. "You're not gonna let her answer for herself?"

"She's busy," Sully answers.

Done taunting Sully and flirting with me, Remy straightens up and lifts his chin at Sully. "Coming to the Castle with Jake tomorrow night?"

I'm close enough to feel the annoyance vibrate through Sully before he answers with a curt, "No."

Griff lifts his chin at me and throws a card on the counter. "If your schedule opens up, let *Jake* know. The job pays $100. Four hours max."

My jaw drops. "A hundred dollars? For what?"

"She's not interested," Sully growls. His grip on me tightens and I snap my mouth shut, dizzy from his hot hard body pressed against mine. Since he's clearly marking his territory, it only seems fair that I rub myself all over him and bask in his crisp, clean male scent, right? That won't be weird, will it?

The guys shrug and take off. Sully watches through the window until they drive away.

"Fucking Jake," he grumbles, releasing me before I twine myself around him like a kitty-cat in heat.

I stumble away, reaching for the card on the counter and stuffing it into my pocket without looking at it. One hundred dollars for four hours. What did Sully turn down on my behalf?

"What was that all about, Sully?"

"Nothing you want to be involved in," he says, walking past me.

I reach out and grab his arm to stop him. "I appreciate you giving me this job, but that doesn't mean you own me or my off-hours."

He stops and stares at me, his jaw working from side-to-side.

I don't get the feeling a lot of people defy or question Sully's decisions.

He runs his gaze over me and swipes his hand over his chin, studying me in a way I've only caught him doing when he thinks I'm not aware. "You want to spend the evening prancing around in little more than your underwear in front of a couple dozen juiced-up guys?"

What the hell?

"No."

"Then drop it."

"Sully—"

He leans in closer. "Not out here. If you really want to discuss it, come see me after Jake gets here and I finish kicking his ass."

Other than finding out why it bothers Sully so much, I don't care to learn more.

I will, however, take him up on the invitation into his office.

SULLY

AUBREY'S COMPLETELY CLUELESS. Not that Remy and Griff are one-hundred percent bad guys. They're just trying to hustle and make money like everyone else. But—and it's a big 'but' to someone like me trying to operate a legitimate business—they run an underground fighting ring. Something my brother participates in from time-to-time and something I've asked him to keep far the hell away from Strike Back.

Remy scoping Aubrey out like she was his next meal was an entirely different matter. As if he might want her for more than just a night of strutting around the fighting ring, flashing some numbers.

Not that I blame him. I've been fighting off my attraction to her since we met. Pressing her little body against me and clutching her hip didn't improve my state of mind. I don't do the territorial, jealous-guy thing. Never have. But for Aubrey, I came damn close.

"Send Jake to see me as soon as he gets here," I order in the gruffest way possible.

She seems hurt, or still pissed with me, but maybe that's better.

I shut the door to my office and pace for a few minutes to calm down. I'm not completely out of the red zone when Jake walks in without knocking.

"Aubrey said to come see you?"

"Shut the door."

He drops his smirk and places his hands on his hips. "What crawled up your ass?"

"You tell Griff and Remy, Aubrey would make a good ring girl?"

He runs his hand over his chin and pulls that "duh" look that's made me want to punch him since we were kids. "I might have mentioned we had a new girl working for us."

"What's the matter with you? You think she's the kind of girl who needs to be mixed up in that shit?"

"I think she's the kind of girl who works two jobs and goes to school, so she could probably use the extra cash. And," he adds with a slight smirk. "I'm tired of looking at skinny, stacked, Barbie doll types on fight night."

"God, you're an asshole." I really hate my brother thinking of Aubrey as nothing more than something pretty for him to admire when he's in the cage.

"True."

"Since when are you taking fights at the Castle?"

"Still like to keep my skills sharp."

"They ever get busted by the cops, you're gonna regret it."

"Nah, cops come place their own bets. Fuck, Remy's got one in the line-up this week."

I snort, not at all surprised. Empire has no shortage of crooked cops and politicians.

"Not everyone keeps their nose as clean as you and Liam."

There's no mature response to that comment, so I ignore it.

He finally drops his attitude. "You know I'll stay clear when Maddy visits."

My lips curl into a smile. "You better."

He tilts his head toward the gym. "What's the deal with Aubrey? You like her or not?"

"Yeah, I like her. But she works for me now and you know I have my mind on other things."

"Bro, you're not like me. You need someone."

"Oh for fuck's sake. Are you handing out advice on my love life now?" I can't think of anything worse or more ridiculous than my little brother offering me relationship pointers.

"Absolutely not."

"Get out of here." I wave my hand in his face, but there's no bite behind my words. As much as he loves pissing me off, I can't stay mad at my brother for long.

A few seconds later, someone taps their knuckles against my door.

"Come on in."

"Can we still talk?" Aubrey asks. Timid this time. Not the fired-up girl who challenged me earlier. It reaffirms that I'm right about keeping her away from Griff and Remy's operation. She'd never survive a night at the Castle.

She hesitates in the open doorway, so I invite her in. "Sure."

Without asking, she closes the door behind her. I should tell her to leave it open, but the words never make it out of my mouth.

"Are you still mad at me?" she asks.

Her voice and downcast gaze tugs at me and I take a few steps closer, placing my fingers under her chin and lifting her face. "I'm sorry I snapped at you. I feel...responsible for you now that you're working for me. That's all."

"I appreciate that, Sully. I really do. I know you think I look young-er than I am, but I can take care of myself. I've been doing it for a long time."

Something about the sad way her mouth turns down bothers me. Again, I realize how little I know about her.

"You and your sister seem tight."

Her face brightens a fraction. "We are. I—I'm not sure where I would've ended up if it wasn't for her."

How do I respond to that?

"Your parents?"

"Let's not talk about them."

"Fair enough."

"Now, ring girl?" she asks, tapping her foot. "What is that? And why does it pay so much?" she asks with a persistence I don't expect.

Why did I think she'd let this go?

Aubrey

I ALMOST FEEL bad for giving Sully a hard time. But if I can hand Celia one hundred dollars by the end of the week, it will be enough to keep our electric on for another two months.

Sully sighs and steps closer. "Griff and Remy run underground fights. *Illegal* gambling. Ring girls get the crowd worked up or announce each round. It's a rough crew. Griff would look after you, but it's still not the safest place for someone like you to be."

Wow. That's so not what I expected him to say. And, wait a second. "Someone like me?"

He reaches out and brushes a stray strand of hair out of my eyes, his hand lingering near my cheek. "A girl who's worried about being jumped because she thinks she's tiny."

"Oh."

Our eyes meet and I'm trapped. Unable to look away.

"Aubrey," he whispers.

He leans in and brushes an unexpected kiss over my lips. A short moan of surprise and pleasure bursts out of me. His mouth is warm and soft. Slow and sweet. Sully takes his time exploring and tasting my mouth. My lips part and his tongue slips against mine.

Another moan leaves me.

I wrap my arms around his neck and slide my hands into the silky thickness of his hair, reaching up on my tiptoes to get closer.

This is totally different from when I ambush-kissed him. This time he's fully present and involved. In charge. Both of us groan as he deepens our kiss. My mind's blank except for the excitement of kissing Sully. Really kissing him. Not a scared, confused, mashing my lips against his.

His firm hand against my lower back presses my body into his. My knees wobble and I grip his arms to steady myself.

A buzz-rattling noise interrupts us and Sully curses, slowly detaching himself from me. "I'm sorry, Aubrey."

I'm not sure if he's apologizing for the kiss or the interruption. But I don't have the opportunity to ask. Still gasping for air, I glance down at his desk and find the source of the interruption.

Someone's calling his phone.

A girl named Madison.

CHAPTER SEVEN
SULLY

"D O YOU...IS THAT your girlfriend?" Aubrey asks with more than a trace of hurt in her voice.

Still reeling from our kiss. I groan at the question.

"No," I say, snatching up my phone. Aubrey tries to push past me and I stop her with an arm around her waist. "Wait."

The tension drains out of her body and when I'm sure she won't run, I answer the phone.

"Hey, Maddy-girl, what's up?"

"Dad! Are you excited to see me next week?"

I'd laugh, except it hurts too much. I miss my daughter all the time. "Of course I am. You know what you want to do while you're here?" I ask, trying to keep my voice upbeat.

"Can we go to the butterfly garden again? Maybe Uncle Jake can come with us this time?"

Maddy's the only person who would ever be able to lure my brother to Dancing Rainbow's butterfly garden. "We can do that."

"Cool!"

I chuckle at the excitement in my daughter's voice at the same time the dull ache of not seeing her for three weeks continues to spread through my chest.

We talk for a few more minutes. Before we hang up, I write down her flight number and the time she should be arriving. Her mother usually books the tickets and sends me the bill. Madison's the one who lets me know when she's arriving.

Aubrey's still in front of me looking bewildered. I'm not sure how much of Maddy's end of the conversation she overheard.

"My daughter," I explain.

"Oh." Her eyes widen. "I didn't realize. Are you. Is she. Are you married?"

"No. It's a…long story. She lives in Florida. I only have her one weekend a month." I shrug, uncomfortable discussing the arrangement. "Never enough time."

The tension in her body softens and she runs her fingers down my arm. "I'm sorry. How old is she?"

"Twelve."

"Oh," she quirks an eyebrow. "Fun times ahead for you."

I groan and roll my eyes. "So far she seems to save the teenage drama for her mom."

Aubrey steps closer, reaches out like she wants to hug me, then retreats. "She probably wants to be on her best behavior when she visits since she doesn't see you that often."

Her observation is on target and said with kindness. The truth of it still hits me like a fist in the gut. "Yeah."

"You hate that she's not comfortable enough to be herself when she's here?"

I shouldn't be surprised. In the short time I've known her, Aubrey's shown herself to be sharp and thoughtful. "Something like that. I wish we spent more time together."

She glances around the office. "Hard to move an entire business."

"Not just that. My family's here. Lauren—my ex—was supposed to move back to New York, but she kept putting it off and now she's remarried. We spent a few years battling it out, but Florida sided with her. I'm lucky to have the time I ended up with. Or so I've been told."

"I'm sorry."

I shake off the anger and sadness about the whole situation. "I shouldn't be dumping any of this on you."

"It's okay," she says softly. "I understand."

And I get the feeling she does. It still doesn't make it right to burden her with my issues.

She keeps staring at me with wide, unblinking eyes and I remember what we were doing before the phone call.

"I shouldn't have kissed you."

Her very kissable mouth turns down and she parts her lips—probably to tell me off, but I hold up my hand.

"It wasn't professional of me. That's not why I hired you. I don't want you to be uncomfortable working here."

"I'm not."

I gesture to the phone still in my hand. "I don't have time for anything else. Anyone else. My daughter and this business are my priorities."

Instead of telling me to fuck off like she should, she tilts her head, studying me for a few beats. "I respect that, Sully. I'd never want to be in the way between you and your daughter."

And she just nailed my biggest concern. The few women I've tried dating in the past were either too eager to play "new mommy" to my daughter or were jealous and tried to make me choose.

There's no choice. My daughter comes first.

What little time I do get to spend with her is precious and I don't want to let anyone interfere with it.

"So, it's not me." She crosses her arms over her chest, putting space between us. "You just don't date because you're a single dad?"

"Pretty much."

"Is that a long-term plan?"

Not sure I understand what she's asking, I cock my head, inviting her to explain.

"Are you planning to spend the next six years alone? Or longer?"

She's not saying anything my mother hasn't already said. Jake's said it too—although he's much more crude in the words he picks.

"You're young and have lots of options, Aubrey. You don't want someone who already comes with responsibilities."

Her whole demeanor changes from one of empathy and understanding to pissed off female. "Wow." She releases an annoyed breath and meets my eyes. "Okay. Thanks for explaining my needs to me."

"That's not what I meant."

"Look," she says, stopping me from explaining myself. "I respect you for taking your responsibilities seriously. I'd never hold that against you. The hot-cold-explaining-my-life-choices-to-me thing I totally hold against you, though."

"You're my employee, Aubrey."

With that, she turns and yanks the door open. "Employer-employee. Got it loud and clear, Mr. Wallace. Thank you."

Aubrey's not dramatic. She doesn't scream the words or slam the door on her way out.

The hurt in her voice echoes just the same.

Aubrey

"ARE ALL MEN ass-hats?" I ask my sister as I approach her workstation at the salon.

"Yes," she answers without turning around. She straightens up and closes the cabinet she'd been sorting through "Which particular ass-hat are you referring to today?"

"Sully."

The corner of her mouth quirks. "Your boss?"

She says *boss* with a dirty eyebrow wiggle that made me laugh the first time she did it. Today, not so much.

I don't want to tell her what happened and have her judge me for once again making poor life choices. But the only other person I'd talk to about this is Bree and she's in class now.

"We kissed."

"Oh, wow." She leans back on the counter giving me her full attention. "How workplace-sexual-harassment of him."

"Stop, it wasn't like that."

"What was it like?"

"Amazing and short." I slick my tongue over my lower lip, remembering the feel of him against me before our interruption. "His daughter called."

Her jaw drops. "He has a kid?"

Exactly. How have I known Sully all this time and not known he had a daughter? "Yeah, she lives in Florida, so he only gets to see her like once a month. So, he's not interested in dating."

She tilts her head and stares at me for a second. "It's hard not to respect that."

"I do. I mean, I want to, but I like him a lot. Maybe he just said it because he's not interested."

"Then why did he kiss you?"

Good question.

One I don't have an answer for.

"You need a break," Celia says after I explain where I'm headed.

"Money's tight enough. You shouldn't have to keep supporting me."

Her face softens. "Honey, I'm managing the place now," she says, gesturing to the small salon around us. "I've built up a bigger client base and I'm making more money than when you moved in with me. You don't have to keep killing yourself. I can take care of the bills until you're done with school."

Tears prick my eyes. My sister's only four years older than me, but when I had nowhere else to go, she didn't hesitate to take me in. At some point in my life, I want to repay her for everything she's done for me. "At the rate, I'm going, I won't be done any time soon, Celia."

She *tsks* and slips an arm around my shoulders, showing me more motherly concern than our own mother ever showed either one of us. "I'm so proud of you. You're doing great. And you deserve a nice guy, who's into you one-hundred percent." She lowers her voice and squeezes me a little tighter. "So, maybe forget about Sully."

Not what I wanted to hear, but she's probably right. "It's hard when now I'm spending so much time with him."

"Do you like the job?"

"I do," I answer easily. "I think I'm actually helping him out and I'm good at it."

"Just...be careful. Don't get carried away. And don't let him mess with your heart."

"He's not like that."

She rolls her eyes. "They're *all* like that. Even the ones who seem nice."

Before I can offer another protest, she pats my back. "Hey, I'll be at that training seminar this weekend. You can have my car. Why don't you go visit Bree?"

"Thanks. I'll see what she's up to."

"Good. You need to do something fun for a change."

"I do fun stuff."

"Making out with your boss doesn't count."

I knew I would regret telling her about our kiss.

CHAPTER EIGHT
SULLY

AUBREY CAN'T SEEM to stop staring at the clock. Probably my fault. She's been uncomfortable around me since the other day.

"Everything all right?" I ask.

"I...do you mind if I leave a few minutes early? I need to make sure I catch the bus."

"What bus?"

She heaves out an exasperated sigh. "To the college."

"I didn't realize any buses ran out there." Johnson County Community College is in a pretty rural area.

"Well, there's only one from downtown to the school in the afternoon and I need to be on it. Normally, I catch it from home."

"How long does that take?"

"Forever."

"You take it home at night too?"

"Sometimes. Usually, Celia picks me up." She tilts her head. "Why?"

Instead of answering her question, I nod at the clock. "Leave whenever you need to. No problem."

"Thanks, I appreciate it."

Back in my office, I send Jake a quick text to find out when he plans to drag his ass in here.

He doesn't respond, but fifteen minutes later he's in my doorway.

"What's on fire?" he asks.

"Nothing. Just need you to watch the place for a few minutes and start my four o'clock class."

"What the? Are you okay?"

I get his concern. I never take off in the middle of the day.

"Just cover for me."

"Yeah, I got your back."

"Thanks."

Aubrey's on her way out of the locker room when I return to the floor. "Hey, ready to leave?"

Her eyes widen. "You said it was okay."

Great, she thinks I'm going back on my word. "It's cool. I'll give you a ride."

She stops and her bag *thunks* on the floor at her feet. "What? Why?"

Before answering, I lean over and grab her bag. "I don't like the idea of you riding the bus alone."

Instead of following me, she crosses her arms over her chest. "Sully, you have a business to run. You don't have time to waste driving me around."

I slip my arm around her shoulders, drawing her closer. "I'm the boss. I can do whatever I want. Jake's gonna watch the place for me."

Reluctantly, she agrees and follows me out to the parking lot. Not that I give her much choice.

"You can't do this every week," she says once we're on the road.

"Sure I can."

She shakes her head. "Why?"

"I told you why. Stop arguing with me. Tell me about your classes."

That must not be a good subject either. She twists her fingers together and stares straight ahead. "I'm taking Intermediate Accounting."

Obviously a sensitive topic, so I try to be careful asking my next question. "And you don't love it?"

"I'm not good at it. It's embarrassing because I'm supposed to be an accounting major."

"Supposed to be?"

"My sister wants to open her own salon eventually, and we thought we'd go into business together. Since I'm scary with scissors in my hands, I thought I could do the books and stuff."

Lucky Celia. If only Jake had half the desire to help out some days.

"Good plan."

"Well, it was. But I suck at it."

"Maybe you have a crappy teacher."

She *hmms* and turns to stare out the window.

"What else are you taking?"

"Business Communications. Now *that* I'm actually good at." She huffs out a sad laugh. "I always wanted to be an English teacher."

"So why aren't you doing that?"

I'm expecting an ordinary excuse like lack of money.

"It's…" she hesitates for so long, I glance over at her. "A long story. I sort of lost my joy for writing and stuff."

The sudden sadness that surrounds her makes me wish I'd kept my nosy questions to myself.

A few minutes later the low stone sign in front of the college's campus comes into view.

"What time are you done?"

"Celia will pick me up," she answers quickly as if she's afraid I plan to return. Well, actually I was considering it.

Her fingers hover over the door handle for a second before she turns toward me. "Thank you so much. I really appreciate the ride."

"Any time."

The urge to kiss her rears up and I tighten my hands on the steering wheel.

"See you tomorrow."

"Can't wait," I say as she closes the door.

It's true too. As much as I find myself trying to figure Aubrey out, I also realize how much I like spending time with her.

Aubrey

I'M TWITCHY WITH leftover nerves from being alone with Sully, but smiling for the same reason when I close the door to his Jeep. Like a silly teenager, I turn and wave as he drives off. I can't believe he left work in the middle of the day to drop me off at school.

He's impossible to figure out. And I probably shouldn't read too much into his kind gesture. One little kiss and a pity lift to school doesn't change the fact that we're nothing more than employer-employee.

I wasn't lying about my Intermediate Accounting class. I hate it. The semester has barely gotten started and no matter how hard I try to pay attention to the lecture on Inventory Valuation Methods, I'm lost.

How am I going to survive this class?

Business Communications is a different matter. Our long-term project involves developing a strategic communication plan for a local business. I have an advantage here since I work for two different local businesses. Do I have the guts to ask Sully if I can use Strike Back as part of my project? Or should I just ask Brantley, my manager at Busy Beans? Strike Back could benefit from it more. Plus, I already have a hundred different ideas running around in my head.

"Hey, Aubrey!" a girl calls out as I'm leaving class. "I thought I saw you earlier."

Ah, Bree's friend, Emily. We've only hung out a few times, so it takes me a second to place her. "If I looked like I was about to cry leaving accounting, it was me."

She chuckles. "Do you want to grab lunch?"

As I'm about to answer, my phone buzzes.

Brantley: *We're slammed. Can you come in and work this afternoon?*

Me: *If I can find a ride, yes.*

Brantley: *I'll feed you.*

Me: *Promises, promises.*

"Ugh." I glance up at Emily. "I'll buy you lunch if you can give me a ride to my part-time job."

She smiles. "Sure. I hate the food here anyway."

We catch up on the way to Busy Beans. Well, she fills me in on her life, and I listen.

"Have you seen Professor Martin? I definitely want to take advantage of his evening office hours."

An uneasy sensation rolls through me. "No thanks. My grades are bad enough right now without risking getting kicked out of school."

She glances over. "I think it's more of a risk for the teacher than the student."

I snort and shake my head. I'm kind of being a drag, aren't I? I force a smile. "Guess I need to check him out."

By the time we arrive at Busy Beans, I'm exhausted. Emily takes "bubbly personality" to a new level.

The coffee shop's packed. I slip behind the counter and loop my apron around my neck, understanding Brantley's desperation.

"Thank you so much, sweet pea," he says, air-kissing my cheek as he sweeps past me. "You're a life-saver."

"Anything for a buck, Bran-man, you know that." I nod at Emily. "I owe my friend lunch for giving me a ride, though."

"I'll take care of her." He shoves me in front of the cash register. "You take care of this line."

I work on thinning the impossibly long line of people waiting to order coffee and pastries for the next hour.

They just keep coming.

Emily waves on her way out and I thank her again for the ride. "Next week!" she shouts.

The pennies clattering into the tip jar every now and then make me question whether coming in on my night off was a good idea.

Pennies. That's what's on my mind when the next customer steps up and orders three blueberry muffins to go.

Something about his voice makes me glance up. A slow smirk spreads across his face as if he'd been waiting for me to recognize him.

"Griff? Right?" I ask, waving my fingers in a half-hearted hello.

"The one and only." He hands over a twenty and tells me to keep the change. I'd like to say I stuff it in the tip jar, but since I'm pretty sure Griff came to specifically see me, it goes right in my apron pocket.

He follows on the other side of the counter as I step away from the register to grab a bag and fill his order.

"You work two jobs?" he asks.

"And go to school."

He lets out a low whistle, that might seem mocking coming from anyone else, but I get the feeling he understands my situation more than he's making fun of it.

"Busy girl."

"Thank you, Captain Obvious," I say, handing over the brown bag. His mouth twitches and he jerks his head to the side. "Do you have a minute?"

A glance up shows the line of customers has dwindled to nothing.

I catch Brantley's eye. "I'll be right back."

"Go on," he encourages with a wink aimed at Griff.

I whip off my apron and slip through the low, swinging door separating me from the rest of the cafe.

Up close, Griff doesn't seem threatening. He's big, sure. Everyone's big compared to me. But he keeps a respectable distance and his gaze sticks to my face. "I'm not sure what Sully told you, but I really can help you out with your money situation."

Given the nature of Griff's business, I'm not sure if the information Sully shared is supposed to be spread around. "How? Are you a pimp?"

He snorts. "No. You ever watch boxing, or MMA, or wrestling? Anything like that?"

"Sure. Once or twice."

He twirls a finger in the air. "The girls who walk the ring, holding up the signs. Encouraging the crowds. That's what I need you for."

"Need me? You don't even *know* me."

"You're mouthy. That's a plus."

I narrow my eyes.

"Jake says you're a good girl, need the cash, and can keep your mouth shut."

"Ahh, there it is. This isn't legal."

"Gray area," he says, waving off my concern.

"There have to be dozens of taller, prettier girls around who would be into the whole bad-boy-danger experience. Why are you so interested in me?"

He drops his smile and sweeps his gaze over me. "Don't sell yourself short." Yes, he adds a smirk to that one. "Seriously though. One of our regular girls is out of town and another one is sick."

"I'm not interested in spending the night prancing around in my underwear in front of a bunch of testosterone-pumped knuckle-draggers. Sorry."

Griff's not even insulted. "Doesn't have to be underwear." One corner of his mouth curls up. "A nice, tight, short dress will do."

I glare at him.

"We look after our girls. Nothing's gonna happen to you. Jake'll be there. He definitely won't let anyone near you."

Interesting that Jake's planning to attend when his brother has such strong opinions on this subject.

Or maybe Sully just didn't want *me* there?

Because he's genuinely worried about me or he's jealous?

Not the last one. That's insane.

"Hundred and fifty," he offers, raising his earlier offer.

Tonight, if I'm lucky, I'll go home with sixty dollars and sore feet.

A hundred and fifty bucks is a lot of money to me at the moment.

"It's fun. A lot of girls think it's exciting," Griff encourages. "Girl like you probably has a lot of questions." He wiggles his fingers in a "give it to me" sort of gesture. "Hit me."

"Do you ever have any girl fighters?" pops out of my mouth first.

The question seems to take him by surprise. He cocks his head. "Actually yes. Anyone who pays up can go in the ring."

Huh. I didn't really expect an answer and definitely not that answer.

"Does anyone ever get seriously injured?"

Another question that he apparently didn't see coming. What kind of girls usually work for him? "Yeah. We have a guy with medical training at the fights. Any injuries above his skill-level get dropped off at the hospital."

Dropped off sounds more like *dumped*, but what do I expect?

"A hundred and fifty dollars?" I ask to be sure.

"In cash." He nods, all serious businessman now. "At the end of the night."

We stand there staring at each other for a few minutes before I let out a breath. "Okay."

"Fantastic. Thank you."

"When and where?"

"I'll text you with the address a couple hours before. Need you there by nine-thirty. Usually breaks around two in the morning."

We exchange numbers and Griff thanks me again before bouncing out the door with his bag of muffins.

I can't stop thinking how mad Sully's going to be.

He's made it abundantly clear we're only employer-employee.

So why does disappointing him bother me so much?

CHAPTER NINE
SULLY

AUBREY'S TRYING TO kill me.

Today, she showed up to work in a bright red polo shirt and tiny black stretchy shorts. As if she's read my damn mind and knew exactly what would drive me insane.

The outfit isn't inappropriate.

Unless you're a perv like she's apparently turned me into.

Jake strolls in around noon, bumping into my shoulder as he stops dead. He squints at Aubrey. "Is she carrying her cell phone in her back pocket?"

Shaking myself out of my latest dirty fantasy involving Aubrey, me, and one of the locker room benches, I mumble, "I don't think so, why?"

"Because that fine, curvy little ass of hers is calling me."

Christ, why didn't I see that coming? "You're a dick. Don't you dare say that to her."

He's laughing so hard, he can barely speak. "I just said it. To get. You going. You should see. The way you're drooling. Over her."

I throw the heel of my hand into his shoulder, knocking him back a few feet. Unfortunately our antics draw Aubrey's attention our way. She smiles and waves at Jake, then returns to whatever she's doing on the computer.

"Seriously," he says after catching his breath. "For a tiny girl, she's—"

"Knock it off, would ya?"

"What?" He throws his arms in the air and turns in a circle. "It's a professional observation."

"No it's not. You're trying to piss me off."

He stops goofing around and gives me a lopsided grin. "Only 'cause it's so easy to rile you when it comes to her."

"Shut it," I growl under my breath as Aubrey strolls over.

"Hey, Jake. Did you just get here?" she asks.

"Yeah, good thing. Looks like my brother's in a mood today."

She gives me a shy smile that punches me in the gut. "Everything okay?" she asks. "You *have* been quiet all morning."

"I'm fine. Jake thinks he's a comedian."

Jake slaps me on the back. "I gotta go. Got someone coming in at twelve-thirty."

After he leaves, Aubrey's gaze lands on me. "Can I show you something I'd like to order?"

"Sure," I mumble, still staring at her legs.

She fidgets and my gaze travels up, landing on her nervous face. "You should really wear pants to work," I blurt.

Her cheeks turn red. "Oh. Uh, I didn't. It's so hot out." The more she stammers, the stupider I feel for opening my big mouth. My inability to control myself isn't her problem.

"It's fine." I nod to the equipment she never touches. "I just don't want you getting hurt or something." Never mind clients who actually use the equipment wear whatever the fuck they want.

"Won't happen again." She hurries away and pushes the door to the women's locker room open.

I step into my office, planning to bang my head against the wall a few times. Maybe knock some common sense loose.

Nothing comes to me, so I return to the floor.

Aubrey storms out of the locker room—wearing long, loose black sweats and plants herself behind the front counter.

Good job, asshole.

I better fix this before it goes any further. "You didn't have to—"

"It's fine," she snaps, cutting me off.

"What did you want to show me?"

"Nothing. It's probably stupid anyway."

"Aubrey," I try again.

71

We're interrupted by students arriving for my one o'clock class. "Are you going to assist me?" I ask Aubrey.

She won't even look at me. "You're the boss. If you want me to, I will."

One of my regulars, Shayla, slides up next to me and threads her arm through mine. "I'll let you demonstrate on me."

"Thanks." I force a polite smile and untangle myself from Shayla. "I'll meet you ladies back there in a few minutes."

"Better make sure you tell Shayla and her buddies about your 'no shorts in the gym' policy," Aubrey mutters without sparing me a glance.

I turn and run my gaze over the women. "I didn't notice."

She huffs out a sad laugh and shakes her head.

I'm torn. Tell her the shorts were bothering me because I couldn't think about anything other than bending her over and yanking them down her legs? Or let her continue to think I don't find her attractive?

Both options are damn unappealing for different reasons.

Aubrey

I REALLY WISH Sully would go away and stop looking at me like I'm an annoying puppy he accidentally kicked.

Of course, that would be easier if I stopped acting like one.

But, damn he knows how to make me feel inadequate.

Finally, he gives up to attend to his trio of tall, leggy blondes. Like hell am I going over there to help out.

Jake saunters my way, leans over and places his elbows on the counter. "Anyone call for me?" he asks.

"Not today."

He glances at the door. "Damn. This dude usually isn't late and doesn't blow off appointments."

"Sorry. Do you want me to call him?"

"Nah." He shakes his head and then stops and stares at me. "Why'd you change?"

"Jesus. What is it with you and your brother? You two have some clothing fetish you need to tell me about?"

"Huh?"

"Nothing," I mutter. "Your brother informed me my shorts weren't appropriate attire, so I changed."

Jake cocks his head toward Sully and chuckles. "Did he really?"

"Don't worry, I'll cover myself in a sack from now on. I know I don't look like the Hilton sisters over there, but jeez."

His eyes widen. "Whoa. Whatever he said, I can guarantee it's not because he thinks you're unattractive."

"Whatever." I tap at the computer and turn the screen toward Jake. "How is it Strike Back has like zero web presence? This site is pathetic."

Not offended by the criticism, he shrugs. "He keeps meaning to hire someone to fix up the website. Hasn't gotten around to it."

"You guys need something to let people know the place even exists."

"We get lots of referrals from word of mouth."

I roll my eyes. "You two act like you're seventy-year-old men afraid of technology instead of almost-thirty business owners."

He throws his head back and laughs. "You're exactly what he needs."

Heat spreads over my cheeks. "What Strike Back needs," I correct.

"Yeah, that too."

CHAPTER TEN

Aubrey

ALMOST CLOSING TIME for Strike Back. Also, almost time for me to be at the fight to make my debut as a ring girl.

So why am I parked behind the gym? Far enough not to be spotted right away but with a good view of the back door.

What am I doing?

I don't have the guts to stroll inside and announce that I'm on my way to do something he expressly asked me not to do. Do I?

Don't put yourself in danger just to make a point.

That sounds like something Sully would say and I hate that he's in my head.

Don't do something stupid just to get even with him for rejecting me.

That one makes me squirm. I glance down at my dress. Short, tight, dark red velvet. My heels are on the seat next to me because I can't drive with them. The ballet flats currently on my feet are much more comfortable.

Did I stop by with the stupid hope that he'll talk me out of tonight? Maybe toss me over his shoulder and have his way with me over his desk instead?

If I don't make up my mind soon, I'm going to be late.

Where does Sully go after work?

Jesus, pretty soon if you flip to nutjob in the dictionary, my picture will be there.

I blow out an exaggerated, heavy sigh. Sitting here reeks of bad decisions. I'll be too mortified if Sully catches me to give him a piece of my mind. Worse if he tells me not to go, I'll probably listen to him and I really do need the money.

Before putting the car in drive, I reach into my purse for my makeup bag and my lip balm.

It's not there.

My memory flashes to my locker.

Shit.

Well, *now* I have an excuse to go inside.

A flimsy, ridiculously obvious excuse.

I put the car in drive and pull up next to the back door. Just because I'm insane doesn't mean I want to walk through a dark parking lot in my barely-covers-my-ass dress.

After a few deep breaths, I open the car door and step out. I leave my heels in the car, because, come on, let's not be completely obvious.

Inside, the lights wink out one by one.

I halt in my tracks.

Should I leave?

When have I ever done what I *should* do?

I run up to the back door and rap my knuckles against the glass.

It's so dark, I barely make Sully's form out as he approaches. I'm standing under a bright light, so I know he sees me.

The door pushes open. "Aubrey? What are you doing here?"

"I'm on my way out, saw the lights were on, and uh, realized I forgot something in my locker. Do I have time to grab it?"

His gaze slowly travels over my body. The tension between us grows as neither of us speaks and he doesn't move to let me in or shut the door in my face.

"Never mind, I'll grab it another time."

As I turn to leave, he pushes the door wider. "No, it's okay. Come in."

"Thanks."

He doesn't move, so I brush past him, ignoring the way my body tingles in all the places we touch.

I hurry down the hallway, my flats whispering over the hardwood floors that gleam in the low light. The locker room door stands wide open with a trashcan keeping it in place. It takes a second to remember why I'm here.

My fingers shake and I mess up the combination three times before the lock finally clicks open.

Reaching in, I grab the small silk makeup bag and check for the gloss I wanted. I mean, if I came all the way in here for it, I might as well make sure it's here, right?

It is and I take it to the counter with the mirror over it and slick some over my lips.

"Aubrey?"

The tube of gloss clatters to the counter, rolls off the edge, and lands on the floor. I bend over, reaching for it and almost smack into Sully's knees.

I wish I'd put my heels on. Standing taller would make me feel less foolish.

"What are you up to tonight?" he asks in a low voice, his gaze roaming up and down my body.

"Uh," I don't lie well. "Stuff."

He cocks his head. "Pretty fancy for just 'stuff.'"

"For an *employer*, you spend a lot of time noticing my clothes."

"Hard not to," he mumbles.

"What's that supposed to mean?"

"Nothing."

Nervous from the way he's staring at me, I wave my cosmetic bag in his face. "Well, I have what I came for. I'm running late."

"Date?" he asks.

"Does it matter?"

He closes his eyes briefly. "No. I shouldn't have asked." His gruff voice is laced with what seems like regret. "Go on."

I open my mouth to confess my plans, then shut it. He'll only try to stop me.

SULLY

Jake: *Is Aubrey with you?*

Me: *No. Why?*

Jake: *She's late.*

I'd ask *for what*, but I have a sinking feeling I already know.

Why'd I let her slip through my fingers?

No wonder she was all dressed up.

The ridiculous possessive streak in me was convinced she had a date. Asking questions I might not like the answers to seemed to be the smarter move.

I stalk out the back door, but too late. She's gone.

To the Castle.

Unfortunately, I know how to find the place.

CHAPTER ELEVEN

Aubrey

THE DIRECTIONS GRIFF sent weren't the most useful, but eventually, I find myself driving down an overgrown dirt driveway. Ten-foot-high chain link fence with barbed wire spirals at the top define the grounds long before the decaying brick building comes into view.

Large, portable floodlights—the kind usually only seen along the highway during night time roadwork—illuminate the circular driveway that loops around the building. The parking lot is full of trucks, motorcycles, and a lot of low-slung sports cars. Nothing too flashy.

I tuck the car into a corner spot, praying no one damages it. Celia won't appreciate me taking her car on this particular adventure.

Threading my car key through a chain, I drape it around my neck and tuck it into my cleavage. My wallet stays in the glovebox. I stuff my heels, a hairbrush, and my makeup bag into a bigger tote and take a deep breath before stepping out of the car.

The leering and low whistles from the guys standing around outside make me wish I'd worn jeans and a hoodie. Surely this place has a bathroom I could've used to change into my ring girl gear.

At the door, a guy stops me with a hand in my face. "Name?"

"Aubrey. Griff asked me to work tonight."

He scowls, but I scowl right back. No one told me I needed a secret password to enter.

"Royal's in the back."

"Royal?"

"That's Griff, but don't call him that here."

"Whatever," I mumble, already regretting tonight.

Griff is nowhere in sight. And I'm not sure where "the back" the doorman referred to actually is since it's one big circular room. Luckily, I spot Jake inside a circle of other fighter-types. He's engaged in an intense discussion with a big, bearded red-headed guy who appears to be inked from neck to fingers.

A bit of a hush falls over the guys surrounding Jake as I approach and he glances up. A welcoming smile spreads across his face.

"Aubrey!" Jake calls out, waving me over. "You made it."

The guys surrounding him part, giving me room to approach. None of them say a word to me.

Jake gives me a friendly squeeze. He seems to command respect here, so his acknowledgment makes me feel less out of place. Protected even.

While Griff claimed he had no other ring girls for tonight, there are a number of scantily clad women milling around. I mention that to Jake and he snorts. "Ring bunnies. They're here for a…different purpose."

"Oh."

His burly friend laughs, and Jake slaps him in the chest. "Aubrey, this is my buddy, Murphy."

He nods at me. "Sully's girl?" he asks, raising an eyebrow Jake's way.

"No. Not Sully's girl," I snap. "His *employee*. Sheesh."

Murphy's not offended. No, he laughs at me and holds up his hands. "I must've been given bad info."

One of the guys who'd whistled at me outside walks by and Jake glares, pulling me into his side. "Sully flip his shit when you told him you were coming tonight?" he asks once the threat has passed. Whether he's feeling protective of me or that was his opponent, I'm not sure.

"I didn't tell your brother what my plans were. It's none of his business."

Murphy nods toward the door. "Well, I'm guessing someone told him."

I'm close enough to feel Jake vibrating with laughter as he watches his brother. "Bastard hasn't come to one of these in years," he mutters.

Sure enough, Sully's striding in the same entrance I used and surveying the vast circular room. I turn away, hoping he'll miss me.

"It doesn't have anything to do with me." My denial sounds weak even to me. I lift my chin at one of the pretty blondes pacing in front of the bathroom. "Maybe he came to pick up a ring bunny to bring home with him for the night."

Jake laughs even harder. "Nah, my brother doesn't bring girls to his house." He raises an eyebrow, waiting for my reaction. I shrug not sure what to make of the information.

Griff waves to me and I wriggle away from Jake. "I better go. Griff wanted me to talk to him first thing."

"Kiss for luck?" Jake asks.

I rear back. "Um, *no*."

He screws his face into a mask of outraged surprise. "Not even one little kiss?" He touches his hand to his chest as if he's heartbroken. "What if I get hurt in the ring and your good luck kiss is the only thing that could've prevented it?"

Murphy bursts out laughing. "Laying it on thick, bro."

"Well, I guess you should be extra careful then." I narrow my eyes. "What makes you think I'd kiss you for luck or anything else?"

He flashes a cocky grin. "No reason."

"Why would...wait, what did your brother tell you?"

"Nothing."

"You're infuriating."

"He's *special*," Murphy agrees, patting the top of Jake's head.

"Are you fighting too, Murphy?" I ask.

"Maybe. I mostly came to scrape Jake off the ground after he gets his ass handed to him."

"Bullshit," Jake shoots back.

Underneath their growly man-teasing, I get the sense they've been friends for a while and Murphy's here as some sort of protection for Jake. I also notice some of his tattoos are similar to Sully's friend, Wrath.

Maybe Sully's not as clean-cut as he wants people to think.

"Better run, Aubrey," Jake says, tilting his head to a determined Sully weaving his way through the crowd.

I pat his shoulder and wish him luck before hurrying away to find

Griff.

He meets me halfway and shakes my hand. "Thanks for showing up."

I can't tell if he's sincere or being sarcastic because I'm late.

"You can store your stuff back here," he says, pointing to a metal desk in the corner. He runs his gaze over my dress. "I guess that'll do."

"Gee, thanks."

His mouth quirks. "I like you, Aubrey. You're totally worth getting an ass-kicking from Sully."

I roll my eyes as I slip my heels on and stuff my bag in the bottom desk drawer. "That's ridiculous." I turn and face him. "So, what exactly does a good ring girl do?"

"Follow me." He waves me closer and I trot after him. We end up in a locker room and I avert my gaze from the half-dressed guys getting ready for their fights.

He stops so abruptly, I almost slam into him. Tottering in my heels to stay upright. I throw out my hand, bracing myself on the wall of lockers to my left.

"Easy, girl," he says, grabbing my shoulder until he's sure I'm steady. "Nervous?"

"Maybe a little." My gaze drifts over the guys crowded in the back. "Are you a fighter too?"

"Not tonight. Remy and I never fight on the same night."

"Your sidekick?"

"More like brother from another mother." He whistles loud enough that the whole room quiets and points to me with both index fingers. "Aubrey's helping Myra out tonight," he shouts with authority. "Treat her nice."

A few of the guys nod my way, but most of them go right back to their conversations with their crews.

"Who's Myra?" I ask Griff.

He nods toward a tall, pretty blonde hurrying over. She's graceful even in her five-inch heels and I feel like even more of a clod for almost tripping in mine.

"Hey, Griff." She tries to plant a kiss on his cheek, but he brushes her off.

"Show Aubrey the ropes tonight," he says.

Myra and I couldn't be physically more opposite. She's so tall she has to stoop to talk to me. Her platinum blonde hair is a mass of wild corkscrew curls down her back. She's friendly and waits to make sure I understand everything she explains before moving on.

"Three rounds. Five minutes each. When the bell rings, grab your sign, hold it up and walk your side of the cage and back twice. Got it?"

"I think so."

"Guys in the crowd might try to cop a feel. If you're not interested, just smack 'em." She grins as if she's looking forward to fighting off unwanted attention.

What was I thinking? I don't belong here.

We step out onto the main floor and Sully pounces, gripping my arm and tugging me to the side. Myra, for some reason, tags along. She runs her hand over his shoulder and tilts her head in a sex-kittenish way I haven't yet mastered. "Sully, Jake said you never come to the fights. How are you?"

He shrugs off her hand but gives her a polite smile. Jealousy flares inside me. Do they have history? He told me he didn't date because of his daughter. Is Myra an exception to that rule?

I thought I'd buried that obsessive-crushing-teenager part of me a long time ago. Sully makes me crazy. Obviously.

"I'm good," he answers. "How've you been?"

"Great. I'm showing Aubrey around tonight." For the first time, she seems to notice how close Sully and I are standing and the possessive hold he has on my arm.

"Can you give us a minute, Myra?" he asks, although it's really more of a demand than a question or suggestion.

"Sure." She glances down at me. "Come find me when you're done."

She hesitates for another second or two, then sashays away, putting a lot of extra sway in her hips. The movement is lost on Sully who's solely focused on me.

"You and fight-night-Barbie seem tight," I blurt out.

His lips twitch, then his face settles into a much more serious expression. "You know why I'm here."

"No, I don't. Explain."

His hold on my arm loosens and he takes my hand. Our fingers intertwine, and his thumb softly strokes my skin. "Things seem calm now, but these fights get out of control sometimes. I don't want you caught up in anything bad."

"Did you follow me?"

"I took a guess." He cocks his head. "You're a stubborn one."

I lift my shoulders. "You told me you weren't interested, so I don't understand why you're here."

"Doesn't mean I want you to get hurt."

Ouch. I mean, I'm touched he wants to protect me. I didn't need the reminder that he's not interested in anything more.

"Besides," he continues. "I never said I wasn't interested. I said I had a lot on my plate." He strokes the back of his hand over my cheek. "You deserve someone who can give you their full attention."

"I—"

An ear-splitting buzz pierces the room, cutting off our conversation. Griff's voice comes out of the loudspeaker. "Five minutes, everyone!"

"I better go." I glance over my shoulder, seeking Myra in the crowd.

"Hey," he says, tugging on my hand. "I'll be right here watching out for you."

"Aren't you going to cheer for your brother?"

One corner of his mouth lifts. "And cheering for Jake, yeah."

A ridiculous impulse seizes me, and I lean up, planting a quick kiss on his cheek. Dating issue aside, I'm sure he had better things to do tonight than come watch over me. "Thanks, Sully."

His hand closes over mine, pulling me closer. For a second, I think he's going to kiss me again.

"Be careful," he says before setting me free.

SULLY

AUBREY TAKES OFF into the crowd. Watching her hips and ass sway under that short, tight excuse for a dress, doesn't kill my urge to chase her down and carry her out of here at all.

Unsanctioned, underground, whatever you want to call it, Griff and Remy's operation is hardcore. The fights have very few rules. For the most part, the fighters who show up at the Castle are talented, but poor kids earning extra money to support their families. This isn't a bunch of rich kids looking to show off muscles they earned with hours at the gym and few of them are here to piss-off mommy and daddy. Those types of fighters don't last long here.

Aubrey's polite but distant to anyone who approaches her. Every now and then she searches the room until she finds me. I nod and she smiles.

I'm so focused on her, I don't notice Jake and Murphy approaching at first. The smirk on my brother's face makes me want to sink my fist into it. "Come to wish me luck?" he asks.

"Christ, you're needy tonight," Murphy grumble-laughs. He holds out a hand to me and I slap it.

"Keeping my brother out of trouble?"

Murphy shakes his head, laughter turning the corners of his mouth up. "We both know that ain't happening." He slaps my back. "Good to see you."

"How'd Aubrey end up here?" I ask Jake.

He scratches the back of his head. "Aubrey who?"

"Stop dicking around."

"I don't think she's the sort of girl who likes to be told what to do."

I lean in and lower my voice. "Don't think I didn't notice you with your hands all over her earlier."

He shrugs off my comment. "You know why."

"I specifically asked you to keep Griff away from her. We both know she doesn't belong here."

"Griff won't let anything happen to her." He flashes another impish grin that doesn't dial back the urge to punch him one bit.

If anyone is looking out for Aubrey, it's *me*.

"Who you fightin' tonight?" I ask to change the subject since it's only pissing me off. Now's not the time to get into it with him. Not when he needs to concentrate on the fight ahead of him.

"Rowdy," he answers, naming a loudmouth bodybuilder neither of us have a lot of respect for.

I snort and shake my head. "That's not much of a match."

"Aw, shucks. Thanks, bro." Jake throws a light jab, knocking my shoulder.

Murphy cocks his head and strokes his chin. "That wasn't exactly an endorsement of *your* skills, Jake," he points out, barely keeping his own expression smirk-free.

I can't help chuckling.

"Fuck off. Both of you," Jake grumbles, flipping us off. He waves his arms in a circle, clearing the space around him. "You two are bad for my mindset."

"When are you up?"

"Second, I think. Ruthless always goes last. Anyway," he pats my back. "Thanks for the brotherly love, but I need to clear my head."

He and Murphy take off and I search the room for Aubrey, finding her strutting in front of the ring with Myra. If anyone's going to help Aubrey out tonight, at least it's Myra. She doesn't have a catty bone in her body. And while she might not appreciate all the times I've brushed her off in the past, I don't think she'll take it out on Aubrey.

Even though I doubt Aubrey knew underground fights existed before tonight, she does a good job working up the crowd in her section. No matter what she does, she seems to always give one-hundred percent. Something the workaholic in me admires a lot.

I glance around the wide open space. Haven't been here in a long damn time. Learned to fight here myself. Back when this building was used for an entirely different purpose.

Fighters I haven't seen in a while come over to shake hands. Ask if

I'm betting on my brother tonight. A few hint that the bad blood between Jake and Rowdy could spark off a bigger fight outside the ring.

Knowing my brother, I can only imagine the underlying animosity has to do with a girl. Or, I should say, *someone's* girl.

Murphy sticking close to Jake makes more sense now. I'm sort of surprised Wrath didn't show up too.

But ultimately, Jake's an adult and knows the risk involved in coming here tonight. If he wants to get his ass kicked, that's his problem.

Aubrey's a different matter.

Everyone in the place saw him with his arm around her earlier. Since it was his way to warn guys that she was off-limits, I won't hold it against him—not too much anyway. But it also paints a target on her curvy little body if things go south after Jake's fight.

A few minutes later, Griff gets in the ring. He's a showman and fires up the crowd before laying out the rules.

"No eye-gouging. No biting. Keep it civil. If I think you're gonna do permanent damage, I end the match. If you ignore a warning or come at me—automatic three-month ban."

The threat of a ban is new, and I can only imagine why Griff added it to the minimal rules. Even so, it's better than most underground matches I've seen. The potential to get ugly still lingers.

Once the match starts, I slowly weave my way through the crowd and come up behind Aubrey.

Her shoulders jerk and she winces every time one of the guys take a hit. Neither of them are even good fighters. They punch and jab the air like it's their first time out of their basement training ring.

"Not quite the same as self-defense class, is it?" I ask, leaning over to speak the words against her ear.

She jumps and turns. Her glossy lips pull into a relieved smile when she meets my eyes. "More violent, that's for sure."

"This is nothing."

"It gets worse?"

"Tried to warn you."

We go back to watching the match. My hands graze her sides and she leans back a fraction. Like it's the most natural thing in the world.

With her back lightly brushing against my front, watching the match in front of us is the last thing on my mind. I curl my hands over her hips, taking a firmer hold. Damn, she fits me just right. She glances over her shoulder, confusion clouding her wide eyes and I back off.

She's here to do a job, not be groped by me.

My attention wanders to the fight. One of the guys takes a shot to the chin. Aubrey squeezes her eyes shut. Her reactions are so different from most of the girls at these fights who get turned on by the violence.

Neither of the fighters have any skill so it's a boring match that earns a lot of boos from the crowd.

Griff circles the area around the cage a few times, finally ending up next to us.

"Where'd you find these fools?" I ask.

He rolls his eyes. "Kids Molly goes to school with."

I raise an eyebrow. "Remy's not letting his little sister hang out here is he?"

"Hell no."

The two kids lock arms and start pushing each other around the ring. Griff groans and shakes his head. "These two fucks."

One of them gets knocked to the ground and Griff puts an end to the match.

"Well, that seemed fast," Aubrey says.

"Just wait until we get two who actually know what they're doing in there," I say.

Her eyes widen. "That got pretty intense at the end. It can be worse?"

"Yes. Longer too."

She shakes her head and glances down at her hands. "I need to do my thing."

"Go ahead. I'll be here."

She tilts her head to the side. Her mouth opens, then closes, as if she's debating her words. "I'm glad you're here," she finally says in a rush.

So am I.

CHAPTER TWELVE

Aubrey

M Y HEART WON'T stop hammering and my stomach won't stop fluttering as I strut my stuff in front of the crowd. Griff announces the next fight, but I'm too nervous and wrapped up in what I'm doing to pay attention.

Honestly, the tingles gathered inside me have to do more with Sully than nerves.

I can't believe he showed up.

To watch out for me?

Is he worried it's really that dangerous? Is he jealous?

It's probably none of the above. He's just a nice guy.

Although the brief way he touched me before suggested something else.

My gaze flickers to him once more. There are plenty of young, good-looking, fit guys running around. Somehow Sully stands apart from all of them. Maybe it's the space people give him, the confidence he projects, or his take-no-shit posture. Whatever it is, it's hard to look away.

He catches me staring at him and flashes a quick, reassuring smile.

The bell rings and I hurry over to stand with Sully for the next fight. He slips an arm around my shoulders and nods at the cage.

Jake's up and my body seizes. I don't want to see him get hurt.

Sully seems to sense my distress and leans down. "My brother has good reason for being a cocky bastard."

"What's that?"

"He's a skilled fighter. Don't worry."

I tilt my head back, meeting his eyes and we stare at each other for a few heartbeats.

A roar from the crowd tears our gazes apart and we focus on the cage.

"The other guy's so big," I whisper to Sully.

The corner of his mouth quirks. "Won't matter. Jake has better skills."

"But—"

"Trust me. Watch."

Jake's friend, Murphy, jogs up to Sully's other side and they nod at each other. After the brief acknowledgment, they both focus on the fight.

I drag my attention away from Sully to Jake, who looks completely at ease as he throws a number of short, quick kicks at his opponent's left leg.

"What's he doing?"

"Rowdy thinks all he needs is size and strength. Jake's going to school him tonight."

"That's not helpful."

Sully chuckles and lifts his chin toward his brother. "He's distracting him with those kicks so he can get in a headshot."

Five seconds later, Jake does just that, landing a punch that opens up a cut under his opponent's eye.

I squeal at the splash of red on the fighter's face, ducking against Sully's side and he squeezes me tighter.

He doesn't laugh or make fun of me for my squeamishness. Scolding myself for being childish, I stand up straight and scan the room. The crowd's moving closer to the ring, the noise ratcheting up several degrees. Murphy edges closer as well, keeping an eye not on the fight, but on two guys standing close to the cage. He bumps Sully with his elbow and Sully acknowledges it with a nod.

"What's wrong?"

"Nothing."

"Take him down!" someone in the crowd screams and several more echo the sentiment. I'm not sure if they expect Jake to do the takedown or the other guy. I hope they're rooting for Jake.

A few seconds later, the big guy launches himself at Jake, tackling him to the floor with a boom and thud that echoes in the room.

"Jake! Oh my God!" I shout, moving closer so I can see if he's okay.

"He's fine," Sully assures me, moving my body directly in front of him. His arms curl around my shoulders, blocking anyone from knocking into me.

"That guy will crush him."

Sully's rumbling laughter vibrates against my back. He leans down, warm breath ghosting over my cheek. "Look closely. He's the one in control."

Once I calm myself, I see Sully's right. The bigger guy's red cheeks and sweaty forehead signal his frustration. In contrast, Jake's completely calm as he rolls side to side, unbalancing the other fighter. Rowdy throws wild punches that don't land and Jake answers with two solid jabs that strike their target. More blood leaks from fresh cuts on Rowdy's face.

"End it," Sully mutters under his breath. "Finish him."

Jake rolls again, capturing and pinning his opponent's arm in a crushing leg lock.

Murphy laughs and Sully curses.

"What's wrong?"

"He's gonna drag it out," Sully explains.

Rowdy struggles and even pinches Jake's nipple with his free hand, but he can't get loose. His face twists into a mask of pain and Griff jumps into the cage to call the match in Jake's favor.

"Why'd he end it?"

Murphy leans over to answer, "Jake was two seconds from snapping Rowdy's arm."

"Oh."

Griff tugs the fighters apart and Jake turns to shake hands with his opponent, which is apparently what's expected no matter how messy the fights turn.

Rowdy gives his back to Jake who shrugs and walks the perimeter of the cage.

The crowd jostles us forward and I notice the two guys Murphy had been watching earlier rush into the cage going straight for Jake.

"Sully!" I shout, tugging on his arm to get his attention.

It only takes him a second to assess the situation. "Stay here," he orders. He taps Murphy on the arm and the two of them take after the guys headed toward Jake.

SULLY

MURPHY'S ONLY A step behind me as we take after the two jerks planning to jump my brother.

Jake—the cocky asshole—is too busy chatting up female fans to notice Rowdy's friends.

One reaches Jake and lands a kidney shot, bringing my brother to one knee.

"Son of a bitch."

His attacker turns and attempts to shove me back, but I step out of his line of movement, throwing out my hand and grabbing his chin. The momentum carries both of us forward. I yank him around and throw him to the ground where I strike. Two swift punches before backing off.

"Stay down," I grind out, not in the mood for a prolonged fight.

Murphy has the other one pinned to the ground with his arm twisted up behind his back.

"You all right, bro?" I ask Jake, holding out my hand. He slaps it and stands.

"I'll live."

"Out!" Griff shouts, pushing Rowdy toward the cage door. His partner, Remy and a few other guys who've been in this circuit for years storm into the cage to take care of Rowdy's friends.

"Sorry," Griff says on his way out.

"Jake!" Aubrey yells when we step out of the cage. She rushes up to us with wild eyes and wet cheeks. "Are you okay?"

My brother puts on an Oscar-worthy performance of moaning and leaning on Aubrey. "I'm better now, thanks, sweetheart," he says as she leads him toward the locker room.

Murphy catches the look on my face and laughs. "Who knew Jake had a death wish?"

"Yeah, who would've guessed." I roll my eyes and Murphy laughs harder.

"I'm gonna stick with Jake. Make sure he doesn't piss anyone else off," he says.

"Good plan."

Aubrey's working her way back through the crowd to me and I can't help but reach out and drag her closer. "Are you all right?"

She stares up at me in surprise. "I'm fine. Jake's in the locker room. You should go check on him and I'll—" she searches the room. "I guess I should look for Myra and ask her what to do?"

I hate letting her out of my sight.

And I think that comes through loud and clear when I don't let go of her right away.

"Sully?"

Reluctantly, I peel my arms off her. "Jake's a big boy. After that mess, I'd rather stay out here and keep an eye on you."

She's too smart to protest. Instead, she thanks me and heads toward Myra. Griff talks to the two girls for a few minutes. While they're busy chatting, two kids who barely look old enough to drive enter the cage and mop up the blood left behind.

When the room is calmer, Griff announces the next fight.

The first fighter is someone I've never heard of, which isn't a surprise since I haven't been part of this world in a long time. The second fighter goes by the ring name "Smokey the Bear" which I assume is some sort of jokey-reference to the fact that he's a local deputy sheriff. Liam's former partner, actually. Brady O'Connor probably spends his afternoons pulling half these kids over for speeding.

At least these two opponents are evenly matched. Age and skill-wise.

It's an interesting fight. Judging by the heavy betting activity, Griff will ask both of them to return.

Half-way through the match, Jake comes up on my side. "I assume you're sticking around until she's done?"

"Ya think?" I answer without turning my head.

"I'm okay, by the way. In case you were wondering."

Slowly, I glance over at him. "Do you need your blankie and teddy bear?"

"Nah." He lifts his chin at a cluster of girls who keep glancing at us and giggling to each other. "A girl will calm my nerves."

"You asking for my permission?"

"No, but a condom would be helpful," he says, holding out his hand.

"Christ, you're irresponsible. Do I look like a pharmacy to you?"

"Nah, just a grumpy fuck who needs to get laid."

"How many hits to the head did you take tonight?"

He grins. "Not enough."

"Got that right," I grumble, digging out my wallet and handing over the lone condom in it.

"Hope you have a spare."

"I'll be fine. Go away."

He does finally get lost and I search the room for Aubrey. She smiles as soon as my gaze lands on her and blows me a kiss.

Several guys turn to see where her affection is directed and I stare each one down.

Brady wins his fight. I hold out my hand to congratulate him and he pulls me in for a quick hug.

"Good to see ya, Sully." He doesn't seem to be concerned that I recognize him.

The volume of the music and chatter increases. I watch Aubrey work the crowd and stay out of her way. Once the final fight starts, I work my way closer.

I've seen Remy fight plenty of times. Hell, I trained him early on. Back when he was an angry, scrawny little bastard looking to defend himself and his baby sister against their drunken father. Since I had my own experiences with a similar home life, I spent a lot of time training Remy where to channel his rage.

The student has definitely surpassed the teacher now. I'm impressed with his skill and focus. If I wasn't so annoyed with him and Griff for bringing Aubrey into this, I'd talk to him about going professional.

Even if I've left that world to try to provide a more stable life for my daughter, I still have connections Remy should talk to.

"He's gotten good, right?" Griff says.

"Yeah. Don't take this the wrong way, but why's he wasting time and taking the risk with underground fights instead of going legit?"

It takes a lot to offend Griff and he's smart enough to know I'm not insulting his operation. "Needs the cash like everyone else."

"If you promise not to try to poach my employees anymore, you're both always welcome at my place to train."

He seems genuinely pleased and squeezes my shoulder. "Thanks, bro." He glances at Aubrey. "She's great. A little timid. You gonna stop her from coming back?"

I flex my jaw. "That's her decision."

"Thanks. I assume you'll hustle her out of here as soon as we're done. Not staying for the after party?"

"Probably not."

"I'll make sure she gets paid right away."

"Appreciate it."

Done messing with me, he grins and bounces back into the crowd.

A few minutes later, Remy knocks his opponent out cold. The crowd loses its shit and I muscle my way through to pull Aubrey out of danger.

"Oh! Wow! I wasn't expecting that!" she shouts. She places her hands against my chest, leaning up so I can hear her. "What a fight—"

Maybe it's the energy in the room. Or how damn beautiful she is, all flushed and smiling, but I wrap my arms around her.

She stops mid-sentence and I can't resist. Leaning down, I cover her mouth with mine. Not a gentle kiss like the one we shared in my office.

This one's full of need, desire, maybe a twinge of frustration from watching her prance around all night in her tight, tiny dress. Maybe frustration with myself for wasting so much time pretending I don't have feelings for her.

Her body squirms against mine and she moans. I kiss her harder, claiming her, not holding back this time. Savoring her sweet taste, I decided not to let Aubrey out of my sight for a second. Hope Jake's around to drive my Jeep home.

Someone clears their throat next to us and I break our kiss. Aubrey slowly slides down, staring up at me, body pressed tight to mine. I'm not even sure she realizes someone's standing next to us.

I glance over at Griff. He's not smirking now. Keeping an arm around Aubrey, I nudge her toward him.

"Ah, thanks for tonight, Aubrey," he says, handing her a few folded bills. "Appreciate you taking the job on such short notice."

"Sure," she answers almost slurring the word. Did I do that to her?

Griff flicks his gaze my way. "Well, you're welcome back anytime, as long as Sully doesn't mind."

"Okay, just let me know," she says, ignoring the question of whether I mind or not entirely.

After Griff leaves, she tips her head back. "I need to grab my stuff. There's an after party…" Her voice trails off and she glances around the room.

The only after party I want to attend is in my bedroom with Aubrey.

I take her hand and tell her to lead the way.

Outside, we stop at her car. It's dark and even though tons of people around us are romping through the wooded area, making plenty of noise, our section of the parking lot is empty.

"This wasn't safe parking all the way out here by yourself," I say.

She lifts her shoulders. "It wasn't this deserted when I got here."

"You should've told me when you stopped by. I would've driven you."

"You seemed to have strong opinions about it." She hurries to add, "But now I understand why."

We haven't spoken about our kiss yet. And I don't need to talk about it to know I want to do it again.

And again.

Placing my fingers under her chin, I gently tilt her head back and seal my mouth over hers. Same as before, she steps into me, sliding her hands up over my shoulders around my neck.

Love the way her little body fits against me. How warm she feels. How sweet she tastes. Cinnamon and honey.

My hands slide down and fit into her waist, then lower cupping her hips. Can't get enough of her.

Every little sound she makes reminds me we're in the open where anyone could walk up on us.

"Stop, Aubrey," I mumble against her lips.

She pulls away, leaning back against her car.

The hurt in her eyes makes me realize my mistake. I never want to make her feel she's being rejected. Not when I want her more than I've wanted anyone in a long time. Maybe ever. But it's not happening in the back of her car or in the woods like we're two drunk teenagers.

I run the back of my hand over her soft cheek. "Come home with me."

"You mean it?"

I lean down and brush my lips against her ear. "I mean it."

She presses her hand against my chest. "Jake said you don't take girls to your house."

When the hell did they have *that* conversation? And why?

"I don't want to take girls to my house. I want to take *you*." My dick flexes against my fly as if he's happy I'm finally admitting how much I want this woman.

She bites her bottom lip and glances away. "Okay," she whispers.

I search the parking lot, but there's no sign of my brother.

"What's wrong?"

"Looking for Jake to see if he can drive my Jeep home."

There's enough moonlight to make out the confusion in her eyes. "Why?"

I can't help but steal a quick kiss before explaining. "I'm not letting you out of my sight."

She traces her fingers over my cheek, stopping at my bottom lip. "Trust me, Sullivan, I won't change my mind."

CHAPTER THIRTEEN
Aubrey

THE URGE TO pinch myself won't fade.

After Sully tracks down his brother, he takes my hand and opens the passenger door for me. I don't even hesitate to hand over the keys to my sister's car. I'm way too excited to operate a vehicle.

I'm going home with Sully.

My lips still tingle from where we kissed.

He's been fighting what he feels for weeks, but now he's taking me to his house.

Was he jealous? Lots of guys had hit on me or asked for my number tonight. I chalked it up to drunken gamblers and brushed them off. I'm only interested in one man. Even if up until now he's done nothing but push me away.

I hate to break the spell, but I have to ask. "Why tonight?"

He glances over. "I lose my mind around you."

"That doesn't sound good."

"I guess it depends on your perspective." He glances over and winks.

"So you were jealous?"

His hands tighten on the steering wheel. "I didn't like the way some of those guys looked at you. But that's not why I want you to come home with me."

I'm too keyed up to pay attention to where we're going and soon he's pulling into a short driveway and shutting the engine off.

"Do you want to come in?" He glances over with a half-smile.

"I…I thought…"

His smile grows. "Nothing's set in stone, Aubrey."

He pushes his door open and comes around to my side, opening my door and holding out his hand.

My heels make a soft clicking over the blue stones lining the walkway to his front porch. He nods at the house right next to his. "My mom's house."

"You live next door to your mother? That's so sweet."

He flashes an unapologetic grin. It makes me like him even more. Which could be dangerous since I already like Sully way too much.

Inside is neat and tidy. Only a few young adult novels on the coffee table indicate a child spends any time here.

"Do you want something to drink?" he asks, closing the door behind us.

"Water would be great. My throat's dry from yelling so much tonight."

He moves through the house with ease and I follow him into the kitchen where he pulls a pitcher of water out of the fridge and plucks a glass out of the dishwasher.

"You did well," he says, handing me the water. "Tonight."

I take a long sip before answering. "Didn't think I had it in me, did you?"

"I just didn't want you getting hurt."

"Honestly, I like Jake. Trust him, I mean. And Griff seems decent enough. But I didn't really feel safe until I saw you there."

He takes a step closer. "You're always safe with me."

I nod and set the glass on the counter. "I believe you."

There's a split second of hesitation between us. An anticipation as he brushes my hair off my cheek, staring into my eyes before bending down to kiss me. His mouth is warm and demanding. One of his hands cradles my jaw while the other presses against the small of my back. He drags his tongue across my bottom lip and I open for him. He tastes like mint. His arms wrap around my body, crushing me against him as our kisses turn deeper, rougher, almost frantic.

I love it.

My hands brush against his sides, stroking down his ribs to settle at his waist. He growls in response, a low rumble in his throat that ripples over me. I dip my fingers under the hem of his T-shirt, my thumbs brushing against his hot skin and he kisses me even harder.

Sully's usually so…polite and reserved. I'm not expecting him to take charge.

But does he ever.

Tilting my head back for a better angle, he kisses me slow and hard. When our height difference is still too much, he growls and wrapping his massive arms around my body, lifts me in the air.

I pull back and stare at him.

"Aubrey, you have no idea how many times I've thought about this."

"You're the stubborn one."

"I am." We're moving through the house and he only stops kissing me to utter a brief explanation. "I thought it was better not to get involved." More frantic kisses. "But I can't resist you."

"Shh," I place my fingers over his lips. "Keep kissing me. I'm all yours tonight."

He hesitates. Does he want me to say I'm his for more than one night? I am. In my heart, I already feel it.

I don't think I can say it yet.

At a doorway, he stops and lets me down. His gaze darts into the darkened room. "Are you sure? This won't change anything. At work. For you, I mean. Either way."

I can't keep up. One second he's take charge and the next he's incredibly sweet and sensitive.

I tilt my head and squint up at him. "Work talk's not very sexy."

He huffs out a laugh and shakes his head. "I'm serious."

"Do you want my resignation first?"

He frowns. "Fuck no." As if the reality of me quitting really bothers him, he draws me into his arms again. "I don't think I could run the place without you now."

"That's ridiculous."

He shrugs as if he's telling the truth and takes my hand. Inside his room, he flicks on a small lamp. A weak circle of light reveals a neat bedroom. It's not college-dorm-room utilitarian, but it's definitely more functional than fancy.

My gaze flicks to his bed and my stomach tightens with anticipation. Maybe a little fear too. Years have passed since my last boyfriend and that was a disaster.

His fingers brush my cheek. "What're you thinking about?"

"You," I answer which isn't a lie. He seems to invade all my thoughts.

"I'm right here." He pulls me to him and his rough fingers graze my thighs. My stomach tightens with anticipation as he grasps the fabric of my dress and slides it up. "This fucking dress drove me nuts all night." Frustration creeps into his tone but his mouth curls with appreciation. In an effortless move, he yanks the dress over my head and tosses it on his dresser. I squeeze closer, kissing his throat, but he pulls back enough to sweep his gaze over my body, drinking me in like he's parched.

Uncomfortable under his stare, I cross my arms over my chest. He leans in closer and brushes a kiss over my cheek. "I want to see you."

He hooks his hands in mine and drags them to my sides. "That's better."

"You're making me nervous."

That seems to bother him, and he draws back. "Why?"

I wave my hands at his tight-fitting T-shirt. "Well, one, you're still dressed."

In a quick, smooth move, he whips his shirt over his head, tossing it on the floor. "Done. What else ya got?"

I'm so busy drooling at his chiseled muscles, my tongue doesn't want to work. "You're all fitness-y and I'm kinda fluffy."

He hooks his arm around my waist and spins me around. "Fluffy? Like a cat?" One of his hands slides down my back and over my butt. "Nope. No tail." He squeezes each cheek thoroughly.

It's so ridiculous, I can't stop giggling and he turns me to face him. "I'm not sure how I feel about you *laughing* in my bedroom." He taps the side of his head. "I had some other noises in mind."

I raise my eyebrows.

"Aubrey." His raspy voice cuts my laughter short. He caresses my cheek with the back of his hand. "You're beautiful and I've wanted you for a long time."

The honest admission steals my words and I blink up at him.

He walks me closer to the bed and nudges me. "Lie back. I need to do something."

"What?"

He doesn't ask again, just lifts his chin. I drop down and to my surprise, he kneels in front of me. Our gazes lock and he leans in, placing a kiss to my inner knee. His lips travel farther, light feathery kisses that leave me trembling. Finally, he reaches my mound and lays another kiss. Even through the satin underwear, I feel the heat of his mouth so close to my core.

"Don't." My voice comes out barely above a whisper. I place my hand over his.

Sully pulls back and stares up at me. "What?"

"I...That. I'm not..." I trail off, unsure of how to explain myself. My heart's racing impossibly fast.

"Aubrey." His rough baritone electrifies my skin. His fingers skim up the sides of my legs, landing on my hips. He tucks his fingers into the waistband of my panties and teases the material from my body. "That day I took you home and fixed your leg. You have no idea how badly I wanted to do this." He stops to nuzzle his face against the fabric barely concealing me and my lady bits freak out.

And yet my mouth won't shut up. "What? Why?"

"You smelled *so* good."

"You could *smell* me? That sounds awful."

He shakes his head and drops his gaze. My breath hitches.

"It was hot. You smelled like sex and sweetness. I wanted to kiss and explore you for the rest of the morning."

His voice. The longing in it. The fluttering in my belly starts up again. He wraps his hands around my upper thighs. "You need to lie back. I've waited long enough to taste you."

"Whose fault is that?" My lips quirk into a smile.

He kisses my inner thigh before staring up at me with so much determination and desire burning in his eyes, it steals the laughter from my lips. "I can't wait to lick you until your legs shake."

"Oh my God," I breathe out. No one has ever spoken to me so bluntly before. "What are you doing to me?"

"Owning every inch of you, Aubrey. Every. Single. Inch."

I open my mouth, but no words come out. He lifts his gaze and I lie back, staring at the ceiling.

"Watch me," he says, spreading my legs wider.

Propping myself up on my elbows, I stare down at him. He doesn't go straight for me though. No, Sully's a patient man who takes his time teasing and kissing my skin until I'm quivering and on the verge of begging.

He uses his thumbs to stroke up and down my lips then leans in and kisses me. Loud, open-mouthed kisses in my most private place.

"Holy shit!" I yelp. My hand dives into his hair, gripping tight.

He grins against me but doesn't stop the sweet torture.

I let my head fall back. Both of my hands twine into his hair. My hips jerk up and I realize I'm grinding myself against his face. He makes a bunch of encouraging noises and slides his hands under my butt, gripping me tight and pulling me closer.

"Oh, fuck, fuck, *fuck*."

He slides a finger inside me and my hips jerk again, slamming into him. Jesus, did I break his nose? He pulls his face away, but keeps gently thrusting his finger in and out. "You're fucking amazing," he says before diving back in.

He's the amazing one. Talented at *all* kinds of kissing. I can't keep track of the sensations and after a while stop trying. The pleasure washes over me in waves, pulling me closer and closer. My body's strung tight. On the verge of something. My hips move in frustrated circles.

He lifts his head, rubbing his cheek against my inner thigh. Light beard stubble tickles my already sensitive skin. "Can you come this way, Aubrey?"

I have no idea. No one's ever asked or tried. The only oral I've received has been a lights-off quick token lick or two before having a cock shoved in my face so I could "return the favor."

Back then, I never thought to ask for more.

Under Sully's hands and mouth, I'm like a flower that blossomed too early. Stung by an unexpected frost, my growth stunted. Sully's the first warm kiss of sunlight. He makes me want things I haven't wanted in a long time. Things I thought were wrong to want. Would lead me to trouble.

I answer with a whimper and he slips a second finger inside me, pumping harder. His mouth seals over me and he gently sucks my clit. Blistering flames of pleasure fizzle through my veins. The only words that come to mind are *explosion, detonate, inferno.*

I always thought the "seeing stars" thing was bullshit, but I see *galaxies* before Sully finally slows down.

"That was beautiful," he mutters. Unconcerned with how wet and messy he's made me, he slides his hands over my core, spreading my wetness, keeping me on the edge. "Are you with me, Aubrey?" he asks in a teasing voice.

"I'm here."

"Are you done for the night?"

I peel open one eye. "Is that an option?"

The satisfied smile slides off his face. He cocks his head and swipes the back of his hand over his glistening lips. "Everything's always an option, Aubrey."

"I want more."

He leans over and slides open his nightstand drawer and tosses a couple condoms on top. One of them he keeps, ripping it open with his teeth.

I watch, transfixed while he shoves his pants down and frees himself.

"Whoa," I mutter without thinking.

He glances up and winks. "That's encouraging."

I don't think he bothers to kick off his pants. Instead, he rolls the condom on quick and grips my thighs, lifting me to the angle he needs to slide right in.

"Oh my God," I moan, my head rolling to the side, eyes closing.

Sully thumps into me harder on the next thrust. "Eyes open. Watch," he demands.

He takes his time, finding what feels amazing for both of us. He's incredibly tuned into what makes me moan the loudest. As I let out another contented sigh, he pulls out.

Frustrated, I sit up. "Why? What're you doing?"

He stretches out on the bed next to me and tugs on my hand. "Get on top of me."

"Are you sure?"

He scrunches his face and shakes his head like he thinks I've lost my mind. Before anything else silly comes out of my mouth, he sits up and scoops me into a kneeling position next to him. "Come on."

I wish I was a little more graceful about it, but Sully groans with pleasure when I finally line myself up and sink down. He gives me a few seconds to figure it out before grabbing my hips and moving me the way he wants.

"That's it," he encourages. "Harder. I know you have it in you."

"I have it in me all right," I joke, wiggling my hips.

He laughs and reaches up to cup my cheek. "I wanna watch you come while you're riding me."

The raw, honest, and dirty demand sends streaks of heat through my body.

Wanting to please him as much as he's pleased me, I move a little faster. "Good. Like that," he says, his eyes falling shut.

I grind my hips into him. "Eyes open," I demand.

The corners of his mouth turn up before he opens his eyes. "Damn, Aubrey," he says with a trace of awe.

He reaches up and cups my breasts, gently strumming his thumbs over my nipples. I lean into him and work my hips up and down. Chasing that feeling of blissful explosiveness that captured me a few minutes ago. Sully's turned me into a greedy girl.

Before long, I'm desperate, frantic for something that seems close but out of my grasp. I work my hips faster, beads of sweat running down my forehead. Sully sits up and cups my cheeks with both hands. "Slow down. I'm not going anywhere. I'm all yours. All night."

SULLY

I COULD'VE COME five seconds after getting Aubrey in my bedroom. But I wanted more for our first night together. Each time she looks at me, there's a certain innocence in her expression that makes me feel like a filthy bastard for all the things I want to do with her. She's so much tighter than I anticipated. I don't think she's a virgin, but she's not experienced either. That much is obvious.

She's riding me as if this is her one and only shot. As if she thinks tomorrow I'll wake up and regret it. When the truth is I don't think I'll ever have enough of her.

The reassurance that I'm not going anywhere seems to help.

"That's better," I encourage. "Nice and slow."

She finds a rhythm she's more comfortable with. One that has me ready to explode. Thank fuck a few seconds later, she gasps and lets out a low moan. She's not a screamer. She's a moaner and a heavy breather. Every noise from her lips is fucking beautiful.

Her eyes roll back in her head. "Ohhh, yes. Sully."

Her pussy squeezes me so tight as she orgasms that it tips me over the edge. "Here," I pant out the word and press my palms to the sides of her face, pulling her down so I can kiss her while I let go. She moans into my mouth and I'm absolutely lost in her.

Foreheads touching, we stare at each other breathing in the same air while our heart rates return to normal. Reluctantly, I palm her hips and pull her off me.

"Give me a second."

My vision swims as I sit up and I blink a few times. Holy shit, she fucked me into one hell of a dazed and confused state.

I stumble into the bathroom to discard the condom and grab a glass of water. When I return, she's laying on her side with a blanket pulled practically up to her chin.

"Are you cold?"

"No," she answers absently, taking the glass I offer.

When she finishes, I take the glass, set it down, then yank the blanket off her.

"Hey!"

"You said you're not cold, so you're hiding from me and I don't like that."

Her mouth opens as if she has a sassy comeback, but her gaze travels down my body instead. I really like the way she studies me. I may not be as cocky as my brother, but I put a lot of hours in at the gym, so I appreciate her gawking.

A lot.

I throw myself down next to her and place my lips on hers. She rolls to her back and I follow, kissing her long and hard. Within a few minutes of our bodies pressed together, my cock's hardening again.

She stares up at me with a sated but mystified expression.

"What's on your mind, Aubrey?"

"I'm not sure how to put it into words. Except, *wow*."

"Wow works."

The uncertain expression returns and she sits up. "It's late. You probably want—"

"To use you as a pillow all night," I finish for her, cutting off wherever she was going. It's a goofy thing to say, but hell, she makes me a little goofy.

She chuckles. "You don't mind if I stay?"

"I'll be offended if you don't."

"I figured with your mom next—"

"Can we *not* talk about my mother right now?"

"Sorry." She glances down. "I figured you won't want anyone to know…" Her voice trails off before she finishes the thought.

"I'll hang a sign out front right now."

She cuts me a sharp look. "Because of your no-dating-clients-or-employees rule."

Fuck, yeah, that seems pretty stupid now. "You're worth breaking all my rules."

"Give me a minute," she says. I watch while she hurries into the bathroom and closes the door.

Stretching out and staring up at the ceiling, I consider how much I've cocked this up when it's really pretty simple. We can control ourselves at work. And I'm not some asshole who'll fire her if things don't work out between us—although right now, the way I'm feeling, I don't see that being an issue.

"Holy—wow."

I turn and find her hesitating outside the bathroom. "What?"

She waves her hands in front of her. "You. All stretched out." Her gaze zeros in on my cock. "Glorious."

"Glorious, huh?" I stroke my hand up and down my dick a few times. "Want a closer look?"

"Definitely."

I crook a finger at her, beckoning her closer.

Nope, this doesn't have to be complicated at all.

CHAPTER FOURTEEN
SULLY

I CAN'T REMEMBER the last time I woke up with someone next to me. Aubrey's still sleeping and damn, she's so pretty it's impossible to tear my gaze away. Zonked out with the morning sun glowing over her skin, she seems so much younger. You'd never know when she finally lets go, how passionate she is inside.

Noise from my living room stops me from continuing my creepy stare-a-thon and I'm careful to slide out of bed without jostling her awake.

Jake's in the living room wearing a predictably annoying grin. I'm sure he noticed Aubrey's car in the driveway and can't wait to hassle me about my "no dating clients and employees" rule.

I'm surprised how little I care what he thinks.

"Looks like you still have company."

"Are you here for a reason?"

"You're not gonna offer me some coffee?"

"No."

He blows out a breath and dangles my keys in front of my face. "I'm dropping off your Jeep."

"Thanks for doing that." I grab the keys and set them on the counter separating the kitchen from the dining area. Jake naturally follows me. "Everything go okay after we left? Rowdy didn't hang around right?" I ask.

"I'm fine." He cocks his head. "You actually brought someone home with you, huh? That has to be a first. Is this my fault for stealing your last condom?"

"Do you have to be such an asshole?" I grumble, heading into the kitchen. Changed my mind on the coffee. I need it to deal with Jake.

"It's part of my charm," he says, following close behind me.

"It's really not."

"Come on, give me details."

"No, perv."

"Not *those* details." He actually drops the cocky expression for five seconds. "I'm serious. You never bring chicks here."

Shaking my head, I consider how to answer. He's right. I don't do relationships and I haven't had a girl at my house since the custody arrangement for Maddy was finalized. "She's not some psycho who's gonna show up when Maddy's here and cause trouble. I trust her."

"You *are* a magnet for crazy chicks."

"Look who's talking." I really want to end our conversation and get back in bed with Aubrey before she wakes up. "I suppose you need a ride to Strike Back?" I ask, hoping he'll take the hint that he needs to go open for me this morning.

"Nah, I'm gonna go next door and visit Mom. She'll give me a ride." He lifts his chin toward the bedroom. "I'll give her the good news about your new girlfriend."

"Don't you dare. I don't need her running over here hinting to Aubrey about how she wants more grandchildren."

He tips his head back and laughs. "Wow, you don't want to scare her away. You're into her."

"Yeah, I'm into her. So if you could not be a dick about it, that would be great."

"I make no promises."

The sound of running water from the bathroom reaches us. Aubrey's awake.

I shove the can of coffee into Jake's hands. "Here, make yourself useful."

Aubrey's about to climb back into bed when I open the bedroom door. She found a faded red T-shirt of mine and slipped it on. On her, it's a dress.

For me, it's an instant hard-on.

"Morning."

The softest, sweetest smile lights up her face. "Good morning." She tugs at the bottom of the shirt. "I hope it's okay I borrowed your shirt. I found it in the bathroom."

"I can't vouch that it's clean."

She pulls the fabric to her nose and inhales, smiling even wider. "It smells like you. I like it."

That's it. We need a proper good morning kiss. Now.

Takes me three steps to cross the room and pull her into my arms. "I really liked waking up with you in my bed."

She pulls back and playfully pokes me in the stomach. "Why'd you leave then?"

I tilt my head toward the kitchen. "Jake stopped by. If I didn't intercept him, he'd have no problem walking in here. Sitting down. Starting a conversation."

Her little body shakes with laughter against mine. "I'd probably die of embarrassment."

Figured she'd be that type of girl. Even more reason I want to get my brother out of my house. "You don't have anything to be embarrassed about."

"No. What I don't have." She points to the pile of her clothes on the floor. "Is any pants."

"Oh." I chuckle and lead her to my dresser, pulling out a pair of shorts I think will fit her if I tie the drawstring tight enough.

"They're not going to fit," she protests. She points at me, then runs her hands over her hips.

"Sure they will. Come here."

I kneel in front of her and she leans on me while I help her into the shorts. "It's a crime to put clothes *on* you," I say as I drag them up her legs.

She tips her head down, watching as I dip close to kiss her belly button. She giggles when I lick her stomach. Gasps when I kiss a little lower.

Her fingers thread into my hair, tugging just hard enough to remind me of the way she went wild under me last night. "Jake definitely has to go," I murmur against her skin. "Need more of you today."

"Don't you need to be at the gym?"

I groan and tie the drawstring into a knot. "Jake's gonna open for me."

"Coffee's ready!" Jake shouts.

Aubrey bursts out laughing and covers her face with her hands. "I can't."

"I'll send him on his way. Give me a few minutes." I lean in closer. "Kiss me first."

She presses her lips to mine and before she can get away, I thread my hand into her hair, tugging her closer.

"Does Aubrey take cream and sugar?" Jake yells, thoroughly spoiling the moment.

"Fucker," I grumble.

"He knows it's me?" she whispers.

"Jake's a lot of things, but stupid isn't one of them."

"I've noticed," she says.

"Be right back."

Jake's thankfully headed toward the door when I stalk into the living room.

"I can take a hint."

"Take my Jeep. I'll ask Aubrey to drop me off later."

"Later? How much later?"

"Keegan's coming in to help with my morning class. You'll be fine."

"Boy, the things I do to help you get laid, big brother."

"Shut up," I say, shoving him onto the porch.

Laughing, he stumbles down the steps and waves at me over his shoulder.

Aubrey's kneeling in the center of my bed when I return to her.

"You can relax, he's gone. Sorry about that."

My gaze roams over her, while she looks good in my shirt, I really want her naked. Naked and bouncing on my cock. For now, I'll start with naked.

I stop at the foot of the bed, and she shuffles closer. "Do you need to get going?"

"Nah, Jake's going to open for me and handle my morning class." I slip my hand under her T-shirt, brushing my fingers against soft, warm skin. "I need more Aubrey time."

"And what are you planning to do with all this new free time?"

I pretend to think about it for a second. "Spend it with you." My fingers trail a little higher gently cupping her breast. "Preferably naked."

To my surprise, she kneels up and strips off the shirt, tossing it aside. I nod and run my hand over my chin. "That's a good start."

She hooks her fingers in the shorts, wiggling her hips. "These too?" she asks in a playful way that makes me lean in and kiss her.

"Those too."

She stops playing with the waistband and puts her hands on her hips. "You first," she says, dropping her gaze to my shorts.

Aubrey

LAST NIGHT WAS pretty dark in here. Now with morning sunlight filling the room, I can really appreciate Sully.

As he tugs his boxer briefs down, any sassy comeback evaporates on my tongue.

Sully. Naked.

Clothed he's impressive. Naked, wow.

He stands there, allowing me to stare and take him all in, and boy is there a lot to take in.

There's something magnetic about his confident stance. Not arrogant. Sexy. Showing off his hard work.

"Well, you're already impressive with your clothes on." I gesture wildly in the direction of his dick. "But naked with some good lighting, you're something else."

"Thank you." He lifts his chin at my shorts. "Your turn."

"There's a lot of daylight in here." My fingers curl in the fabric at my waist. "I don't look as good naked as you do."

He doesn't respond. Instead, he places one hand on the bed and one on my leg. "No, you look better."

Curling his fingers, he drags the shorts down my legs. I fall back on the bed, laughing. He drapes himself over me, holding himself up with powerful arms on either side of my head. "What's with you? I can't keep my hands off you. And you keep questioning yourself."

"Sorry."

"Don't apologize." He moves his hips in slow circles letting me feel his growing erection. "I like everything about you."

I reach up and trap his face between my palms. "I like everything about you too."

"Good." He reaches over to the nightstand and the anticipation of what he's about to do has me spreading my legs wider. Something he notices and given the way he tears into the wrapper, seems to please him.

"How do you feel this morning?" he asks while tugging on the condom.

"I could feel better."

"Yeah? Something I can help with?" he teases, covering my body with his again. His cock brushes against me and I moan out an incoherent bunch of nonsense.

He does it again, sliding through my wetness.

"Stop teasing," I beg.

His mouth curves into a wicked half-smile. "That's the best part."

SULLY

WE ONLY END up getting out of bed because Aubrey's alarm goes off.

"Crap! I'm supposed to be at the coffee shop at eleven."

I cup her cheek and pull her close for another kiss. "Go grab a shower, I'll make breakfast."

She hesitates and I raise an eyebrow. "Do you mind grabbing my bag from the backseat of the car? I have a change of clothes in there."

"Sure. I would've grabbed it earlier for you."

Her shoulders lift. "I like wearing yours."

"I like you in them." In fact, I want to see her in them again tonight. "What are your plans after your shift?"

"I guess go home and check on the apartment."

"How about you come over and I'll make you dinner?"

She blinks. "You sure you want me here two nights in a row?"

I lean in and press a kiss to her cheek. "Yes, I want you here." Two nights in a row, hell I wouldn't mind waking up with her every morning.

She leans into my touch and ducks her head. "Okay. I'll come by the gym and follow you." She glances up and her cheeks turn pink. "I was too excited last night to pay attention to how we got here."

She's too damn sweet and I kiss her again before letting her go.

All too soon, she's driving me to the gym and pulling into the back parking lot. She's late, so she doesn't shut the car off.

"Hey." I reach for her face. She smiles when I touch her. A beautiful, sensual smile that reminds me of last night. Her lips part right before I press mine against them. I take my time, memorizing her taste. Wanting her to feel this kiss for the rest of the day.

"Have a good day," I say when we part.

She blinks a few times. "You too."

Jake catches me at the back door, grinning wide enough to make me groan.

"Nice of you to show up." He peers out the back door. "Where's she going?"

"Coffee shop."

He nods but is surprisingly quiet. Never a good sign.

"Everything okay here?" I ask, glancing over my shoulder to see if he's following me to my office.

"Both classes were full this morning." His voice lacks the annoyance I'd expect after covering two full classes for me.

"Morning, handsome." Keegan's slow grin and wide body filling up my office doorway stops me in my tracks.

I turn and glare at my brother. "Can't you keep your mouth shut?"

"What?" Jake can't fake an innocent expression to save his ass, but he gives it a solid try. "He wanted to know where you were."

"Assholes," I grumble pushing past Keegan.

Keegan's rumbling laughter irritates me. Eventually, when he realizes I have no details to share, he leaves.

I have a few afternoon appointments, so I focus and prepare for those.

Jake sticks around and helps out more than usual, which immediately makes me suspicious.

CHAPTER FIFTEEN
Aubrey

I BARELY SLIDE through the back door of Busy Beans on time. Brantley shakes his head while I loop my apron around my neck and take my place at the cash register. He's not mad, but he'll definitely tease me later.

After the mid-morning rush, customers come and go at a slow, but steady pace. Around three o'clock, the bell chimes and I glance up. Griff's holding the door open for a tall, slender, dark-haired girl who can't be more than sixteen. She breezes right up to the counter and studies the baked goods before telling him what she wants.

A slow grin turns his mouth up when our gazes finally collide. "Afternoon, Aubrey. I wasn't sure if you'd be working today."

"I'm here."

He taps the glass case. "Two blueberry muffins."

The girl tugs on his sleeve and he amends his order to three muffins. "Anything else?"

"Large black coffee and a Caramel Mocha Frappe," he orders with a straight face.

"Skinny frappe? Fighters have to watch their weight, right?" My lips quirk. "I assume it's for *you*."

"Ah, funny girl," he jokes. "I guess we didn't scare you too badly last night."

"Nope. I don't scare easy."

The girl flounces off to the end of the counter to wait for their drinks.

I raise an eyebrow. "She's a little young for you, no, Griff?"

He doesn't laugh. "She's Remy's baby sister. What kind of guy do you think I am?"

"Well…"

He snorts and shakes his head. "That your way of saying you're interested, Aubrey? Jealous?"

Now it's my turn to snort out a laugh. "No, I'm good. Thanks."

He slaps his hand over his chest. "Damn, girl. You didn't even get to see what I can do in the ring."

"I'm sure it's breathtaking."

He grins a little wider. "I saw you and Sully making eyes at each other all night."

I can't even hide the smile on my face.

"Real talk?" he asks, leaning in closer.

"Sure."

"Sully's a good guy. I got a lot of respect for him."

I cock my head and nail him with a glare. "Is that your way of saying I need his permission to work the ring again?"

"*Nooo*, I'd never put it that way."

"Griff," the girl calls, a note of exasperation coloring her voice.

"Be right there, Molly," he answers without looking away.

"Someone has you wrapped around her finger."

He laughs, not at all embarrassed. "Pretty much."

"Hey, is Remy okay after last night?" I ask.

The question seems to surprise him. "Yeah, last night was nothing. He's taken much worse beatings."

Molly returns and hands him his coffee. This time she actually acknowledges me. "Did you get to see my brother fight last night?"

"Sure did. He's really good."

She slants a look at Griff. "I wouldn't know. I'm not *allowed* to go."

I'm not sure how to answer her. "It was a rough crowd. I'm sure your brother doesn't want you to get hurt."

She rolls her eyes and nods. "That's their perpetual excuse."

Griff chuckles and ruffles her hair. She slaps his hand away and snags the bag of muffins off the counter.

"Gotta go," Griff says. "Tell Sully I might take him up on his offer and I'll stop in sometime this week."

"Do I even want to know?"

He grins and takes off after Molly while I shake my head.

My smile remains until my shift is over.

I'M EAGER TO see Sully again, but since Celia's away, I also want to check on our apartment. Maybe grab some clothes and stuff too.

On the stairs, I run into Ty about to take Gambler for a walk. "Hey, where you been, Aubrey?"

"Uh, I just got off work."

He cocks his head and stares at me for a few seconds. "Where's your sister?"

"A work thing. She'll be back tomorrow night."

"Ahh, okay. I was wondering why it was so quiet over there."

"Are we really that noisy?" I tease.

"No, I just worry about the two of you alone. That's all."

A warm rush spreads through my chest. Ty's been pretty nice to us since we moved in. Not in a creepy trying-to-get-in-our-pants-way, but a friendly-overprotective-neighborly-way. "Thanks, Ty."

"You need something while she's gone, let me know." His gaze sweeps over me one more time. "Are you seeing Sully?"

My cheeks heat up so fast I'm sure I'm the color of a beet. "A little."

What kind of stupid answer is that?

He winks at me. "Gotcha."

Gambler pushes his head against my leg, begging for some petting and I reach down to scratch behind his ears. "You being a good boy?" I ask.

"No," Ty answers, but his voice is full of affection for the pup. "He ate half my couch this afternoon."

"Seriously? Shoot, I can start walking him again."

"No way. I can't have you get hurt again. I'll figure something out." He gives the leash a gentle tug. "Right now I'm gonna take him for a run and hopefully tire his ass out."

"Good luck."

I hurry through the apartment, grabbing a few things and inhaling a quick snack. I'm a little alarmed about how much I want to see Sully.

It's only been a few hours. I can't seriously miss him already?

Setting that thought aside, I take one last look around the apartment and trot downstairs.

I'm at the gym fifteen minutes later.

Sully's busy with a client, so I sit behind the desk. Technically, I'm not on the schedule today, but if I'm here, I might as well help out, right?

"Hey, Aubrey," Jake says, sneaking up on me.

"Why are you being so creepy?"

His devilish smile intensifies. "No reason."

I can't picture Sully discussing details of our night together with his brother. He seems too mature for that. Still, it makes me uneasy and I cross my arms over my chest.

"Shoot, I'm just messing around, Aubrey," Jake says, picking up on my shift in attitude right away. He glances over his shoulder. "I think you're good for him."

"Really?"

"Yeah, I mean it. You've been good for the gym too. I actually notice the difference when you're not here."

Pleased doesn't even begin to describe what the compliment does to me. "Thank you." My professional aspirations have taken a beating the last few years, so it feels good to be useful and appreciated.

A hand slides over my hip and Sully's scent drifts into my space. Warm breath skates across my cheek. "I missed you." Sully's voice is pure heat and I lean back against him. His arm bands around my waist and he kisses my neck.

My eyelids flutter shut. "I missed you too."

Someone clears his throat, startling me out of the trance I slipped into the second Sully touched me. Sully straightens up and drops his hand. He seems as surprised as I do.

Jake's smirk indicates he has a lot of opinions to share about our public cuddling.

I quickly scan the gym, no one seems to have noticed our intimate greeting.

"Can I see you in my office, Aubrey?" Sully asks. He's already headed in that direction, not waiting for my response. Too embarrassed to say anything to Jake, I follow.

Dammit. I know how important it is to Sully not to get carried away at work. Although to be fair, he touched me first.

Sully closes the door behind us. My mouth opens to apologize even though I'm not sure why. Maybe this right here is exactly why he was so cautious about us getting involved.

Before I have a chance to say anything, he seals his mouth over mine and pushes me up against the door. His hands go to my hips, sneaking under my shirt, his thumbs gently brushing my sides. Every thought disappears. There is only the need to kiss and be kissed by him. By the time he pulls away, we're both breathing hard.

"Lost control out there," he rasps. He brushes his thumb over my cheek. "I always suspected you'd turn me into a rule breaker."

"Sorry."

"Don't be sorry. It's all on me." He takes my hand and leads me over to the couch across from his desk. "How was your day?"

"Well," I say, drawing out the word in a teasing way that makes him smile. "It improved significantly about ten minutes ago."

"Yeah?" He raises an eyebrow. "And?"

"It got *exponentially* better about ten seconds ago." I gesture over my shoulder to the door.

He pulls me down onto the couch with him until I'm straddling his lap.

"Sully." It's a weak protest, because I love being close to him no matter where we are.

His hand threads into my hair, pulling me down for a kiss. He parts my lips and strokes his tongue against mine. This isn't a soft-appropriate-for-the-workplace kiss. It's an invitation-to-get-naked kind of kiss. Blistering and passionate. Reminding me of all the other ways he used his wicked mouth on me last night.

Keeping a gentle hold on my hair, he pulls back and studies my face for a moment. "You're blushing. What are you thinking about?"

Not bold enough to make eye contact, I lean in and whisper my thoughts against his ear. "How good you felt inside me last night."

He answers with a groan and kisses my neck. His hands palm my butt, shifting me forward so I can feel the effect my words have on him.

"What a good kisser you are," I continue. "*Every*where." A wild rush of pleasure consumes me at the memory.

He licks and kisses more spots along my neck, down to my shoulder before pulling back. No one's ever looked at me quite like this. Eyes shimmering with desire, lips warm with appreciation "I'm dying to kiss you *everywhere* again."

My heart kicks and tingles race over my skin. He's such a perfect blend of forceful and sweet. "Looking forward to it," I whisper.

SULLY

A MAN CAN only withstand so much temptation. I'm giving serious consideration to stripping off Aubrey's clothes and spreading her out on my desk.

My brother has a death wish because a few seconds later he knocks and opens the door before he's invited in.

With one hand covering his eyes, he says, "Sorry, sorry. Not looking."

Not in a joking mood, I growl, "Knock it off."

He drops his hand and lets out a huge, fake a sigh of relief. "Oh, thank God, you still have clothes on. There's a customer who wants to talk to you."

I shake my head and motion for him to close the door behind him.

"I'll be right out."

"You're busy for a Saturday afternoon," Aubrey says, shifting out of my lap. She stands and runs her hands over her clothes as if I wrinkled them with the power of my indecent thoughts.

My gaze shoots to the door. Jake left it slightly ajar. "Do you want to leave and meet up later?"

"I don't mind staying."

As much as I want her to stay, I don't want to take advantage of her sweet nature. "I don't want to make you work on your day off, especially after you already worked your other job today."

"I want to help you out," she says softly.

"Don't feel like you have to." I gesture between us. "That's not what this is about."

She chuckles. "I appreciate that, but you think too much."

"I can't help it. Especially when it comes to you."

CHAPTER SIXTEEN
SULLY

THE SECOND MORNING waking up next to Aubrey is even better than the first.

"This is by far, the best way I've ever woken up," she murmurs. I climb up her body, dropping little kisses along the way.

"Tell me more about you." I don't pose it as a question. We didn't do a whole lot of talking once we came through my front door last night.

She freezes, but recovers quickly, hiding the hesitation with a short laugh. "What do you want to know?"

"Start small."

Her mouth twists down and her little fist comes flying at me. I grab it mid-air and kiss the back of her hand. "That wasn't a size joke. You fit me perfectly. In a second I'll show you again just how well we fit."

"Oh." She leans in, brushing her lips over my shoulder, distracting me.

"Give me something."

I'm done avoiding whatever this is between us. No, I'm *all in*. I want to be closer to her but not just in the physical way. I take her head back and kiss her soft lips. Slowly savoring her, I continue kissing her neck and when she finally moans for me, I pull back.

She sighs, and I cover her mouth with my finger. "Give me something," I repeat.

"I'm prepared to give you *everything*." Under me, she wiggles her hips to emphasize the *everything*.

"I want *more* than sex from you. Tell me something simple."

She throws her hands in the air. "You know where I live, where I work, my favorite flavor of ice cream, what my major is. What more do you want to know?" Her bottom lip juts out and I barely resist taking another taste.

"What's your favorite color? We'll start there."

Her shoulders drop in obvious relief. "Red."

"You look good in red. Favorite season?"

"Fall."

"There, was that so hard?"

"What about you?"

"Black and summer." I don't give her time to cut me off. "When's your birthday?" I ask.

"January." Her eyes soften as she stares off at something in the distance she can't quite touch. "I hate winter. Just once I want to spend my birthday somewhere warm. On the beach. From sunrise to sunset."

I squeeze her to me and pat her butt. "I'd definitely be down for you in a bathing suit and some sand under our toes."

"January's kind of far away," she whispers.

Not liking what her words imply, I kiss her forehead. "Not really."

"Now we know more about each other. Happy?"

I chuckle against her neck, pushing her heavy hair out of my way. Under my touch, she shivers. "Cold?"

"I'm so hot for you it's not even funny."

I open my mouth to tell her I feel the same way, but she presses her fingers over my lips. "Sully, question time's over."

I kiss her fingertips, her palm, and the inside of her wrist. Her body tenses and I glance up, meeting her troubled eyes.

"I thought of something else to tell you about me," she whispers.

"What's that?" She looks so scared and vulnerable. Whatever she has to say, I want to assure her it's okay.

"Please don't break my heart."

Aubrey

HAS ANYTHING MORE pitiful ever come out of my mouth? Probably.

"You're the heartbreaker here," Sully says. Somehow his words reassure me that I'm not alone in what's happening between us.

I glance at the clock and poke him in the chest. "We can't be late again."

He groans and shuts his eyes. "Sometimes being the boss really sucks."

Tickling my fingers over his chest, I lean and kiss his cheek. "Yeah, but you're really good at it."

"You're killing me."

We end up arriving at Strike Back on time.

Around three, Celia sends me a text to let me know her flight is on time.

I hate interrupting Sully, but I want to let him know I'm leaving.

"Sully," I call out.

He sets the weights he was using down and in the couple seconds it takes for him to scrub a towel over his face I admire his glistening muscles.

"What's up?" he asks.

"I need to go pick up my sister."

"Sorry, I forgot." Something, maybe disappointment, clouds his eyes. "I don't suppose I can entice you to come to dinner tonight? Nothing fancy," he hurries to add. "I usually get together with some of the guys on Sunday nights."

"So, not a date. Just friends?"

I think he realizes what I'm asking before I do. "Girlfriends are allowed to come."

I step closer and grab onto his T-shirt, twisting my fingers in the material, bringing him closer. "Are you calling me your girlfriend?"

"Is there something else you'd rather I call you?" he teases.

"Does that mean I can tell people you're my boyfriend?"

"You can." He hesitates and pulls back. "Is someone asking?" A hint of jealousy colors his question.

I'm not one to play games or stoke the flames of envy, so I answer honestly. "I ran into Ty yesterday, and he asked if we were seeing each other. I wasn't sure what you wanted me to say."

He frowns. "Yeah, you can definitely tell *him*."

I tip my head back and poke him in the side. "Aww, are you jealous of my neighbor?"

"No."

"I'm pretty sure he's into my sister. So I wouldn't worry about it too much."

He shakes his head, but it feels like there's more he wants to say on the subject of Ty. "If Celia's interested, she's welcomed to join us tonight."

"Okay, I'll let her know."

He walks me out to my car. "I'm going to miss having wheels," I joke as I open the door.

"Be careful." He presses a quick kiss to my cheek and opens my door for me.

CELIA'S PLANE IS *not* on time. I grabbed a caramel Frappuccino from the airport Starbucks for her and it's currently melting in my hand while I wait.

Finally, the screen announces her plane's arrival and my heart rate slows. It's still another fifteen minutes before I spot her. I raise my free hand and wave, hoping she can see me.

"Hey! I was getting worried about you!" I give her a tight hug.

"Ugh, the last thirty minutes were awful. I'm so happy to see you!"

I thrust the drink into her hands and she beams at me. "You must love me. I know how you feel about the big coffee giant," she teases.

"Don't tell Brantley." My manager at Busy Beans would die if he knew I set foot inside a Starbucks.

My sister travels light, so we don't have to wait for her luggage. She's vibrating with energy, practically skipping to the car. "I'm so happy to be home."

I toss her the keys and she adjusts the seat before sliding into the driver's side.

"How was your weekend? Do anything fun?"

Sully. And yes, he was fun.

"I, uh, yeah. It was good."

She glances over. "Sounds like there's more to it than that. What'd you do?"

"Hung out with Sully, mostly." I wince and wait for her to lecture me.

"Mr. buff, gym dude? The guy you're working for part-time?" she asks drawing out the questions, pretending her memory's a little fuzzy on the subject.

"Yes," I answer with a hint of impatience.

"Go, Aubrey," she mutters. "He's pretty damn hot."

A relieved breath whooshes out of me. "He is. He's really sweet though too. I like him a lot," I add in a quieter voice.

"Good. God, Aubrey. It's been a long time, you *should* be dating."

"I've dated." Or at least I've tried to.

She blows out an I-call-bullshit breath. "You have to stop punishing yourself for something that wasn't your fault."

She's wrong of course, but I'm not going to argue with her. I'm moving on with my life and that's all that matters. "He invited us to meet up with him and his friends tonight for dinner if you're interested."

"Sure. I'm still too keyed up to go home for the night." She's quiet for a second. "Wait, is his degenerate brother going to be there?"

"Stop. Jake's actually really nice."

"Yeah, because he knows if he touches you, Sully will kill him. To everyone else with a vagina, he's probably a dick." She stops and snickers. "Or tries to stick his—"

"Yeah, yeah," I interrupt. "Save it, funny girl."

She spends the rest of the drive home filling me in on her conference. All about new products she plans to try. She wants me to stop by the salon one morning so she can use me as a hair model for a class she's supposed to teach.

"Sure. As long as it's not braiding. Last time I thought you were going to rip my scalp off."

"No braiding. I promise."

At home she switches into planning-a-night-out-mode, tearing through outfits in her closet at warp-speed.

"You have such great legs," she says, tossing a short denim skirt at me. Well, on her it's short, on me not so much. "Wear that."

"With what?"

"Uh." More stuff goes flying through the air. "This." She throws a peacock blue halter top my way. "That color makes your eyes pop."

I cock my head. "Do I want my eyes to pop? Sounds painful."

"Ha. Ha. Go get dressed."

In my room, I stop and send Sully a text to let him know we'll be there.

Can't wait to see you, he writes back.

Warmth spreads through my chest.

I can't wait to see him either.

AN HOUR LATER we arrive and to my surprise, Sully meets us at the door.

"Hey," he says and with no hesitation, sweeps me up against his body, pressing a quick kiss to my lips. He touches his forehead to mine long enough to murmur, "Missed you."

Swoon, swoon, swoony-swoon. Seriously, I'm a pile of mush inside. "Missed you too."

Behind us, Celia clears her throat. Yeah, we're kind of causing a scene. Sully slowly sets me down and holds out his hand. "Nice to see you again, Celia."

She eyes him with a brief moment of suspicion before shaking his hand. "I see you've gotten closer to my sister," she says.

I elbow her in the ribs—which she ignores.

Sully's not offended. He gives her a lopsided smile. "Do I measure up?"

"I guess we'll see."

He chuckles and takes my hand. "We always try to grab the big booth in the back. Keegan and Jake are already here. Liam said he and Bree will stop by later."

Wow, I've been so caught up with Sully, I haven't even told Bree.

Jake's eyes widen when the three of us approach and he sits up straighter. "Keegan, you know, Aubrey. This is her sister, Celia."

Keegan actually stands and shakes her hand.

Jake nods and settles back against the booth. "Nice to see you again."

She briefly narrows her eyes, then flashes a smile at him. "You too."

"The waitress has been slammed tonight. Ordering at the bar might be quicker," Keegan warns us.

Sully asks Celia what she wants, then me. "I'll go with you," I offer.

It ends up being pointless for me to go with him. I'm too short for the bartender to even spot me in the crowd unless I jump up and down.

After Sully places our order, he slips an arm around my shoulder and leans down to kiss my temple. "I got you."

I love the way he makes me feel. Safe, warm, and protected.

When we're finally handed our order, I grab the pitcher of beer and let him take the rest.

"Thanks," Celia says, grabbing the pitcher from me. I slide in next to her.

"We tried to divide and conquer, but the bartender kept looking right over me."

"You've gotta be more aggressive," Sully teases. "Get right in their face."

"It's so unfair." I laugh and slap Sully's arm. "You have like ten inches on me. They can't even *see* me over the bar."

He leans in and brushes a kiss over my cheek. "You're perfect," he whispers in my ear.

Jake sets his beer on the table with a *thunk*, drawing our attention his way. "Ten inches? More like ten and a half or eleven." He holds his hands about two feet apart. "The Wallace brothers are *extremely* well hung."

I cough and look away.

Sully reaches behind Celia and me and shoves Jake's shoulder. "No one was talking about that. What's the matter with you?"

"No offense to you, Sully," Celia says with a smile. She casts a less pleasant look Jake's way. "I find guys who feel the need to brag about their dick size usually aren't packing much. *Or* they're unimpressive in the sack because they think their big tool is all they need to get the job done."

"Oh, he's a big tool all right," Keegan says. He lifts his chin at Sully. "I like her."

Jake casts a sideways glance at his friend before responding to Celia. "I'll prove your theory wrong any time you want, sweetheart."

Celia leans into me and loud enough for everyone at the table to hear says, "I'm guessing Sully has the bigger package and that's why Jake feels the need to overcompensate."

While Sully and Keegan groan, I choke and reach for my water.

Unfazed, Jake reclines, spreading his arms over the back of the booth. He trains his mischievous eyes on my sister, staring her down. "Baby, anytime you wanna see my dick, all you have to do is ask."

"*No one* wants to see your dick," Keegan assures him. "Stop begging girls to look at your junk all the time. It's embarrassing."

Sully's more direct with his brother. "Knock it off," he warns.

Jake's smug smile only grows wider, but he doesn't offer up any more invitations into his pants.

"There they are." Keegan nods toward the front of the bar.

"Thank God," Sully grumbles. He leans down. "Sorry about my brother. He's not usually this obnoxious."

"Celia can handle herself. If you haven't noticed."

"Yeah," he mutters, glancing over at them.

Liam and Bree make their way through the crowded bar to our table and Bree's eyes widen when she sees Sully's arm around me. She grins and flashes me a quick thumbs-up.

"Never been so happy to see you two." Keegan casts a dramatic eye roll toward Liam. "You saved us from having to listen to Jake bragging about the size of his tool all night long."

Celia snickers into her hand before throwing a quick wave. "Hey, Bree, good to see you again."

"Why is Jake talking about his tool at dinner?" Liam asks.

"He was trying to impress me," Celia explains. "But it takes more than a large tool to capture my interest."

Everyone, except me, laughs while Liam and Bree squeeze into our round booth next to Keegan, pushing Jake closer to Celia.

God, I hope the two of them behave.

Bree touches the ends of her hair and smiles at Celia. "I need to come see you again, Celia."

"Anytime."

"What do you do, Celia?" Keegan asks.

My sister beams. "I'm a hair-stylist."

"Are you any good?" Jake asks with a smirk.

My sister slowly turns and studies him. Without answering, she reaches out and runs her fingers through his hair. He leans into her like a big ol' jungle cat—eyes closed and all. "You cut this yourself with hedge-trimmers or something?" she asks.

His eyes snap open, but they're dancing with laughter instead of annoyance. "No." He lifts his chin Sully's way. "He cuts it."

Sully shrugs. "I've done it since we were kids."

Something about that hits me right in the chest. Can Sully be any sweeter?

Even though he didn't extend an invite, she reaches over and runs her hand over Sully's head. This time, I slap her hand away before she has a chance to comment.

"You do men's hair too?" Bree asks.

"Don't get any ideas," Liam says. "I like where I go just fine."

Keegan tucks his hands up under his chin. His eyes widen and his mouth kicks into a childish grin. "Gee, what's next, boys and girls? Can we share makeup tips too? I'm in desperate need of tips on how to achieve the perfect smoky eye."

While the rest of us burst into laughter, Celia shrugs. "You asked."

"I need to run to the ladies' room." Under the table, I tap Celia with my foot. In her shin. I nudge Sully to let me out of the booth and Celia follows.

"Why are you flirting with him when you clearly don't like him?"

"Who?" she asks.

"Don't 'who' me."

"That was *not* flirting." She waves a hand in the air. "He needs to be taken down a notch or two."

I stop her with a hand on her arm. "Celia, I really, really like Sully, which means I'll probably spend a lot of time around Jake. Please don't make it miserable."

Finally, she stops and really looks at me. "I'll try." She glances back at the table. "I guess as long as he keeps his mouth shut, he's not bad to look at."

"That's the spirit."

Celia teasingly shoves my shoulder. "I see someone I know, I'm going to stop at the bar and say hello."

"See you back at the table."

SULLY

"HAVE YOU LOST your mind?" I growl at Jake while he watches Celia and Aubrey disappear into the crowd.

"What?" he asks with an innocently raised eyebrow.

"Don't fuck your brother's girlfriend's sister. Christ, why do we have to spell everything out for you?" Keegan snarls.

"I didn't. Yet," he mutters.

Keegan shakes his head. "Your ego is huge."

"Oh, it's huge—" Jake starts.

"Don't," Liam growls, cutting off my brother's dirty innuendo.

Bree snickers into her hand. "Nothing Jake says surprises me by now."

Jake turns his laser focus Bree's way. "Is she seeing anyone?"

For some reason, Bree takes the question seriously. "I don't think so." A wicked smile curves her lips. "But Keegan has a point. If you date Aubrey's sister, it might be awkward later." She shoots a devilish look my way. "You know, if Sully asks you to be his best man and Aubrey asks her sister to be her maid of honor..." She drifts off, letting the suggestion hang in the air.

Jake and Keegan howl with laughter, assuming the way-too-soon-for-hinting-about-a-wedding bothers me. Liam casts a sideways glance at his fiancée.

Our waitress drops off the rest of our order, almost putting an end to any more premature wedding planning.

I glance down the hall, but there's no sign of Aubrey. I notice Celia over by the bar.

"Whoa." Jake jabs his elbow in my side. "Is that Amy heading to the ladies' room?"

"Don't try to distract—" I start to say, but stop short when I spot Amy and realize, it's not an ill-timed joke from my brother. "Aw, fuck."

Liam and Keegan both laugh.

"Better go diffuse *that*," Jake suggests.

"You really think she'd say something to Aubrey?"

"She didn't seem too fond of you last time," Liam reminds me.

Bree scowls and stabs her fork into her salad without a word.

The whole situation is awkward. Nobody else offers any other bits of advice. I stalk through the bar, but by the time I make it down the hallway, there's no sign of either of them.

This isn't a big deal, right? Amy has no reason to talk to Aubrey. It's not like Amy and I were ever in a real relationship.

Definitely *don't* say that to Aubrey. It sounds awful.

The door opens and Amy steps out. Her lips curl into a smirk when she sees me.

She jerks her thumb toward the door. "*Aubrey's* in there all alone if you want to give her a Wallace Wallbanger."

I take a few steps closer. "What did you say to her?"

She touches her fingertips to her sticky, pink lips. "Who me? Not a thing."

Aubrey

A BEAD OF sweat rolls down my back and I hurry to re-tie the stupid halter-top my sister talked me into wearing. Thank God I noticed it was loose now, in the privacy of the bathroom. Flashing the entire bar would've been an awful way to remember my first night out with Sully.

Ugh, more sweat. The bar obviously doesn't waste a penny pumping any cold air into their closet-sized restroom.

Finally, I secure the knot at the nape of my neck and squeeze out of the tiny stall.

And stop dead.

A girl I don't recognize is perched on the edge of the sink, even though it looks one rusty bolt away from toppling over. Who is this chick with the skinny arms crossed over her ample chest and heavily made up eyes glaring like she's trying to make me evaporate with the power of her mind?

"Excuse me," I say, pushing past her. She twists her body out of my way with a huff, as if I'd told her to fuck off—which maybe I should have.

"Are you with Sully?" she asks.

Suspicious of her intentions, I answer with a careful yes.

"I'm an old friend." She holds out her hand. "Amy."

I hold up my wet hands as a weak apology for refusing the hand-shake. "Aubrey."

Her eyes widen, and her lips flatten into a thin, angry line. "That's a name you don't hear often."

I'm used to people commenting on and confusing my name—Audrey, Avery, Ashley, Abby, I've heard them all—but it's never seemed to piss off anyone before. "Yeah," I mumble, squeezing by to grab the paper towels.

She takes a step back and in the mirror I watch her gaze roam over my back, which is kind of creeping me out. "How long have you known Sully?"

"A while." Obviously she *knows* Sully, but there's no way in hell I'm going to ask for details.

Her mouth twists and her eyes narrow to slits. "So, you're his new fuck-in-the-bar-bathroom girl? Because that was *me* for the last year or so. On and off." She lovingly traces her fingers over the edge of the sink in case I can't interpret her meaning.

Whoa. That's way too much information for a stranger to tell me about my boyfriend. And, *ewww. Yuck.* I didn't need to know that.

The thought of them together burns like acid. And let's pretend it's sweat stinging my eyes not tears.

Is that what Jake meant with his whole "my brother never takes girls home with him" thing? Am I supposed to feel special?

Slowly, I toss the towel in the trash and pull a comb out of my purse. "I don't know anything about that," I say, faking disinterest. I flick the comb through the ends of my hair, ignoring her and hoping she'll go away.

When she doesn't leave, I stop and stare at her. "Do you need to use the bathroom? Or did you just stop by to tell me you have carnal knowledge of my boyfriend?"

Amy jolts and her eyes widen. Maybe she doesn't know what the word *carnal* means. Or maybe no one's ever stood up to her before. Either way, I've put up with too many bitchy girls like her in the past to allow myself to show that I'm rattled.

She shrugs—the lamest comeback ever—and flounces out the door.

"Whatever," I mutter shoving the comb in my purse and staring at myself in the mirror for a few beats. My stomach's still fluttering after the confrontation. Finally, I reach for the door.

Sully's waiting for me on the other side.

My anger and humiliation bubble up and I tamp it down. He's a grown man. Of course he's bound to have an ex or two running around.

Although, a warning that he used to bang one in this very bar on a regular basis, and that she might be the confrontational type, might have been a polite head's up.

He steps forward and holds out his hand. "Everything okay?" he asks in a cautious manner. So, obviously, he suspects his psycho bang-buddy had some words for me.

"Sure, I have girls follow me into the bathroom to tell me they've fucked my boyfriend all the time," I say in a low, even tone.

He closes his eyes briefly. "I'm sorry."

"Should we ask the owner to erect a shrine in there?" I flap my hand at the bathroom door. "According to Amy, it's sacred territory."

This time he winces, so I guess it's true. "I didn't know she'd be here or that she'd say something to you."

"Obviously."

I will not cause a scene. I will not.

"Let's go. My sister's going to wonder where I am and I think we should be there as a buffer, so she doesn't castrate your brother."

The corners of his mouth lift in a hint of a smile. "You sure? Do you want to talk?"

"About your ex? Nope. Not even a little." I hesitate and then ask the only question that matters. "Are you two done? I don't know how to navigate the 'seeing other people' game."

"The thing with her ended a while ago." He takes my hands in his and stares into my eyes. "I'm not seeing anyone but you, Aubrey."

"Good," I whisper.

He leans down as if he's going to kiss me.

"Still too soon," I mumble.

He sighs and takes my hand. Together, we walk back to our table.

I stop dead a few feet away. Sully's eyes are on me, so he doesn't notice at first. "Are you kidding me?" I ask.

"What?" He glances at the table and groans. Wedged between Celia and Jake is a smug Amy, lapping up all the attention.

Celia glances up and smiles as we approach. "You okay, sis?" She turns to Amy. "This is Amy, she works in the store next to my salon."

"We've met," I grumble.

CHAPTER SEVENTEEN
SULLY

MY MOTHER WAS adamant about raising her two rambunctious sons into good men. Not assholes like my stepfather. She had a lot of rules for us. The top three were: be honest, be considerate, and take responsibility.

Tonight, I think I've cocked up all three. Although this situation never occurred to me, it should have.

Aubrey hesitates to slide into the booth and I can't really blame her. "Celia," she says in a low voice, catching her sister's attention. "I don't feel well. Do you mind if we go home?"

Celia snaps into big sister mode and scoots out of the booth. "Sure, hon."

I place my hands on Aubrey's shoulders and lean down to speak against her ear. "Don't go. I'll fix this."

She shakes her head without saying a word.

Celia opens her purse and pulls out a few dollars, but I hold out my hand to stop her.

"I've got this, Celia. Don't worry about it."

"You're leaving?" Bree asks. She nudges Liam so she can get up and give Aubrey a hug. "We'll catch up later this week?"

"Sure."

Amy watches the whole scene with a triumphant smile, while Jake, helpful brother that he is, keeps trying to distract her.

I hate having Aubrey leave like this.

"Celia can stay. I'll take you home," I say to Aubrey.

Celia lets out a big yawn and wraps her arm around Aubrey's shoulders. "I'm exhausted from my trip. I should probably get home anyway."

They say goodnight to everyone. Over Aubrey's protest, I walk them outside.

"Aubrey, can we talk?" This is *not* how I wanted things to work out tonight. I planned on Aubrey coming home with me again. And every night for the foreseeable future.

"I need to go," she says. "I didn't want to cause a scene in front of everyone. But I won't sit there with that woman and pretend everything's normal when I know what she's trying to do."

"I didn't—"

She cuts off the lame apology I was about to give her. "I know you didn't." She glances down. "I'm not mad at you. I just want to go home."

We're, what? Two days into this relationship and I'm already fucking up. "We'll talk tomorrow."

She nods and turns toward the car, but I grab her hand and pull her back to me. "You can't leave without a proper kiss."

Finally, she smiles and even though it's hesitant and unsure, it's the most beautiful thing I've seen all night. Our lips meet. This is no quick goodbye kiss. It's long and slow and deep. Trying to make up for the things I can't say right now.

She lets out a stuttering sigh and backs away. "Good night, Sully."

Aubrey

"SO, ARE YOU planning to tell me what really happened?" Celia asks as soon as we drive away.

I sigh and sit back, closing my eyes. "I don't want to talk about it."

"Come on, one minute you two are so stinking adorable, I want to choke you and the next you can't get out of there fast enough."

Celia will work the truth out of me eventually, so I might as well just spill it now. "Your pal, Amy, cornered me in the bathroom to let me know she and Sully used to be fuck-buddies." It sounds ridiculous once I finally get the words out.

"Holy shit, are you serious? I'm so sorry. I never would've invited her over if I'd known that."

"It's not your fault. It's not even that big a deal."

"Sure it is." She reaches over and pats my leg. "I can already see how much you like him, so that must've been a shock." She huffs out a laugh. "Poor Sully. Here he was being all sweet, staking his claim on you in front of his friends, and it backfired." She shakes her head and chuckles some more. "Poor bastard."

"Shut up. Now you're making me feel worse." I consider her words while she makes the turn into our apartment complex and parks the car. "You really think that's what he was doing?"

"Letting everyone know to stay away from you? Uh, yeah. I don't think he took his hands off you for five seconds. That's probably what set Amy off if he was never like that with her."

Huh. I ponder that all the way up the stairs.

CHAPTER EIGHTEEN
SULLY

DISAPPOINTMENT PULLS ME out of sleep when I reach over and find the other side of the bed cold and empty.

Two nights.

Two nights is all it took for me to get used to waking up next to Aubrey.

Will she even show up for work today? After last night, I wouldn't blame her if she called out. Lucky for me, I don't think she's the type to bail on her responsibilities.

"Damn, brother. You haven't been this big of a pussy over a girl since high school," Jake says as soon as I sit down for breakfast at our mother's.

"Language, Jake," my mother scolds. She turns her curious face my way. "What girl?"

"Her name is Aubrey."

"The girl you hired to work for you?"

"That's the one." I grab my water and take a long swallow to prepare for the questions coming my way.

"Is she on birth control?"

Jake bursts out laughing.

I choke on my water. "Jesus, Mom, really?" Not the question I expected her to lead with. What's she like? When can I meet her? How old is she? Any of those would've been preferable.

"Can you blame me?" she asks with a raised eyebrow. "That's just as much your responsibility as hers. If you can't talk about it, maybe you shouldn't be having sex."

I grit my teeth. I love my mother, but sometimes the stuff that comes out of her mouth… "I can talk about it with *her*. I do *not* want to talk about it with *you*," I clarify.

She averts her eyes and tugs at the pendant hanging from a delicate gold chain around her neck. "Well, if I'd talked to you about that stuff earlier, maybe—"

"Ma, stop." I will *not* have my mother feel guilty about the mistakes Lauren and I made as teenagers. "Your hands were full raising the two of us." I tilt my head Jake's way.

He gives me a why-are-you-throwing-me-in frown. "*I* know how to wrap it up."

Instead of whapping him upside the head, like she should, she reaches over and squeezes his hand. "Fair enough." She stands and pats my shoulder on the way to the kitchen.

I glare at Jake. "Really, dick?"

Still laughing, he leans forward. "At least she got it out of her system. Maybe she won't hound Aubrey too bad."

"Yeah," I answer with a healthy bit of sarcasm. "I'm sure she'll rein it in."

"I don't hound people, Jake," she shouts from the kitchen.

In a lower voice, he says to me, "Think Aubrey's still mad about last night?"

"Hope not."

"Guess we'll find out."

"What did you do, Sullivan?" my mother asks.

I groan and glare across the table at my brother.

LATER THAT MORNING, I have a gym full of people trying to undo the damage from a weekend of over-eating and drinking.

Aubrey shows up a few minutes early for her shift. Prettier than ever. How does she do that?

"Can we talk?" she asks.

I hope this isn't the part where she quits.

She follows me into my office. Before I even close the door, she touches my arm. "I'm sorry about last night."

I didn't realize how much I missed having her hands on me. "You don't have anything to be sorry about."

"I shouldn't have left like that."

After leaving the bar, I considered how I'd feel if she was the one with an ex who confronted me that way. I'd probably be cooling off in the county jail right now. So no, I don't blame her for being upset.

"I understand." I don't need to say more than that and I sure as hell am *not* bringing up Amy's name. It hasn't escaped my notice that she didn't ask any questions about Amy or what I did last night after she and Celia went home.

"You can trust me," I assure her.

"I already do."

Good. I don't ever want to give her a reason not to.

In a lower voice, she adds, "This is a little new to me."

I'm not sure how to respond. Is she trying to say she's never dated before? Or just that *we* are new as a couple?

"It's new to me too."

Finally, she meets my eyes.

"I missed waking up next to you," I say. Fuck it, after last night I want to tell her how I feel and be honest about everything.

"I missed you too," she whispers, taking a step closer.

I cup her jaw, running my thumb over her cheek. "Kiss me."

She doesn't hesitate to wrap her arms around my neck. This is exactly what I wanted. Her body pressed against mine. I lean down and gently brush my lips against hers. Gentle turns to wild as I slide my hands down to cup her ass, lifting her up and into me.

Someone knocks on the door and opens it before I pull my lips away from Aubrey's. Dazed, she glances around as if she forgot where she was.

Jake grins at us. "Guess she's not still mad."

Aubrey glances over her shoulder. "*She* was never mad at Sully."

I chuckle, flex my arms around her, and lift my chin at Jake. "Get out."

Jake's jaw drops. "You have—"

"Get. Out."

He finally shuts the door.

Aubrey squirms in my hold. "Come on. You have a business to run." She pats my chest. "Work time, Mr. Wallace."

"One more kiss."

She leans up on her tiptoes and presses a quick kiss to my cheek. "If you're good, you'll get more later."

"Now that's what I call motivation."

Aubrey

I'M STILL FLUSTERED from my talk with Sully. And Jake walking in on us. Even though he hasn't said a word.

Part of my job is to sort through the emails sent to the gym. If I don't, they won't get answered. Sully didn't even remember the password when I started. This morning, the first message is from Trinity Photography.

Sully/Jake,

Sorry it took so long. Here's your link to the gallery. Let me know if you want any shots touched up to use for promotional purposes. If it hasn't been sold, it's yours.

Thank you again!

Trinity.

Intrigued, I click the link.

"Wow."

It's a gallery full of a mix of candid and professional portraits of both Jake and Sully. From serious to relaxed. Different lighting and settings.

"You found our dirty little secret," Jake says.

Startled that I didn't notice him peeping over my shoulder, I elbow him in the ribs. "Warn a girl." I peer up at him. "What secret?"

He chuckles. "Wrath's girl is a photographer. She talked us into modeling for book covers that she designs."

"I've met Wrath. I'm sure she didn't have a hard time *convincing* you," I tease.

Jake throws his head back and laughs. "He's a big, scary bastard, right?"

The answer to that is "duh" but I'm not about to insult his friend.

"That's really cool. The photos are amazing."

He lifts his chin and gives me a cocky smirk. "Thank you, darlin'."

Rolling my eyes, I return my attention to the photo gallery. "These would be great promotion for the gym and Sully's self-defense classes."

"I keep telling him that. He doesn't want to be a sell-out."

My head's spinning with ideas. And wondering if I could turn this into my Business Communications project that's due at the end of the semester.

"What's so exciting over here?" Sully asks, slipping an arm around my waist, effectively bumping his brother back a few steps.

"Jake was telling me about your modeling career."

Sully shoots a dirty look at Jake. "Can't you keep your mouth shut?"

"What? She found them on her own. Thought she might appreciate some context to all the shirtless photos."

"Sully," I say, resting my hand on his arm to draw his attention away from Jake. "These are great. I think you could do a lot with them to promote the gym."

He's shaking his head before I even finish the sentence. "Not you too."

While his mouth is busy protesting, I swear I see a hint of interest glimmering in his deep brown eyes, so I decide to go in for the kill.

"You need more of a social media presence. These are definitely attention-grabbing." I rub my hands together really warming up to the idea and all the possibilities. "We could do a series of short videos. Maybe once a week where you teach a quick self-defense move. Something to entice people to sign up for your classes. Or maybe—"

"Ease up there, Aubrey," Sully says, touching his fingers to my lips.

Before he says anything, Jake pipes up. "You don't want to whore out your man for new customers. I'd make a better face for the business anyway."

"It's not 'whoring him out,' it's *introducing* him to potential customers," I argue.

"But I'm the better-looking brother," Jake insists.

"Debatable." I add an eye roll which makes both brothers laugh.

Sully turns serious again and focuses his penetrating stare on me. "You're excited about this idea, aren't you?"

"I think it could be helpful." I glance down, willing Jake to go away so I can talk to Sully in private.

"Give us a minute, Jake," Sully says as if he'd read my mind.

"I have an ulterior motive," I say once Jake's out of hearing range.

Sully raises an eyebrow, inviting me to explain.

"I really do think it could benefit Strike Back. Plus, I've been struggling to come up with a project for my Business Communications class and this could be it."

That must not be what Sully expected, because he stares at me for a few seconds without saying anything. "You feel that strongly about it? To risk your grade?"

"I don't think it's a risk at all."

He nods slowly. "Okay. Whatever you need."

"Yeah? You trust me?"

"Absolutely."

I can't help it, I'm so excited, I clap my hands and jump around in a little circle. "This is going to be great. I promise."

"You got him to say yes?" Jake asks. Not waiting for my answer, he smacks Sully's shoulder. "I've been nagging you to join the rest of the world in the twenty-first century forever. Suddenly a pretty girl asks and you're all for it?"

"Looks like it," Sully answers without taking his eyes off me.

SULLY

I PROBABLY SHOULD'VE been more cautious when I told Aubrey I'd do whatever she needed to get her project off the ground. Because once I give her the green light, she's relentless.

After I say yes, she's on the phone with Trinity, securing a handful of photos to use on the website I've neglected for years. And by the time Aubrey leaves for her afternoon classes, she has an Instagram account with a week's worth of scheduled posts ready to go.

By midweek, she has me agreeing to shoot five short video sessions to post to the YouTube account she apparently also set up at some point. I'm impressed and charmed by her enthusiasm. While I've been stuck figuring out the nitty-gritty details of running the business since the beginning, she has a really unique way of envisioning the bigger picture.

Jake seems equally bewitched. Probably because she talked him into doing his own series of videos.

"This is a lot more work than it seemed," Jake grumbles as Aubrey directs him in the rearranging of equipment.

I have to smother my laughter. "But you've been asking me to do this for *years*," I mock him with his own words and barely keep the grin off my face. "Welcome to the twenty-first century, little brother."

"Yeah well, I follow lots of those fitness channels. Figured any idiot can post some clips and make some money. But more work than I realized goes into those little five or ten-minute segments."

My brother can be a lot of things, pain in my ass, troublemaker, lady-charmer, but he's not lazy. So his complaints only emphasize how much work Aubrey's putting into this project.

A project to grow *my* business. Yes, she also secured her professor's approval to use it for her project, but ultimately it will have long-term benefits for Strike Back. Which means a lot to me.

Watching the two of them bicker back and forth, but Jake ultimately doing whatever Aubrey asks him to do, is its own form of entertainment. For me anyway.

"Hey, come here," I say when she sends Jake out on a break.

Her gaze darts around as she approaches. "Is this okay? I'm sorry I took over this room, but it has the best light—"

"Stop," I say, cutting her off. "I wanted to say thank you."

Pink spreads over her cheeks. "I haven't really done anything yet."

"You've done more in a couple days than I've managed to do in a few years. I'm blown away. And I really appreciate it."

"You're welcome."

"You know, it's occurred to me that I haven't taken you out on a proper date."

She raises an eyebrow. "The Castle doesn't count as a date?"

"No." I wrap my arms around her a little tighter. "You're not going back there, are you?"

"I have the feeling Griff won't extend another offer any time soon. He's too afraid of you."

"What makes you say that?"

She ducks her head and laughs softly. "He came to visit me at the coffee shop the day after. Said it was out of respect for you, but I know fear when I see it."

She's teasing, but I'm too concerned about why Griff's visiting her at her other job to laugh. "Why didn't you say anything?"

"Honestly? I haven't thought about it since." She pokes me in the stomach. "I seem to forget about everyone else when I'm around you."

I wrap my hand around hers, lifting it to my mouth to kiss her fingertips. "I can work with that."

"Figured." She tips her head back. "So when and where for this date?"

"This—oh, shit. I have Madison this weekend." I've never forgotten one of my daughter's visits before and I can't say I'm feeling too good about that right now.

"Okay," Aubrey says without hesitation. "Next weekend." She reaches up and kisses my cheek.

"Break it up!" Jake hollers. "Let's finish this, Aubrey," he says.

She glances over at him and collapses into a fit of giggles. "Did you oil yourself up?"

"No," he answers evenly. "It's *sweat*. I banged out some push-ups in the parking lot."

She shakes her head and points to the tripod holding her camera. "You're supposed to save it for the camera."

"Putting on a shirt wouldn't hurt either," I mention.

I should've kept my mouth shut because Jake uses it as an opportunity to show off even more. "Bro, we know you got the genes. If you work a little harder, you can look as good as your little brother."

Unimpressed, Aubrey rolls her eyes. "Less yapping, more working," she scolds.

Convinced she can handle him, I excuse myself to make a phone call.

CHAPTER NINETEEN

Aubrey

THE WEEK SEEMS to be ending a whole lot better than it began. I've made significant progress growing Strike Back's online presence. Jake started teasingly calling me the gym's Social Media Manager, which I have to admit I secretly love. I'm not positive I've earned the title yet, but I plan to.

"Can we talk?" Sully asks, shutting his office door behind him.

"Sure." I've been trying to keep things professional between us at work, but I wouldn't mind if he swept everything off his desk and threw me on top of it for an afternoon quickie.

He runs his knuckles over his chest for a few seconds. I've never really seen Sully nervous before. Oh, God, have I made too many changes? Stuck my nose too far in his business? Is he firing me? Or worse, breaking up with me?

"You already know Maddy's coming to visit this weekend." He glances at the clock. "I actually have to leave in a few minutes to pick her up from the airport."

"Okay."

He finally meets my eyes. "I feel like such an asshole even saying this, but, I've never introduced Madison to a girlfriend before. And I'm not ready to—"

"Sully," I say, taking a step closer. "I totally understand."

His eyes widen and his hands land on my hips, pulling me in closer. "You're not mad?"

"Not at all. I figured you'd be busy this weekend."

"I'll still be here Sunday morning for class. My mom takes Madison to church."

"So, I'll see you then and you can tell me all about your weekend on Monday."

He seems so relieved, he blows out a long breath and kisses my cheek.

Honestly, I'm relieved too. Meeting his daughter seems like a huge step I'm not ready for yet. What if she hates me?

"Thank you so much." His voice nothing more than a low hum. He wraps his arms around my waist, pulling me closer.

Not only do I respect him even more for being so protective of his daughter, it absolutely melts my heart.

"Are you excited?"

The corners of his mouth lift. "Always." He lets out a heavy sigh. "I have so much to do around here, but every time she visits, I feel like there's so much I want to cram into such a short amount of time."

"I can understand that."

"Jake's a big help, but he likes to see her too, you know?"

"Sure." I squeeze him a little tighter and tip my head back, resting my chin on his chest. "I'll do what I can to keep things running smoothly for you."

"Thank you. I appreciate that."

I pull back and poke him in the chest with my pinky finger. "Although, I don't provide the same visual eye-candy for the ladies that you do."

He snorts and grabs my hand, kissing the backs of my fingers. "You're the only one I want to gobble me up."

We both snicker at the silly comeback.

"Are you planning to tell Madison her dad's a big Instagram star?"

"Hell no. She'll probably die of embarrassment." He squints at me. "I take it the clips are doing their job?"

"Big time."

He shakes his head as if he's embarrassed. Another thing I love about Sully. He's extremely humble. Exactly the opposite of his brother.

He glances at the clock and groans. "I really do have to go."

"Okay." I attempt to pull away, but he hums in disapproval and tightens his arms around me.

Slowly, he leans down and presses his lips to mine for a slow, lingering goodbye kiss.

JAKE STICKS AROUND, so I don't expect Sully to return tonight.

"He told you about Maddy?" Jake asks when there's a lull in the gym.

"We talked about her."

"You're cool with it?" he asks.

"Cool with what?"

He shrugs. "Him having a kid."

"Why wouldn't I be?"

"I don't know. A lot of girls can't stand competing for attention. Don't want the reminder he was ever involved with anyone else."

"He's almost thirty. I assume he's had other girlfriends by now."

He snorts then turns serious. "Lauren was his first serious girlfriend. They dated all through high school. He was crushed when her family up and moved to Florida his senior year."

I swallow hard as I absorb that information. Sully hasn't provided me with a lot of details and Lauren was obviously a big part of his life for a long time. "Is that how she ended up living down there?"

"Yup. Never told him she was pregnant when she moved. Didn't tell him when Madison was born. She only bothered to let him know he had a daughter a few years later when she sued him for child support out of nowhere."

My fingers trace over the achy spot blooming in my chest. "That's awful." Awful for Sully. And awful for Madison.

"Yeah, Sully lost his fuckin' mind. Spent a fortune running back and forth to Florida to fight for custody and to be part of Madison's life."

"He mentioned some of that."

"Knowing my brother, he probably didn't want to bad mouth Lauren, even though she deserves it for what she did. That's not the kind of guy he is." At his sides, his hands squeeze into fists. "I want you to understand the situation. Sully isn't some jackass deadbeat dad."

"I'd never think that about him."

Jake nods as if he's satisfied I'll treat his brother and niece right.

Maybe other girls would find Jake's interrogation insulting, I'm touched by how deeply he cares for his family. Maybe on the outside, there doesn't seem to be anything other than good looks, muscle, and flirty-arrogance, but there's obviously much more lurking inside of Jake.

I'm not sure how to put that sentiment into words without sounding condescending. While I'm puzzling it out, the back door crashes open.

"Uncle Jake!" a girl shouts. In a blur of motion, she races across the room, launching herself at Jake so hard, he almost falls backward.

"Holy shit, kid." He laughs and holds her at arm's length. "Look how tall you've gotten."

She pulls back and adopts a more casual pose. "I'm almost as tall as Mom now."

I'm not sure what I expected Madison to look like. Sully said she was twelve, so this tall, willowy young woman isn't what I pictured. Except for her light, aqua eyes, she strongly resembles Sully. Right down to her dark, wavy hair and lightly tanned skin. Only a bit of roundness in her baby face gives away that she's not quite a teenager yet.

I glance at Sully who's standing behind them and he flashes a quick, reassuring smile.

After some light teasing and mild rough-housing with her uncle, Madison's gaze lands on me.

"Oh, hi." She glances at her dad in a *who's-this-chick?* way.

"Maddy, this is Aubrey," Sully introduces.

My discomfort ratchets even higher. Am I supposed to shake her hand? My palms are sweaty. Damn. "Hi. How was your trip?"

Maddy shrugs and tosses her hair over her shoulder. "No biggie. I do it all the time."

"Aubrey's helping out here," Sully explains.

"She's managing the social media too," Jake adds.

"Huh. About time," she says, dismissing me and returning her attention to her father. "That reminds me, I need a digital detox this weekend." She reaches into her pocket and pulls out her cell phone while Jake and I duck our heads and laugh.

"Is that right?" Sully says, holding his hand out for the phone. "Your mom know you plan to have your phone off?"

She shrugs. "Mom has your number." She pats her backpack. "I finished most of my homework on the plane."

"You want to use the office?" Sully asks.

"Can I use your tablet for one last thing?"

"Okay." Before leading her into the office, he turns and raises an eyebrow—a subtle check-in. I wink in response which makes him laugh.

I return to my spot behind the desk and flip on the television.

"You okay?" Jake asks.

"I'm fine." I nod toward the office. "She seems excited to be here."

"Yeah. It's always madness when she's with him," he says with an affectionate smile. "Sunday afternoons are rough, though. She used to try every trick to stay longer when she was little. Stomach aches, ear aches, tantrums, forgotten stuff at home." He glances over his shoulder. "She doesn't do that anymore, but he's still torn up every time he drops her off at the airport."

For a parent who actually cares about their child, I can't even imagine how much that hurts. "It must feel like watching a piece of his heart fly away," I whisper.

Jake cocks his head. "How poetic," he says. Not in his usual teasing way.

Uncomfortable, I stand and jiggle my shoulders.

"Tight?" he asks.

"I guess. I've been on the computer a lot lately." I give him a pointed look. "Managing the social media and all."

He chuckles and motions me over to the wall. "Here, let me show you a few things you can do to prevent an RSI." He gently pushes me until I'm leaning against the wall.

"Flat against the wall," he encourages. His fingers lightly graze the top of my head and whisper over my shoulders. "Butt and heels against the wall too," he directs without touching me in either spot.

"Good. Now raise your arms parallel to the floor. Bend your arms." He positions me so my elbows are bent at a ninety-degree angle. "Keep the backs of your hands against the wall. Feel the stretch in the front of your shoulders and chest?"

"Yes." Ow, this seems so simple, but it actually hurts a little.

"Breathe, Aubrey. Now, draw your elbows into your sides. Focus on squeezing your shoulder blades together."

"How long?"

"Hold it for a couple seconds."

By a couple, he means forever. Apparently I'm in poor shape. How embarrassing.

"Just means you spend lots of time working hard on the computer," Jake says gently. No judgment in his tone at all.

"Now, push your arms up but maintain your position against the wall."

Across from us, the door to Sully's office opens and closes with a soft click.

"What are you doing?" Sully asks. His voice is low, but I don't need to glance over to sense his irritation.

He stalks over to us. "Get your hands off her," he says, slapping Jake's arm.

"Chill, bro. I was helping her with something."

"Help from a distance."

That's enough of that. "Sully, knock it off." I drop my arms and pull away from the wall. "My shoulders were bothering me. Jake was showing me some exercises to help."

His expression softens when his gaze lands on me. "Sorry."

"Why are you apologizing to her? I'm the one you snapped at," Jake grumbles, brushing off his sleeves.

"Shut up," Sully growls without looking at his brother.

"Maddy busy with homework?" Jake asks.

"Yeah, don't bug her."

"I won't. Geez," he grumbles, walking away.

"As a younger sibling, let me give you some advice—you shouldn't pick on your little brother," I say once we're alone. "It's not nice."

"Pick on him," he echoes, shaking his head.

I reach up and rub his shoulder. "You seem tense."

He shrugs, and his gaze searches the room before finally landing on me. "I don't like hiding what you mean to me."

There's that swoony-swoop in my stomach again. "It's not about you *or* me. Do what you think is best for Madison. I'm okay with whatever feels right to you."

He stares past me as if he's considering his options. "Maybe next visit. You can hang with us. Let her adjust to the idea?"

I lean up and give him a quick kiss on the cheek. "I'd like that."

SULLY

AUBREY'S UNDERSTANDING MEANS everything to me. It also helps me relax, knowing she's at the gym this afternoon. Although I'm still irritated with my brother and not all that thrilled about leaving him alone with her. Which is stupid. Jake's done plenty of shitty stuff over the years, hitting on a girlfriend has never been one of them.

"If it's slow tonight, just close early," I say to Aubrey.

She salutes me and gives my hand a quick squeeze before letting go.

I stride over to the office and tap on the door, pushing it open. "Ready to go?"

Maddy spins around in my chair a few times before answering. "We can't stay here?"

"Grandma's waiting to see you."

"Oh!" She hurries to pack up her stuff, which somehow in the last half hour ended up everywhere. Finally, I get her in the Jeep and headed toward home.

"Are you dating Aubrey?" Madison asks once I leave the parking lot.

"What?" I turn and give her a quick look. "Why would you ask that?"

"She's pretty."

"Yeah," I answer carefully. "She is."

"You should have a girlfriend."

"You and Grandma are the only ladies I need in my life right now." Shit, that feels awful. I don't like lying to my daughter or denying what Aubrey means to me to anyone. Even if I think it's the right thing to do at the moment.

"Dad," she says in her dramatic-breathless-eye-rolling way. "At some point don't ya think you should get married?"

"Why are you worried about me getting married all of a sudden?" My relationship with Maddy is so important to me. I see so little of her, I don't ever want her to feel like I'm neglecting her or that I'm distracted by someone else.

"Mom's got Robert. And you're like, all alone up here when I'm in Florida."

"I'm not *alone*. Uncle Jake's like lice, I can't shake him."

She giggles then turns serious again. "You know what I mean."

"Grandma lives right next door."

"*Daaaaaad*. You're not taking me seriously."

"Yes, I am."

"So you'll think about it?"

"Think about what?" I tease.

"*Daaaaaad*. Ask Aubrey out. Old people still do that, right?"

"Careful who you're calling old, little miss."

"Well, Aubrey's not old. Robert is like old enough to be my grandfather."

Inside I'm laughing, but I force myself not to say something inappropriate about her stepfather. "I don't think he'd appreciate that. And it's not really true."

"Maybe if you guys got married," she says in an excited rush. "I could come stay with you more often."

Hold up. What?

I wait until I pull into my driveway and shut the Jeep off before addressing that last part. "Madison, what makes you say that?"

"I dunno." Her eyes shine with unshed tears. "I just miss you. I only get to see you like once a month."

Shit, shit, shit. I haven't messed with our custody arrangement in years, because at the time I'd been granted visitation, I'd been lucky to carve out the time I had. As a young, single father half a country away, the court had made me jump through hoops back then. Honestly, I don't have the money to battle Lauren again. The last time we went to court, it took every last penny I had.

But obviously, I need to figure out something.

"I miss you too, sweetheart. You want me to talk to your mom about maybe having you come visit another weekend a month?"

Her eyes widen, and I wonder if she already tried to talk this out with Lauren and got shot down.

"You'd do that?" she asks.

"If that's what you want. I'd love to be able to spend more time with you, Maddy. I don't want to disrupt your life though."

"It's not disrupting my life," she says. "I love visiting grandma and Uncle Jake. None of my friends have a cool uncle like mine."

I bark out a quick laugh. "Make sure to tell him that."

My mother's front door swings open and Madison jumps out of the Jeep, racing across the lawn to say hello.

I reach into the back and grab Maddy's stuff. "I'll be over in a few," I call out to my mom, who just waves at me.

By the time I make it to my mom's, Madison's busy chattering away and helping in the kitchen. I sit back and watch them, thinking about Madison's request to visit more often.

Owning the gym means I pretty much work there seven days a week. Jake helps alleviate a lot of that burden, but he has his own stuff. Without my mother's help, I'd be screwed. Can I really ask her to give up another Sunday every month to help me out? Maybe I don't need to. It was harder when Maddy was younger, but she's old enough to come with me on Sunday mornings. Hell, she's suggested I start a kid's self-defense class a couple times now. Maybe that's something she and I can work on together.

I wait until after Maddy's asleep to bring it up with my mom. "Madison told me today she wants to come visit more often."

My mother raises an eyebrow. "Did you talk to Lauren?"

"Not yet. I don't want to call while Maddy's here in case we get into an argument."

She rests her hand on mine. "You're a good father. I'm proud of you."

"Thanks, Ma." The corners of my mouth lift in a tired smile. "She asked me if I was dating Aubrey."

"Really? I'd think at her age she wouldn't want you dating anyone."

"She's worried I'm lonely."

At that, my mother scoffs. "I'm smart enough to know *neither* of my sons are ever lonely. Even if I don't want details."

I give her the side-eye. "Says the woman who asks what kind of birth control I'm using at the dinner table."

She flashes an unapologetic smile.

"How does Aubrey feel about Madison? Is she upset you're occupied this weekend?" she asks.

"I told her I wasn't ready to tell Madison about us yet. She was fine with it."

My mother nods, clearly impressed. Not many people impress this woman. "That's a very mature response. When do *I* get to meet Aubrey?"

"Maybe next weekend? We can do dinner?"

"I'd like that. The sooner, the better. The weekend after, I'm going to Cape Cod with Jenny."

"Ugh. You know I'm going to worry about you the whole time, right?"

She laughs and pats my cheek. "I'm the parent. I do the worrying."

I grab her hand, giving it an affectionate squeeze. "I'll never not worry about you, Mom."

Aubrey

JAKE AND I close down the gym together. Celia picks me up, but Jake's so eager to see his niece, he doesn't stick around for one of their flirty-arguing conversations.

"Aw, that's kind of cute," Celia admits once I explain. "So you met Sully's daughter?"

"She breezed in like a little tornado." I chuckle, remembering how nervous I felt under her scrutiny. "She's kind of intimidating for twelve."

Celia executes a neat U-turn in the middle of the street and heads home. "That's because you want her to like you."

"True. Meeting her made it seem so…real."

"Uh, that's because she's real." She glances over. "Are you having second thoughts? It's a big responsibility to get involved with someone who has a kid."

I consider her question before answering. Sully already showed me this afternoon how much he wants to consider both of our feelings. "Honestly, no."

"You're not insulted he didn't want to introduce you as his girl-friend?"

"Not at all. We've been together barely a week. It made me respect him more, honestly."

"Oh, boy. That sounds like your ovaries talking."

"What? Why?"

"He's a good dad." She wags a finger in the air like she's reading from a script. "Ergo, he'd be a good dad to *your* kids."

"Duh, of course he would."

She laughs and slaps the steering wheel. "Wow. One week my ass. You're already making babies in your head."

"Shut up. I am not." Well, now that she said it, I kind of am.

All the fun gets sucked out of our night as soon as we get home. Celia flips through the mail and stops at one long, white envelope.

"Aubrey," she says and my skin prickles at the serious tone she uses.

"What is it?"

"I don't know. It's from the parole board."

"You're kidding. He can't be..." My voice trails off as I do the math in my head. Yeah, I guess it's possible. "Shit."

"Do you want me to open it?" she asks.

Too upset to speak, I just nod.

She opens the letter and scans it quickly. "That motherfucker," she grumbles.

"What?"

"They're asking if you want to come testify on his behalf."

"What! That's insane. There's supposed to be a restraining order even after he's released." At the time, I'd been furious my parents insisted on that part. Now, I'm grateful. At least they did one thing useful.

She hands over the letter without any further comment. It's exactly what she said. An invitation to come testify.

"I can't go there, Celia. Not even to argue against his release. I can't. I don't want to—"

"Okay. Calm down. Write a letter." She nods to the envelope in my hand. "All the info is there. They'll have to take it into consideration."

"I hope you're right."

CHAPTER TWENTY
SULLY

AS USUAL, YESTERDAY went by way too fast. After dropping Maddy off at my mother's, I arrive early at Strike Back to prep for the morning self-defense class.

Aubrey's withdrawn and quiet when she arrives. We talked briefly last night after Maddy went to bed and she seemed okay. Did she rethink our situation? Was meeting my daughter too much for her?

I'd hate it if that was the case, but it'd be better to know now rather than later. Especially if I approach Lauren about more visitation with Maddy.

The thought puts me in a foul mood. Something I don't have time to indulge in when I need to focus on the class.

A talk with Aubrey doesn't seem possible since I need to leave early for family dinner at my mother's before taking Madison to the airport.

"Bree's not coming this week?" I ask Aubrey, trying to coax a smile or something out of her.

Her mouth quirks. "No. She has a big paper or something due."

We're stopped from any more conversation by other students arriving.

It's another scorcher today. Maybe that's why class is small. I wrap up early and pull Aubrey aside.

"Everything okay?"

Her big eyes meet mine and I finally get a genuine smile out of her.

"Yeah, class was good." She pokes a finger in my side. "I let some of your students know you're finally on Instagram. Hopefully word will spread."

I pull her in closer. "Missed you yesterday."

Her eyes go soft and she melts into me. "I missed you too."

"What'd you do?"

"Nothing exciting. Caught up on my laundry." She fluffs her pony-tail. "Talked Celia into trimming my hair."

"Sorry, I didn't notice with it up."

She tilts her head as if she's confused. Shit, now that she's called attention to it, I can almost feel my hand twisting around her ponytail while I take her from behind.

I cough and glance away. "It's slow. Want me to show you that maneuver I mentioned in class?"

"How to get out of the ponytail grab? Sure."

We're alone in the gym, so I take my time walking her through the steps.

Damn, she smells good. The fundamental urge to get as close as possible makes me skim my hands over her sides. My fingers tease under her shirt, barely brushing over her ribs and back down to grasp her hips.

She rests her hand on my chest. Right over my heart that I'm sure she can feel thudding against her palm.

In my hands, she feels light and delicate. My muscles tighten as I pull her closer.

"Sully?" she whispers. A warning that we're not exactly alone.

She blinks up at me and her lips part. I'm a centimeter away from pressing my lips against hers when the back door opens, and voices reach us. Aubrey stumbles backward and rights herself about a second before Maddy and my mother pop into the workout room.

"Daddy!" Madison flies into my arms. I squeeze her tight, never knowing when she'll decide she's too old to call me daddy or let me hug her in public.

"You're like a little freight train, you know that?"

Maddy just laughs and hugs me tighter.

Aubrey slowly backs away and I reach out to stop her.

I lift my chin. "Everything okay, Mom?"

My mother's shrewd gaze sweeps over the scene in front of her be-

fore answering. "We stopped for ice cream and she wanted to see you."
My mother glances at Aubrey, a faint smile curving her mouth. "I hope
it's okay."

"Yeah. It's great." I motion Aubrey closer. "Mom, this is Aubrey. I
hired her to help out at the front desk."

Maddy finally relaxes her python impression and turns to face Aubrey. "Hey again."

"Aubrey," my mother says. "I've heard a lot of nice things about you.
Sullivan says you've been a big help."

"Oh." Aubrey's hands flutter in the air for a moment. "That's good
to hear. It's nice to meet you, Mrs. Wallace."

My mother can be good at recognizing when people are nervous and
she lets Aubrey off the hook. "Where's Jake?"

"He's here somewhere."

"Do I hear my favorite ladies in here?" Jake asks, poking his head out
of the locker room. "Give me a second."

Madison strolls away to inspect some of the new equipment I've
added since the last time she was here. "Be careful," I can't help calling
out.

She throws me an eye-rolling head shake. "I know."

Aubrey hides her laughter behind her hand and I shrug.

"I should go back to work," she says. "Nice to meet you, Mrs. Wallace."

Before my mother has a chance to open her mouth and stop her,
Aubrey scurries to the front desk.

Mom curls her hand around my bicep. "Am I that terrifying?" she
whispers.

"I don't think she expected to meet you today, that's all." I glance at
Aubrey, who's busy cleaning the counter.

"I didn't want to make her nervous. Maddy really did want to come
see you."

I give her hand what I hope is a reassuring pat. "I love when you
stop by. Wish you did it more often."

"Don't start with me, Sullivan. I'm up to thirty minutes a day on that treadmill you forced into my house."

I can't help laughing and holding up my hands in defense of the accusation. "That's not what I meant. And I didn't force anything." I nod at Jake, who's coming our way. "He was in on that too."

"What'd I do now?" Jake asks, kissing Mom's cheek.

"Nothing," she says, beaming at him. "I wasn't sure you'd be working here this afternoon."

Jake suffers under the misguided delusion that I'm the favorite son, so I keep my working-is-a-stretch comment to myself.

"I'm here."

My attention is drawn to Maddy approaching Aubrey. Noticing the tension in my posture, my mother follows my line of sight.

"Does she like kids?" she asks in a low voice.

Jake chuckles and I glare at him.

"I think so. She wanted to be a teacher." It's not like we've been together long enough to discuss Aubrey's feelings on kids. She's such a sweet person, I can't imagine her not liking them. Besides, as Madison is fond of reminding me, she's *almost* an adult.

Aubrey

I TRIED TO give Sully and his mother some space. At least appear like I'm doing my job. I feel ridiculous standing here in front of the woman while I'm wearing my workout clothes. A sweaty mess. About five seconds from making out with Sully when she and Madison showed up. Something I'm sure anyone can tell by my bright pink cheeks.

Maddy strolls up to the front counter, watching me with curious eyes for a few seconds before pivoting toward her uncle.

"Uncle Jake! You're supposed to teach me some moves," Maddy says, twirling, chopping, and kicking the air.

"Since when do you want to learn anything?" Sully teases.

"Uncle Jake will make it *fun*, not work," she sasses back, making me smother a laugh. Even Maddy knows Sully is the serious instructor at

Strike Back.

"Let's go, princess," Jake hollers. He points toward the smaller workout room and she scampers over.

Then I'm alone with Sully and his mother. Maybe being scrutinized by a twelve-year-old isn't so bad.

Mrs. Wallace moves closer and gives me a friendly smile. What has Sully said about me? Oh my God, does she recognize me from sneaking out of her son's house in the wee hours of the morning a bunch of days this week?

"I hope you don't mind that we stopped by?" she says softly. At first, I think she's apologizing to Sully, but she's facing me.

"Oh. No. Of course not."

I finally find some courage and smile at her. "It's nice to finally meet you."

She's a pretty woman. Sully has her hair and strong bone structure. That's when I notice the dullness in her left eye. Is she partially blind? Heat crawls up my neck and I avert my gaze. Now I feel stupid. Did I stare too long? I don't want to make her uncomfortable. God, my palms are so sweaty.

"Is my son treating you well?" she asks.

"Very. I mean yes. I like him...I mean I like the job a lot." *Oh my God, stop talking, Aubrey!*

Her mouth tips into a knowing smile as if to say 'I know you're dating him.' It's not unkind, though. More like relief.

I glance at Sully and he's smiling. As if this is normal and he's thrilled to have all of us in one place.

The front door opens, saving me from embarrassing myself any more.

Until I realize who decided to stop by.

Celia's gaze pings from me, to Sully, to his mother and back to me.

"Hey, Celia," Sully calls, waving her over. "Good to see you again."

He makes the introductions while I stand there willing my body to melt into the floor.

"What's up?" I ask Celia. Not even the offer to use my employee discount brings her into the coffee shop to visit me as frequently as she's shown up here.

"Nothing. It was a slow afternoon. I helped the girls clean up, then jetted out. Thought I'd take you to dinner when you're done."

It's not that we don't go out to dinner from time to time, but it's still suspicious.

"Sure." My gaze strays to Sully. "I'm done in about an hour."

"Whoa! I guess it's family day at Strike Back," Jake calls out. "Hi, Celia."

Celia throws me a desperate *I'm sorry* look before giving Jake a cool greeting.

He wanders over with Madison who tries to pull a sneak attack on Sully. He turns at the last second and catches her, grabbing her and swinging her around, mushing kisses on her cheek. "You think after a few lessons with your uncle means you can sneak up on me? Huh?" he teases.

Maddy giggles uncontrollably while Sully flings her around. "Stop! Gross!" she yells in between more wild giggles.

Just when I thought he couldn't get any more irresistible.

He steadies her and points her toward my sister. "Madison, this is Aubrey's sister, Celia."

"Do you work here too?"

My sister is immediately charmed by Maddy. Not a surprise, after all, she has more experience with younger kids than I do.

"No, I'm a hair stylist at a salon in the mall."

"The fancy one or the five-dollar cuts one?" Jake asks.

Celia barely throws him a look. "*Not* the five-dollar one."

"I'll have to stop in." He pats his head and smirks at Sully. "I've been told I'm in need of a new stylist."

"You're in need of something," Sully growls.

By the small smile flickering over her lips, Mrs. Wallace seems amused. "I have an idea. Why don't you girls come over for dinner?"

"Oh, no. I don't want to—" I start to say, only to be cut off by Maddy.

She bops up and down. "Yes! Grandma makes the best buttermilk fried chicken." She glances at her grandmother. "That's what we're having, right? It's Sunday."

"If you want to do that, then we have to go home and start now," she warns.

"Okay."

My "I-don't-want-to-intrude" attempt to get out of dinner is cut off by my own sister.

"That sounds delicious. Thank you so much, Mrs. Wallace," Celia says.

Traitor.

"Can we bring anything?" I ask.

"Nope. Just yourselves." Mrs. Wallace places her hands on Madison's shoulders and steers her toward the back door.

"Later!" Madison calls out.

Sully' chuckles as he watches them go. "Be good and help Grandma," he calls out. From his tone of voice and the emotion in his eyes, it's obvious how much he loves his mother and his daughter.

TWO HOURS LATER, my sister's dragging me out of the car and up Mrs. Wallace's front porch steps.

I smooth my hands over the skirt of the black and white dress my sister forced me into when we stopped home.

She smacks my hands away from their human iron impression. "Stop fidgeting."

"Are you sure this looks okay? I feel like I'm trying too hard."

"You look sweet and wholesome."

I cock my head and let out a dry laugh. "Like I said."

She rolls her eyes and pushes me up the sidewalk.

"Smile, pumpkin," she prods after knocking on the door.

"I *am* smiling."

"You look like you're headed to the dentist."

"I blame you for this," I hiss.

"Daddy!" Madison yells as she opens the door. "Aubrey and Celia are here!"

She opens the door wider, inviting us inside. "They're in the kitchen."

"Thanks."

I don't know what to do. Am I supposed to make small talk with her? I wish I'd brought something. What do twelve-year-old girls like? I was one once, so I feel like I should know.

Celia elbows me in the ribs, nudging me along while Maddy flops on the couch and returns to whatever she's watching on television.

"Welcome!" Mrs. Wallace says.

The spicy, warm scents and sizzling from the kitchen remind me that I haven't eaten in a few hours. My stomach growls loud enough that Celia glances over.

Jake's at the counter opposite his mother, chopping vegetables.

Celia stops dead, mouth hanging open. "You cook?"

He winks and flashes a cocky grin. "I have *lots* of talents, sweetheart."

"Jacob Cordero Wallace. Behave," Mrs. Wallace warns.

Celia and I titter with laughter while Jake grins. "Yes, mother."

She swats him with a dish towel which only makes him laugh harder.

"How was the rest of the afternoon?" she asks.

"Okay," I answer lamely. I wish I'd brought a gift. Instead of running home to change, I should've grabbed some flowers or something.

"Aubrey, would you please hand me that jar?" she asks, pointing to something on the counter.

The request startles me out of my stupor and I hand it over without embarrassing myself further.

A heavy, warm hand slides up my back, landing on my shoulder. "Hey," Sully says against my ear. "Thanks for coming."

I turn slightly, almost catching his lips for a kiss, but pull back at the last minute. Now's not the time. "Thanks for having us."

He squeezes my shoulder again, his thumb gently rubbing the tension gathered in my neck. "Relax," he murmurs. "Or she'll start firing off questions."

Maybe it's silly, but his warning helps me relax.

All of this is perfectly normal, right?

CHAPTER TWENTY-ONE
SULLY

"YOU LOOK PRETTY," I whisper in Aubrey's ear.

She glances down and fidgets with the dress. "I wish I'd gotten something for your mom instead."

I'm not sure what she means exactly, but it doesn't take a genius to see how freaked out she is. Guilt nags at me. I hadn't planned on family dinner so soon. Maybe she should've had more time to get comfortable with the idea. "You don't need to bring anything here," I assure her. "She's really just happy to have more people to feed."

Next to us, Celia snorts. "We're not used to that." She elbows her sister and Aubrey shoots a warning look at her.

"Is there something we can do, Mrs. Wallace?" Celia asks.

Mom nods to the cabinets behind me. "Set the table, please. Sullivan can show you where the dishes are."

I take down the plates and glasses they need, show them where the silverware is, and then excuse myself to see what Maddy's up to.

"What'cha doing in here, kiddo?" I drop down next to her on the couch, tickling my fingers over her feet.

She jabs her little toes into my leg to fight off the tickle assault. "Nothing."

"I thought you wanted to have guests over."

"I do."

"Are you all packed?" I ask gently.

Her mouth turns down. There it is. Sunday afternoons are bittersweet. Dinner with my mother and Jake, but we usually head to the airport right after. While she doesn't throw the tantrums she did when she was little, she does tend to get rather quiet and withdrawn. I didn't protest when my mother invited the girls to dinner because I thought having Aubrey and Celia over might help take Maddy's mind off leaving, but now I'm worried it's actually making her feel worse.

"All my stuff's in the Jeep," she says.

"When'd you do that?"

She shrugs.

"You know, Celia's a hair-dresser. Why don't you ask her about those pink highlights or whatever that you want to get?"

She slides her gaze my way. "Yeah?"

I normally wouldn't suggest something I suspect my ex won't approve of, but I'm desperate here.

"Okay." She shoves off the couch and trots into the kitchen and I follow.

"Oh, there you are," my mother says. "Dinner's ready." She pats Maddy's shoulder. "Will you grab the iced tea, honey?"

"Sure."

Somehow Celia ends up next to my brother. I'm sure that won't be awkward when he gets his tongue ripped out for saying something stupid.

Aubrey seems a little lost and I nudge her into the chair next to me. Maddy sits on my other side, next to my mother and asks if she can say grace.

"Of course you can," my mother answers.

The words my daughter usually says are sweet and to the point. Today she amends them slightly.

"Thank you for the meal we're about to eat. For Grandma who worked hard to make it. And thank you to family and new friends here to share it with us. May we stay strong and healthy." She turns and grins when she's finished.

"Thank you, Madison." There's a catch in my mother's voice that says she's also having a hard time with Maddy leaving in a few hours.

"Drumstick!" Maddy calls out.

"*That's* why you wanted to say grace," Jake says. "I knew it."

"Nuh-uh." Maddy shakes her head.

"Guests first," my mother prompts, nodding at Celia.

When everyone's plates are full, Maddy peers over at Celia. "You said you do hair, right? Do you ever dye hair pink and stuff?"

"Sure," Celia answers. "It can be a longer process than people realize, though." She tilts her head and studies Madison for a minute. "You have such pretty hair, I'd hate to use so many chemicals on it. I could get you some nice extensions instead. If they're done right, they blend right in and you can't tell the difference."

"Ooo! I like that idea." She swivels her head my way. "Can I?"

"We'll see. If your mom's okay with it, then yeah."

"Cool!"

I shake my head. More likely, Madison will forget all about it by the next time she visits.

And isn't that a depressing thought.

My mother pats her hair. "Maybe I should come visit you before my trip."

"Any time, Mrs. Wallace," Celia says. "I'll leave you my hours if you want."

"Thank you, dear."

I catch Jake's eye and we nod at each other. Knowing my mother, she'll come up with an excuse *not* to treat herself. It'll be up to us to make sure that doesn't happen.

"So Aubrey, did you really get my dad on social media?" Maddy asks, leaning over so she can see Aubrey better.

Aubrey coughs. "Uh, yes. I have a few ideas to attract more people to the gym. We started a YouTube channel too."

"That's kinda cool."

"We're each contributing short videos." Jake smiles at Aubrey. "She's a real ball-buster."

"Jacob," my mother warns.

Celia chuckles. "My sister can be very determined when she really believes in something."

All this attention on her has Aubrey blushing bright red. "I think it will be a good way to grow the business." She pushes some food around on her plate. "And it's helping me out with one of my projects in school."

"What are you studying, Aubrey?" my mother asks.

"Accounting." She huffs out a sad laugh and gives her sister an apologetic shrug. "I'm not very good at it, though."

Celia waves it off. "I told you to switch your major. If you do well with Strike Back, I'll have you manage my social media next."

"Celia wants to open her own salon eventually," Aubrey explains. "And since no one wants to let me near their hair with sharp implements, I was going to try to help some other way."

My mother beams. "Ah, like my boys in business together. I love that."

I've never been clear whether my mother knows it's Jake's illegal fighting career that's funded his business ventures. Including the cash he's invested in Strike Back.

As we're finishing dinner, my phone buzzes with a text that Maddy's plane is due to arrive on time.

"All right, let's help Grandma clear the table." I stand, but my mother waves me off when I try to collect her plate.

"I've got this. You two need to get on the road."

Aubrey and Celia stand too. "We'll take care of this," Aubrey says.

"Come give me a hug," Jake says to Maddy. Like every time she gets ready to leave, he looks like he's about to cry. Not that I'd ever say that out loud.

While they're busy talking, I help Aubrey with the dishes. "I'm sorry I have to leave—"

"We're fine. I want to help your mom out. That was like the best dinner I've had in ages."

"Hey," Celia says, bumping her hip against Aubrey. "See if I microwave you a dinner ever again."

Aubrey rolls her eyes at her sister.

Madison pokes her head in the kitchen. "Bye, Aubrey. Bye, Celia. It was nice meeting you."

Celia smiles. "You too. Come see me next time you visit and I'll hook you up with the pink extensions."

Finally something makes Maddy bounce with excitement again. "I can't wait."

I squeeze Aubrey's hand and say a quick goodbye before heading out with Madison.

My mother walks out to the Jeep with us for extra Maddy hugs. "I'm going to miss you. Be a good girl."

"I'm always good, Grandma."

"You can call me too. You know I hate texts and face-chats."

"Facetime, Grandma."

"Whatever."

After Madison hops in the Jeep to mess with the radio, I pull my mother aside. "Please go easy questioning Aubrey."

Her eyes widen in indignation. "What? I didn't ask any questions during dinner."

I tilt my head in Maddy's direction. "Yes, but now that you don't have a certain audience…"

"Oh, stop. I'll behave." She tilts her head, staring at me for a moment. "I could tell she was nervous, but she seems very sweet." A wistful sort of look passes over her face. "I like the way she looks at you."

"How's that?"

"Like she really cares about you and she respects your relationship with Maddy."

I'm not sure how to respond, so I give her a quick hug and kiss on the cheek. "See you a bit later."

Aubrey

"Is it rude if we make a run for it now?" I whisper to Celia.

"Yes." She shoves another plate in my hand. "Dry that."

Much to my surprise, Jake's helping us with the dishes. We have a nice little system going. Celia washes, I dry, Jake puts them away.

"Relax," Jake says. "If my mother didn't like you, you'd know."

"That's not reassuring."

He chuckles and places the last dish in the cabinet. "Thanks for helping me do that," he says.

"Why, because otherwise you'd do it by yourself?" Celia asks.

"Yes," he answers simply.

"Oh, thank you, girls," Mrs. Wallace calls out as she returns to the kitchen. "You really didn't have to."

"No problem. Thank you for having us," Celia says.

"Was Maddy okay?" I ask before thinking it over. I hated the sadness that seemed to surround her when she had to say goodbye.

Mrs. Wallace tilts her head as if she's surprised I noticed. "She'll be okay."

She walks us to the door and right before we step outside, pulls me in for a hug. At first, I'm startled and don't know what the heck to do. But I hug her back just as tight. She's warm and motherly. Two things I've never really known.

"See you soon," she says.

Celia gets a quick hug too. "I left my number and hours on the counter, if you still want to stop in," Celia says.

"Thank you, dear."

In the car, Celia and I both stare at each other in awe.

"God, you better marry Sully," she finally says. "His mom's such an amazing cook. Can you imagine our mom ever feeding us fried chicken?"

"No," I grumble. Anything more than a handful of lettuce on my plate always ended in a lecture on how much prettier I'd be if I lost weight. And when that didn't work, a few summers at fat camp hammered home the message.

CHAPTER TWENTY-TWO
SULLY

SAYING GOODBYE TO my daughter never gets any easier.

For seven years now I've been taking Madison to the airport at the end of her visit and sending her home.

Still hurts every time.

So she doesn't get upset, I try to bury my feelings and keep our conversation superficial. After our talk on Friday, she didn't ask me again about the extra visits. I didn't bring it up because I hadn't discussed it with her mother yet.

At the security gate, she jumps up and gives me the biggest hug. I almost lose it.

"Love you, Daddy." She sniffles. She calls me that less and less, so I squeeze her tighter.

These moments I love and hate the most.

"Love you too," I whisper. She's growing up so fast. Next time I see her, she might not let me hug her like this, so I soak it all up now.

Pulling back, I kiss her cheek. "Be good."

Her smile's strained and half-hearted. "I'm always good."

I give her another quick hug and check to make sure she has everything before setting her free.

Once she's through security, she jumps and waves before running for her gate.

The Empire airport isn't that big and I'm able to watch her almost the entire way.

A few minutes later, my phone pings.

Madison: *On the plane.*

I walk out to my Jeep and finally call Lauren.

"Hey, Sully. Is she on her way home?"

"Yup. Her plane just took off."

"How was she?"

I've been going over how to approach this since Friday night. How to gain more visitation without pissing Lauren off or getting dragged back into family court.

"Great. We had fun."

"That's good. Well—"

I cut her off before she gives me an excuse to get off the phone. "Lauren, do you have a minute to talk?"

"Sure." Her wary tone doesn't disguise her curiosity.

"Maddy asked about coming to visit more often—"

"I'm sorry."

What the hell is she sorry for?

"It's fine. I *want* to see her more. Can we work something out?"

She sighs into the phone. "How's the gym?"

"All right," I answer slowly, not sure why she cares. "Still struggling, but getting better."

"Do you have more people to help you run things?"

"Jake." I cough to cover my discomfort. "And a new person I hired to help out."

"Do you have the *time?*"

The insinuation that I somehow neglect Madison when she visits, pisses me off. "I'll *make* the time, Lauren."

She lets out another sigh. I wish we were doing this face-to-face so I had some clue of what's going through her head. On the other end, she's quiet for so long, I pull the phone away to make sure we're still connected.

"How about the weekend after next?"

Shit, my mother has plans to be out of town that weekend, but there's no way I'm turning down this opportunity.

"That would be great. It won't mess her up with school or anything, right?"

"No, it should be fine. Are you sure about this, Sully?"

"Yeah, I'm sure." Great, she probably thinks I'm trying to weasel down my child support payments or something.

As if she heard my thoughts through the phone, she says, "We don't need to go back to court and make it official yet. Let's try it out a few times and see how it goes."

"That's fine." Lauren and I mostly get along. Well, except for the part where she hid my daughter from me for four years and then seemed surprised and annoyed that I wanted to be a part of Maddy's life when I found out she existed.

Not that it still burns my ass or anything.

Even so, I've heard enough horror stories from other single parents that I don't suffer any guilt over my next request. "Can you send me something in writing, though?"

"Sure. Is e-mail okay?" she asks with only a hint of the irritation I expected.

"That works. Thank you, Lauren."

She sighs again. "I should probably be thanking *you*. She's been a handful lately."

"Really?" News to me. Except for a random smart-ass comment—which I blame Jake for—Maddy's easy to spend time with.

"Figures she behaves when she's with you. While I get the back talk, door-slamming, and attitude."

I'm not really sure what to say about that. Since I only see my daughter two and a half days a month, there's not a whole lot I can do to remedy the situation or take the pressure off Lauren. "Do you want me to talk to her?"

Lauren snorts. "Sure. Maybe it'll mean more coming from you." I'm so close to saying that it didn't need to be this way. She could've moved back to New York when she said she was going to. Maybe not hidden the existence of my daughter for the first four years of her life. Let me be more involved. Any of those things. But rehashing the past doesn't help anyone. It's not worth arguing over again.

I just want more time with Madison.

"I'll give her a call tomorrow."

"All right. I'll let you tell her about the extra visits, okay? Just in case you change your mind. I don't want her to get her hopes up—"

"I'm not going to change my mind."

"Good night, Sully."

She hangs up and I blow out a frustrated breath. At least it went better than I expected.

An extra weekend with my daughter. I'm grinning from ear-to-ear and I can't think of anyone I want to share this news with more than Aubrey right now.

It's about forty-five minutes to her place from the airport. Did she even make it home yet, or is she still at my mother's getting grilled?

She doesn't answer the text I send, so I decide to go straight to her place and find out.

When I bound up the stairs and knock on her door, she opens it within a few seconds.

"Sully!" Her big brown eyes shine with happiness and surprise. "I didn't expect to see you."

"Is it all right that I stopped by?" My gaze drops to the tank top and tiny shorts she's wearing, and my mind immediately shifts in another direction.

"Hey, Sully. Can't stay away, huh?" Celia teases.

"You manage not to kill my brother, Celia?" I joke back.

"Barely," she grumbles, dropping onto the couch.

I jerk my head toward the stairs and trace my fingers down Aubrey's bare arm. "Want to go for a walk with me?"

"Sure." She ducks behind the door and grabs a hoodie.

"It's still hot out," I warn her.

She gestures to the tank top. "It's kind of thin."

"That's why I like it." I keep my tone low, only meant for her.

A brief smile flickers over her lips, but she doesn't respond, other than slipping the sweatshirt over her head and shoving her feet into a pair of woolly boots.

"Seriously, it's still like eighty degrees out."

"I always wear these around here at night."

I hold out my hand and she takes it. "I'll be back in a little bit," she calls to Celia before shutting the door.

We're quiet as we take the stairs. The wind kicks up when we step into the courtyard, blowing her hair all around. She tips her head back, breathing in the sweet, humid night air.

"Doesn't smell like fall yet," she says.

Her serene smile and closed eyes sends a sizzle of arousal down my spine. The shorts that stop mid-thigh don't hurt either.

"How'd it go?" she asks.

I don't answer right away. Usually I'm bummed after sending Maddy back to Florida and head straight to the bar to meet up with Jake and Keegan. Tonight, the second I saw Aubrey the usual pain washed away. "It's never fun. But I talked to Lauren and she agreed to let Maddy visit more often."

"That's great." She squeezes my hand and seems genuinely happy about the news.

"We planned on the weekend after next."

"Awesome. Does Maddy know yet?"

"No. Lauren wants me to tell her. She's afraid I'll back out or something."

Aubrey rolls her eyes but doesn't comment. I love that she's on my side without talking shit about my daughter's mother.

We're a few feet away from my Jeep when I stop and pull her closer. "I missed you."

"You just saw me a few hours ago." She pokes her pinky finger against my chest. "Work, Sunday dinners, late-night walks in dark parking lots. Soon you're going to get tired of me."

"Never." I tip my head back, staring at the inky sky. The weeks and months ahead rush through my mind and I can't imagine not wanting Aubrey to be a part of every single moment.

CHAPTER TWENTY-THREE

Aubrey

SULLY'S SO SERIOUS tonight. I can't believe he stopped by to see me after we spent the day and evening together. That I was on his mind after dropping his daughter off, when I know how hard that must be on him.

I reach up and brush the back of my hand over his cheek. A light layer of scruff tickles my skin as he leans into my touch.

"Madison's a lot of fun."

A smile twitches at the corners of his mouth. "Fun, yeah. She keeps me on my toes."

There's nothing but affection for his daughter in his words. I love that. Adore how much he cares about his whole family. Spending time with them tonight allowed me to see him in a different light. More than the man who sets my blood on fire every time he looks at me. He's such a good man.

Thunder growls above us and the wind whips against our bodies. The leaves from the trees at the edge of the parking lot rustle.

He inhales deeply. "Guess there's a storm coming."

"The breeze feels good. You were right, it's hot." I slip my sweatshirt over my head and when I find my way out of the material, Sully's holding out his hand.

"I'll carry it for you." Heat blazes over my skin where his gaze lingers.

Such a simple gentlemanly thing to do. Doesn't crack any "I told you so" jokes. Just folds up my shirt and carries it in one hand while holding on to me with the other.

A few seconds later, lightning severs the darkness and more thunder rattles the air. Warm, wet needles of rain prickle over my skin. In an instant, I'm soaked.

I yelp and Sully holds my sweatshirt over my head, leading me to the Jeep. He throws the door open and I fling myself inside, breathing hard. Heat and humidity cling to the interior and the backs of my thighs stick to the seat. Sully jumps in the driver's side and twists to grab something off the backseat.

"Sorry about that. I didn't expect the sky to open up so violently." He hands me a towel and I rub it over my face, chest, and arms before shoving it his way.

When he doesn't take the towel, I glance over. Drops of rain cling to his hair, curling it at the ends, turning it almost black in the weak light. He inhales sharply and runs his gaze over my breasts. The tank top might as well be a napkin for all the good it's doing in the coverage department.

"I'm soaked."

"I see that." His voice comes out raw and strained. The weight of his stare hardens my nipples. No man has ever looked at me with so much desire blazing in his eyes.

He reaches over and cups my breast, rubbing his thumb over the tip.

I suck in a sharp inhale. My heart hammers. Without thinking about it, my gaze drops to his lap.

He lifts and twists his big body into the backseat and pats his thigh. "Join me."

Skeptical, I stare at the cramped space. "Is there room?"

"Let's find out."

Well, at least he hasn't been back there with anyone else.

"I don't think I've done this since high school," I blurt out as I climb into the back. He stares at me with a twist to his mouth and I realize what I said. "Never mind."

He tugs at the hem of my shorts and since they're nothing more than terrycloth held up by cheap elastic, they slide down my hips.

"Sully." I squeal and push his hand away. "I don't want my entire apartment complex to see my bare ass."

"The windows are too fogged to see anything." He pats his thighs again. "Come on."

It takes some fancy contortion, but I straddle his lap, looping my arms around his neck. "Now what?"

"Kiss me."

His hand cups the back of my head and he pulls me closer. His lips brush mine. Soft at first. One kiss leads to another. Deep, drugging kisses that make me forget we're in the back of his Jeep with a wild storm swirling around us, beating at the windows. His other hand strays to my hip, then slides under my shirt, drawing the wet fabric away from my heated skin.

I brush my tongue against his and he moans into my mouth. Rough hands cup my breast, teasing my nipple. "No bra?"

"I wasn't expecting to go out again."

"I like it."

Reaching between us, I rub my hand over the bulge in his pants. He groans even louder. "Want something?"

"Yes."

"Say it."

My cheeks sting with heat and I press my body against his. Slowly, I trail kisses over my neck and jaw, working my way to his ear. Taking the time to gather up my courage. "I want to ride your cock."

It's the first time I've ever been brave enough to be so direct.

"Fuck." Underneath me, his body jolts. He strips off my shirt, tossing it in the front somewhere, then works my shorts down. I can't undo his belt and zipper fast enough, so he brushes my hands away. "There's a condom in the middle console."

"Spare for emergencies?" I tease.

He gives me a sharp look. "I slipped it in there this morning."

"Where?" I ask digging through all the stuff he keeps stored in the space.

"Altoids tin. Didn't want—"

"Got it." Peppermint fills my nose. "Yum. Minty fresh."

"Give me that." He snatches the condom from my hand and presses a rough kiss to my cheek.

I'm mesmerized as he reaches behind his neck to pull his T-shirt over his head, leaving his hair all tousled and sexy. He rips into the condom, smoothing it on fast before urging me over him.

"That's it," he murmurs.

He slips his fingers between my legs, finding how wet I am—from him not the rainstorm—and groans.

His lips capture my nipple and he sucks hard. "Oh!" I sink my hands into his thick hair and he moves to my other breast licking and sucking.

The second his cock nudges against my entrance, I gasp.

"Nice and slow," he says. "I know you can take me."

We're both slick with sweat, heat sizzling between us as he fills me inch by heavenly inch.

His head falls back, and he groans with pleasure. For a second, I don't move, enjoying the feeling of fullness. His hands fit into the curve of my waist, gently urging me up. "Fuck, Aubrey. I need you to ride me."

I lift my arms gauging where the roof is, so I don't ram my head into it.

"Come here." He urges me closer, sliding his hands down my back to cup my butt. Our lips meet. My sweat-slick skin clings to his as I work my hips, finding a rhythm that works for both of us. We rock together, raw energy sparking between us.

Intense pleasure barrels down on me and I dig my fingers into his shoulders.

"Harder," he urges. "Come for me, Aubrey." His voice is tight with concentration. "Let go."

My screams echo in the tight confines of the car as I splinter apart. Sully doesn't show me any mercy though. He keeps pounding up into me and my orgasm soars. My voice breaks, my cries turning hoarse. In a matter of minutes, he's turned me into a wild, moaning creature.

He finally lets loose with a roar. His teeth graze my shoulder. Breathing hard, he rests his sweaty forehead against mine.

I'm limp, boneless, draped over him.

Keeping one arm firmly wrapped around me, he reaches over and pops the side window open a crack. I take the opportunity to run my hand down his forearm, savoring the muscles that just worked so hard to please me.

"You all right?" he asks.

Am I?

"That was…" Shoot, what was I even going to say? I collapse against his chest, listening to his heart beating fast and strong beneath me. His strong arms provide a safe, tight shelter.

After a few moments, he kisses the top of my head. "Talk to me."

"I'm okay." I peek up at him. "That was…something."

"Yes, it was." He shifts under me. "Give me a second."

"Sure." I throw myself to the side, groaning at the tightness in my hips from straddling him for so long.

Sully glances over, a wicked smile on his lush lips. "Do I need to work you out more often?"

"I think so."

He reaches out and rubs his hand up to my hip and down my leg, soothing. "You're pretty all naked and sweaty in my backseat."

I chuckle and don't even search for something to cover myself with. Why would I when he's staring at me with so much approval and desire in his eyes?

He hesitates, and his intense brown eyes turn serious. "You know that's not why I came to see you tonight, though, right?"

"I don't mind if it is. That was pretty hot."

"It was," he agrees. He leans over and grabs a roll of paper towels off the floor. I hand him his shirt, then reach into the front to retrieve my soggy tank top. He stretches into the front to start up the Jeep and crank up the air-conditioning.

"Come here," he says, settling back down next to me and holding out one arm.

I snag my shorts and wriggle into them before snuggling against his side.

As we cool off together, he strokes his hand through my hair. "You want to grab some stuff and come stay at my place tonight?" he asks.

"I can't…" I hesitate, unsure of how to explain my morning plans. "I promised to help Celia with something and I have to go into school and work on an assignment after."

A low growl of disappointment eases out of him.

I reach up and trace my fingers over his cheek. "I'll see you at the gym in the afternoon."

"I don't know if I can go that long." He's teasing, but there's a sweet catch in his voice—like maybe he really means it. "How were things with my mom after I took off?"

"We left right after you. She sent us home with leftovers and made us promise to return."

He chuckles. "Sounds about right."

SULLY

IT'S SAPPY, BUT I'm not ready for this moment with Aubrey to end. Since I can't talk her into coming home with me, I'm content cuddling in the car with her instead.

"Madison wasn't upset we came over for dinner, was she?" Aubrey asks after a few minutes.

"Not at all." I kiss the top of her head again. "What made you ask that?"

"It was her last night here, I didn't want to intrude."

"My mother's pretty persuasive when she wants to be."

Her small body shakes against me. "I noticed. She sure keeps Jake in line too."

Now I'm laughing. "Yeah, but he'll do anything for her."

"I have the feeling both of you will."

I sigh, considering sharing some of my past with Aubrey. Something I don't do with anyone, well, ever. "I don't know if you noticed or not, but she's blind in one eye. Happened when Jake and I were kids…"

And it's my fault.

"…I worry about her," I finally finish.

Aubrey's confusion is clear from her cute wrinkled-nose face. My explanation made no sense.

"Ah, here I thought you just lived next door so she could help you with Madison."

The comment doesn't surprise me. It's not far from the truth, either. "That's part of it. It's an odd story, actually. We moved there when I was thirteen and Jake was twelve. After a bad…well, some stuff happened." I quicken my words, not wanting to share *those* painful details yet.

"The woman next door was a widow with no family, so my mother sent us over to help her out and stuff. They got to be good friends. When she passed away, she left the house to my mother."

"Wow, that was nice."

"A huge surprise too. By then I was fighting for visitation with Madison and I was having trouble showing the court I had a stable environment. I was living in the back of the gym because I'd sunk all the money I had into it."

"Not a suitable place for your daughter."

"Right. So Mom sold me the house for a dollar. She went down to Florida a bunch of times with me to hearings. I was only twenty-one, so it was a fine line between arguing that I had a support system in place to help me with Madison, but she wouldn't be coming up here just to be dumped off at my mother's." I run my hand through my hair, just thinking about that time in my life still pisses me off. "The judge didn't care for me too much."

As if she can sense my irritation, Aubrey rubs her hand over my chest. Her soft touch actually soothes away the unpleasant memories.

"Your mom obviously loves Madison a lot."

My lips quirk into a smile. "Yeah, she finally has the girl she always wanted. Jake and I didn't look as good in frilly pink."

She laughs and cups my cheek, rubbing her thumb over my bottom lip. "I bet you could pull it off."

I hate that we're always talking about me when there's still so much I want to know about her. "So now that you've met everyone important to me, what about your family?"

She shifts away from me. "You've met Celia."

"What about your parents?"

"They're not dead or anything. We're just not...close." There's sadness twisted up in her words and I squeeze her a little tighter. "I was a...difficult teenager and they're not really the forgiving type."

I can't imagine what she would do that would be so unforgivable.

No matter how much I wanted to keep my distance from Aubrey in the beginning, I can't help wanting to protect her, love her, and murder anyone who makes her unhappy.

Love.

Well, shit.

CHAPTER TWENTY-FOUR

Aubrey

"I DON'T THINK I can do this," I say to Celia the next morning.

"Yes, you can."

I'm not testifying. I can't. But since I received the notice so late, I'm afraid my letter won't arrive in time. Celia agreed to drive me to the parole hearing this morning and help me hand-deliver it.

"Got everything?" she asks.

She has to drop me off at school right after so she can get to work on time.

"Yup. All set."

The time I spent with Sully last night pushes me through all my anxiety. That part of my life needs to be over and it's time I stand up for myself.

Testify on *his* behalf. What a joke.

"You want to stop by and visit Mom, on the way back?" she asks as we pass the Thruway exit leading to the town we grew up in.

"That's a great big *nope*." I flip my middle finger in the direction of our childhood home and she laughs.

"I'm proud of you," she says a little later.

"Why? I'm being a total coward." I flap the letter I'm holding in the air a few times. "A fucking letter. Seriously?"

"They gave it as an option, Aubrey," she says with exaggerated patience. "Obviously, it's common."

She glances over. "You tell Sully where you were going this morning? Does he even know?"

"Hell fucking no. Are you kidding?"

"Aubrey," she sighs.

"Not yet." I can't bear to reveal my shameful past to him. For just a little longer I want to live in the happy space we've created.

"He sort of screams wholesome, doesn't he?" She wrinkles her nose. "Makes you wonder what happened to Jake."

"He's not *that* wholesome," I mutter.

She gives me a sly smile. "You *did* return to the apartment looking rather disheveled last night."

Heat tickles my cheeks. "We got caught in the rain."

"How romantic," she sighs.

"Stop making fun of me."

"Oh, I'm not. I'm jealous." She presses her hand against her chest. "The way he can't take his eyes off you, I imagine he's very *attentive* in the bedroom."

"Stop imagining my boyfriend in the bedroom at all," I grumble.

"You know what I mean."

"Yes. He's…talented at all the things."

"So he knows where everything is?" She snickers at her little joke.

I actually shiver thinking about last night. "Oh, yes. He knows where everything is and what to do when he gets there."

"God, I hate you right now."

When we arrive at the hearing, I lose my nerve. Celia ends up going inside to deliver the letter for me. I feel like a coward, so I use the time to check up on Strike Back's Instagram account. I answer a few comments and check to make sure Monday's post will go live as scheduled.

I pull out my notebook and jot down a few ideas that come to me while I'm scrolling through other similar accounts. I'd like to set up some sort of live chat, but I think Jake will be more agreeable to that than Sully will.

I've walked a fine line with the tone of the posts. Clearly, I want to showcase the guys' abilities and keep things fitness-oriented. But let's be honest, I'm also using them as man-bait to attract an audience. Part of why I was so hesitant to talk about it with Madison and Sully's mom last night. I'd probably traumatize poor Maddy if she knew my plan involves turning her dad and uncle into Internet sex symbols for profit.

Jake's friends, Griff and Remy, are supposed to start training at Strike Back. Would it be weird if I tried to talk them into contributing a video? I tap my pen against my notebook. What's a non-sleazy way to approach someone and ask to take some video of them while they work out? Oh, and if you can please do it shirtless, that would be great, thanks.

Maybe I should start by asking Jake and Remy to spar in front of the camera. It would definitely appeal to their vanity.

Celia's door opening startles me out of my planning session and I flip my notebook closed.

"I'm glad you didn't go in." She starts the car and backs out of our spot.

"Why? Did you see him?"

"Not really."

I don't ask for more details, because I honestly don't care. Is it too much to ask that I be allowed to move on and forget that embarrassingly stupid time in my life?

"But they took my letter?"

"Yes."

"Good. Thank you so much for helping me do this." My voice breaks and I almost start bawling.

"Hey." She reaches over and pats my leg. "It's okay. I'm so proud of you."

"Why? I'm practically flunking out of community college, working two part-time jobs—"

"Aubrey, stop," she snaps, cutting me off. "Drop accounting, please. I think you're onto something with the social media thing. It combines a lot of skills you're already good at. You've always been creative and artistic."

"I'm not artistic."

"With words, I mean. You used to write the most beautiful poems and stories."

"You know why I can't anymore."

"Don't let him take that away from you too. Stop running away and trying to force yourself into doing something you hate."

"It's a lot of money I wasted then." Just thinking of all the hours on my feet at Busy Beans to pay my last tuition bill makes me queasy.

"Better to let go now than to keep sinking money into something you're never going to love doing."

"I'll only be taking one class this semester if I drop accounting."

"Then take the one class and knock it out of the park."

"You really think I can make a career out of that?"

She shrugs. "Who knows? Things change so fast anymore. But marketing, presenting products and ideas, the psychology behind it, that doesn't change. You're smart and intuitive. Focus there."

Her pep talk sparks something inside me.

I flip my notebook open and jot down a 'to do' list.

It's been so long, I almost forgot what hope feels like.

CHAPTER TWENTY-FIVE
SULLY

I'M WAITING BY the security gate for Maddy's flight to land when my phone lights up.

Disappointment settles in that it's not Aubrey.

"Hey, Lauren. I'm waiting at the airport."

"Oh, good. I'm glad I caught you before she gets there."

"Why? What's wrong?"

She sighs. I'm about to ask why she bothered calling if she doesn't want to spit it out.

"Nothing's wrong. It's just been an exhausting week. She's moody, emotional, temperamental. I thought I should warn you."

I can't tell if she's exaggerating. "Thanks for the head's up."

"Hey, you wanted an extra weekend with her."

"That hasn't changed."

"Give it time." She laughs, a grating sound under the circumstances. "Or maybe not. I'm sure she'll be on her best behavior for *you*."

"I'll talk to her."

"You can try."

"Lauren." I blow out a frustrated breath. "What do you want me to do?"

"Nothing." She pauses and chuckles. "Still planning to introduce her to your girlfriend this weekend?"

"Yeah," I answer carefully. She didn't have a problem with it when I brought it up the other night. I hope she's not going to give me grief now.

"Okay. Well, good luck."

There's not much more to say. We hang up and I pace while I wait for Maddy's plane to land.

Forty-five minutes later, she shouts, "Daddy!" and comes running through the security gate, hurling herself against me.

"How was your flight?"

"Good."

"Did you check any luggage?"

"Nope. I didn't want to waste a second." She reaches over and pats her small rolling suitcase. "Everything is in here. Or here." She jerks her thumb over her shoulder at her backpack.

I have the urge to remind her about the suitcase full of stuffed animals she used to bring with her, but I don't.

"Where's Uncle Jake?" she asks, shrugging off her backpack.

"He's at the gym." I take the pack and set it on top of her suitcase before leading her outside. Madison stopped holding my hand in public sometime last year.

"Can we stop there first?"

I hesitate before answering. It's not unusual for us to stop there.

"Is Aubrey still working there?" she asks once we're in the Jeep.

"Uh, yeah. I kind of wanted to talk to you about that." Shit, why does explaining my relationship to my daughter feel so damn awkward?

Probably because I've never done it before. Never planned to do it either.

She casts a sideways glance my way. "Did you ask her out?"

"Sort of. Yeah." I cough. "We've gone out a few times. So, I was thinking, how do you feel about her coming with us to the Big E tomorrow?"

She sits forward to play with the radio. "Sure. Will she go on any of the rides with me?"

"I thought you were too old for little kid rides?"

A blush creeps over her cheeks and she shrugs.

"So, your mom says you've been spirited lately."

She cocks her head and rolls her eyes. "Spirited?" She adopts a tone of voice very similar to her mother's "Are you sure she didn't say *'moody, emotional, and temperamental?'"*

"Anyway," I say, ignoring her last comment because damn does she have Lauren pegged. "You need to treat your mother with respect."

"Daaaad," she whines.

"Don't *Daaaad* me."

"But, she sends me chores by *text*." She flips through her phone and then shoves it in my face. "That's so *not* what texting is for."

Brushing the phone aside, I pin her with a stern look. "Maybe you're nicer via text and she's tired of the back talk."

She spreads her hands wide in front of her to emphasize the full extent of the injustice. "She makes me do chores around the house Ella never has to do."

"Maybe it's because you're older and your mom thinks you're more capable than your little sister. Ever think about that?"

"No." She crosses her arms over her chest and stares out the window.

"Are chores your biggest complaint?" I ask.

"Give me a minute to think on it."

I smother a laugh as I pull out of the parking lot. "Chores are good for you. Builds character."

"Ugh."

"When we were your age, if Grandma ran out of chores for Jake and me to do, she used to—"

"Send you next door to Mrs. Shepherd's house to work," she cuts me off with a bored tone. "I've heard this a million times."

"Mowing the lawn, shoveling snow, carrying groceries—"

"Interest level exceeded over here, Dad."

"You get my point."

"Yes. Point gotten."

"What point was that?"

She huffs. "Be nice to Mom and chores are good for me."

"You got it. Lecture over."

Aubrey

"CAN YOU DO another set, Griff?" I move to a spot where I can film but not be in the way of the shot. "Are you getting tired?"

He jumps and grabs the bar over his head. "I can go all day long, Aubrey." He flashes a cocky wink while continuing to run through sets of controlled leg raises. "All night too," he adds, not even breathing hard.

"Show off," Jake mumbles.

"Need me to demonstrate how it's done, old man?" Griff snarks back.

"You looking for an ass kickin'?"

"Bring it." He raises up and playfully kicks out at Jake.

These goofy, candid videos might be more interesting than what I originally planned, so I keep filming them as they banter back and forth.

Jake had been the one to ask Griff for me if he'd mind helping with some promotion for the gym. At least I didn't have to be the sleaze asking, "Hey, you're hot. Wanna whip off your shirt and let me get a few short video clips of you to post online?"

"Let's spar," Jake suggests.

In the last two weeks, Jake talked his brother into branching out and installing a practice ring for guys like Griff and Remy to come work on their training. I wasn't clear on the details of why Sully was against it at first, but he's definitely seen an increase in business as a result.

Paying customers. Not that I'm nosy—it is after all part of my job to keep track of his schedule—but Sully does a *lot* of pro-bono classes and low-cost training. Not just the couple of classes he teaches here. He also takes part in special programs at women's shelters, college campuses, and police departments in the area. Pretty much any non-profit who asks, he'll say yes to. Which is sweet, believe me, I almost melted into a puddle of goo when I realized how much time he spends on charitable endeavors. But it doesn't bring a lot of revenue into the gym itself. Sully has a stellar reputation in the community because of his work. Now I want to help him leverage that into making Strike Back more profitable.

"Are you nervous?" Jake asks.

"A little."

"Don't be." He lowers his voice. "My brother likes you. A lot, Aubrey. I haven't seen him act this way about a woman, well, ever."

Can I break my face from smiling too much? Because Jake's words have me ready to explode with happiness. "I like him too," I whisper.

"He's never introduced Maddy to a girlfriend before," Jake continues.

That nervous flutter starts up in my belly again. Yes, I've already met Madison, but this is different.

Jake turns, fully facing me now. "You need to understand something. Sully's a strong guy. Inside and out, but his heart's not bulletproof. If you can't handle this, tell him sooner rather than later."

"I don't have a problem with it."

He stares at me for a few seconds before nodding and backing away.

The back door opens and my heart kicks up. I didn't expect Sully to return to work after picking Madison up at the airport this afternoon.

"Hey, Aubrey!" she calls out. I swear the kid's grown another inch since I saw her. So unfair.

"Hey, Madison. How was your trip?"

She shrugs off the question. "Same old. Where's Uncle Jake?"

"He's working with a client." More like trying to beat the crap out of his buddy, but that seems like an inappropriate thing to say to Maddy.

"Hi." Sully's warm voice slides over me like caramel. He approaches slowly as if he's assessing how to handle this situation.

Did he tell Madison we're dating?

"Dad says you're coming with us to the Big E tomorrow," Madison says sort of answering my question.

"Is that okay with you?"

She cocks her head as if she never considered having a choice in the matter. "Sure. Have you ever been?"

"A long time ago."

"Me too. The timing never usually works out." A little more enthusiasm creeps into her voice. "But this time it does."

"Yes, it does." Sully musses her hair and she leans against him. "Who's Jake working with?"

"Griff. Jake talked him into letting me take a few short videos for our Insta."

Sully chuckles. "I thought *I* was supposed to be the star of the show?"

He's teasing because we both know he'd be perfectly happy if I never filmed him again. There's nothing vain or arrogant about Sully.

"There's a bill for some of that netting on your desk," I remind him.

"I'll take care of it."

Madison glances at her dad and back at me as if she's trying to decide which one of us is the least boring option.

"Can I stay with Aubrey, Dad?"

He gives me a quick look before answering, "Sure."

Shoot, what am I supposed to do with her? She's too old for me to toss some coloring books at, right?

My mouth twitches into an uncomfortable smile. "Are you thirsty?" God, I hope not. All I have to offer are water or protein shakes.

"There's my princess!" Jake yells across the gym. He jogs over and scoops Maddy up. "Why didn't you come see me?"

"Aubrey said you were busy."

"I'm never too busy for you."

Thanks, Jake.

"Holy sh…shoot," Griff stutters. "Madison, right? I haven't seen you since you were little."

Jake hooks his arm around her. "She's *still* little. Get lost."

Maddy's cheeks turn pink and she pushes away from her uncle. "Are you a friend of Uncle Jake's?"

"I think so," Griff jokes, rocking back on his heels. "I'm not so sure at the moment. I was about to kick his—"

"Dream on," Jake says, cutting him off.

The phone at the front desk rings and I hurry to answer, hoping Jake and Griff don't kill each other. Why am I surprised Jake's so overprotective of his niece?

After answering some questions from someone who found us through Instagram—*yay!*—I hang up. Griff strolls over with his hands in his pockets. "I'm gonna take off. Can you send me one or two of those clips? I'll help promote Strike Back through my account too."

"That'd be great. Thank you."

He half-smiles at me. "Thank you for taking them. Sully's lucky to have you."

My cheeks heat up and I mumble, "Thank you."

"Here, let me see your phone." He leans over the counter to grab it and tries to flick it on.

"Um, a person's phone is private." I place my hands on my hips. "What do you think you're doing?"

I'm only teasing, but he sets it down on the counter and holds up his hands.

While I'm flicking through some of the photos to send him, Maddy joins us. At first, I think she's here to talk to me, but she brushes her hair over her shoulder and peeks up at Griff, batting her lashes.

"So, what do you do?" she asks.

Oh God.

Oh no.

Watching two people flirt is awkward under most circumstances. Watching a twelve-year-old flirt with a guy who's friends with her dad, is downright painful.

It'll be painful for Griff too if Sully catches this scene.

"Uh," Griff says, inching away. "I have to get going." His frantic gaze finds mine as if to say, "Help me out here."

"Aubrey," Sully calls. "Can you come here for a sec?"

Griff's eyes are practically screaming, "Don't leave me alone with Sully's daughter!"

"Actually, I need you out here for a minute, if you can," I answer.

Sully approaching our little trio finally derails the train wreck. Maddy sighs in disappointment and wanders into the gym while Griff sighs in relief. "Thank you," he whispers. "Jesus. I don't want to be mean to her, but—"

"What's up, Aubrey?" Sully asks, stopping Griff from elaborating. Not that he needed to.

"Uh." Crap, I should've had a better plan. "Griff needed to talk to you about something."

I leave them to clean up the locker room and Maddy follows me inside. "He's *so* hot," she whispers. "Does he come here a lot?"

"Not really." I glance back at Griff and Sully. "He's a little old for you, Maddy. Plus, he's a friend of your dad's."

She purses her lips into a pout. "So?"

That explanation should've been sufficient. Apparently, I need a better one.

Here I'd been hoping to befriend Maddy this weekend, not lecture her so she ends up hating me.

"Are you excited about the fair tomorrow?" I ask, hoping to distract her.

"Yes! Can't wait."

That's better. I can't help smiling at her enthusiasm.

Sully pops his head in the locker room. "Hey, Maddy, ready to head home?"

"Sure."

He lifts his chin at me. "You leaving for the coffee shop soon?"

"Oh, shoot." I glance at the clock. "Thanks for reminding me."

On my way out, he hooks me around the waist, drawing me closer. "You work too hard." He leans down. "Your man should take better care of you," he says against my hair. The words combined with the emotion in his voice turn my knees to jelly.

"I can take care of myself," I whisper.

"I know you can." The corners of his mouth kick up. "I'm being selfish. I want you all to myself."

"You'll see me tomorrow." My gaze strays to the front where Maddy's talking to Griff as he tries to back out the door. "Besides, I have a feeling your hands are already full this weekend."

CHAPTER TWENTY-SIX

Aubrey

DID I REALLY agree to spend the day with Sully and Madison?

I keep staring in the mirror. Playing with my hair. Up or down? What makes me look older?

"You look so cute," Celia says.

"I don't want to look cute. I want to look capable."

"Capable of what?"

"Spending the day with my boyfriend and his almost-teenage daughter."

Her lips twitch and she brushes my hair off my shoulder. "Want me to put your hair up in a bun or something? Give you a stepmother makeover?"

"I'm not her—" Wait a second. If Sully and I keep dating... If we eventually... "Oh, shit."

"Just occurred to you, huh?" She nods in sympathy as she starts gathering my hair. "How about a simple braid?"

"Sure." I reach into my pocket for an elastic and hold it out to her.

"You look good in orange."

I glance down at the burnt-orange romper and fiddle with the double spaghetti straps holding it up. "You swear it doesn't make me look like a human pumpkin?"

She snort-giggles. "No. It's adorable. The ruffled edge is so cute. Gives you the appearance of legs for days. Guys love that."

"Even with the flat sandals?"

Somehow she keeps the exasperation out of her voice. "Yes. You're going to be walking all day. Those will be comfortable, plus you look cute but sassy."

"Sassy," I grumble.

Right as she's tying off the braid, someone knocks on our front door.

"I'll get it. Finish up in here," Celia says.

"Deep breath. You look fine. This will be fun," I tell my reflection. I smear on more sunscreen and a few more dabs of lip gloss, then realize I'm stalling.

Sully's smooth and easy voice draws me into the living room. His eyes widen and his gaze roams over me in an appreciative way. Maybe I don't look like a pumpkin after all.

"Where's Madison?" I ask.

Please tell me she didn't get mad I was joining them and decide to stay home.

"In the car. Last chance to monopolize the radio," he answers like it's no big deal.

"Have fun, guys," Celia says, shoving my purse and a bright yellow sweater-cardigan in my arms.

"Bye, Celia." Sully fires off a quick wave before taking my hand. "You all right?"

A pent-up breath whooshes out of me. "I'm nervous," I confess.

He stops at the top of the stairs and places his hands on my shoulders. "Why?"

I lift my gaze, meeting his concerned brown eyes. "I've never done this before."

One corner of his mouth lifts. "Neither have I."

Unsure of how to respond, I stand there staring at him. My gaze lingers on his forest-green button-up shirt. The color brings out golden flecks in his already vibrant brown eyes. Inside the apartment, I hadn't taken the time to fully appreciate how good he looks. How did he even find a shirt to accommodate his broad shoulders and thick biceps? With the way he has the sleeves rolled up to show off his forearms, I won't be able to concentrate all day.

"Aubrey?" His deep, raspy voice pulls me away from drooling over his arms.

He squeezes my shoulders. "Maddy already likes you. She was happy you were coming with us, honest. I wouldn't do anything to make either of you unhappy or uncomfortable."

His sincere words and expression melt some of my anxiety. "Let's go."

Maddy scoots into the backseat when she sees us coming and waves at me.

"It's so nice, I thought you'd have the top off."

He rolls his eyes as he opens the door for me. "*Someone* doesn't like to get her hair all windblown and messy anymore. She even complains about having the windows down." He teases.

In response, Maddy fluffs her hair and sticks her tongue out at him.

"I totally understand," I say as I climb into the Jeep. "I have extra pony-holders if you need one."

Am I a suck-up or what?

She takes the elastics I hand her and ties her hair back. "Thanks."

Once we're on the road, windows down and radio cranked to eleven, I'm able to relax a little more. Madison and I have eerily similar taste in pop-rock music. I'm not sure what that says about me, but we have fun serenading Sully all the way to Massachusetts.

Several times, I catch him glancing over with a smile on his face.

Once or twice, his hand grazes the side of my bare leg.

The closer we inch toward the fair, the heavier the traffic. Madison leans on my seat, practically bouncing out of the vehicle with excitement.

"*Pleeeeease* can we park near the Clydesdales? I want to see them first."

"Starting with the biggest horses, huh?" I ask.

"They're so beautiful."

While she rattles off details about Clydesdales, I lean over to Sully. "They're only here every other year, right?"

"They're here. I checked." He flicks his gaze to the rearview mirror. "Believe me, I checked first."

I chuckle and sit back to look up a map of the fair. "Keep going on

Route 147. It looks like we want the Gate Nine lot."

"Thank you."

We slow to a crawl and Maddy recites a list of fair food she plans to indulge in.

"Where are you planning to put all that?" Sully asks.

"I'll burn it off with all the walking," she shoots back.

He chuckles and shakes his head. "I don't want you to get sick and be miserable the whole way home."

"I'll pace myself," she assures him.

I cover my mouth to hold back my laughter.

"The key, Aubrey," Maddy announces. "Is to skip the really junky fair food in the front and go for the good stuff back in the Avenue of States exhibit."

"Ahh, okay. So, you have a plan?"

"Yes."

"Fried dough isn't junky?" Sully asks.

"No, Dad." I don't have to turn around to visualize her eye-roll.

I tap his arm. "Sacrilege. Fried dough is the *best* part of going to the fair."

He flashes a quick grin. "Maddy, don't forget we're supposed to bring home a cream puff and eclair for grandma."

"Okay."

"She'll kill me if we go to the fair and don't bring them back for her," he explains to me. He glances at Madison. "What do you think we should bring Uncle Jake?"

In my peripheral vision, I catch her tapping her chin as if she's giving it a lot of thought. "Apple cider, maybe? Or maple pepper. I'll think of something good. And I want to get real maple syrup for Mom."

"Sounds like a plan. You write it all down?" Sully asks.

"Duh. No. It's all in my head."

He chuckles and nudges me. "Can you grab my wallet? It's in the middle console."

"Sure." We roll to a stop at the entrance to the parking lot just as I find his wallet. "I brought money. I can—"

"Give me that." He plucks his wallet from my hands and passes a twenty to the man in the booth. A few seconds later, we're waved into the parking lot and directed to a wide grassy parking area near the gate. "See, pays to be early," he says to Madison.

"Yeah, yeah," she grumbles. My seat tips back as she loops her arms around the headrest. "He had me up at the butt-crack of dawn, Aubrey."

I chuckle but don't comment. Somehow it feels inappropriate to say I've learned her dad's an early riser.

Sully glances over at me, his eyes simmering with heat. Maybe he was thinking the same thing.

When he's satisfied he's found a spot where we won't get boxed in as the fair gets more crowded, he leans over. "Give me a second to talk to Maddy."

I grab a comb out of my purse and mumble, "Sure."

SULLY

THE DRIVE WENT better than I expected. Can't deny how awkward I felt about this whole thing this morning. Feeling more reassured now.

Maddy jumps down from the Jeep, pawing through the small purse at her side. "I can't find my sunglasses," she mutters.

"Check the—"

"Got 'em!" She slips them on and grins at me.

"They look good." I crook my finger at her. "Come here for a second."

"What?" she asks, stepping closer.

I lean down and lower my voice. "Listen, I know you're a big girl and don't do the hand-holding thing anymore—"

"Daaaad, really?"

"Let me finish, Madison."

She crosses her arms over her chest and taps her foot. "I'm listening."

"This is a big fair and it's going to be insanely crowded today. I need you to stick near me or Aubrey. No running off."

Her body tenses as if she's trying to come up with a smart retort. I pin her with what I hope is my stern-dad stare and wait.

Finally, she drops her arms. "I won't. Promise."

"Thank you."

She tugs at the front of the blindingly neon-yellow shirt she chose this morning. "Just in case, you should be able to see me from like a million feet away."

"Clever," I mutter with an eye roll.

"Ready?" Aubrey asks, coming around the front of the Jeep.

"See," Maddy says, pointing at Aubrey. "She's wearing a bright color too. That way you can't lose either of us."

Aubrey blinks and stares down at her outfit—the one I wanted to strip her out of the second I saw her this morning. Something about so much bare leg on display makes me want to run my hands all over her smooth skin.

"Oh. I guess this was a good pick, then," she says.

A breeze picks up, rustling through the heavy canopy of trees I parked under. It's a perfect fall day in New England.

"Ready?"

"Yup!" Madison chirps. She grabs Aubrey's hand and drags her toward the entrance gate.

Sure, she won't hold *my* hand in public. I chuckle and follow them.

Once we've bought our tickets and maps, we stop to formulate a plan for the day.

Aubrey listens while Madison rattles off all the things she wants to see and eat. Listens and looks at my daughter as if each one of the words rushing out of her mouth matters and she's not just humoring her.

My chest squeezes. This morning, I'd been intent on reassuring Aubrey, so I held back my own fears about today. So far our fears were unnecessary.

"All right." I take out my wallet and hand Madison spending money for the day. "Spend it wisely."

She grins and stuffs the bills in her purse. "Thanks!"

This Midway at the Big E is your typical fair. With the same vendors and games set up you see at most fairs. While Madison claimed she was too old for this and wanted to head to the animal barns and craft shops first, now she swears she has to ride the Vertigo Swing Tower. It's fine, it gives me time to check-in with Aubrey.

"Still okay?" I ask.

She beams up at me, a whole lot more confident than she seemed when I picked her up. "Great. I haven't been here since I was a kid."

"Sure you don't want to go on any rides?"

She shakes her head and chuckles self-consciously. "I don't think I'm tall enough for half of them."

"Stop," I warn, hating how self-conscious she seems about her size.

Her gaze flits around the immediate area and she leans up on tiptoes. "I'm only interested in one very *specific* ride," she says low enough for only me to hear.

A rumble of approval eases out of me and I plant a quick kiss on her lips. "You're the perfect size for *that* ride."

Madison joins us, looking a lot less thrilled than when she bounded up the stairs for the swings. "What's wrong?"

"Nothing. It was cool. It went high enough to see the whole Midway, but I'm too old for these baby rides."

She's pale and I wonder if she got scared but doesn't want to admit it.

"Feel okay?" I ask.

Madison scowls and doesn't answer. Instead, she takes the map from Aubrey's hands and declares the horses are our next stop.

Aubrey shrugs at me and follows.

The scents of farm animals, barbecue, and a variety of fried foods fill the air. Aubrey takes a bunch of photos of Madison and me, which I appreciate. I always seem to forget. She snaps even more photos of Madison and the two of them discuss the best filters, poses, and angles to use.

I casually hook my arm around Aubrey's shoulders. "Still having fun?"

"I am. Really. Stop worrying so much."

"I'm not worried."

She rubs her finger right between my eyebrows. "What's this then?"

"Hunger."

"I guess we better feed you then." She pinches my bicep. "Need to keep you big and strong."

Leaning down, I press a kiss to her temple. Love the way she teases me. "I do need to keep my stamina up."

She raises an eyebrow. "You stay *up* like a champ."

I cough-laugh and look away.

Madison asks for more pictures of the horses and I take a few of her to send to her mom.

We promise Maddy we can return to the horses after we eat. Although, I have a feeling something else will have captured her interest by the time we finish lunch.

The avenue of states is all the way on the other side of the fair. We weave through the crowds of people to stand in line for lobster rolls, loaded baked potatoes, and blueberry pie.

"I'll grab a table outside," Aubrey says, pointing to the back of the building. "Madison's still in line for her potato."

I swing my gaze to the left and easily pick Maddy out in the line. "All right."

Madison's picking up her order when I'm handed our lobster rolls and I meet up with her. "Want me to carry those?"

"I got it. Where's Aubrey?"

"She said she was grabbing a table."

"I hope it's in the shade," she grumbles.

I stop and take her in once again. It's a warm fall day, but not that hot. Living in Florida, she's conditioned to much hotter temperatures than this. "Are you sure you feel okay?"

She blows me off and storms outside, leaving me shaking my head.

Aubrey stands and waves us over to a table in a shady corner of the lawn.

"Want to look for those gifts next?" Aubrey asks. She nods to one of the houses in front of us. "The Vermont state house is right there.

Probably the best place for maple syrup."

Madison nods and drags her fork through her potato without really eating any of it.

"You want to trade?" I ask, holding out my lobster roll.

"No. I'm fine." She flicks her gaze at Aubrey. "The New Hampshire house. We should go there too. They used to have maple cotton candy and really good fudge."

"Sounds good. I can't remember the last time I had fudge," Aubrey agrees.

We finish lunch—well, Aubrey and I finish, Madison didn't make a dent in her food—and I take the trays to the trash cans. Aubrey meets me there and smiles.

"Ready for a sugar rush?"

"You're my sugar rush," I whisper, giving her a quick kiss.

Madison's already half-way to the next shop when we catch up to her. "What did I say about walking off?" I say.

"I didn't," she snaps, jerking out of my hold. "We said we were going here next."

Bewildered by her behavior, I back off for now.

"Is she okay?" Aubrey asks in a low voice.

"I don't know. Maybe we should head home after this."

"Oh boy," she mutters. "Good luck with that. I think she has her heart set on going back to see the horses."

"Well, if her attitude doesn't improve, we're not going to see anything else."

"Give her a break. Maybe she's overwhelmed."

Maybe Aubrey's right. Maddy seems to chill as we collect her maple sugar goodies. She even offers to split her cotton candy with Aubrey. Part of me worries Maddy's not handling Aubrey joining us today as well as I thought she was. Too much too soon or something.

We finish winding through the state houses and move over to craft alley. Madison stops at one of the jewelry shops and immediately zeroes in on a butterfly pendant suspended from a fine silver chain. She's so enchanted by it, I have to get it for her.

"Do you want that?" I ask.

She shakes her head. "I don't have enough left."

"I want to get it for you."

"Are you sure?"

Maybe I should check with the shopkeeper before I commit. He takes it out of the case and lets Maddy try it on. I plunk down my credit card and wait for him to ring it up.

"Oh, that's so pretty on you," Aubrey squeals.

My gaze drifts around the small shop. Should I get something for Aubrey too? I'd rather give it more than a couple seconds of thought, so I dismiss the idea.

The shopkeeper returns. He's also the designer, so he explains to Maddy how to clean the pendant and throws in some polishing cloths.

Outside, Madison slips her arm through mine as we walk toward the next shop. "Thank you, Dad. I really love it."

"You're welcome."

"Do you mind if I slip in here?" Aubrey asks, nodding to a shop that sells special shea butter lotions and bath stuff.

Maddy wrinkles her nose and pulls me toward a toy stand. "Meet you in the middle," I say to Aubrey.

I glance down at Madison who's squeezing a white, fluffy, stuffed owl. "I thought you were too old for toys?"

"It's for Ella. She loves owls."

Love for my daughter expands and fills my chest. She complains about her little half-sister a lot, but that she's still thinking of her and wants to spend her last couple dollars on a gift for her is sweet. "It's pretty. I'm sure she'll love it."

"She better," Maddy says, making me laugh.

We meet Aubrey at the shop she stopped at as she's checking out. "Anything good?"

"Body butter." She unscrews the cap of one of the jars in her bag and sticks it under my nose. It's a soft coconut-vanilla scent. Almost impossible to detect with the air full of sizzling briskets, sausages, and popcorn. "It's nice."

And now I'm visualizing all the ways I want to butter up Aubrey's body.

"Can I?" Madison asks. "Ooo, that smells good."

Pink spreads over her cheeks and Aubrey opens her bag. "I bought a jar for you too, if you like it. It's strawberry—"

"Oh, yes. Thank you!"

After Maddy gives it a thorough sniff-test—and I say a secret *thank you* that it smells nothing like the body butter I'm planning to slather all over Aubrey—I transfer the jar to one of her bags, then pull Aubrey closer. "You didn't have to do that."

She shrugs. "I wanted to."

We follow the sidewalk that leads to bigger outdoorsy vendors. Tractors, sheds, hot tubs, stuff like that. Aubrey stops at the hot tubs. "I definitely need one of those one day."

I can vividly picture her in it and have to glance away for a second.

"We have one," Maddy says. "I'm not allowed in it for more than ten minutes though."

"You'll probably cook yourself if you're in it much longer," Aubrey teases.

Maddy giggles. "Ella's not allowed in it at *all*."

"Big sister privileges."

They walk ahead, talking about sister stuff, I guess. We stop to buy squares of fudge and Madison looks around for a bathroom.

"I'll go with her," Aubrey says, reaching up and giving me a quick kiss on the cheek.

A few minutes later, Aubrey emerges alone. "She's coming," Aubrey assures me.

"Come here." I hook my arms around her waist, yanking her closer. Our foreheads touch. "Are you having a good time?"

"I am. Are you?"

"Yes. I—"

"Jeez. Do you *have* to stop and make-out like every fifteen minutes?" Maddy's snide voice pulls us out of our bubble.

"What?" I'm not used to my daughter using that tone with me.

"Sorry," Aubrey mutters, pulling away.

"No." I grab her hand, keeping her where she is. "What's wrong, Madison?"

"Nothing. Just, jeez." She won't meet my eyes but glances down the Midway instead. "Can we keep moving, please?"

I guess we're back to awkward.

Aubrey

I THOUGHT WE were getting along and having a good day. Suddenly Maddy seems absolutely miserable and everything I do annoys her.

Her foul mood worsens until she bursts into tears and demands to go home.

Sully closes his eyes and takes a deep breath. "Madison. Calm down."

She wails even louder, drawing a lot of attention our way.

My frantic gaze searches the area and I nudge him toward a bench in the shade.

A huge white sign for the Big E cream puffs grabs my attention and I mutter, "Thank you, Jesus!" under my breath.

"I'm going to go grab those cream puffs and eclairs you wanted," I say, eager to sound helpful instead of desperate to get away. "Should I meet you here or by the car?"

Sully shakes his head. "It's a straight shot out the gate and to the right. So if we're not here, we'll be headed to the car."

"Okay." I glance down at Madison who has her face buried in her hands. I want to comfort her, but I'm not sure it will help. "Maddy, do you want anything?"

"I don't care!"

Yikes, okay.

"Madison! Stop being rude," Sully scolds. God, this just keeps getting worse.

"Be right back."

It turns out "be right back" was a little too optimistic. The Big E cream puffs are their own attraction at the fair. The windows are all glass so you can watch the desserts being made. Any other time I'd be fascinated, but now I just want to grab the puffs and go.

I finally make it to the window to place my order. Worried dehydration brought on Maddy's mood change, I ask for three bottles of water as well.

The bench is empty, so I carry the giant white pastry boxes all the way to the parking lot.

Sully and Madison are still having words outside the Jeep. Can I find a bus back to Empire? I'm really not looking forward to the ride home.

"Aubrey, let me grab those," Sully says as soon as he sees me. Madison groans and slams the door after she hops in the Jeep. Sully rolls his eyes.

"No better?"

"Nope." He huffs out a frustrated laugh. "Her mother tried to warn me about this last night."

A couple of questions flutter at the edge of my tongue. But they're invasive and none of my business, so I keep my mouth shut.

In the car, I pass a bottle of water to Maddy who takes it without a word. "Do you need anything else, Maddy?" I ask before Sully opens his door.

"No."

It's an uncomfortable two-hour drive home.

"I'm so sorry," Sully says, walking me to the steps leading up to my apartment. He keeps glancing at the Jeep, where Madison's asleep in the backseat.

"It's okay. Maybe a trip like that was too ambitious for our first outing."

"First, huh? You saying there will be another?"

My face falls. Wow. Stupid assumption.

Sully must realize where my thoughts ran. He grabs my hands and squeezes. "No, no. I meant *you'll* give *us* another chance? Me and Madison?"

"Oh!" Now I feel silly. "Of course." I let out a sigh. "Maybe next time we'll stay local or just do dinner or something. Or I don't have to—"

He squeezes my hands again and draws me closer. "Thank you."

A horn blows, startling us apart. Sully's eyes close and a grim expression settles over his face as he turns toward the Jeep. "I guess she's awake."

I pat his chest. "Good luck, Dad."

Not to be deterred, he leans down and kisses me. Quick but sweet.

When we part, I can't help smiling. "I know your mom's out of town, so if I can help you in any way, call me. I used to speak twelve-year-old girl pretty fluently. Maybe I can give you some tips over the phone."

He throws his head back and laughs. "Thank you."

Feeling reassured that Sully and I will be okay, I trot up the stairs, waving when I get to the top to let him know I'm all right.

Celia's rushing around the living room when I walk into our apartment. "Shit, you scared me! I didn't think you'd be back until a lot later," she says.

"Whoa, what are you so dressed up for?"

She stands up straighter, smoothing her hands over her black sleeveless peplum top and black pencil skirt. "Date."

"With who? I need details."

She rolls her eyes. "This guy who keeps coming into the salon to see me. Persistent asshole." The words come out more affectionate than mean.

"If he's an asshole, why are you going?"

"I don't know. I'm intrigued." She narrows her eyes. "Now, spill. Why are you home so early?"

I toss my stuff on the couch and then drop down next to the bags and kick off my shoes.

"We had a good time. Then, I don't know. Madison seemed mad or something. It kept getting worse, so Sully decided it was better to take her home."

"Aww." She sits next to me and pats my leg. "I'm sorry. She seemed so nice last time. Maybe it's just hard to see her dad with someone after having all of his attention for so long."

"Yeah, that's what I figured. We were getting along. I was trying so hard not to be 'Dad's obnoxious girlfriend.' You know, give them some space. Not be all clingy with him or kiss up to her *too* much."

She chuckles. "You've put an awful lot of thought into it."

"Of course I have. I actually like her too. When she's not being a brat," I add.

"What did Sully say?"

"I think he was upset. Or embarrassed. I don't know. I don't think she's ever acted up on him before."

She wrinkles her nose. "You think she's PMSing?"

"Maybe. I don't know her *that* well. I couldn't figure out a tactful way to ask."

"Have mercy on poor Sully if that's the case. I hope it's not her first one."

I chuckle and bump my shoulder against her. "You remember when that happened to me?"

"How could I forget? You thought you were dying. Mom's whole 'you're a woman now, get over it,' was less than useless."

"Remember she told me if I wasn't so fat, I might've started later?" I can joke about it now, but back then it was a pretty traumatizing thing for an eleven-year-old to hear from her mother.

Celia rolls her eyes. "That was so stupid. And not even remotely true." She wraps her arm around my shoulders and gives me a quick hug. "My car keys are on the peg. Since it seems Sully has his hands full tonight, why don't you go out or something?"

"I'll think about it."

CHAPTER TWENTY-SEVEN

Aubrey

LATER THAT AFTERNOON, my phone rings and I snap it up, pleasantly surprised it's Sully after the awkward way our afternoon ended. "Hey, I didn't expect to hear from you until Monday."

He lets out a frustrated laugh. "I'm kind of having an issue."

"With Maddy? Is she okay?"

"She's fine. I think. She won't talk to me."

"Why?"

"This is awkward. My mom's not here and you're a girl…"

I think I know what's coming and steel myself not to laugh. Celia was right after all.

"She got her period and I guess she didn't bring anything with her. She won't tell me what she needs. I can't reach her mom to ask her. So I tried to run to the store and grab some stuff, but I guess the supplies I picked up were *wrong*." He lets out a defeated groan. "And now she won't talk to me."

Giggle-suppression failure.

"Aubrey," he pleads. "It's not funny."

"Poor Maddy. She's probably embarrassed and uncomfortable." And am I totally awful for thinking that maybe, hopefully, hormones are the reason Madison seemed so annoyed with my presence earlier?

"The only thing she said was 'pads with wings' and apparently what I grabbed doesn't have the *right* wings."

"The right wings *are* critical," I tease.

Obviously not in the mood for joking around, lowers his voice. Almost begging. "Would you mind coming over?"

"Not only will I come over, I'll even stop at CVS and pick up some supplies."

He lets out a relieved breath. "Thank you. Wait, you need me to come pick you up?"

"Nope. Celia's out on a date and left me her car. Do you have a heating pad?"

He takes a while to answer. "Probably?"

"That sounds like a no. I'll bring one."

AN HOUR LATER I'm knocking on Sully's front door with four plastic bags of girly supplies in my hands. Plus, groceries.

Sully's eyes widen when he takes everything in. "What did you get?"

"All sorts of goodies. You can grill some steaks for us later," I say, handing over one of the plastic bags. "I'll go talk to her."

He cocks his head, staring down the hallway. "Are you sure you want to go in there? She's even less-friendly than she was when I dropped you off."

"She probably wasn't feeling well before. If the situation's too hostile, I'll drop the bags inside her door and run." I hold up my right hand. "Promise."

His shoulders drop, and he shakes his head, a small smile playing at the corners of his mouth. "Thank you."

Pretending I'm more confident than I'm actually feeling, I march down the hallway.

"Last door on the right," Sully reminds me.

"I've got this," I mutter to myself. I know how much this sucks. If it hadn't been for Celia, explaining what was happening to me and buying me the right supplies, I probably would've crawled into a hole and begged for death once a month from the age of eleven on. My parents were certainly no help in that department.

All I can think about is how upset Maddy must be to finally have the extra time with her dad and have this ruin it for her.

I glance back at Sully who's shifting from foot to foot, an anxious expression on his face, hands jammed in his pocket. Clearly he wants to do the right thing for his daughter and has no idea where to start.

I tip my head back and close my eyes for a second. *Please don't let me screw this up.*

I tap on the door a few times.

"What!?" Maddy yells.

Crap. Shifting the bags to one hand, I push the door open.

Don't show any fear.

"Hi, Madison. I know I'm probably the last person you want to see right now. But I came over to help."

Her eyes widen, and her tear-stained cheeks turn even redder. My heart squeezes at her obvious mortification.

"My dad *called* you?" she wails.

"He thought I could help." I hold up the bags. "I brought goodies."

She picks her head up and raises an eyebrow. "What kind of goodies?"

"There's chocolate fudge brownie ice cream in the freezer."

She jerks her chin. "What's in the bags?"

"Truffles. Maxi's with wings, Advil, a heating pad."

She wrinkles her nose. "Heating pad?"

I shrug. "It always helps me."

She scoots over and I approach slowly, setting stuff down on the bed first like some sort of offering to appease the goddess of hormonal teenagers. She peers into the bags, grabbing the bag of chocolate truffles first.

It's brief, but I swear she actually smiles.

She grabs the pads next and breathes a sigh of relief. "Thank you. The ones Dad bought were diaper-size." She holds her hands about three feet apart. "I mean seriously, I could go canoeing with these things."

I can't help laughing. "I'm sure he tried his best, honey."

"Give me a second. I'll be right back." She scoops the important bags up and runs across the hall, leaving her bedroom door wide open.

While she's gone, I unwrap the heating pad and find a spot to plug it in.

"Is it safe?" Sully whispers from the doorway.

"I think so, but I wouldn't linger if I were you." I squint at him. "Did you go into the feminine hygiene aisle or the adult incontinence aisle at the pharmacy?"

"What?" He runs his hands through his hair. "I don't know. The package said 'overnight protection' I figured that would work until—"

He stops abruptly when he realizes I'm teasing. "It's not funny."

Across the hall, the toilet flushes and Sully zips away. Can't blame him.

Maddy floats back into the room. "Soooo much better. Thank you."

She flops down on her bed, pulling the covers up to her chin. "Does this ever not hurt so bad? I feel like my insides are being ripped out."

"I know." I hand over the heating pad and show her how the controls work. "See if this helps. Give it a few minutes to warm up."

She rifles through the rest of the bags and wrinkles her nose at the tampons. "I don't use those yet. Mom says I shouldn't."

"Oh. I wasn't sure." That's weird, but I'm not about to contradict her mom. "If you're not supposed to, don't. Leave them here so you have them in case of emergency when you're older."

"Thank you."

"No problem."

She pops open the Advil and takes what she needs.

Mission successful. Don't overstay your welcome.

I start edging my way toward the door.

She stares at me for a few seconds, then glances away. "You don't *have* to go."

She scooches over and taps the space beside her. I perch on the edge of the bed. "I was going to watch Labyrinth. Have you ever seen it?"

The movie is older than I am. "Lots of times."

She rolls her eyes. "Dad always makes fun of the Goblin King."

I imagine some of the humor and metaphors in Labyrinth that goes over Madison's head are outright horrifying for Sully. Not to mention the codpiece. I choke back a laugh.

"He calls him *King Tightpants*."

The laughter I'd been hanging onto by a thread bursts out and Maddy joins in.

"Watching it with Uncle Jake is even worse. He makes fun of *everything*."

"I bet he does."

Her hand drifts over the heating pad resting on her stomach. "This does feel better."

To my total surprise, Madison snuggles up to me. Cautiously, I sling an arm around her. "Thank you, Aubrey."

"No problem."

She tips her head back, staring at me for a few seconds with shining eyes. "I'm sorry I was mean to you before."

I'm so shocked by her apology it takes me a second to respond. "You weren't mean, honey."

"I guess I was jealous you get to spend so much time with my dad."

It's a pretty adult thing to admit and I hug her a little tighter. "I'm sorry. I never want to intrude on your time together."

"It's okay."

"I bet it's really hard being so far away except for a couple days a month."

"It is," she says, sitting up. "I really wish we lived closer. Mom talks about moving back to New York all the time, but my stepfather doesn't want to and Grandma Jean is there…"

I'm so at a loss for words. It's not like I've earned the right to offer any opinions and I'm so afraid of saying the wrong thing and making the situation worse.

"That's rough, Maddy. You know your dad loves you a lot, though. He's really happy about the extra visits. I hope that continues to work out for you guys."

"I've been looking forward to it for weeks and now I feel bad." She crosses her arms over her chest and throws herself against the bed. "Mom said if he spends more time with me, he'll realize he's gotten off easy all these years."

That sounds mean, but then again, I'm not the one dealing with the hormonal teenager on a daily basis.

"And now I yelled at him." A few tears roll down her cheeks and she quickly swipes them away. "So she's right."

"People say stuff they don't mean when they're mad or upset sometimes, Maddy. It doesn't mean they don't love each other."

In response, I get a grunt-grumble, that I assume means she agrees.

"Labyrinth?" I ask, picking the remote control off the nightstand. I glance around the room. "You've got a nice set-up in here."

"You've never been in my room before?" she asks with a raised eyebrow.

It feels like a trick question. Damn, this kid's sneaky.

"No." Heat crawls up my neck to my cheeks. Every time I've been at Sully's house, we've been too eager to get to *his* bedroom. No time for a tour of the house. "Your dad told me it was your room, but that's it."

She takes the remote from me and brings up the Netflix menu to find our movie.

"I feel like we should have popcorn."

She nudges the bag of chocolates into my hands. "Chocolate's way better."

"True. Do you want something to drink, though?"

She scrunches up her nose and thinks it over. "Maybe some milk?"

"Okay. Give me a minute. Don't start without me."

I slip out of the room, immediately bumping into Sully.

"Is she okay?" he asks. He runs his gaze over me. "Are *you* okay?"

"I survived. I'm grabbing some milk." He follows me down the hall. "She wants to watch Labyrinth."

In the kitchen, he hands me two glasses and leans against the counter while I pour the milk.

"Should I be concerned she likes that movie so much?" he asks.

I lean up and kiss his cheek. "Nah, it's all about a young girl coming into her own power and saying *no* to the dazzling King Tightpants."

He chokes, then full-out laughs. "I guess I ruined it for her last time."

"Maybe a little."

"Hey, come here." A more serious expression settles over him and he reaches out to take my hand, pulling me closer. "Thank you for doing this. You don't have to. It's not your responsibility."

"I like her and I—" *Love you.* "Want to help."

Unaware of what almost came out of my mouth, he gives me a soft kiss on my cheek. "I appreciate it. I still haven't heard back from Lauren. And my mother rarely does anything for herself, so I didn't want to bug her on her trip."

"I'm glad you called me."

SULLY

I'VE NEVER FELT so inadequate. Or more aware that my little girl isn't so little. She's growing up and I don't know what to do.

At least Madison's not crying anymore, because if there's one thing I can't take, it's tears from my daughter.

I could strangle her mom right about now though.

Once it seems Aubrey's safely back inside Madison's lair, I stalk into the living room and throw myself on the couch to stare at the television.

My phone vibrates over the coffee table and I pick it up.

Lauren. About fucking time.

"What's wrong, Sully?" she asks. "You blew up my phone. Is Maddy okay?"

"She's fine. Although you might've warned me our daughter started getting her period."

Typical Lauren blows out a dismissive breath. "She just started in February. She's been so irregular, and you see her so infrequently, I never thought it would be an issue."

Nice dig about how infrequently I get to see my daughter. "You still couldn't give me a head's up? She's my daughter. I should know these things." I don't *want* to know any of it, but I don't have a choice.

Besides, it would have been nice to have the right stuff here so Maddy didn't have to be so stressed out when she already felt so miserable.

Lauren groans. "She asked me not to tell anyone. I think she's hoping it will disappear as mysteriously as it arrived. Honestly, she's been very dramatic about it."

I grit my teeth, surprised Lauren's so cold about this. "Well, she's in a lot of pain and pretty miserable."

"As is *every* woman when they have their period. She's not dying. Give her some Advil. She'll be fine."

"Isn't she a little young for this?"

"That's when I started."

Well, hell. What do I say to that? "Oh."

"Do you need me to talk to her?"

Shit, I do *not* want to tell Lauren I had to ask my girlfriend to come over and help me.

"I finally got the right stuff for her and she's napping now." There. Answered the question and avoided telling her about Aubrey.

"See," she says, drawing out the word for maximum condescension. "I knew you'd figure it out."

"Thanks a lot."

"Listen, while I have you on the phone, can we talk about Thanksgiving?"

I groan. "Sure, what about it?"

"Well, I know it's not your turn to have her for Thanksgiving, but Robert and I wanted to go to Aspen to go skiing, and Madison—"

"Hates skiing," I finish for her.

"Exactly."

"So, you want me to take her for Thanksgiving this year and you have her for Christmas?" This sucks because it's the second Christmas, I won't have Madison. But maybe I can fly down to Florida and see her for a few days instead.

"No. Keep Christmas."

"Are you sure?"

"I'm sure."

So many things come to mind. Part of me wants to get it in writing because I don't trust her not to change her mind at the last minute. Part of me hurts for Madison that it seems her mom doesn't want her around when it's inconvenient. But more than anything I'm excited about the holiday with my daughter.

"What about Ella?" Maddy's younger half-sister has only visited once before and Maddy did *not* appreciate having my attention divided between the two of them—maybe she gets enough of that at home. But I don't want to leave Ella out or separate the girls at the holidays. "Is she going skiing with you?"

"No, she's staying with Robert's parents."

"Okay. She's welcome here if that changes."

"Thanks, Sullivan. We both know Madison won't care for that, but I really appreciate it." This time, she sounds genuine.

"My mom will be thrilled to have Maddy here for Thanksgiving."

She laughs softly. "How is your mom?"

"Good."

"Well, tell her I said hello."

"Will do."

We go over the flight times for tomorrow night, then hang up.

I wander back down the hall, surprised Aubrey hasn't emerged yet.

And then I overhear their conversation.

"There's this boy I like, but he only likes girls with bigger boobs, you know?"

Aubrey laughs softly. "He doesn't sound worth your time."

"But he's really popular," Maddy persists. "And sends me these notes sometimes."

Fuck no, I'm not ready for this. My back hits the wall and I close my eyes.

"Oh, honey. I know it's exciting and fun, but don't let that be your sole focus. Worry about yourself first."

"Did you have a boyfriend before my dad?"

"Uh, yeah."

"A lot?"

"A few. But I really regret the one I had in high school." That makes me open my eyes. We've never done the "past relationships" talk. Mostly because my last "relationship" was in high school and ended with the girl I thought I was in love with moving away and having a baby she didn't bother to tell me about for four years.

"Ohhh," Maddy moans and I have to fight the urge to storm into her room. "This hurts *so* bad. One of my friends says there are these pills you can take to make them go away."

"Uh," Aubrey lets out a nervous chuckle. "It doesn't completely go away. But you're too young for that."

"Are you sure? Because I *hate* this."

"I know it sucks. But look at the bright side. The first day is usually the worst, so it should get better from here. And it means you're a healthy young woman."

I could kiss Aubrey for trying to come up with some good things for Maddy to focus on right now.

Maddy groans. "I'm not ready to be a *woman.*"

Couldn't agree more, kid.

"And," Maddy continues. "I don't even have decent-sized boobs to make up for it yet."

Christ, I'm not ready for this.

"You'll get there."

"Did you?"

Aubrey lets out a nervous laugh. "I felt like *poof,* they showed up one day, unexpected."

And now I'm picturing my girlfriend's breasts. Nothing creepy at all about this situation.

"I don't even want babies," Maddy continues.

Good, because you're still my baby.

Aubrey laughs harder. "I know exactly what you mean."

"You don't want to have babies with my dad?"

My daughter's words hit me like a bucket of ice water to the face. Do *I* want more kids? Finding out about Madison, fighting to be part of her life has taken up so much of my energy, I've never even let myself consider whether I want any more children.

Aubrey would be such a good mother.

"Whoa. Slow down, Maddy." Aubrey's hesitation is hard to miss. "We haven't been dating that long."

"So? I wouldn't mind a little brother. Please, just not another sister."

"You don't get along with your little sister?" Aubrey asks, sidestepping the little brother thing effortlessly.

Now that the idea's in my head, I can't shake it as easily. What would it be like to do it all over from the beginning? To do it *together* with Aubrey?

Guilt settles in my chest. How could I ever experience our child's first laugh, first word, first steps without being reminded of how I missed every single one of those things with Madison?

"How do you feel now?" Aubrey asks.

Madison lets out a big yawn. "Sleepy."

"A nap always makes me feel better. We can watch the movie when you wake up."

"Are you staying?"

"Uh, for a little while. Sure."

They're quieter and I can't make out any more words.

A few seconds later, Aubrey emerges from my daughter's room with a slight smile on her face.

"Oh!" She jumps when she sees me. "I didn't realize you were still here," she whispers.

To overcome, I bend down for a kiss. "Thank you," I mouth against her lips.

She raises an eyebrow, but I take her hand and pull her away from Maddy's room.

"She's napping," Aubrey whispers.

"I heard."

"What's wrong?"

"Nothing." I step back and run my hand over my chest, thinking of how to frame what I want to say to her. "Thank you so much for everything. For talking to her. I felt so helpless before. I hate that she won't talk to me, but I'm happy she's comfortable talking to you."

Her mouth quirks and she taps my chest. "No girl wants to talk about that stuff with her dad. Even a cool dad like you."

We end up in the living room. I pull her down on the couch with me and wrap my arm around her shoulders. Aubrey yawns and I feel bad about dragging her over here after we had such a long day. "Tired?"

"A little." She wiggles her feet in front of us. "We did a lot of walking."

I reach down and draw her feet into my lap, gently working my thumbs into the arch of one foot and then the other.

She moans softly and leans back against the end of the couch.

"You think that's why she was so testy?" I ask as my fingers keep working.

"Probably." She opens her eyes and watches me for a few seconds. "I think she was really looking forward to the extra visit and was afraid her period would ruin it."

I'm so not ready for any of this.

"I finally heard from Lauren. I guess this started a while ago, but it's not a regular thing, so she didn't bother telling me."

"That makes sense."

"Does it?"

Aubrey shrugs. "Some girls are really secretive about that stuff. It's embarrassing to them. Some don't care. I wondered if that's what was going on today, but I didn't want to ask and make it worse."

"You did?" Shit, why hadn't it occurred to me?

"Well, the mood swings. The tears…I've had some experience there." She chuckles softly.

"She's my little girl. I'm not ready for this," I finally admit.

"Mother nature waits for no man," she teases.

"I mean, she's too young." I realize my hands have stopped moving. Aubrey slides her feet out of my lap and sits up, facing me.

"She's growing up." Aubrey pauses. Bites her lip. "I didn't want to say anything, but I guess you missed her flirting with Griff yesterday?"

My head snaps up. "What? I'll kill—"

"Stop right there." She presses her palm against my chest. "He didn't *encourage* her at all. Believe me. He tried really hard to put her off without being mean."

Yeah, I've known Griff a while and that sounds exactly like how he'd handle that situation. "Thank God it was him and not some other asshole."

"Right, but my point was, she's not a little kid."

"I heard you trying to steer her away from boy talk."

She shakes her head. "Not for your sake. For *hers*." There's an undercurrent in her voice that makes me think for some reason, this is important to her. Personal almost. Definitely need to explore that later.

"Anyway, Lauren asked if I wanted Maddy for Thanksgiving."

"Oh, that's great! I've never asked what you guys do for the holidays."

I explain the arrangement we laid out in our custody agreement.

"Does that mean you won't have her for Christmas?"

"No, she said we'll leave everything as is."

"That's great." She seems genuinely pleased and it's nice to have someone who isn't my mother or brother to talk about this stuff with for a change. Aubrey's not jealous. Doesn't see my daughter as a threat or competition for my affection. She listens without judgment and offers helpful insight.

I'm already half in love with her and this…this might push me right over the edge.

"ARE YOU HUNGRY?" Sully asks.

"Actually, yeah. I'll see if Maddy's awake."

I run down the hall, but she's still sound asleep. At least she looks more comfortable now. Quietly I sneak into her room and turn off the heating pad, setting it on her nightstand in case she needs it later.

"She's out cold," I say when I find Sully in the kitchen.

He hesitates. "I'll wrap up her dinner and feed her when she wakes up."

Rain pelts the windows, dashing our plans to grill outside on the patio.

"Looks like we're eating in," Sully quips.

"Sounds good to me."

We cook together side-by-side, easily talking about the good parts of our day at the fair and our plans for tomorrow.

I rub up against his side, peering down at his chopping skills. "You're good at this."

"My mother insisted her boys be self-sufficient." He winks at me. "A gift to our future wives."

There's a flutter in my stomach at the way he explains his talent. "I knew I liked your mom."

He wiggles his eyebrows. "I do laundry too."

I bump him with my hip.

The teasing smile slides off his face. "I like having you here, Aubrey."

"I like being here with you."

The timer on the stove beeps at us, utterly ruining the moment.

Dinner's quiet. The scents of sizzling steak and sautéed mushrooms doesn't draw Maddy out of her room. After dinner, I check on her and she's still snoring softly.

"I've never seen her nap before," Sully says. "She's always been extremely anti-napping. It's for babies, you know."

Nervous laughter bubbles out of me. The man's been inside me for God's sake, but it still feels weird to talk about this with him. "When I was her age, I used to get really bad cramps. A nap always helped."

"Oh."

I shrug. "My mother's solution was to exercise more, but I ended up passing out once. She left me alone to nap after that."

"That's crazy."

"I told you we're not close. Celia's the one who took care of me and explained stuff. My mom's solution was to lose weight to stop getting my period."

His face twists in outrage. "That's not only stupid, it's dangerous."

"Looks have always been more important to her than anything else." I shrug again—it's getting to be a nervous tic around this subject.

We end up back in front of the television, flipping around for something to watch.

"I swear some nights our entertainment is just reading movie blurbs and watching trailers on Netflix," I joke. "Celia can never commit."

He snorts. "Jake can't sit still long enough to watch anything. If I don't choose wisely, he'll get up and start pacing."

"How'd you two end up so different?" I say it teasingly, but a weight seems to press down on Sully. His smile fades and he drops the remote next to him.

"We're actually half-brothers."

"Really? You look so much alike I never thought about it."

He *hmms* and flicks at a loose thread of denim by his knee. "My dad died before I was born."

"Oh. I'm so sorry."

He shrugs as if it's something in the past he's already dealt with. "A friend of his married my mother. Gave me his name. They had Jake about a year after I was born. So, it's not like I ever knew any different." There's a wry twist to his lips. "Well, he reminded me I wasn't his frequently enough, so I didn't forget."

"That's pretty shitty since he married your mom when she was pregnant."

"Yeah, he was shitty in a lot of ways."

He stares straight ahead, and I wait silently to see if he wants to continue.

"Did you…did your mom leave him?"

"No. He's dead."

"Oh." I don't bother saying I'm sorry this time. "Your mom's a strong woman. It sounds like she's been through a lot."

"She has. There's nothing I wouldn't do for her."

An eerie tone creeps into our moment. One where it seems I have a lot of puzzle pieces in front of me but no idea how they fit together.

CHAPTER TWENTY-EIGHT
SULLY

I HAD NO intention of turning our conversation so heavy. Or dredging up anything from my past. Those secrets should stay buried. They're not important to who I am now.

"Come here," I say, pulling her closer. She tucks her feet up under her and crosses her arms over her chest. "Are you cold?"

"A little."

"Here," I reach behind me and drag a blanket over both of us.

"Oooo, it's so soft and fuzzy." She runs her hands over the fleece and tucks it up around her shoulders.

"Do you want me to grab you a sweatshirt?"

"No, this is good."

My gaze drifts to the screen and I pick up the remote again. "Want to watch some of this show with me? Maddy asked to watch it, but I wasn't sure if it was age-appropriate."

A smile tugs at the corners of her mouth. "You're a bit of an old-fashioned dad, aren't you? She has a TV in her room."

I shrug. "It has a parental lock, so she can't access stuff rated above a certain level."

"Ahhh, kids are smart though and know how to go around those things."

"I'm sure. But for my sanity, let's pretend that's not true."

I flick the button to start the show and while it's engaging enough, I'm more interested in staring at Aubrey.

"Why are you watching me?" she asks without turning her head.

"Because you're pretty." I cup her jaw, turning her head my way.

"You know that, right?"

Her lashes flutter and she won't meet my eyes. "I guess so."

"Aubrey."

"I don't feel compelled to wear a bag over my head or anything—"

Demonstrations have always worked better for me than words, so I cut her off with a kiss. She falls right into it, reaching up to stroke my face. "You're the sexy one," she murmurs against my mouth.

I'm breathing hard when I pull away, touching my forehead to hers.

"Yes," she continues, running her fingers under the edge of my T-shirt. "That shirt you wore today was *really* sexy. I felt a little guilty for wanting to pop all the buttons loose and maul you at the fair."

I like this bolder-says-what's-on-her-mind version of Aubrey. A lot. "Tell me more."

She swoops in, kissing along my jaw. "I would've like to ride the Ferris Wheel and do some over-the-pants stuff while we—"

My mouth crashing into hers cuts off the rest of her sentence. We tangle together under the blanket and I shove my hand down her yoga pants, slipping into her underwear.

"Sully," she whispers against my lips. "What are you doing?"

"*Shhh.*"

"Madison's right—"

"That's why the…*shhh.*" I pick my head up and stare down the hall. "We'll hear her stirring. Trust me."

She lets out a soft whispery laugh and kisses my chin.

Even though she said she was cold earlier, her skin burns hot under my roaming fingers. Silky and warm. I slip my hand between her thighs, teasing and playing with her.

"Sully," she gasps as I thrust two fingers inside her. Her eyes close, head falling against the back of the couch, leaving her neck vulnerable to my mouth.

"Can you come nice and quiet for me?" I whisper in her ear.

"Not…if you…not if you keep doing *that.*"

I grin. "Doing what?" I push in a little deeper, curling my fingers to graze over her G-spot over and over. "What am I doing, Aubrey?"

Her head rolls from side to side, but she can't seem to find any words. Twisting my wrist, I grind the heel of my hand against her clit.

Her mouth forms this perfect O and she sputters. "Oh, shit. That's good. Right there."

"Quiet, remember?"

In response, she reaches down and grabs my cock. Even through my jeans, her touch burns and without thinking, my hips jerk.

I push my fingers into her again, rubbing and grinding. On a mission to make her breath catch and her eyes roll back in her head. Her thighs tremble and her other hand clutches my shirt. Her back arches and her entire body jerks against me.

"That's it." The agony and joy on her face has me grinning like an idiot. Her orgasm is long and steady. Her whimpers faint.

After a minute I withdraw my hand from her pants and she blinks. Big brown eyes stare up at me, soft and hazy. "You're dangerous," she whispers.

Down the hall, Maddy's door opens, reminding me we're absolutely not alone. "Give me a second." I press a quick kiss to her cheek before hurrying in the kitchen to wash up and calm down.

Aubrey's still alone in the living room when I return. She scans me head to toe, stopping on my crotch. Her mouth quirks. "Come here."

"Did she go back in her room?"

"I think she's in the bathroom."

I sit next to her and she tosses half the blanket over my lap. "Thank you," she whispers against my ear. "Next time's all about *you*."

"I plan to collect."

The bathroom door opens and a few seconds later, Maddy pads into the living room. "I'm hungry," she announces.

"Do you feel better?" I ask.

Instead of getting pissed like before, this time she just looks tired. Her gaze strays to Aubrey. "Yeah. Thanks."

Her eyes narrow at how close Aubrey and I are on the couch and I brace myself for another meltdown.

Aubrey flips the blanket off her lap and moves over, patting the space between us. "Come. Sit."

To my surprise, she snuggles up to Aubrey. I think Aubrey's shocked too because it takes her a second to adjust and slip an arm around Maddy.

"I wrapped your steak up. You want to eat it out here and watch your movie?" I ask.

She turns and stares at me for a few seconds, fingers tapping against her leg. "Are you going to make fun of Jareth again?"

I raise my right hand. "Nope. I swear there will be no King Tight-pants jokes."

"*Daaaad.*" Finally, she cracks a smile.

"Okay. No *more* jokes."

"Can I have steak and eggs?" She wrinkles her nose. "Instead of whatever vegetables you probably made?"

"Sure."

She follows me out to the kitchen and leans her hip against the counter, watching me pull items from the fridge.

"I talked to your mom."

She rolls her eyes and crosses her arms over her chest. At first, it looks like a defensive posture. Until I notice her bottom lip quivering. "Did you tell her I went all hormonal teenager on you?"

Shit. My plan was to tell her about Thanksgiving, not have her think I called her mom to complain about her.

"No. Not at all. I did have some questions for her, though." I see no point in lying about it.

Maddy rolls her eyes. "Did she tell you I'm dramatic and complain too much?"

"Uh, not exactly."

"Yeah right," she grumbles. There's the bottom lip wobble again. And now her eyes shine too.

"Come here." I pull her in for a hug and at first, she's resistant, but finally, she relents and hugs me back just as tight. "I love you no matter what, Maddy. You know that, right?"

She slides her cheek against my shirt, in what I think is a yes.

"Your mom loves you too—"

"No, she doesn't."

"Madison. You know that's not true."

A strangled sob comes out of her and I keep rocking her back and forth. A lot like what I used to when she was little and hurt herself.

"I know you're going through a lot of changes—"

"Please, not the *changes* speech."

"But," I continue, ignoring that. "You can always talk to me."

"Fine," she says, louder this time. "I hate this and don't want any of it. It sucks."

Yes, yes it does.

"And," she continues, really on a roll now. "I'm the first one in my class who got it. Mom sent me with a pad in my pocket one day. And I was so scared it would fall out that I kept touching it to check it was there. So my teacher thought I had a *bomb* or something on me and made me hand over what was in my pocket. She kept badgering me in front of everyone. So I slapped the pad in her hand and everyone saw it and made fun of me for like a week!"

Well. That was a lot to absorb.

How bad do I want to fly to Florida right now and have a chat with this teacher for embarrassing Maddy like that?

"That does suck. I'm sorry, Maddy."

"Mom went and yelled at Mrs. Smith. I'm so happy I don't have to see her at school anymore."

"That's good."

"Mom keeps lecturing me about babies and staying away from boys so I don't get pregnant while I'm in high school like she did."

Ouch. That's an uncomfortable topic.

I've spent a lot of time being pissed at Lauren for not telling me she was pregnant. But listening to Maddy now, I get a small glimpse of how Lauren probably felt. Alone and afraid. I would've helped her, but I was still a kid myself and she was so far away.

I hug Maddy a little tighter.

When she quiets, I glance down at her red, tear-streaked face and silently lead her to the sink to wash her face.

"Better?"

She sniffle-hiccups.

"Still hungry?"

"Yes." Her gaze slides to the freezer. "Aubrey said there was ice cream."

"After dinner."

A dramatic sigh accompanies her eye-roll. "Fine."

"Your mom and I talked about Thanksgiving," I try again.

"Ugh. I don't wanna go skiing—"

"Right. You're going to come here instead."

"Really?" she asks with a note of caution in her voice. Again she sniffles. "But doesn't that mean I won't get to come for Christmas again?"

"No. You'll still come for Christmas."

Finally, something makes her smile. She bounces and clasps her hands like she's praying. "Please, please let it snow this year!"

"I thought you didn't like snow?"

"I love snow. Doesn't mean I want to slide down a mountain of it with nothing between my butt and the ground except some skinny sticks strapped to my feet."

I chuckle at her description.

"I want to build a snowman, roll around in the snow for a few minutes, then come inside and drink hot chocolate."

Now I'm laughing even harder. "I'll do my best to make that happen."

Aubrey

"OH, NO SARAH! Don't do it. One mistake's gonna lead you on a journey of suffering and confusion!" Maddy shouts at the television, giggling through every word.

Sully peers at me over her head and smiles as if he can't believe he got roped into watching this movie again, but there's nowhere else he'd rather be.

After the movie, Madison sits up and stretches. "Are you staying over, Aubrey?" She glances at her dad. "I'm not a dumb kid. You can stay here if you want. You don't have to go home because of me."

I chuckle and sit up, grabbing my shoes. "You're definitely not dumb. But no, I have to return Celia's car so she can get to work in the morning."

"Oh."

"Do you need a ride in the morning?" Sully asks.

"No, I'll walk. I have my shift at Busy Beans in the afternoon too."

"Ooo…Dad can we visit Aubrey? I want one of those mocha frappe thingies."

"I don't think we want to bug Aubrey at work."

"No, it's fine," I say, unsure of whether I should contradict him. Maybe he has something else he'd rather do with Maddy before sending her home. "Sunday afternoons are pretty slow if you want to stop in after the gym closes."

Sully stands and walks into the kitchen.

"Her flight's at eight," he calls out. "We can stop by on the way."

"I'm done at six."

"Oh! Will you come to the airport with us?" Madison asks.

Whoa. Why is Sully in the kitchen when I need him here? I want to say yes. But what if he prefers to say goodbye to his daughter without me intruding? "Sure," I answer cautiously. "If you want me to."

A grin lights up her face before she turns more serious, lowering her voice. "I hate leaving him and saying goodbye. But if you're there, then he won't be alone after I go."

Oh my God. Has a sweeter sentiment ever been uttered?

Spending time with Madison has been one big roller coaster of emotions this weekend. But somehow this sweet, sensitive, firecracker of a kid has totally stolen my heart.

Just like her dad.

CHAPTER TWENTY-NINE

Aubrey

B USY BEANS WAS in the middle of a mad rush for pumpkin lattes when I started my shift. Thankfully, it's calmed down, so I have time to catch up on some of the cleaning.

"Hello, Aubrey."

Time stops. The air in my lungs freezes.

That voice.

It shouldn't be invading my space. It should be locked up with the psycho who owns it.

My heart stutters when I look up into his bold blue eyes. Once I'd thought they were beautiful and I couldn't believe how lucky I was to have them trained on me.

But now I know better.

He snuck into my life and my heart when I was too young to resist him. Too inexperienced to understand the warning signs. I'm not an insecure, love-starved fifteen-year-old teenager. Not anymore.

I steel my spine and will my voice not to betray my fear. "What are you doing here?"

He lifts his shoulders and glances around at the cafe. His gaze returns to me, sweeping over my apron.

"I'm here to see you," he says as if it makes perfect sense.

My heart drums a terrified, erratic beat. This shouldn't be happening. He shouldn't be here. I shouldn't have this reaction to him. Not now. Not after everything I've struggled through to get to this point in my life.

I concentrate on calming my ragged breathing. He holds no power over me. Not anymore.

"You're not supposed to be here." I wish my voice held more strength. But at least it didn't crack.

"Where else would I go, Aubrey? I've missed you."

"You're crazy. You have to go." My voice takes on a harder edge.

He stares at me as if he didn't hear a word. His gaze flicks to the pastries and back to me. "I don't think working here is good for you, darling. You've gained a lot of weight."

Oh hell fucking no, he didn't.

Planting my hands on the counter, I lean over. "Maybe that's because I'm a woman now and not a kid you can take advantage of."

"Take advantage?" He smirks. "That's rich."

My cheeks heat up with every memory of the way fifteen-year-old me once loved the attention of this man.

And the way he reeled me in over and over, taking what he wanted and leaving me in pieces.

At least now, I have the mental fortitude to resist. And thanks to Sully's training, I'm not as afraid as I once was. I may be small, but I can pack a swift kick.

"You look like shit," I say with a smile. "I'm guessing prison didn't afford you a lot of outside time."

A cold smile spreads across his face and he leans in close enough that his breath slips over my skin like poisonous vapor. "I'm going to enjoy wiping that insolence of your face. With my cock."

He reaches out to twirl a piece of my hair around his finger. "You'll like that."

Yanking my hair out of his hold, I pull away and cross my arms over my chest. "Never. Going. To. Happen."

His jaw ticks and he taps his fingers against the counter.

Pure hatred flares in his eyes. "Four years, Aubrey," he seethes. "Almost two years in jail waiting for trial before I took the plea."

"Still not long enough."

"What happened to the girl who refused to testify against me?"

"She grew up."

Again, he continues as if he didn't hear me, leaning in and lowering his voice to a seductive tease. "Thank God you *didn't* testify. My lawyer said that's the reason I skated on the statutory rape charge."

Shame and anger blaze over my skin. My parents refused to allow me to testify. They were too busy shipping me off to a mental hospital.

My punishment for embarrassing them.

"You have no idea what I went through after you lost your damn mind." My harshly whispered words force him to retreat.

"Your parents tried to keep us apart. I love you. What was I supposed to do?"

"Not be a psycho? Stay away from me in the first place? Abide by a code of ethics?"

The condescending head shake I remember so well makes an appearance. "Aubrey. We have so much time to make up for. Let's not spend it arguing."

Once his manipulative tone and obvious disappointment with me would have had me scrambling to do whatever he wanted.

Not anymore.

He glances at the clock behind me. "What time are you done? We'll go to dinner and talk this out."

"No."

He raises an eyebrow. "No?"

"I'm here until closing." Why am I making up excuses? No is a complete sentence for fuck's sake!

He turns, taking a second to read the hours on the front door. "I'll be back at nine."

After that announcement, he pivots and walks out the door.

I stand there in a trance, unable to process what just happened.

Being with Sully has made me forget all the mistakes I collected as a teenager.

But now the biggest mistake of my life has returned to collect *me*. Cold nauseating fear thrums in my veins. Even though I won't be here when he shows up tonight, I know this won't be the last I see of Darren.

I glance around, embarrassed anyone could've overheard us. But it's slow now. My manager is outside on a smoke break and the only two customers in the place are wearing earbuds while they bang away at their laptops.

More than that, I want to call the cops. Call *someone*. I can't believe no one warned me he was being released. I thought he was supposed to stay away from me. Maybe I should've read the paperwork a little closer.

The bell over the door chimes again and this time I pick up the phone under the counter. Fuck this, he does *not* get to harass me at work.

But it's Sully and Madison. I've never been so happy to see two people in my life.

Shame washes over me. In no way do I want a ghost from my past haunting my present. Or intruding on the future Sully and I might have together.

The urge to spill it all to him rises in me, but I don't even know where to start.

Brantley returns from his smoke break, reeking of peppermint and nicotine. He nods to Sully. "Don't see you in here often."

"I'm here to steal Aubrey away."

Brantley chuckles. "She's mine for another fifteen minutes."

As Sully orders for both of them, my heart rate finally returns to normal. "She decided on the way over a strawberry frappe would be better," he says. "Make it quick before she changes her mind."

Chuckling, I hand the order to Brantley and pull a slice of lemon cake out of the case. "This will go well with it."

I can't help scanning the big, plate glass window at the front of the shop. The last thing I need is Sully running into the biggest mistake of my life. And I sure don't want to expose Madison to him.

When Brantley realizes Sully's sticking around, he releases me early. We're almost outside when Madison decides to run back to the bathroom.

Alone on the sidewalk together, Sully takes my hands and leans down to kiss me. "Missed you today," he murmurs just loud enough to hear over the rustling trees and hum of the occasional car driving by.

This is what I need. This man. He's already erased the awful feelings that came over me from seeing Darren. All the crap I survived must have been worth it because it brought me here to Sully. I won't allow my past to ruin us. "Missed you too. How was your day?"

"A lot calmer than yesterday." He breathes out a sigh of relief. "We talked a lot."

Madison bursts out of the coffee shop. "It must be so much fun to work there. I can't wait until I'm old enough to get a job."

I can't help laughing. "I'm pretty confident you'll feel differently in a few years."

"Maybe," she concedes.

Maddy's upbeat on the way to the airport, excitedly mentioning all the things she wants to do in two weeks when she comes back. Sully smiles the whole way.

The painful memories and bad feelings stirred up earlier settle down, leaving behind only a tiny, nagging trace of dread.

CHAPTER THIRTY
SULLY

"THANK YOU FOR coming with me," I say once Madison's plane takes off.

"How could I say no after she was so sweet to ask me to join you guys?"

"Well, I didn't want to mess you up with work."

"You didn't. And it would be worth it anyway."

I take her hand and for the first time don't feel completely hollowed out as I leave the airport.

"Have you ever watched the planes?" I ask.

She frowns. "You mean as they take off?"

"Yeah." I point toward the exit to the parking lot. "There's a viewing area at the end of the runway. You can watch them take off right overhead."

"Okay, let's check it out."

Maddy's plane is long gone by this point, but we pull in anyway. We're not alone. The short, wide gravel area has cars lined up along the fence. Lots of spotters have cameras ready to snap photos of the planes taxiing down the runway and lifting into the air.

We find a spot and I boost Aubrey onto the hood of the Jeep so she can watch without the fence blocking everything.

Although loud, it's also surprisingly peaceful watching a few of the planes take off against the night sky.

After a smaller jet flies over us, I turn and find Aubrey watching me.

"Ready to go?"

"Sure."

I help her down but don't let go of her right away.

"Spend the night at my place?" I ask.

Her full lips twitch. "I thought you'd never ask." She rests her hand on my shoulder and leans up to whisper in my ear. "I'm pretty sure I owe you some favors."

"That's not why I asked, but I'll happily accept any favors you're giving out." Not to mention, the second the words left her lips my cock stood up and saluted.

She keeps up the sweet torment all the way to my house. We barely make it in the front door before I'm stripping off her shirt and yanking down her pants. "You smell like coffee and butter," I rasp, dragging my tongue against her neck. "Taste like sugar."

"Mmm…" She makes the sexiest noises in response to every kiss and lick.

We make our way over to the couch and she gives me a gentle shove.

"My turn to do the tasting," she whispers, dropping to her knees in front of me.

Brown eyes blaze up at me with intense need. Every muscle in my body tightens with anticipation.

I lean forward and trace my finger over her plump bottom lip. "I dream about your sexy lips wrapped around my cock a lot."

Her lips part and she sucks my finger into her mouth, snapping my last bit of control. "Need your mouth somewhere else on me, Aubrey," I growl.

That kicks her into action. She works my zipper open. Like the gentleman I am, I help her out by lifting my ass and shoving my jeans and briefs down. She takes over, fully stripping them off.

More playful teasing while she flicks her tongue over the head of my cock, leaving me close to begging for more.

"You're killing me."

Her eyes widen as if she has no idea that I'm dying here. Dying to work my cock between her soft, wet lips.

Finally, she slides her mouth over my cock. I hiss from the pleasure. The wet heat of her mouth. The softness of her tongue as she swirls it around the tip.

Powerless to do much, my head falls back against the couch and I groan. "That's good. So good. Don't stop."

She wraps her hands around my shaft, working them up and down in time with her hot mouth. Each time trying to take more of me than before. I grunt and thrust up, catching her by surprise.

She squeaks but doesn't let up on my dick. Every zip of pleasure I react to makes her moan. As if she's enjoying it as much as I am.

"Jesus." So good. For a second, I open my eyes. She's watching me, assessing what I like. What makes me groan the loudest. This isn't going to last very long.

As if she knows the fuzzy thoughts floating in my brain, she sucks harder. Moves faster. Hums. Encourages me to blow.

"Ah, fuck!" My eyes pop open and my hand settles on the back of her head. Pleasure blasts down my spine. My body turns to stone, every muscle tight. A guttural groan is the only warning before I empty down her throat.

Even then she doesn't let up. My hands tangle in her hair, my hips thrust as she keeps wringing every drop from me.

Breath stuttering. Heart pounding.

Done.

I fall back on the couch and try to remember my own name.

"Aubrey," I rasp, opening one eye.

She blinks and wipes her thumb against her bottom lip. The corners of her mouth curl up in satisfaction.

Every molecule in my body protests moving from this spot. My limbs refuse to cooperate, and my brain struggles to find words.

"Bedroom."

She nods in false sympathy. "You need a nap?"

That snaps me out of the-best-blowjob-of-my-life fog. "Nap?" I sit up. "You think I need a nap?"

A burst of energy flares inside of me and I scoop her off the floor, carrying her to my bedroom.

Inside, I flick the light on and she squints.

"The big, glaring light isn't all that romantic," she says.

"Maybe. But I want to see every inch of you."

"You've already seen every inch of me."

"I know." I kiss her cheek. "That's why I want to see you again." I kiss her other cheek, "And again." I keep alternating words and kisses until she's laughing so hard she almost falls out of my arms.

I set her on the bed and she kneels in the middle.

"Take your bra off."

She hooks her thumb in the strap, sliding it off her shoulder and then back. "This bra?"

"Do *not* play with me, woman," I growl and dive for her, closing my teeth over one nipple hidden by sheer black fabric.

She arches her back and I palm her other breast. "Take it off."

"I can't."

"Sit up."

To do that, she needs me to get off her. Reluctantly I roll to the side and watch her struggle to unhook her bra. She flings it across the room and I help myself to her bare breasts.

"Don't tell me you can't work a bra," she teases.

"I prefer you here and fully present in the moment with me."

Her teasing expression softens and she strokes the back of her hand against my cheek. "Believe me, there's nowhere else I'd rather be."

She opens her mouth again as if she has more to say, but I cover it with my own, kissing her hard. I pull back, resting my forehead against hers, staring into her eyes. "I love you."

Her breath catches and for a second, my heart stops. That feeling has been bubbling up inside me for a while, but I hadn't meant to voice it right now. I pictured something a little more romantic.

"I love you too," she breathes, pulling me down for another kiss.

"I'm also starving for you."

She laughs at first, but the laughter turns to gasps and sighs as I kiss my way down her body. Dragging my fingers over her smooth skin, I stop to lick and taste her along the way.

I lift her hips to pull her underwear down, tossing them on the floor.

There's no hesitation from her this time, she opens her legs for me and I reward her with a long, slow lick. "That's my girl." I don't have the willpower to take my mouth off her, so my words are muffled. She rakes her fingers through my hair and presses her hips up.

"Good." God, I love her all sweet and eager.

I use my thumbs to spread her wide, exposing her. Never mind the spectacular blowjob that should've left me spent for the night, I'm so hard it hurts.

She's wild and squirmy tonight. I have to wrap my arms around her thighs to keep her still.

"Oh, God. Oh, fuck. Sully, I can't."

"Yes, you can." In fact, the way her leg muscles tighten and she shoves herself against my face, I'd say she's damn close.

Thank God, because I'm on fire with the need to fuck her.

I flick my tongue over her swollen clit faster and faster until she just snaps. She gasps and stutters my name, her whole body trembling through her release.

Perfect.

Exactly what I needed. Her wet, satisfied, and ready for more.

Aubrey

I HAVEN'T EVEN caught my breath before Sully's over top of me, cock nudging against me, slipping in the evidence of how much pleasure he gives me and how much more I want.

All my senses are heightened, and I've never felt more alive. Heart racing, sweat rolling over my skin, impatient for him to be inside me.

"Hurry."

He half-smiles and grabs a condom from the nightstand. Using one arm, he tries to shift our bodies toward the headboard.

"Work with me, Aubrey," he grunts.

Even as I'm dying to have him inside me, I giggle at his frustration. "What are you doing?"

He gives up trying to move us and reaches down, positioning himself.

Dark, simmering eyes stare down at me. "I need to be inside you so bad, I'm afraid I'll fuck you right off the bed."

I'd laugh, except he's too intense to be joking.

"Hang on," he grits out as he pushes inside me.

My hands grip his biceps, hard as stone from holding himself back.

"Give it to me," I pant.

He's hot, hard, and solid everywhere.

Another long thrust hits a sensitive spot and I moan, lifting my hips to get more of that sensation.

"Like that?" He grins and does it again. And again.

I'm trembling. On the verge of climax when I hear something that sounds an awful lot like a door closing.

Not the bedroom door.

Farther away.

"Sully," I whisper.

"Right here, babe."

"No!" I thump his chest with my hand. "I think someone's in the house."

He stops and cocks his head to the side.

Rigid and completely still, we both listen for another sound.

Unfortunately, my nether-regions have their own agenda and tighten around him.

He groans and closes his eyes. "I can't concentrate if you do that."

"Sullivan?" someone calls out.

He curses and leaves my body so abruptly I have trouble processing what happened.

"Sullivan, are you home?"

"Oh, shit," I mutter, recognizing the voice.

"Yeah," he calls out, yanking on a pair of shorts and quickly tying them.

For some idiotic reason, I scamper under the covers and pull them up over my head.

How much did Mrs. Wallace overhear? I'll never be able to look her in the face again.

SULLY

"MA? WHAT ARE you doing?" I ask as I close the bedroom door.

She whirls around. "There you are! I wanted to let you know I was home. You didn't answer..." Her voice trails off and she stops mid-step. Her shrewd gaze sweeps over me.

I'm sure my hair's sticking up in every direction. If that doesn't clue her in, my sweaty, bare torso and hastily thrown on gym shorts should do the trick.

Her gaze drops to the floor where Aubrey and I left a trail of clothes from the front door to the couch.

She covers her mouth with her hand. "Is Aubrey? Did I? Were you?" Her voice rises in pitch with each half-question.

It's been a while since my mother was tongue-tied. But the moment is way too awkward to fully enjoy.

Her cheeks flame red. "I'm so, so sorry. Forget I was here," she says, backing toward the door.

Unlikely.

"I'm glad you're home safe. We'll talk in the morning," I say.

"Okay. Tell Aubrey I'm sorry."

She slams the door behind her and I wait a few seconds before hurrying over to engage the chain lock. Never bothered to use that before, but I sure as fuck will from now on.

Not that I think Mom will ever stop by unannounced ever again.

Aubrey's still hiding under the covers when I return to my bedroom. I close—and lock—the bedroom door behind me.

"You can come out now." I'd laugh, but the mother—ha!—of all blue balls weighs me down as I approach the bed.

"I'll never be able to be in the same room as your mom again." Her voice is muffled from under the covers, but her mortification is clear.

"If it makes you feel better, I think she was just as embarrassed."

Aubrey pokes her head from underneath the blankets. "That doesn't make me feel any better. I actually like your mom and now she's going to think—"

"That you make her son very happy. Trust me, that's all she's worried about." I grin. "And more grandbabies, because she's definitely worried about that."

The look of pure horror on Aubrey's face makes me think maybe I should've kept that last one to myself. But then she laughs it off. "You'll have to be the one to break it to her then. I don't think my lady parts will ever work right again."

"Sounds like a challenge to me." I rub my palms together to show her how eager I am.

She opens her mouth to say something and I place my finger over her lips. "We can talk about it later." I point to my almost-ready-for-action-again dick. "I'm in actual pain here."

She snorts, then bursts into full-blown giggles. "Oh, dear. We can't have that." She reaches for the waistband of my shorts and tugs. "I think it's imperative we finish. Otherwise, we might not ever be able to do it again," she says in a grave tone.

"Laugh all you want, but it's probably true."

She snickers and tugs at my shorts. "I bet with minimal effort, you can have me hot and bothered again."

I slide the shorts down my legs and her eyes widen. She tosses the sheets back and sits up, reaching for my cock. "Yup, that should do the trick," she says, licking her lips. My eyes squeeze shut as she works her hand up and down my shaft.

"Harder," I urge, placing my hand over hers. Her thumb grazes the sensitive spot underneath and I hiss with pleasure. "Don't stop."

I reach over for another condom. Opening my eyes to rip it open, I find her watching me.

"You okay?" I ask, feeling like a dick. Instead of worrying about my hard-on, which let's face it, it was going to return the second I got a glimpse of Aubrey's naked body, I should've focused on working her up again.

I'm not at all prepared for what comes out of her mouth.

"I'm on the pill."

My dick is all "'Yes, please!'" while my brain is like, "'Fuck no. Last time you believed a chick and went in commando resulted in a daughter you didn't get to see for the first four years of her life.'"

Trust issues much?

"I don't mind," I say.

Her cheeks turn pink. Knowing Aubrey, that probably took a lot of courage.

Fuck.

She waves her hand in the air as if she's trying to dismiss whatever just happened.

"Another time."

Even though my dick is *not* pleased about being smothered in latex after Aubrey's offer, I'm harder than a motherfucker.

I grab her hips and haul her to the edge of the bed. "Wrap your legs around me."

She hooks her feet together, heels resting above my ass and pulls me closer.

"Not so fast." I tease her entrance with the head of my cock until she's squirming under me.

"Sully," she pleads.

I push inside. Slow this time, watching the pleasure flickering over her face. She arches her back and her lips part.

"Ohh. Right there."

I lick my thumb and place it over her clit, rubbing in the fast, tight circles I've discovered she really likes.

She gasps, and I keep going. Slow and steady. Pulling almost all the way out before pushing in deep.

She reaches out to me and I take her hands. "Like that?"

"Yes," she whispers.

"You're going to come for me, right?"

"Yes."

"Good." I thrust in deeper. Faster. Keep rubbing and thrusting.

Her heels dig into the small of my back and I fall down over her, gathering her in my arms.

She trembles. Writhes under me. So close, but not quite there.

Then she breaks with a sweet cry of relief. I bury my face against her neck, grinding into her harder and faster until I let go. Squeezing my eyes shut as the orgasm overtakes me.

As I keep pumping into her, I wish I'd taken her up on the no condom offer. All sorts of images run through my head. Coming inside her. Filling her. It's something primal. Mating instinct? I don't fucking know. I want all of it though. Want all of her.

Mine.

I touch my lips to her forehead, trying to orient myself. Catch my breath.

Regain my sanity.

CHAPTER THIRTY-ONE
SULLY

WAKE WITH Aubrey snuggled up against my back. The warm weight of her feels so right next to me.

As smoothly as possible, I turn, watching her for a few minutes.

She blinks and smiles when she sees me. "Morning."

"Move in with me," I say.

She raises her eyebrows.

"I miss you when you're not here and I love waking up next to you."

"Wow," she whispers. "That's some good morning."

"I'm serious." I brush a few stray strands of hair off her face. "Move in with me."

She sits up, pressing the sheet against her breasts. "I don't know. Your family has a knack for walking in when we're in delicate situations."

She's teasing me. I sit up and kiss her shoulder.

"I'll buy better locks. And a Do Not Disturb sign."

She turns, but there's no hint of teasing. "What about Madison? Won't that be weird for her? Will it screw up your custody arrangement?"

I don't get the sense she's trying to dodge my question. More like she's genuinely worried about these things.

And it makes me love her even more.

"Let me worry about that stuff."

"Okay."

"Okay, you'll move in?"

Her lashes flutter and a smile flickers over her lips. "Yes." She hesitates. "Just give me a little time to break it to my sister."

"Whenever you're ready."

She turns over and I draw her into my arms. At first just to hold her, but other parts of my anatomy have different ideas.

I kiss her shoulder blade and up to her neck, moving her hair so I can kiss behind her ear. Not so subtly, I rub my morning wood against her ass. "Did you offer up something last night?"

"Such as?" A cautious note colors her question.

I decide not to fuck around and go right for the important information. I trust her not to lie to me. "I haven't been with anyone but you since my last physical."

"Oh," she whispers. "Me either."

Reaching down, I hook my arm under her knee, lifting her leg. "Arch your back."

My other arm snakes under her body, cupping her breast and anchoring her to me. Molding myself to her, I continue nibbling on her neck. My cock nudges her entrance and she presses back even more, inviting me to drive in. I stop, overcome with how fucking amazing she feels bare.

"Fuck," I groan against her shoulder, grazing my teeth over her smooth skin.

She wiggles and I lift her leg higher for a better angle.

One of her hands reaches back, gripping my arm. "Fuck. That feels. That feels amazing," she whispers.

No sounds except us. So hot. Like we're melting into each other. She leans back, and I nuzzle her, leaving faint abrasions from my rough morning stubble on her skin.

I'm not sure how long we're like that—half cuddling, half fucking—until she shudders against me. I push her over on her stomach and stuff a pillow under her hips. She arches her back, granting me access to push back inside. My hands fit into the curve of her waist, holding her in place while I pound into her with unrelenting strokes. Under me, she bucks, moans, and encourages me with dirty words.

"Oh." She claws at the pillows, grasping and pulling them toward her. "Oh." Her moans go on and on, triggering my release. I hold myself up, tense as I empty everything I have into her.

When I'm finished and can see again, I kiss my way up her spine. "I want to wake up with you like this every day," I whisper.

She turns, watching me over her shoulder. "Sounds good to me."

Pulling out, I tap her ass once, then again because it feels so good. "Love your ass," I mumble.

She glances back. "I can't get rid of it no matter what I do, so I guess that's good for me."

Shaking my head, I sit next to her on the bed, rubbing my hand over her back and ass. "You have any idea how many times in class I had to stop myself from grabbing this hot ass? Don't you dare try to get rid of it." This time, I grab a handful and she squeals, laughing and slapping my hand away.

"Mine," I growl before planting a kiss on her cheek.

"You're full of it."

Wow, she seriously questions herself. Something I've noticed since I met her. Not the usual fishing-for-compliments insecurity some girls display. Something much deeper than that.

I rub my finger over her cheek. "I don't lie, Aubrey."

"But you didn't want anything to do with me."

"That's not true at all."

She raises an eyebrow, challenging me to explain. I sigh and trace my fingers down the line of her spine, trying to decide how much I'm willing to share.

Aubrey

I MAY HAVE reached a new level of pathetic and needy. The man told me he loves me last night. Asked me to move in with him this morning. Gave me one of the most intense orgasms of my life—in fact, I'm still quivering from it, which is why I haven't found the strength to move yet.

But seeing Darren yesterday messed with my head. I might have shoved the encounter out of my mind for a few hours last night, but his words won't stop echoing. And, oh, how I hate letting that particular ghost haunt me when I'm with Sully.

He seems so torn and I'm almost afraid to hear what he has to say. The soothing way he keeps stroking his hands over my back seems to help.

"It's not because I wasn't attracted to you," he explains. At first, his voice seems tentative as if he doesn't want to reveal too much, but then he shakes his head and continues. "I wasn't using not getting involved with clients as an excuse. I meant it. This is a small community with a lot of big mouths. You know all those free classes I do at the shelter and the Y? They're not gonna let me do that if I gain a reputation as some sleaze who hits on all the students."

I turn over and sit up, dragging the sheet over me. "Why do you do so many of those free classes?" I admire him for it, especially since it comes at the cost of not growing his business in ways that will earn him more money. His dedication stems from something deep that I want to understand.

His stepfather. Sully already gave me the answer the other day. I just didn't hear him.

"Did your stepfather hit your mom?"

He runs his hand over the back of his neck and looks away. "Yes."

"Her injury. Her eye. Did he do that?"

His jaw locks tight and he nods.

I reach out, run my hand over his arm and twine my fingers with his. "I'm sorry."

"It's a long time ago." He seems to shake himself out of the memory. "He ended up dead. I went into juvenile detention."

"Jesus. Why? For protecting your mother?"

He shrugs. "A man was dead." He snorts. "The 'Castle' where they hold the fights? That used to be a Juvenile Detention center. One of the more vicious ones. It got shut down when the feds investigated and found out just how many broken bones and teeth were caused by the so-called youth counselors."

"Oh my God. No wonder you wanted to stay away," I whisper, feeling awful that I made him go there when it probably brought up a lot of bad memories for him.

"That's not the main reason. To Griff and Remy it's their way of flipping off the system. But yeah, I'd rather not be reminded of my stay there. Although it is where I took up an interest in martial arts."

"How old were you?"

"Around eleven." He lets out a humorless laugh and turns his head. "A guard there offered to 'train' me. It was really more of an excuse to kick my ass."

"But you were so young."

"Youngest one there for a while." He forces a bitter smile. "Everyone knew I was there for killing my stepfather. People tended to steer clear of me."

"I'm sorry."

"It feels like a lifetime ago." He closes his eyes. "I didn't *want* to be defined by that one thing for the rest of my life. The counselors used to say it was a warm-up of what the rest of our lives would be like—in and out of prison. It drove me to prove them wrong. It's why I get so pissed with Jake—"

"Because the fighting could get him in trouble?"

"That and...other stuff, but yeah."

I understand exactly what he means by not wanting to have your whole life determined by one bad incident. It's why I've lived the last few years trying to escape and bury my own painful past. Hiding it from anyone in my "new" life.

Now that Darren's resurfaced, I might not be able to hide any longer.

"Sully?"

"Too much too soon?"

"No. Not at all. Thank you for trusting me." Now it's my turn. "I—"

His phone rings and I snap my mouth shut.

"Hey, Maddy," he answers. A genuine smile lights him up.

Her voice is loud enough to hear her excitement but not the actual words. While Sully talks to her, I get up and run to the bathroom, clean up, and throw on a T-shirt.

He's dressed but still on the phone when I emerge. "Okay. Yup. Heading out in a few. Talk to you later. Love you too."

He's grinning when he ends the call. "School was closed today. She's pissed she didn't know about it sooner so she could've stayed an extra day."

"Aw. What happened?"

"I don't know. Sinkhole? Water main break? Something like that. She wasn't very specific."

The lingering happiness from talking to his daughter still surrounds him. I don't want to ruin it by finishing our conversation. Or maybe I'm just a coward. Either way, he doesn't mention it and I let it go.

I can always warn him about my past later, right?

CHAPTER THIRTY-TWO
SULLY

Before starting breakfast, I slip on a T-shirt and a pair of sweats and jog next door. I knock loud enough to rattle the little glass panes in the door.

My mother opens it and scowls at me. "Really? Is that your way of hinting I should knock next time?"

My lips curl into a half-smile. "No, not at all."

She shakes her head and lets me in. "Everything okay?"

"Yeah, I just wanted to see how your trip was."

"Fun, but I can tell you about it later." She glances at the kitchen clock. "You're usually on your way to the gym by now."

"I know."

"How was Madison? I'm so upset I missed her."

"She was…a trip. I'll have to explain later. But she and Aubrey seemed to get along well. Maddy seems to like her."

"Oh." Her mouth curves into a soft smile. "That's good. I was worried she'd be a bit prickly about it."

"Well…"

She laughs and pushes me toward the door. "You can tell me later."

"I asked Aubrey to move in with me."

That stops her in her tracks. "You did? That seems fast."

Her reaction surprises me. The woman has been hinting that I needed to "settle down" for years now. "I thought you liked her?"

"I do." She tilts her head and runs her hand over my hair. "I'm never going to stop worrying about you, though."

Since I understand the sentiment, I don't give her any grief.

She cocks an eyebrow, hopeful expression playing over her face. "Does she want more kids?"

"Jesus, Mom. Would you stop with the grandbabies?"

"I'll take that as an 'I don't know.'"

"Her *first* concern was whether moving in with me would upset Madison. My already-existing daughter." I shake my head. "She's really sensitive to Maddy's feelings."

"That *is* important. But what about your needs?"

"We have enough chemistry to blow up a building."

She frowns. "That's not what I meant. Get to know her more…and not in the biblical way."

"I know the things that matter. She's smart. She's supportive—I can't tell you all the stuff she's done to help me grow the gym. She treats me well. She treats my daughter well. Christ, she even likes Jake. What else is there?"

I don't want to admit it, but her comment bothers me. There's a grain of truth in it. Aubrey can be very-tight lipped when it comes to talking about her family or past. But bits and pieces slip out here and there. I figure that will continue the longer we're together.

"What's her family like?"

"I don't think she's close to her parents at all. They sound like assholes. But you saw how tight she and her sister are." I cock my head. "Do you really think I should judge anyone based on their family ties?" That came out more dickish than I meant and my mother flinches. "I'm sorry. I didn't mean it that way."

Instead of kicking me out—like she should after that remark—she hugs me. "I'm sorry. The news took me by surprise. If you're happy, I'm happy for you."

"Thank you."

"I'm not apologizing for wanting more grandchildren though."

I shake with laughter as I pull away. "Wouldn't expect you to."

She reaches up to ruffle my hair again. "She's a pretty girl. You'll make beautiful babies."

"Oh, for God's sake."

"Since you're still here, how was Maddy? Did you have fun at the fair?"

I huff out a laugh and roll my eyes. "It was something." Maddy will probably kill me, but I'm hoping for advice from my mother. "She got her period and was…upset."

Her hand flies up, covering her mouth. "Oh, no. She's too young for that. Poor baby. Was that her first?"

"I guess not. Lauren didn't bother to warn me."

Not a fan of the woman who denied my mother prime-baby-cuddling years, my mother rolls her eyes as soon as she hears Lauren's name.

"It was…an event. Maddy was very upset." I jerk my chin in the direction of my house. "Aubrey came over and helped me out."

"Oh. That was very sweet. Was Madison mad?"

"No. They seemed to bond or whatever."

Her eyes widen. "Well, that's good. Poor Aubrey. You really threw her into the deep end, didn't you?"

"Little bit." I glance at the clock. "I really have to go."

"Okay. I'll give Maddy a call later."

"Call her now. School's closed. I just talked to her a little while ago."

As if on cue, my mother's phone rings and she smiles when she checks the screen. "Ah, it's Maddy."

I lean in and kiss her cheek. "I'll talk to you later."

She's already on the phone with her granddaughter. Subtle as a brick, she asks if anything exciting happened on her visit.

Aubrey

"DO WE HAVE time to stop by my place?" I ask. "I really want to grab some clean clothes."

"Yeah, of course. Sorry about that. You should grab some extra stuff to leave at my place."

"Sure," I answer a little too enthusiastically. Sully's been quiet since he returned from his mother's this morning. God, after last night, she probably told him I'm a brazen hussy and he should dump me.

"Was everything okay with your mom?" I ask, glutton for punishment that I am.

His mouth quirks into a quick smile that doesn't quite reach his eyes. "Yes. She wanted to know how you feel about babies."

"They're cute." Wait a second. "Oh, how I feel about *having* babies you mean?"

He laughs but doesn't confirm.

"How do *you* feel about having more kids?"

"Honestly, I've never thought about it. I guess I'm afraid it would make me realize all the stuff I missed out on with Madison. And I've already spent enough time being angry with Lauren."

He's such a good man.

"Yes," I whisper. "I want to have kids someday."

He glances over. "Good to know."

We don't take the conversation any further before we get to my apartment. Celia's car is missing, and guilt crawls over me that I've barely seen her in two days.

We enter the apartment, and since we're running late, I head straight to my bedroom for clean clothes.

In the living room, Sully chuckles.

"What's so funny?" I call out.

"Dearest little sister," he reads. "I hope that hot stud of yours plowed you good this weekend. I miss your face. In case you forgot who this is, your sister, Celia."

"Oh my God," I shriek, running out of my bedroom. "I can *not* believe you read that!"

He still laughing, but manages to get out, "Hot stud, huh? Is that how I'm known around here?"

"Give me that." I grab the mail out of his hands. Good thing too, because right underneath my sister's embarrassing note is a postcard from the Department of Corrections informing me that one Mr. Darren Bar has been released from prison and should I have any problems, call the local police department.

A freaking postcard. You've got to be kidding. And, oh my God, what if Sully had read this?

"Everything okay?" Sully asks, rubbing the back of his hand over my cheek. "You're so pale."

Shake it off. "I'm just embarrassed you read that." Shame and guilt do a mean little tap dance over my heart for lying.

I consider my options as I return to my bedroom. Call the police later and let them know that *he* already paid me a visit. Surely that's against his conditions of parole? After that, I'll tell Sully all about my sordid past.

Wearing clean clothes and a full backpack I meet Sully at the door. His phone rings. "Think it's Maddy again?" I ask as he answers it.

He shakes his head and mouths, "Jake."

"I'm on my way there." He pauses, eyebrows shoot up then down. "What are you talking about?" His frown deepens and he motions me out the door. We hurry down the steps and into the Jeep while he listens to whatever bad news Jake has to deliver.

"I'll be there in like five minutes. Did you call the cops yet? Fuck, yeah all right." He disconnects the call and tosses his phone on the dashboard. Slamming his fist against the steering wheel, he lets out a curse.

The sick feeling of dread that settled in my gut yesterday intensifies with the force of a thousand destructive secrets. I'm not even sure I need Sully to tell me what happened. Somehow I just know Darren's involved.

"Someone broke in and vandalized the gym last night," Sully finally explains as he tears out of the parking lot. "Jake says it's pretty bad."

I swallow hard and force out a question. "Does he know who did it?"

"With the kind of company he keeps, who fucking knows."

My guilt intensifies, then ebbs. Maybe Sully's right and it has something to do with Jake, not me. I saw the way that guy went after him at the Castle after Jake won his fight. As much as I like Jake, I have to admit he involves himself in some shady business. And I'm sure what

I've learned barely scratches the surface.

But deep down, that inner voice I've worked so hard to listen to, says I'm wrong.

As Sully pulls into his space, he mutters another curse. "I'll kill Jake if he brought this on. Christ, Maddy was here yesterday. He promised to stay out of anything that would put her in danger."

Please let me be wrong. Please let it be something unconnected to me—I glance over at Sully's enraged expression—*or Jake.* Let it be a case of regular vandalism. Junkies looking for cash. Bored teenagers on a crime spree. Something impersonal.

Broken shards of glass from the back door glitter in the morning sunlight against the blacktop.

Sully slams the Jeep into park, kills the ignition, flings open his door and storms out of the car, stalking into the building.

I follow him inside, pausing to jump over a pile of broken glass, and stop when I bump against him.

Beside me, he's statue still, staring at the destruction.

Trashed doesn't come close to describing the scene.

Blue gym mats shredded. Front desk smashed to smithereens. Holes in the walls where weights were thrown into the drywall. Shattered mirrors. The door to the ladies' locker room torn off its hinges.

But the absolute worst?

Two words painted in dripping black letters against the bright white wall.

I'm responsible after all.

I brought this on.

My past, my mistakes have destroyed everything he's worked so hard for.

It's the exact same message Darren sprayed on my parents' front door when they tried to end our relationship.

SHE'S MINE.

CHAPTER THIRTY-THREE
SULLY

UTTER DESTRUCTION.

That's the only way to describe what's in front of me. The gym. Everything I've built over the last nine years—trashed. Some psycho went through like a hurricane, denting, ripping, shredding, and breaking everything he could get his hands on.

I've worked hard. Worked my ass off. Tried to give back and keep my nose clean. This isn't the work of kids who broke in to fuck around and vandalize for fun or to alleviate their boredom. The computers are smashed, but not stolen. Hell, even the petty cash box is still here. I can't understand this level of hatred.

It borders on insanity.

Then my eyes focus on two words painted on the back wall. Against the stark white paint, the words look obscene.

SHE'S MINE.

My gaze travels to Jake. "Is this you?" I ask in a low voice.

He immediately holds his hands up and steps back. "No way, bro. I got a strict no cheaters policy. I can't think of a single person who'd do this to you."

He's completely serious. Not a hint of fucking around. But obviously his mind went there too, so I don't suffer too much guilt over the question.

What if this had happened when Maddy was here? Even the thought makes my blood pressure spike.

Aubrey's quiet. Too quiet. She's probably terrified. The place she works and spends a lot of her time in has been violently violated. I wouldn't blame her if she's mentally drafting her resignation letter.

But then I glance at her.

Tears roll down her cheeks and she shakes her head.

Her eyes. She won't look at me.

She knows who did this.

My gut says I'm right. Besides the message, this carnage feels awfully personal.

Police radio crackling, Deputy Sheriff Brady O'Connor strolls in the back door and whistles. "Holy shit, Sullivan."

"I had to call him," Jake says quietly. "You're gonna need a report."

"I'll be right back," Brady says.

I pull Aubrey aside. Acid burns my throat and my chest tightens. "Do you have any idea who did this?" I ask in the calmest voice possible under the circumstances.

Her body trembles and she nods miserably. She fixes her gaze on the floor, allowing her hair to cover her face. "I'm so sorry," she whispers.

"What the fuck?" I rage, and she flinches. Have I ever raised my voice around her before? Probably not. I shouldn't be now either.

"Bro, calm down," Jake says, grabbing my arm. "It's not her fault. Whatever it is, isn't her fault."

"Like fuck it's not. Who did this, Aubrey?" At the same time I'm yelling at her, I'm scared to death that she has anyone in her life capable of such violence.

I don't know her at all.

She didn't tell me. Doesn't trust me. When I've trusted her with so much of myself. I've had her at my house. With my family. And the whole time she knew there was some psycho after her?

"I'm sorry," she says again without looking at me. She bursts into tears and runs out the front door—one of the few things left intact.

What the actual fuck?

"Christ, Sully. Really? What the fuck's wrong with you?" Jake shouts.

"Look around you!" I yell back.

"Oh my God," someone says behind us. "What happened?"

"Celia," Jake says. "What are you doing here?"

Her wild gaze searches the room, cataloging the damage. "Looking for Aubrey." As soon as she sees the message on the wall, she closes her eyes and lets out a defeated sigh. "Motherfucker."

I shoot an I-told-you-so glare Jake's way.

"Who, Celia?" I ask.

"Where is she?"

"What the *fuck* did she drag me into?" I ask a little louder.

Her eyes narrow and she places one hand on her hip. "Don't you dare put this on her." She steps closer, poking her finger against my chest. "You have *no idea* what hell she's been through. No idea what that sonofabitch did to her. *None.*"

"No, I don't. Because she never fucking told me!" But even as I fling the words at Celia, I question myself.

Fire rages through my blood, incinerating me from the inside out. Not because of the damage to my business.

Because all the little warning signs make sense.

How desperate Aubrey was to take those extra self-defense classes.

Her hesitance to talk about her past. To reveal too much.

Her lack of self-confidence.

And a thousand other little things that should've clued me in.

Stupid me, I figured she'd been burned by a guy.

Not involved with a sociopath.

A searing rush of protectiveness surges from deep inside me.

"Who is he?" I ask a whole lot calmer now.

"Never mind. If she didn't tell you, there must have been a reason."

"Bullshit, Celia." I take a few steps closer. "Tell me, please."

She bites her lip and glances at the door. "I need to find her. Make sure she's okay."

Brady—who apparently walked back in without me noticing—wraps his hand around my arm before I have a chance to grab Celia and shake the information out of her.

I'm vaguely aware of Jake chasing her out the back door.

"Aubrey's your girl?" Brady asks.

"Yeah. She works here too."

"I need to speak to her."

"You and me both."

Aubrey

HYSTERICAL AND TERRIFIED, I run down the street. I pass Busy Beans and speed up. It's not safe there anymore.

Obviously, Darren spent time watching my every move before visiting me at the coffee shop. To know where I work. To know I'm involved with Sully.

Was involved with Sully.

Am in love with Sully.

Can't think about Sully right now. Picturing his beautiful, furious face right before I ran out threatens to tear my heart open.

Darren—the bastard—ruined my life before. Took all my plans and hopes for my future and ground them into dust. Six years later, he's managed to blow up two things that mean so much to me with one destructive act. My relationship with the best man I've ever known and a job that finally made me feel like I have a purpose in life.

Gone.

Sully will never forgive me.

Not that I blame him.

CHAPTER THIRTY-FOUR
SULLY

A STEADY, DULL pain throbs behind my eyes while I go over Brady's endless questions. More guys from the sheriff's department show up to catalog the crime scene.

My business is now a crime scene.

It's completely different, yet still somehow reminiscent of the night my stepfather died. Except this time, no one cuffs me and throws me in the back of a patrol car.

I'm not a bruised, terrified boy covering for my mother this time either.

Everything around me slowly comes back into focus. Jake's standing next to me calmly answering more questions. He's safe. Not bloody from another beating at the hands of his father. My mother's safe at home. Probably still on the phone with Maddy.

My gaze falls on the stuff strewn around. The equipment I haven't even started making payments on yet. The mirrors Jake and I installed by ourselves. Everything I did on my own or with Jake's help.

But it's just stuff.

Things that can eventually be replaced. It's the hard work I put into the place that hurts the most. The reputation I've built. Who wants to take self-defense classes from someone who can't keep his own business safe?

"Fuck," I mutter.

Brady walks away to take a phone call and Jake shoves me into my office.

"You all right?" he asks.

"No."

He crosses his arms over his chest and cocks his head. "You're an asshole."

"I know."

"Go fix it and make sure she's okay." He nods to the door. "I can handle this right now."

"Did Celia tell you anything?"

He shakes his head. "Just to go fuck myself." His lips quirk into a completely inappropriate smirk. "Christ, she's fucking hot when she's pissed."

One stupid comment from Jake actually makes me laugh. "Dick."

He drops the smile. "I don't know what this was about. We can both stand here and make guesses all day long. Won't fix a damn thing. What I *do* know is that girl cares about you a *lot*. Cares about this place probably as much as we do."

"I know."

"Then get out of here and go grovel your ass off." His hard tone softens to something almost compassionate. "For once, let your little brother handle things. I'm not completely useless."

"You're not useless. A pain in my ass, yeah, but never useless."

Instead of laughing, he nods to the door. "Go on."

Aubrey

MY TEARS DRY as I spill my whole miserable story to Bree. Liam stayed for some of it, then left to take a phone call.

"Oh, Aubrey. No wonder you don't like dredging this up." She tilts her head and the sympathy in her eyes doesn't feel as awful as I thought it would. "I can't believe they let him out of prison. The justice system really is messed up."

I feel terrible dumping this on Bree after everything she's been through, but she and Liam didn't hesitate to take me in when I called.

"You'll be safe here," Liam assured me.

At my feet, their Rottweiler, Kimber, stretches and rolls to her back, showing off her belly.

"Hussy," Bree teases, reaching down to rub the contented pooch. Kimber sneezes and sits up, leaning most of her weight against my leg as if petting her is my new full-time job.

Heck, it might as well be.

"I should've told Sully sooner. Warned him."

"How could you know? This isn't your fault, Aubrey."

"He came to see me at the coffee shop the day before. I should've told Sully after his daughter went home."

My cheeks heat up, we'd gotten carried away, and I wanted to avoid sharing this painfully embarrassing story just a little longer.

Bree's thoughtful as she chooses her next words. "The only thing a guy like Sully's going to be upset about is that he wants to be the one to protect you and he can't do that if he doesn't know."

Petting Kimber seems to ease some of my anxiety and while I'm scratching behind her ears, she turns to look at me, tongue hanging out as if to say "Told ya."

A car door slams outside and Liam's tense voice can be heard, as well as another angrier voice.

My heart slams against my ribcage. Is nowhere safe?

Kimber's ears perk up and she stares at the front door. Her lip curls in a low snarl.

"Relax, Kimber," Bree orders.

She drops her ears but keeps her eyes trained on the front door.

SULLY

EACH TIME I call Aubrey's phone, it goes straight to voicemail. Not a surprise.

I head right to her apartment, prepared to do some serious groveling.

Judging by the look on Celia's face, she's not at all happy to see me on her doorstep.

"What do you want?" she asks, leaning against the doorframe to make it clear I'm not invited inside.

"I need to talk to Aubrey."

"She's not here."

Cold fear knifes through me. I shouldn't have let her leave before. "Where is she?"

The tone of my voice changes her demeanor quickly. She drops the hostile posture and motions for me inside. "She's somewhere safe."

Christ, how bad is this?

Pretty fucking bad, asshole. You saw what this guy did to the gym.

"Where?"

She sighs and shakes her head. "I shouldn't tell you."

"Yes, you should."

She continues to stare at me, trying to make up her mind. "He knows where we live."

I fight the urge to ask *who,* but seeing Aubrey is the only thing that matters right now.

"I took her to Bree's place. Liam will keep her safe."

Shit, that stings.

"*I'll* keep her safe."

"You better."

On my way out, Celia stops me. "I called the sheriff's department to let them know who to look for. Aubrey's planning to go to them in the morning and give a full statement."

"Thank you for doing that. But all I'm worried about right now is Aubrey."

"Good."

LIAM'S OUTSIDE WATERING the lawn, washing his car, or some other typical outdoor chore when I pull up in front of his house.

I jump out and storm over his crisp, precision-cut green grass while

Liam watches with a crooked smile.

"Where is she?" I bark out.

He answers with a blast of ice-cold water to my chest, soaking me from the chin down.

"Motherfucker! Seriously?" I sputter and shake off as much as I can, but my shirt and shorts remain glued to my skin.

He drops the hose and shrugs. "You looked like you needed to cool off."

"Fuck you. Where is she?"

The hosing might have seemed like a prank, but as Liam stalks closer, it's clear he's actually pissed.

"What did I tell you?"

"Trust me, there's nothing mixed-up about how I feel about her," I answer, remembering exactly what conversation he's referring to.

He cocks his head and studies me for a few beats. "She's inside with Bree."

Since I'm soaking wet, courtesy of him, I don't bother with a thank you.

"Don't get water all over my living room!" he shouts after me.

I glance at him over my shoulder. "Guess you should've thought about that before hosing me."

Without giving thought to the Rottweiler Liam and Bree recently adopted, I throw the front door open.

A hundred pounds of muscle covered in black and tan fur comes hurtling toward me.

"Kimber, no!" Bree shouts.

"Shit!" I stop and stand still, holding up my hands. "It's okay. Good girl."

Kimber stops. Thank God. The danger of having my face eaten off has been subdued thanks to Bree's command. The Rottie still gives me a thorough sniffing before returning to Aubrey's side.

"Sorry," Bree says. "She's—"

"Just doing her job."

Liam comes up behind me. "Oops."

"You're a dick," I growl over my shoulder.

"She wouldn't hurt you." He chuckles. "She *will* make you piss your pants though," he says a little louder while glancing down at my shorts.

"You asshole." I lift my chin at Bree. "Your fiancé hosed me down outside."

"Sounds kinky. Should we leave you boys alone?" she deadpans.

Aubrey ducks her head and a small smile flickers over her lips. The only good thing about this whole adventure.

"Aubrey," I say, begging her with my voice to at least look at me.

Bree stands and hooks her fingers in Kimber's collar. "Come on, girl. Daddy's going to take you for a walk."

"I am?" Liam asks.

"Yup." She hustles him out the door and they close it behind them.

I rush over to Aubrey and kneel down in front of her.

She bursts into tears. "I'm so sorry."

"Shhh." I take her hands in mine. "Aubrey, look at me. I'm sorry. I shouldn't have yelled at you."

"But it *is* my fault."

"No, it's not."

"Your whole…everything…"

"It's just stuff. I'm more worried about *you*. I'm completely in the dark here."

She sniffles and swipes at her damp cheeks. "I wanted to tell you. I should've warned you."

"So tell me now." I stand and pull her up off the couch. "But not here."

"Okay." Her gaze roams over me. "Did Liam really spray you?"

"Yes," I grumble. "Come on. We'll go somewhere and talk." I stop mid-step. Just because I've come to my senses, doesn't mean she's going to forgive me for acting like such a jackass. "If you want, I'll bring you back here when we're done. If this is where you want to stay."

She shakes her head, but says, "Thank you."

Bree and Liam are walking up the driveway with Kimber when we come out of the house.

"Everything all right?" Bree asks.

"We're going to talk," Aubrey says.

Bree gives her an encouraging hug and whispers something in her ear I can't make out. Aubrey nods. "I'll be okay."

"I leave for my shift at 3:30, but Bree will be back around six if you're still staying over," Liam says.

Yeah, I kind of want to punch him for that, but I'm also glad he's willing to help Aubrey out, so I restrain myself.

Once we're on the road, Aubrey reaches over and touches my leg. "You should really take me to the sheriff's department, so I can give my statement today."

"Celia said she gave them a name."

"You must have so much to do…"

"Jake's taking care of it. Right now, the only thing that matters is you."

CHAPTER THIRTY-FIVE
SULLY

S ILENCE WHISPERS BETWEEN us as I steer the Jeep into the parking area next to the Empire International Airport. The exact spot where we watched the planes take off the other night is open, and I slip into it.

I kill the engine. Send Jake a short text, then shut off my cell phone.

"Sully, you can't. What if Jake needs to reach you?" she protests.

Right now I haven't earned the right to kiss her, but I do it anyway. "It's fine."

Heaving myself out of my seat, I climb into the back and hold out my hand to her. "Come here."

"It's not really the time for a backseat make-out session."

I don't laugh. "Just talking."

A smile tugs at the corners of her mouth and she takes my hand, allowing me to pull her into the back with me.

I wrap an arm around her and she curls into my side, resting her hand on my still-damp chest.

Our breathing fills the silence as I wait for her to begin. When she's ready.

"I met him when I was fifteen." Her words are cautious and slow at first. As if she doesn't dwell on these memories often and doesn't want to dredge them up now.

"My friends and I went to this big music festival," she continues. "It was one of those outdoor-all-day-into-the-night concerts. We had tickets for lawn seats and one of my friends thought we could sneak in and grab some empty seats closer to the stage."

"Typical teen antics."

She snorts. "I guess. We got caught. But the security guard said he'd let us stay."

"I sense he slapped a condition on it?"

Anger twists her features as she nods. "If I gave him a kiss." She squeezes her eyes shut. "He was older. Good-looking. All my friends kept flirting with him, but he was only interested in me. It…I had never had that happen before."

Sounds like a first-rate predator to me.

She swallows hard. "I lied about my age. So, getting involved with him, that's on me. My fault."

"Bullshit." She's twenty-two now and barely looks eighteen. I highly doubt she passed for anything resembling legal back then. But since I've learned that's a sore subject for her, I keep the observation to myself.

Ignoring my outburst, she continues.

"He knew all the hiding places. During intermission, he took me downstairs, beneath the venue."

A sick feeling rolls through my gut at where she's headed.

My body must tense or betray my thoughts in some way, because she sits up. "We didn't…not that night. But we did more than kiss."

Jealousy, that I have no right to, burns my throat. "Go on."

"We kept seeing each other after that. Secretly. I knew my parents would freak out."

"Exactly how old was he?"

"Twenty-eight."

"Jesus Christ."

"It gets better," she says with no humor behind the words. "When I started school in the fall…he was one of my teachers."

I sit up, turning to face her. "Are you fucking serious?"

Her teeth sink into her lower lip and she drops her gaze. "Yeah, he was my English teacher. We just sort of stood there and stared at each other. I told him I was in college. And he never explained the security work was a his summer job."

"What happened?"

"I was more upset about it than he was. I'd never…I'd never thought about any of my teachers that way before…It was *weird*."

No kidding.

"After class, he asked me to stay and laid into me for lying about my age. He had just started teaching there and he was scared of losing his job."

Maybe he shouldn't have been trolling for teenagers at concerts if he was so worried about his job and reputation.

"Didn't any of your friends recognize him?"

"No. These were friends from junior high. My parents sent me to a private high school."

"Go on."

She licks her lips and averts her eyes. "It was so awkward and uncomfortable to be in his class that I tried to transfer out of it. He was furious when he found out." She rolls her eyes. "He gave me this sad sob story about how he was so in love with me that he needed to be able to see me every day if he couldn't be with me. And I—stupid, gullible teenager that I was, fell for every line."

Predator. Slimy, manipulative, cunning fucking predator dressed up as a teacher.

I cup her cheek and force her to look at me. "Aubrey," I say as calmly as possible. "You were a kid and he was your teacher. He was the adult in the situation. He knew better."

"I don't want to sound like a pathetic cliché, but I think I've mentioned my parents weren't the super-loving type."

My thumb twitches over her soft cheek as I wait.

"My mother's emotions ranged from cold to indifferent." She blows out a breath. "Having this man declare how much he loved me and how beautiful I was, how he couldn't stop thinking about me. It was all…"

"Seductive."

Her cheeks burn red. "Yes." Her fists clench and unclench. "I told him *I* was sorry and I wouldn't leave his class."

I struggle to keep my face neutral. "What happened?"

"Nothing for a little while. He always praised my work. I loved poetry and spent a lot of time writing my own in my journal. Typical angsty teenage stuff."

I try to smile to break some of the tension. "I didn't know you're a poet."

She stares right into my eyes. "I'm not. Not anymore."

Wrong thing for me to say.

"We ran into each other outside of school one afternoon and things…ignited." Her gaze drops and she whispers, "He took me back to his apartment."

Hot rage consumes me, and I struggle to get my breathing under control.

"After that, we snuck around and saw each other on the sly. He told me how I was so much more mature than women his age and loved how smart I was and how much we had in common."

I barely restrain my eye roll. "That's the same load of shit every predator uses."

She stares at me.

Mimicking the sharp, whiny tone I've heard one too many times from pathetic men, I list their tired excuses, "'She came on to *me*. What was I supposed to do? She dressed provocatively. She acted older than her age. How could I possibly know she was underage? How could I resist?" I pin her with a sharp look. "Those excuses are bullshit attempts to shift the blame to their victims."

I stop and take a breath and find a gentler tone of voice. "I don't care how 'mature' you were, it's not the same as being an actual adult. Teachers go through all sorts of training. He knew better."

She seems to consider my words. Christ, I can't believe she's been living with the weight of all this guilt for so long.

"How long did that go on?" I finally ask.

"All through my sophomore year."

"Seriously?" No one in her life noticed the fucking pedophile hanging around her?

"Beginning of my junior year." She licks her lips and moves away from me. "I thought I was pregnant."

You've got to be kidding.

281

"My parents found a used test stick and flipped their shit. They badgered me until I cracked and confessed."

Tears stream down her cheeks and I pull her back into my side. "What did they do?"

"Well, they called me a slut and asked what I had done to seduce him. Why he'd risk his career because of me."

For a second, I can't draw in any air. "Excuse me?"

"I argued that we were in love." She gives me a weak smile. "When they confronted him, he didn't deny it. He seemed happy."

This piece of shit must be ten different shades of fucked in the head. "I'm sure that went over well."

"They forbid him from seeing me. They wanted it to stay a secret, so they didn't go to the school or police. But he came unglued." She meets my eyes. "He vandalized our house. That's how I knew it was him this morning. That's the same message he left on their front porch."

"Christ."

She hugs herself, rubbing her hands over her arms and stares down at the floor, her voice flat. "The situation exploded. My parents filed a complaint with the police. The school got dragged into it. This salacious story was everywhere. The news devoured it and labeled it a 'sex scandal.' A forbidden student-teacher romance."

I cough, uncomfortably familiar with how lies and half-truths can destroy a life.

"His 'we're in love' speech didn't go over well with the police. They arrested him."

"About fucking time," I grumble.

"It just made everything worse. This was a small town. Once his name hit the news, students put it together. How he always doted on me and showed me favoritism. My name spread like wildfire."

"You were a kid, papers couldn't print that." Conviction hardens my voice.

She snorts. "They didn't have to. I went to private school. My father had a pretty successful financial planning firm. Lots of my classmates' parents were clients of my dad's firm. He started losing those people first. Then when the news crews showed up, he lost even more business."

"Too fucking bad."

She shakes her head. "He blamed me. They had to sell our vacation house in Connecticut and I think my mother was more upset about that than what was happening to me."

Some people don't deserve to be parents.

"I had to sit through endless, humiliating interrogations. In the end, my statements made it worse for him." She straightens her spine. "After a few months, my parents stopped cooperating with the DA. They pulled me out of school and had me committed to a psychiatric facility."

Of all the shocking things she's revealed, this hits me the hardest. I all but explode out of my seat. "He's the one who needed to be committed."

"It swept all my parents' problems away. I couldn't be compelled to testify and embarrass them further. The DA plead the case down. The news coverage dried up."

Every fucking adult in her life failed her. "So everyone walked away unscathed but you?"

She shrugs, but her eyes shine with unshed tears. "I brought it on myself."

"Aubrey. That's not true." I touch one finger under her chin, tipping her head back to see her face. "You were, what, three years older than Madison is now?" I swallow over the rage burning in the back of my throat. "Believe me, if some twenty-something asshole went after her that way, I'd kill him. Your parents should've *protected* you. Not blamed you."

She nods, but I don't think my words hit home for her. "Celia filed for guardianship to get me out. But she was too young, and they denied her." A brief smile flickers over her lips. "At least I knew someone cared about me."

"She's a good sister."

She half-smiles. "Celia visited me as much as she could. Eventually, I started paying attention in the group therapy sessions. So many stories were similar to mine. The grooming behavior. The manipulation…the controlling and terrorizing. Needing to know where I was and who I was with every second of the day. The subtle put-downs that made me think no one would ever love me but him. So many behaviors I excused because they seemed romantic and meant he loved me. It was…devastating. To think I'd been so naïve."

Aubrey

I'M EXHAUSTED AFTER dredging up so much emotional garbage.

After expelling a long breath, I wrap up my story. "When I turned eighteen, the hospital had to let me go. My parents were done with me. My father had salvaged his business, but they'd shelled out a fortune. They told me in no uncertain terms I was on my own from then on. I wasn't allowed to move back in."

"Are you kidding me?" Sully asks.

"Celia took me in. She'd already cut ties with my parents years before." I snort and shake my head. "And I always thought she was their favorite."

"It doesn't sound like they were meant to be parents."

"No kidding. Celia and I say that all the time." My lips twitch into a weak smile. "That's why we both like your mom so much."

He squeezes me tighter. "Go on."

"I didn't know what to do with myself." A violent shiver works over me. "The thought of being a teacher after all that made me ill."

"That's why you picked accounting? Something completely different from poetry?" Sully asks with gentleness and understanding.

I never thought of it in those terms. "I guess so."

His unwavering stare doesn't stray from my face. "For the record, you'd be a great teacher. You're exactly the kind of person kids need, but I understand why it would bother you."

"I never imagined he'd be released so soon." Bitter regret singes my voice. "And I never, ever thought he'd come looking for me right away."

"He's a sick bastard."

I close my eyes and try to block the rising burn in my throat. "I should've warned you. He'd always get jealous when I talked to boys in class. He'd grill me for hours after school if he thought a guy even smiled at me. As soon as he came into Busy Beans the other night, I should've warned you."

Sully doesn't accept that. As my pulse races and my throat seals shut, he pulls me against his chest.

"I don't blame you, Aubrey. It had to be a shock. To see him after all that time and with an adult's perspective. And you said he used to grill *you*. He didn't confront those boys?"

"Well, he failed at least two that I know of."

"Wow, a coward *and* an asshole."

Heavy, unrelenting regret and shame spreads over my skin. "Sully, I was going to tell you. I just hadn't figured out how. I wanted to tell you this morning after you shared so much with me." I finally meet his eyes again. "It's not an excuse, but Maddy called, and you seemed so happy talking to her, I didn't want to ruin the moment. And we were running late...I'm not making excuses...I had no idea he'd—"

"Hey, stop," he murmurs, putting a halt to my crazy rambling.

I rest my head against his chest, accepting the comfort he's offering.

"Aubrey," he says after a few minutes of silence. "Have you...did you date anyone after him?"

"A few times." I sigh and shake my head. "One relationship turned serious." Swallowing over the lump in my throat is almost impossible. "But when I told him, he acted like everyone else. That I'd been the slutty temptress who ruined some poor guy's life."

"Is that why you were afraid to tell me?"

I risk glancing up and find the full weight of his gaze on me. "Maybe a little." My hands flap uselessly in the air while I try to come up with the right words. "Not that I think you're like that, but—"

He takes both my hands in his. "I understand."

"I believe you." I hesitate, unsure of where to go from here. "What do we do now?"

"I'm not letting you out of my sight until he's back behind bars."

My pulse quickens at his stern voice, but the love in his eyes assures me he only wants to protect me.

For the last few years, I've wandered aimlessly through life, feeling like a stranger inside my own skin. Lost and angry with my parents and Darren, but mostly angry at my own actions.

These last few months, Sully's shown me who I can be. Who I want to be. As if he's handed me the keys to the door leading me back to myself.

"Thank you for listening and not running away."

He pushes my hair out of my eyes. "I love you."

Those are the words I need the most. To know that after hearing what I allowed to happen, he doesn't hate me.

Tears threaten to fall, but I will them away. "I love you too. Real, solid, glowing love, Sully. Where I'm weak, you've given me strength."

He touches his forehead to mine and speaks low heartfelt words. "You fit the missing piece in my life. You inspire me and make me believe anything is possible, Aubrey. I am *never* walking away from you."

CHAPTER THIRTY-SIX

Aubrey

Dearest Aubrey,

I have to admit, I'm hurt and disappointed. I thought the letter your sister delivered to the parole board was something your family concocted to keep us apart again. After speaking with you, it's clear you've been brainwashed. While I held onto our love during some of my darkest moments, you apparently moved on with your life. I guess now it's time for me to do the same.

I've requested and been granted permission to move out of the area. You won't have to fear seeing me again.

You used to be such a kind, beautiful soul and even though you've turned on me, as much as I want to hate you, I can't.

I hope that new man of yours never hurts you the way you've wounded me.

Always,

D.

If I roll my eyes any harder, they're going to fall out of my head.

"For fuck's sake," Sully growls, snapping the letter out of my hands.

We stopped by to pick up more of my things to bring to his house. Celia handed me the letter as soon as I walked in the door.

While Sully reads the letter—muttering curses under his breath the entire time—I flip over the envelope and study the postmark. "It was mailed in Poughkeepsie on Monday."

"Setting up his alibi probably," Celia mutters.

"Hopefully that's where he moved. It's at least two hours away."

"Not far enough," Celia and Sully both grumble at the same time.

I shrug and take the letter from Sully, slipping it back into the envelope. I'll drop it off at the Sheriff's department later. Maybe the letter will help track Darren down. His parole officer claims Darren checked in on time. But no one's questioned him about vandalizing Sully's gym yet.

"He's a bigger dipshit than I thought if he thinks that letter will make us believe he didn't trash Sully's place." Celia crosses her arms over her chest and shakes her head. "I wish he had delivered it in person so I could've kicked him in the balls."

Sully chuckles and pats her shoulder. "Thanks."

She reaches out, pulling me into a hug. "I hate him for doing this to you again," she says.

I heave out a breath. "Me too." I turn and catch Sully's eye. "I'm so sorry—"

"No." He holds up a hand, cutting off my apology. "This isn't your fault. Besides, I have a few days off while the insurance company jerks me around and my mother has been more than happy to put me to work."

"See, I always told you momma's boys make good boyfriends," Celia says loud enough for Sully to hear and laugh.

I laugh with them, but inside I feel awful. Even if he refuses to admit it, his main source of income is gone because of me.

Sully's hand touches my shoulder. "It's only temporary, Aubrey. I can always pick up a few classes at Wrath's gym or find a few workshops to teach."

I appreciate the effort to relieve my guilt.

But as soon as we return to his house, I pull out my laptop.

"What are you doing?" he asks.

"It's time to work on part two of my Business Communications project."

He narrows his eyes, but a teasing smile plays over his lips. "I don't know if I'm in the mood for one of your video sessions." He leans in and tickles his fingers over my ribs, making me laugh.

Pushing him away, I nod to the screen. "I have plenty of footage. I need to edit it into useful content."

"Need help?"

"Sure. You can help me come up with some compelling descriptions."

He takes a seat next to me and bumps my shoulder. "See, we're a perfect team. I give you the boring fitness jargon and you punch it up into something interesting."

My nose stings. The simple compliment means so much to me. "Thank you."

We work together for most of the afternoon. Accomplishing so much helps alleviate some of my guilt.

Our night is almost perfect.

If only Darren wasn't out there waiting to ruin everything.

CHAPTER THIRTY-SEVEN
SULLY

A WEEK LATER, we're finally given the all-clear to start repairing the gym. Aubrey's ex had finally been questioned but swore he had no knowledge of what happened or even who I was. The letter Aubrey gave his parole officer didn't seem to be enough to convince him. I've been told the Sheriff's department is still looking into it, which gives me little comfort. Most importantly, he hasn't tried to contact Aubrey again.

Oh yeah, I was warned to stay far away from the guy. As if I'm the problem and not that lunatic.

Today, I have more important things on my mind.

After wrapping up some car shopping, I walk into Strike Back to find a team of people already hard at work.

Wrath's size makes him the first one I identify. "What's going on?"

He turns and flashes one of his scary-ass biker smiles. "Hammering up some drywall, bro." Deep, rumbling laughter follows his words. "Where ya been?"

Murphy ambles up next to him and nods at me. "Jake promised us food and alcohol in exchange for our labor."

"Bullshit," Jake calls out. "You're here because of your deep love and respect for me."

"Okay," Murphy says, rolling his eyes. "Whatever you say."

My gaze darts between my brother and the two bikers in front of me. "What's going on?"

"You take a hit to the head when this went down?" Wrath asks. "We're repairing the walls." He speaks each word slow and deliberately as if I need the extra time to comprehend them. "Got two prospects coming over to paint on Thursday. So this needs to get done now."

"I can't ask them to do that."

"*You're* not. I am. They wanna patch in one day, they do what they're told. They don't want an ass-kickin' they'll make sure they do a good job." He slaps Murphy's shoulder. "Besides, my little ginger Road Captain's gonna stick around to supervise."

Murphy's eyes widen. "What now?" He scratches a hand over his beard. "I'm *not* a prospect. Why do *I* have to listen to you?"

Wrath ignores him and focuses on me. "Don't worry, Sullivan. I'll give you a nice, legit bill for the insurance company when we're done."

Great, probably a way to help the Lost Kings MC launder some money. Just what I need.

But you know what? I don't care. Every contractor I've contacted is booked out for months. I can't afford to stay closed that long. Wrath's in business with my brother. He doesn't have to be here doing menial work to help my gym when he has his own to run. He's doing it out of respect for Jake and I'm not about to turn down his help.

"Thank you." I hold out my hand and Wrath shakes it. "Appreciate it."

"Ruthless and Royal!" Jake shouts, drawing our attention to the front door.

Remy and Griff stroll in. Remy shakes his head. "Damn, you weren't kidding about the damage." He lifts his chin in Jake's direction. "Who'd you piss off now?"

Jake shrugs off the question and I appreciate him not offering up Aubrey's personal story for discussion.

"Jesus Christ," Remy says, squinting at Wrath. "You're a fucking legend. Don't suppose you're willing to come out of retirement?"

Wrath raises one blond eyebrow at me in a who-are-these-little-punks expression that actually makes me laugh.

I gesture to the half-demolished gym around us. "We're closed if you haven't noticed."

"We're here to help," Griff says. "Got loads of experience fixing walls." He jerks a thumb in Remy's direction. "Redoing his grandmother's house. Hideous wallpaper everywhere."

Remy's hand shoots out, giving Griff a quick shove. "Don't you insult my grandma."

"I'm not, asshole."

Jake slaps Remy and Griff on the shoulders and pushes them in Wrath's direction, ending their bickering. "These are my little protégées I told you about."

Griff scowls at Jake. "There's nothing little about either of us, old man."

Jake smacks him on the back of the head and nods Murphy's way. "This is Murphy. He's joining us full time at Furious."

"You fight?" Remy asks.

Great, maybe all the underground fighters in the area can start using my gym to socialize.

Shaking my head, I duck into my office. Jake follows me.

"You're not mad, are you?" he asks.

"No. Thank you for arranging this."

He shrugs like it's no big deal. "Wrath likes it when you owe him a favor."

My mouth twists into a wry smile. "I'm sure." My amusement fades as I flip through the stack of bills in my hand. I'll deal with them tomorrow. "I have to pick Aubrey up from school. But I'll be back later."

Outside my office, Wrath laughs. "I knew I was right about you and the little pixie."

"Shut up." I chuckle and slap him on the back as I head out.

Jake cocks his head toward the parking lot. "Are they delivering it today?"

"Yup, should be within an hour or so."

He stops me with a hand on my chest. "You know I'll look out for her too. Give her rides to school. Whatever you need, right?"

"Yeah, I know." I pull him in for a quick hug. "Thanks. I'll be back later to help. Text me if I need to pick up any supplies."

AUBREY'S WAITING IN her usual spot, talking to her friend, Emily, and another girl I don't recognize. I pull up to the curb and flip through the radio while I wait for her.

The door creaks open and she peers in at me. "Why didn't you honk or something?" she asks, passing me her backpack, which I set behind her seat.

She climbs in and kisses me before I have a chance to answer and by the time we're finished I forgot the question.

"Sully?"

"Huh?" Only this girl could kiss me stupid.

She closes her door and clicks her seatbelt into place. "Why didn't you honk to let me know you were waiting?"

I scowl at the question and steer away from the curb. "You were talking to your friends. It's not a big deal."

"I know you have a million things to do. I really can take the bus."

"No."

She sighs.

"Not with that asshole still on the loose. No way."

"All right." She pulls her hair into a ponytail and slides the window down.

"How was your day?"

"Good. Great, actually. My professor's really enthusiastic about my progress with the project. Impressed, actually."

I reach over and squeeze her leg. "That's great. Proud of you."

She runs her fingers over the back of my hand. "I feel bad you're driving me all over the place, but I like spending the extra time with you."

My hand's still resting on her leg, and I twist my wrist, inviting her to twine her fingers with mine. "I like it too."

Her words almost stab a blade of guilt in my chest for the gift I'm about to give her.

As I pull around the building into the parking lot, Aubrey leans forward, peering out the windshield. "Wow, who do all the trucks and motorcycles belong to?"

"Jake has a few of his friends helping out."

"That's sweet." She points toward the back of the parking lot. "Why is there a car with a bow on it in your parking lot?"

I crack a smile, guessing Jake's the one who slapped the big silver bow on the front of the shiny red Jeep Renegade.

"I don't know." I fake confusion. "Let's check it out."

I park a few feet away from it and we climb out. She glances back and forth between the two vehicles. "It's cute. Kinda looks like your Jeep had a baby."

"You think so?" I rub my hand over my chin like I'm deep in thought.

She narrows her eyes at me. "Why are you being weird?"

"Am I?"

"Don't you want to figure out who it belongs to?" she asks, walking over to the vehicle.

I jog over, catching her around her middle and lifting her in the air. I kiss her cheek, shoulder, and finally, her neck. "I already know who it belongs to," I whisper against her ear.

"You do? Who?"

I set her down and pull the keys out of my pocket. "You."

She blinks at stares. First at the keys, then at me. "I don't...wait, what?"

"You need a car. You're adding more classes to your schedule next year." My lips quirk. "Your social media manager job requires travel."

"Sully, I can't accept such a huge gift from you."

"It's not a gift. It's a perk of your job." I dangle the keys in front of her.

She laughs. "My job can be done from a computer."

"Yeah, but your boss is a real prick who makes you run all these other errands."

Finally she snatches the keys out of my hands. "That's not true." She tilts her head. "You really bought this for me?"

"Yup." I point toward the road, in the direction of the car dealership a few blocks away. "Brought mine over for an oil change and this little beauty had just been turned in at the end of its lease. It reminded me of you."

"Because it's tiny?" she jokes.

"Because it's your favorite color," I correct. "I've been buying cars from Henry since I was a teenager. He worked out a deal for me."

She bites her lip and looks at the car again.

"Come on." I place my hand on the small of her back. "Let's check it out."

She's hesitant at first. Her voice trembles as she reaches up to kiss me. "This is the sweetest…thank you so much."

I cup her cheek and hold her for a longer kiss. "You're welcome. Go on, get in."

She opens the door and slides into the seat. "It was leased? It doesn't even feel broken-in."

"That's why I jumped on it before Henry cleaned it up and put it out on the lot."

She runs her hands over the touchscreen in the middle and down the controls below it. "I guess I should tell Celia I don't need a ride tonight."

"She already knows."

Her eyes widen. "What? How?"

"She met me at the dealership before I signed the papers."

"Why?"

"I wanted to make sure you'd like it."

"Sully." She sighs. "That's so sweet. I can't believe she kept it a secret."

Me either. "Let's take it out."

She peers up at me. "Will your shoulders even fit in here?"

I snort and walk around to the passenger side and get in. "It's surprisingly roomy."

"Where to?" she asks.

"Wherever you want."

CHAPTER THIRTY-EIGHT

Aubrey

I'VE DRIVEN IT every day for about a week, but I'm still not used to my car. It's so red and pretty. I can't help smiling every time I see it. My bright, shiny reminder of how sweet and thoughtful Sully is.

How lucky I am.

After spending most of my weekend with Sully and Madison, I promised my sister I'd stop by the apartment to help her go through some boxes.

Then we're meeting Sully and the guys at their favorite bar for dinner.

I pull into the spot closest to the sidewalk. Even though I haven't heard anything from Darren since he sent his last letter, Sully still worries so, I text him that I'm here.

Barking echoes through the courtyard and as I jog up the steps, I recognize Gambler's bark. As rambunctious as the dog can be, he's not usually noisy.

Cautiously, I creep up the remaining stairs and look around before stopping at Ty's door. Gambler barks even louder and there's a rattling from inside the apartment, like he's trying to escape his crate.

Worried about the dog, I pull out my cell phone and call Ty.

"What's going on, Aubrey?"

"Hey, I just stopped by to meet Celia and Gambler's going nuts in your place."

"Shit. I'm at the station. Do you mind checking on him for me? The landlord's already on my ass about having a pit bull. I don't need a noise complaint too."

"Of course. I didn't want to go into your apartment without telling you." I walk over to Celia's door and open it, reaching inside to grab Ty's keys on the peg by the door.

"I appreciate it, Aubrey."

"I'm going in now."

"I'll stay on the phone with you."

"Hey, Gambler," I call as I enter.

He stops barking and sits up straight, tail whipping from side to side.

"Are you okay, boy?"

He whines in response.

"Need to go out?"

"Don't, Aubrey," Tyler says. "If he's that worked up, I don't want him dragging you down the stairs."

"I'll be careful."

"Is he okay?"

I inspect the black metal bars of his crate before unlocking the door. Gambler falls into my arms, wiggling and wagging his tail. His big, pink tongue slurps the side of my face, making me giggle.

"He seems fine. I'm sticking around for a while. I'll bring him next door with me and keep an eye on him. If that's okay with you?" I ask.

He breathes out a sigh of relief. "Thank you. I'm leaving here in a bit."

We hang up and I grab Gambler's leash. He sits and waits while I clip it on. "Someone's been going to obedience class," I mutter, rubbing the top of his head. "So polite."

I lock Ty's door and lead Gambler outside. He immediately heads for the stairs.

"Easy, boy."

After a quick walk around the parking lot, we head upstairs. At my front door, he growls.

Did I leave it ajar when I grabbed Ty's keys?

A trickle of fear drips down my spine. I can't remember closing the door. I was on the phone and distracted, so I probably didn't pull it shut.

Gambler growls again and scratches his paw against the door, pushing it open even wider.

Nothing looks out of place. Then again, I haven't been here in a few days.

My phone vibrates, startling me. Heart hammering, I answer. "What?"

"Rude much?" Celia laughs. "What's wrong?"

"I'm at the apartment."

"That's why I called. I'm running late."

"Oh."

"Is everything okay?"

"I'm not sure. Gambler was barking like crazy when I got here. I called Ty and I'm bringing him over to our place for a while."

"He did that last night, too," she says. "Ty's been working a lot. Figured poor G was just wound up. Ty took him on a run this morning, so he should've been tired."

I close the door behind me, dropping Gambler's leash so he can run around the apartment. Laughing, I ask, "How do you know so much about Ty's schedule, sis? Hmm? What have I missed around here lately?"

She snorts. "Give it a rest, little Miss Matchmaker." There's yelling in the background and she groans. "Gotta go. See you in a bit."

Laughing to myself, I wander into the kitchen and grab a glass of water and a couple biscuits we keep for Gambler.

I find him stationed outside my closed bedroom door.

"Yup, that's my room, boy."

He glances over and whines.

"Want a cookie?" I wave the treats in his face, but he ignores them.

"Your loss." I return to the living room and pull out my laptop, setting it up on the coffee table. Plopping down on the floor, I pat the carpet next to me. "Come here, boy."

He chuffs, but trots over, sitting right up against my side. I wrap one arm around him and pet his chest. "Such a good boy," I mutter along with a bunch of other cutesy doggy compliments. "Want your cookies?"

While he munches on the treats, I log into the gym's YouTube account.

"Holy shit!" I squeal, startling Gambler.

We've finally reached a hundred-thousand subscribers. I send Sully a text, not that he pays attention to the numbers the way I do. But it's a big deal, so I want to share it with him.

Good job! He writes back.

As if the subscribers are there because of me instead of the sweaty, shirtless workout videos of Sully, Jake, and their friends.

Giddy with excitement, I scroll through some of the comments on the most recent video, answering questions and pointing people toward our website for more information.

Thump.

Gambler's ears perk up. He hasn't stopped staring at the hallway since he sat down and now it's starting to creep me out.

"It's okay, boy. Chill, you're making me nervous."

He whips his head around and licks my chin a few times before returning to staring at the hallway.

"Yuck," I mutter, swiping at my face, "I love you, but the slobbering has to stop."

Tickticktick.

My gaze shoots down the hallway.

What the hell is that?

Gambler growls low in his throat, the fur down his back stands straight up.

"Easy, boy," I whisper, pulling myself to my feet. "Stay," I order.

He rolls his doggy eyes my way as if he's saying, "You're not the boss of me."

I creep toward the hallway and find my bedroom door open a crack.

There's no way Gambler opened the door earlier. I glance back at him. *Right?*

"Did you do that?"

At this point, I'm talking to the dog to keep myself calm.

Blood pumping like crazy, I press my hand against my bedroom door and push it wide open.

The knob thuds against the wall and the door gently swings back toward me.

Everything seems fine. I'm still creeped out.

Maybe Gambler and I should go wait *outside* for Celia.

Liking that idea better and better, I turn to go back to the living room.

Time to grab Gambler's leash, and my purse. I'll go park my butt somewhere that doesn't make me jump every five seconds.

A whispering-shuffle behind me is the only warning before my hair is yanked. Hard.

I stumble, the hold on my hair the only thing keeping me on my feet. A sharp scream of surprise and outrage bursts out of me. It's such a shock to my system, my mind blanks. Forgetting all the maneuvers I've learned from Sully, I reach back, digging my nails into flesh. My attacker gives my hair a vicious twist and I let out another yelp.

Gambler barks and his galloping paws thud over the carpet. I'm spun and shoved toward my bed and the door slams shut.

Gambler's heavy body hits the thin door with a jarring thump. His paws scratch furiously over the cheap particle board. Whines and barks echo through the apartment.

Breathing heavy, Darren engages the lock and backs away from the door.

My gaze shoots to the lock.

A quick twist of the knob and Gambler will take care of the problem for me.

The bed dips as Darren sits next to me. Instinct has me jerk away, but he yanks me back by my hair.

Stupid ponytail.

"I didn't know you had a dog, Aubrey," he whispers against my ear. And, *ew*, is he *sniffing* my hair?

"There's a lot you don't know about me," I whisper.

He tightens his hold on my hair and a prickle of pain trails against the side of my neck. Warm wetness spills over my skin.

He cut me!

"I'm looking forward to us getting reacquainted."

"You're out of your mind. After what you did to my boyfriend's gym, the police are still investigating you."

Maybe I shouldn't have warned him that he's still a suspect, but I'm desperate to say anything to convince him to release me.

Instead, he backhands me hard across the face. My head snaps sideways. Sharp, stinging, ear-ringing pain explodes in my head and I fall to the side.

Stop. Think.

I can't.

This isn't like anything I've trained for.

"*I'm* your boyfriend. Me, Aubrey. Six years I've been waiting for you. We were going to get married."

"I was sixteen!"

"You were having my baby," he whispers. "We were going to be a family."

"What?"

Oh, Jesus. The stupid pregnancy test that prompted the unraveling of our affair.

"What did you do? Did you kill our baby?" he asks.

"I was never pregnant. It was a false-positive."

He goes stock still, sucking in a deep breath. "You ruined my life because you couldn't read a simple test?"

Wow. I don't even know where to start with that nonsense.

Outside the bedroom, Gambler frantically attacks the door.

Cheap door. Cheap lock. It's only a matter of time before he opens it.

I hope he goes for Darren's throat.

"I read it fine. It was wrong. It happens sometimes," I grumble, pissed at myself for bothering to explain. "You seem to forget I was a sixteen-year-old student, and you were my twenty-eight-year-old teacher," I say with more force in my voice.

"Age is just a number. You loved it."

Good God, he really has no remorse.

Instead of guilt and sadness. This time anger bubbles through my veins. Maybe back then I was willing, but I sure as hell am not now. I haven't written to him or contacted him in over six years.

A "normal" guy would've gotten released from prison and moved on with his life, not sought out his victim to pick up where they left off.

"Thanks to you, I can't teach anymore," Darren says in a matter-of-fact tone. If he's expecting an apology, he's out of luck. I'm fresh out of any sympathy for him. "But I'll figure out a way to provide for you and our family."

It seems the crazy train is moving full steam ahead.

The door rattles again and Darren stares at it. Enough is enough. I use the distraction to center myself before lashing out with my right foot.

It's a kick I've worked on a lot with Sully. Darren's leg is a smaller target than the heavyweight bag Sully has me practice on, but my foot connects with a solid crack to his knee.

Darren shrieks and grabs his leg. "Bitch!"

I shove myself off the bed, diving for the door. Darren reaches for me, hand grazing the back of my shirt, but I shake him off.

Movement in my peripheral vision has me throwing myself at the door, but I fall short and Darren lands on my back.

For a second I can't draw in any air. The shock of hitting the floor with one-hundred and fifty pounds of psychotic baggage on my back steals my breath.

While my brain processes the situation, my fingers claw into the carpet, desperately trying to drag my body out from underneath Darren.

"Not so fast." His fingers circle my wrist and yank it behind my back. My other hand remains trapped under my body. I squirm and struggle to free myself and he wrenches my arm harder. "Behave!"

"Fuck you. Get off me!"

"Shh." The back of his hand brushes the side of my face. "You're going to come with me and we'll start our new life together."

"Um, *no.*" I struggle, gaining a precious inch of ground.

"You'll remember how good things were, Aubrey. We need time to get to know each other again."

"I gotta tell you, Darren, if you're trying to woo me, this really isn't the way."

"There's the spark I remember," he says in his smug-condescending-teacher way that used to fill me with shame. Ugh. Now, it just pisses me off.

I flip and squirm my way onto my back.

"That's it," he says.

He can think I'm acquiescing if he wants, but from working with Sully, I've learned this position gives me more leverage. I may be tiny, but my legs are pretty damn strong. Even better, Darren's focused on the door. I pull my knees up, then kick out as hard as I can, hitting him square in the chest.

I'm rewarded with a sharp whoosh of air shooting out of him as he falls backward. No time to gloat, instead I scramble to my hands and knees. I grab for the knob and twist hard. Gambler rockets into the room, snarling and barking.

Behind me, Darren shrieks and struggles to get to his feet.

I cringe at Darren's screams and Gambler's growls.

I turn as he lashes out, kicking Gambler in the shoulder.

"No!" But my cry is useless. Gambler barely notices the kick and instead latches onto Darren's ankle.

Darren screams and drags himself toward my closet door. He shakes Gambler off and as the dog goes back for another bite, Darren makes it into the closet.

My closet door thumps shut. Gambler hits it with his front paws. Furiously he scratches at the wood, eager for another chunk of the man on the other side.

"Good boy," I wheeze out. "Come here." I clap my hands, but the dog ignores me.

Instead, he sits in front of the door and whines.

"Never mind. You stay there while I call 911."

"I'm going to fucking kill you, bitch!" Darren yells.

"Come and get me," I shout back, feeling wildly out of control.

"Oh, wait you can't. Gambler's waiting right outside the door."

"He bit me!" Darren shouts, indignation coloring his words.

Maybe Darren's right and I'm a bitch, but damn if I'm not grinning ear to ear.

CHAPTER THIRTY-NINE
SULLY

STRIKE BACK IS almost back to normal.

"Pass me a new roller," Liam asks, holding out his hand.

"What the fuck are you doing that you're going through them so fast?" Keegan wings one across the room.

"Hey!" Jake yells. "Stop throwing shit."

"No, just a roller," Keegan jokes. Then he throws one of the fluffy paint rolls at Jake's head.

"Aren't you happy we came by to help?" Liam asks with a big grin.

"Yeah, it's a real treat," I grumble and check the time.

"What's wrong now?" Jake asks, clapping me on the back.

"Just thinking of stopping to see Aubrey."

He rolls his eyes. "You're like a desperate teenager, bro. Let the poor girl have a night hanging out with her sister."

"Sully," Brady calls from the currently empty weight room. "Come look at this."

While I'm on my way over, his police radio crackles. I only catch the last number of the code the dispatcher gives. "—Nine at 33 Calloway Gardens, Apartment B."

"Shit, that's Aubrey's address." I'm already reversing direction before I finish the sentence.

"Sully!" Brady calls after me. "I'm on it."

"What's going on?" Jake asks.

"Aubrey."

Brady's radio crackles again, but I'm already headed out the back door.

I tear out of the parking lot with Brady on my tail, lights and sirens filling the air.

The road's empty and he passes me.

It's a short drive and I almost flip the Jeep making the turn into her apartment complex.

I'm behind Brady, pounding up the stairs and vaguely aware people are standing around the courtyard watching the drama unfold.

More sirens in the distance.

Aubrey's door flies open before Brady even bangs on it. Her jaw drops.

"An officer's here. Thank you," she says into the phone.

"Aubrey."

"Oh my God." She throws herself at me. "What're you doing here?"

"Reunion can wait. What's going on?" Brady asks.

"Darren broke in. Attacked me. Gambler has him cornered in the closet." She shivers and I hug her tighter.

Brady meets my eyes and raises an eyebrow. "Who's Gambler?"

She points to the door across the hall. "My neighbor's dog. He was barking like crazy when I got here, so I brought him over until Ty got home."

"What kind of dog?" Brady's hand grazes the can of mace at his hip.

"He's a pit bull, but he's very friendly."

Brady grumbles something and heads toward the bedroom.

"Wait!" Aubrey yells. She turns in my arms, frantic. "I don't want them to hurt Gambler. He's done nothing but protect me."

"He won't," I assure her. "Brady knows how to handle dogs."

"Let go." She squirms out of my hold. "I'll grab his leash and take him out of the bedroom."

Brady holds up his hand. "I can't have you getting hurt. Stay with Sully."

An outraged snort is all the warning she gives before ducking past Brady. He shakes his head but doesn't attempt to hold her back.

She shoves the door open and claps her hands. "Gambler. Come on, boy. It's safe now."

A few seconds later she returns with Gambler wiggling and trotting next to her. "Good boy," she keeps repeating.

She sits in the far corner of the couch. Gambler puts his head in her lap, happily wagging his tail while she pets him.

I'm torn between going to her or punching this motherfucker in the face when Brady finally drags him out.

Brady seems to sense my dilemma. "Wait here."

Aubrey entire body trembles and I shrug off my hoody, wrapping it around her shoulders.

"I'm fine, Sully."

Fine my ass. I crush my mouth against her lips. Her fingers cling to my shirt, keeping me close while she whispers some of what happened. "He...he wanted to take me with him."

"I'm so sorry." I press my forehead against hers. "I never should've let you out of my sight."

"I can't live like that," she protests.

She could've been seriously hurt. Or that asshole could've taken her with him to God knows where.

I wrap my arms around her tighter, assuring myself that she's safe.

"Get off her!" someone roars behind me.

Oh, fuck yes. Bring it on.

Aubrey reels back, eyes wide and focused on something beyond my shoulder. I turn to face the man who's responsible for ruining so much of Aubrey's life.

No time to plan a method of attack. Instinct takes over. I push Aubrey behind me and catch Darren with a hard left hook.

It's almost comical how fast he hits the ground. Granted, he's handcuffed, but hey, he came at me.

"Sully!" Brady shouts.

Darren grunts and plows his foot into my stomach.

"Back off," I growl at Brady.

I grab Darren by his neck and haul him to his feet. "Contact her or come near her again and it'll be your last mistake."

"All right, Sully," Brady says in the same tone he used with the angry pit bull a few seconds ago. "I got this. Take care of your girl."

"If you got it, why'd he come charging at me?"

Darren stupidly opens his mouth. "She's not his girl." He glares at me. "You're not good enough for her. She's mine. She'll always be mine."

"You don't listen very well, motherfucker." I land a quick jab to his throat that finally shuts him up. It also closes off his air supply and he collapses in a fit of coughs and sputters.

"Oops." I give Brady an unapologetic smile.

"Dammit, Sully," Brady says with a smirk. "Now I have to fill out a report."

"Make sure you use my full name." I protected my girl and I won't regret that.

Brady gives me a lopsided grin. "Clumsy asshole tripped on the stairs. Happens all the time."

Behind him, another deputy sheriff laughs. "Bet he bangs into the car roof too."

"Damn, you really are clumsy." Brady snickers. "Maybe the jail infirmary can check that out for you." He hauls Darren to his feet. The coward's still wheezing and the two officers drag him out the door.

"Sully," Aubrey whispers behind me. My eyes close for a brief second. I hate that I exposed her to more violence, even if it was fast and justified.

One of her soft hands presses between my shoulder blades and a calmness washes over me. "Are you okay?" I ask as I turn around.

She throws her arms around my neck and buries her face against my chest. "Thank you."

"For?"

She shakes her head and burrows tighter against me.

"Paramedics are here," Liam says from behind me.

I lift my head. "Where'd you come from?"

"Are you kidding? We were right behind you guys."

I glance out the door and Keegan waves at me.

"Thanks."

Gambler rubs his head against my leg.

"It's okay, boy. They have him," Aubrey says, trying to soothe him and probably herself.

A spot of dried blood on her neck catches my attention. "Jesus, did he cut you?"

Her eyes are glassy and unfocused. "I think so," she whispers.

"I'll get someone for her," Liam says. He points my way. "You stay put."

"Aubrey! Oh my God. What the hell?" Celia shouts from the hallway. Liam leads her inside and she rushes to her sister, hugging her tight.

Gambler nudges the sisters with his nose and whaps his tail against the couch, demanding acknowledgment of his heroics.

Tears run down Celia's cheeks and she hugs Aubrey again. "Did he hurt you?"

"I'm fine." Her gaze lands on me and she finally smiles. "I used that heel-strike sidekick we practiced. It's pretty effective."

Relief, pride, terror and so much love for this woman all tumble through me at once. "Good job."

Celia sobs and then shifts, yanking me into a hug. "Thank you."

I awkwardly pat her back. "Aubrey's the one who did it."

Aubrey leans forward and taps her sister. "That's enough gratitude. Get off my man."

Celia releases me and shoves Aubrey. "I almost had a heart attack when I saw all the cop cars downstairs."

The paramedics show up and treat Aubrey's cut. She refuses to go to the hospital and after filling out all their paperwork, they finally leave.

People will clomp in and out of their place all night.

"Come on. You two are staying with me."

CHAPTER FORTY
SULLY

S OMEHOW MY MOTHER'S heard everything by the time the girls and I arrive at my house. She insists on making dinner, but Aubrey's dead on her feet, so I tuck her in before wandering into the kitchen.

"Is she okay?" Celia asks, biting her lip. "I should check—"

"She's asleep. Let her rest." I place a hand on her shoulder and steer her into a dining room chair. "You too."

"I'm way too wound up to rest." Brittle laughter flows out of her mouth. "I can't believe this." She blinks up at me. "Did she…tell you the whole thing?"

I cast a glance in my mother's direction. She's busy pretending not to listen to our conversation. She'd been pretty upset when the gym was vandalized. Not that she blamed Aubrey, but I don't feel like opening the door to her voicing any doubts about our relationship. Especially with Celia here.

After dinner, Celia's phone beeps. "I need to run back to the apartment."

Torn, I stand. I don't want her to go alone, but I don't want to leave Aubrey. She seems to sense my hesitation. "Darren's in jail. I'll be fine."

My mother's unusually quiet after Celia leaves.

"Thanks for making dinner," I say, giving her a one-armed hug.

"Of course." She braces her hands on the counter and shakes her head. "Sullivan—"

"Ma," I warn in my *don't start* voice, because I can already tell I won't like whatever she has on her mind.

"Have you thought this through?"

"Thought what through?"

She blows out a frustrated breath and turns to face me. "I could see Jake dating her. But you have Madison to worry about. You can't have some woman bringing psychopaths into your life."

Deep breath. She doesn't mean it. She's worried about me.

"So I should abandon her when she's having a rough time? Seems unfair. That's not the kind of man you raised me to be." The words come out a whole lot calmer than I'm feeling. "I'm surprised at you, Mom," I say in a low voice.

"Don't throw that in my face," she warns.

"I'm not. *Yet.*"

"Sullivan." She blinks and stares at the ceiling for a few seconds before speaking. "Did you blame me for what happened with Jacob Senior?"

"Yeah," I answer honestly, "Sometimes. I wondered why you didn't leave him sooner."

"I never should've married him."

No kidding. I force a smile. "Yeah, but then we wouldn't have Jake."

"Thank God he turned out nothing like his father," she mutters.

"He's trouble of a different nature for the ladies."

She scowls. "That's not funny."

I take her hand, forcing her to look at me. "What's going on?"

"I'm worried your childhood…that *I* gave you some white knight complex that will get you killed one day."

When I stop laughing, I pin her with a stern look. "No white knight complex, Ma."

"Bullshit," she says.

"Well, I didn't even know about this guy."

"That's another problem, don't you think? She should've warned you." She throws her hands in the air. "This is *worse* than what Lauren did."

"Stop right there. This is not even in the same neighborhood of what Lauren did. She kept my daughter from me for years, Ma. *Years.* Aubrey had no idea any of this would happen. She was embarrassed to tell me about something that happened when she was a teenager."

Her eyes snap to mine. "Teenager? I thought it was an ex-boyfriend?"

"He is, but she was fifteen and he was her teacher."

"Oh my." She presses her hand to her chest and takes a step back.

I wait, watching her closely. One of the ugly truths I've learned in all the self-defense classes I've taught at shelters and other programs is how judgmental women can be of other women in situations similar to their own. I don't expect that from my mother, but honestly, I wasn't expecting this reaction from her at all.

"Where were her parents?"

"Good question."

"I—"

"It was a dark time in her life where the people who should've protected her didn't. She's worked hard to put her life back together."

"You've worked hard too, Sullivan. Worked hard for everything you have. You can't—"

"Stop." I'm close to done with this conversation. My jaw tightens as I fight to remain calm. I don't think I've ever been so pissed with my mother before. "She couldn't know any of this would happen. Everyone has a past. She didn't blow me off when I told her I had a daughter. Didn't flinch when I told her I killed my stepfather—"

"Sullivan! You didn't."

"Why shouldn't I? It's part of my past."

"But it's my past too."

Completely at a loss, I pinch the bridge of my nose.

"I never should've let them put you in that detention center," she whispers.

Ah, now we're getting somewhere. We've never really talked about it. When I was released, I came home and everyone acted as if I'd been away at summer camp. "What was a better alternative? *You* going to prison, so Jake and I could muddle our way through foster care? Thanks, but I did just fine."

"I'm sorry."

"Don't apologize for—"

"I *am* sorry. For all of it. I should have protected both of you better."

I wave off the apology. "I don't think Jake even remembers half of it."

"No, you took the worst of it trying to protect me and that never should've happened. That wasn't your job." She sighs and peers up at me. "You love Aubrey?"

"Yes."

"Trust her?

"Yes, Ma."

"Then I'm sorry I questioned her." Her hand strays to the pendant around her neck, twisting it back and forth. She blows out a long breath. "Ever since…I've just wanted to protect you and make up for all the awful—"

"You don't have anything to make up for. You're a good mother. Always have been." I wobble my hand back and forth. "A little too up in our business sometimes, but good."

She pushes my hand away and wrinkles her nose. "Fifteen, huh? Why is he even out of prison?"

Aubrey

I WAKE UP disoriented with a pounding headache.

Sully's room.

It all comes back to me in a rush.

Well, that explains the headache.

My stomach growls and I flip the covers off and go search for Sully.

I stop short in the hallway when I hear his mother's low voice, simmering with anger.

"That's another problem, don't you think? She should've warned you. This is worse than what Lauren did."

Ouch. That's harsh.

Sully defends me. But cold doubt swirls in my stomach. Am I bad for him?

As quietly as possible, I retreat to his room and grab my cell phone. Sitting on the bed, I flip through my contacts, my finger hovering over Bree's number. Maybe I should go stay with her and Liam instead of staying here and causing more trouble for Sully.

He's close to his mom and I shouldn't cause friction between them.

I spend a painfully long amount of time staring at my phone.

No. Fuck that.

I toss my phone on the nightstand and march back down the hall-way prepared to tell Mrs. Wallace how much I love her son.

But by the time I arrive, she seems a little more on my side.

"Hey." I lean against the wall just inside the kitchen and offer a weak wave hello. "Hi, Mrs. Wallace."

To my surprise, she comes over and envelopes me in a warm, moth-erly hug. "Are you okay, honey?" she asks.

I can't keep up with this woman. Pulling, back, I nod, searching her face for some sign this is an act. But her eyes shine with affection. "I hope you're not upset, but Sullivan explained…a little to me."

"No, that's okay," I whisper. My gaze shoots to Sully and he gives me a tight nod.

She sighs. "He kind of had to. I'm a bit of a momzilla and voiced some opinions on what you might have dragged my son into. But he set me straight," she says, barely taking a breath. "I'm sorry, honey."

Is she apologizing to *me*?

I glance at Sully again. He stood up to his mom. For me? When I've caused him so much trouble?

I can't even be upset with her. She's just looking out for her son. Because that's what a *good* mother does.

"That's okay, Mrs. Wallace. I'd have some questions too, if I were you."

She hugs me tighter and over her shoulder I see Sully sigh with relief.

"You must be hungry," she says, running her hand over my hair.

"A little. I think that's what woke me up. Something smelled good." I glance around the kitchen as she releases me. "Where's Celia?"

"She ran over to the apartment," Sully explains.

"Do you need help, Mrs. Wallace?" I ask as she retreats to the stove.

"No. You stay there. Let me feed you."

Sully watches his mother for a second before taking the chair next to me. "Are you okay?"

I flick my gaze to his mother and back to him. "I think I'm going to be just fine."

CHAPTER FORTY-ONE
SULLY

"**Y**OU SURE THAT'S the one, Maddy?"

"Yup." She presses her finger against the glass right over the vintage-style red garnet ring we picked out for Aubrey. "She'll *love* that one."

The cushion cut stone has a halo of tiny diamonds surrounding it and more set into the slim band. It'll look perfect on Aubrey's hand.

"Yes?" the saleswoman asks.

"That one."

"Are you nervous, Dad?" Maddy asks while I'm paying for the ring.

"Nope." Well, I'm concerned Madison won't be able to contain her excitement and will spill the beans before I propose.

But I also wanted her to feel included, which is well worth the risk of Aubrey learning about my plans.

Aubrey

"PACK YOUR BIKINI, baby!" Sully shouts when he comes in the door.

"Uh, what?"

He strides into the kitchen, wearing a big smile, eyes full of mischief.

"We're going to the beach for your birthday."

"Where? What beach?" Excitement bubbles up inside me. "I have—"

"No classes until Tuesday."

"But what about your classes?"

The gym's back on track and doing well since the re-opening. We're busier than ever. Not really a good time for Sully to take a vacation.

"Murphy's covering. Tickets are paid for. Hotel is booked, so don't try to talk me out of it."

Excited, I throw my arms around him for a kiss. "Thank you."

He pats my ass a few times. "Come on, go get ready."

"We're leaving now?"

"In two hours."

"Sully," I scold. "I can't pack that fast." But I'm laughing and already running to the bedroom as I say it.

Two hours later we're waiting to board our plane to Tampa.

"I've been checking the weather all week. It's actually pretty chilly down there right now," Sully says.

I glance at the wide plate glass window at New York's frozen winter sky. "Is it warmer than negative two degrees?"

"Yup."

"Then I can't wait."

THE NEXT MORNING, Sully has me up early to watch the sunrise on the beach. The sand is so soft under our feet, it feels like flour.

It's January, so we're one of only a few people walking along the surf. We're probably the *only* ones in shorts and T-shirts.

The sunrise happens both gradually and fast, breaking the dark blue night sky with bursts of yellow and orange.

"It's beautiful," I whisper.

Sully must be as awed as I am because he doesn't answer. I turn and find him down on one knee.

"Looking for shells?" I tease.

He holds up a small black velvet box. "Nope, try again."

With shaky fingers, I reach out and he takes my hand. "I never knew what my life was missing until I met you. Your kindness and creativity inspire me every day. You're the only person I want to watch all my sunrises and sunsets with. Will you marry me?"

Tears roll down my cheeks the second I realize what he's doing. I blubber out, "Yes." Then fall to my knees in the sand beside him.

"What are you doing?" he asks.

"I love you."

"Good, because you just said yes and you can't take it back." He grins as he plucks the ring out of its box. "Careful, I don't want to drop it in the sand."

My left hand won't stop trembling as he takes it and slips the ring on my finger. "It's so beautiful. How'd you know I wanted a—oh my God! Maddy. I'm such an idiot." I frown.

He grins even wider. "I'm shocked she managed to keep it a secret for so long."

"But that was months ago."

"I knew I wanted to propose at the beach. It's been killing me. I wanted to do it that night we went to lights in the park. And then I thought maybe New Year's Eve—"

I dive at him, knocking him back against the sand and pepper his face with kisses. "This is perfect."

His arms wrap around me, warm and secure.

"Can we get married on the beach too?" I ask.

He leans up and presses a kiss to my lips.

"We can get married anywhere you want."

EPILOGUE

Aubrey

STRIKE BACK HAS finally reached two-hundred and fifty thousand subscribers on our YouTube channel. A quarter of a million people in record time.

Sully also scored a lucrative sponsorship deal. They'd outfitted the gym with tons of new equipment after we fixed the place up.

And tonight Strike Back is throwing a party to celebrate. We're live-streaming parts of it on the channel.

"Congratulations, man," Griff says, shaking Sully's hand.

Sully's arm tightens around my shoulders. "All her, Griff. This is Aubrey's doing."

Griff nods at me. "You gonna turn this into a full-time business?"

"Maybe." I tip my head in Wrath's direction. "I've been working on a plan for Furious Fitness. I just haven't sold him on the videos. Trinity's supposed to help me convince him."

Griff chuckles. "Good luck with that."

"Go, circulate," Sully says. "But see me later, I have something I want to discuss with you."

"Got it."

Sully turns to me, cupping my face and rubbing his thumb over my cheek. "I need to see you in my office."

"What's wrong?"

"Not a thing." His simmering stare and lowered voice suggest exactly what he has in mind.

"Oh." My gaze darts around the room. "You think that's a good idea when it's so crowded?"

"I think it's a *great* idea." He steers me toward the office and slowly twists the knob. "What the fuck?" He shoves his shoulder against the door, pushing it open enough to get an eyeful.

Sully and I stand there, mouths open, staring at the sight in front of us.

Jake glances over his shoulder, shielding my sister from our view. I'm pretty sure that heap of cloth on Sully's desk is her dress.

"Can't you take a hint?" Jake jerks his chin at us. "I shoved the chair against the door for a reason."

Slowly, we back away and shut the door.

We stand there and stare at each other for a few seconds.

"Let's never speak of this," I finally say.

He chuckles and leads me away from the door. "What are we going to do?"

I shrug. "About what?"

"Aubrey, I'm serious. I love my brother, but commitment isn't in his vocabulary."

"Uh, I'm pretty sure my sister's allergic to relationships so I wouldn't worry about it."

His gaze strays to his still-closed office door. I rest my hand on his arm.

"Not our problem, Sully. Whatever goes on between them, won't impact us. Promise."

"Promise," he echoes.

I glance back at the office again. "Boy, that's going to make Sunday dinners awkward. Not to mention our wedding."

His gaze darts around the room and lands on the back door. His mouth slides into a sly smile. "Come on, I have something I want to show you outside."

Skeptical, I squint at him. "Is it in the backseat of your Jeep?"

He flashes the impish smile that warms me from head to toes and makes me love him even more each time I see it. "You'll have to come with me to find out."

BUSY BEANS
COFFEE SHOP

ALSO BY AUTUMN JONES LAKE

THE LOST KINGS MC SERIES
Slow Burn (Lost Kings MC #1)
Corrupting Cinderella (Lost Kings MC #2)
Three Kings, One Night (Lost Kings MC #2.5)
Strength From Loyalty (Lost Kings MC #3)
Tattered on My Sleeve (Lost Kings MC #4)
White Heat (Lost Kings MC #5)
Between Embers (Lost Kings MC #5.5)
More Than Miles (Lost Kings MC #6)
White Knuckles (Lost Kings MC #7)
Beyond Reckless: Teller's Story, Part One (Lost Kings MC #8)
Beyond Reason: Teller's Story, Part Two (Lost Kings MC #9)
One Empire Night (Lost Kings MC #9.5)
After Burn (Lost Kings MC #10)
Zero Tolerance (Lost Kings MC #11)
White Lies (Lost Kings MC #12)

STAND-ALONES IN THE LOST KINGS MC WORLD
Bullets & Bonfires
Teller and Murphy both appear here.
Warnings & Wildfires
Wrath and Murphy both appear here.